Acclaim For the W
MAX ALLAN

"Crime fiction aficionados are in for a treat…a neo-pulp noir classic."
—*Chicago Tribune*

"No one can twist you through a maze with as much intensity and suspense as Max Allan Collins."
—*Clive Cussler*

"Collins never misses a beat…All the stand-up pleasures of dime-store pulp with a beguiling level of complexity."
—*Booklist*

"Collins has an outwardly artless style that conceals a great deal of art."
—*New York Times Book Review*

"Max Allan Collins is the closest thing we have to a 21st-century Mickey Spillane and…will please any fan of old-school, hardboiled crime fiction."
—*This Week*

"A suspenseful, wild night's ride [from] one of the finest writers of crime fiction that the U.S. has produced."
—*Book Reporter*

"This book is about as perfect a page turner as you'll find."
—*Library Journal*

"Bristling with suspense and sexuality, this book is a welcome addition to the Hard Case Crime library."
—*Publishers Weekly*

"Fuck," he said.

Jon had been kneeling, looking at the discarded sacks. Now he joined Nolan.

"What?"

"I think she was dragged through here." He pointed to the brush; a sort of path had been made, if you looked close: bushes were bent back, branches broken, snowy earth disturbed.

Nolan followed the path, pushing roughly, impatiently, through the foliage, twigs and branches snapping like little gunshots. Jon followed.

At the bottom of the incline was the curve of the road that went up into Nolan's exclusive little housing development.

"Oil," Nolan said, pointing to a black puddle glistening on the icy pavement. "A car was parked here. She should have noticed it when she drove by. They were waiting for her."

"Waiting? Who? What are you talking about?"

Nolan bent and poked around in the snow at the edge of the curb. He found what seemed to be a frozen wad of white tissue or cloth; he picked it up, sniffed it.

"Jesus," he said.

Jon said, "Will you please quit saying 'fuck' and 'Jesus' and tell me what the hell is going on?"

He held the thing under Jon's nose. "Sniff," he ordered.

"Jesus fucking Christ," Jon said. "Chloroform."

"They snatched her," Nolan said.

"Who snatched her?"

"If I knew that," Nolan said, "I'd know who to kill…"

Mad
MONEY

by **Max Allan Collins**

A HARD CASE CRIME NOVEL

A HARD CASE CRIME BOOK
(HCC-158)
First Hard Case Crime edition: April 2023

Published by

Titan Books
A division of Titan Publishing Group Ltd
144 Southwark Street
London SE1 0UP

in collaboration with Winterfall LLC

Print edition ISBN 978-1-78909-146-5
E-book ISBN 978-1-78909-147-2

Design direction by Max Phillips
www.maxphillips.net

Typeset by Swordsmith Productions

The name "Hard Case Crime" and the Hard Case Crime logo are trademarks of Winterfall LLC. Hard Case Crime books are selected and edited by Charles Ardai.

Printed by CPI Group (UK) Ltd, Croydon CR0 4YY

Visit us on the web at www.HardCaseCrime.com

Introduction

The book you are holding, *Mad Money*, is the final volume in Hard Case Crime's project to publish all of my Nolan novels. They brought out my first new Nolan novel in more than 30 years, *Skim Deep*, at the end of 2020, and then began reissuing the earlier titles, two to a volume, the following year. Handsome new editions of *Two For the Money* (collecting *Bait Money* and *Blood Money*) and *Double Down* (collecting *Fly Paper* and *Hush Money*) came out in 2021, and *Tough Tender* (collecting *Hard Cash* and *Scratch Fever*) followed in 2022. That brings us to *Mad Money*, which collects *Spree* and *Mourn the Living*.

Spree is the longest—and for the three decades until *Skim Deep* came out was the last—of my Nolan novels. Many readers consider it the best of the series, and I wouldn't disagree.

The idea was to do a book on a larger scale than the 60,000-word fast-and-lean paperbacks of the previous entries. I'd written the first several Nathan Heller novels at this point, and those were fairly massive books—not long after *Spree*, I would write the Heller novel *Stolen Away*, which would be the longest first-person private eye novel ever written.

In addition, Donald E. Westlake, writing as Richard Stark, had written *Butcher's Moon* (1974), a longer-form novel about his thief Parker than he'd ever before attempted. It turned out to be the final novel in the series, at least for a while, but its larger landscape was inspiring. After all, the Parker novels had been one of the two major influences on Nolan (the other being the Sand novels by Ennis Willie).

The Heller novels, added to my high-profile scripting of the *Dick Tracy* comic strip, had suddenly given me some leverage in the mystery writing field. This proved to be a passing fancy, but I took full advantage, and thanks to Nate Heller, I was able to return to two characters of my early career, characters whose development had been stunted by, frankly, having their series cancelled. That led to my writing *Primary Target* (retitled *Quarry's Vote* in its current Hard Case Crime incarnation) and bringing my hitman Quarry back to nasty life. And it led to my resurrecting Nolan and Jon for one more caper in *Spree*.

There was talk at the time of relaunching Nolan as a series. The editor at Tor had made an offer on the early books and we signed a new contract. Tor had been doing the mass-market paperbacks of the Heller novels, so it was all in the family. Then Tor got outbid for the next Heller reprint by Bantam Books, and things got contract-cancelling chilly. No more Nolan novels, at least not at Tor.

All of that talk, however, had followed my submission of the novel. When I wrote *Spree*, I did so with the full expectation that it would indeed be the final Nolan. Because of this, I wanted to leave him in a place where readers might be able to imagine how the rest of his life might play out. And also, I wanted to give him one last score, one really major caper, to cap off his career.

Most of the Nolan novels are at least in part caper novels. They are not, however, what I would call classic caper yarns in the tradition of *The Killing*, *Rififi*, or *Ocean's Eleven*, where the caper itself is a high-concept outlandish affair. Nolan's capers were down-and-dirty—robbing a small-town bank, looting a hillbilly hideout. I wanted him to go out in style.

In the mid-'80s, shopping malls were a very big, successful deal. And the notion of heisting an entire shopping mall was a most appealing one for Nolan's final caper. I went out to my local, then-flourishing mall in Muscatine, Iowa, and was surprised by how easily I got the security guys to show me around and explain all their systems and tricks. I remember coming home and saying to my wife Barb, "Maybe I should scrap the novel and just heist the fucking place."

Well, what the hell—I wrote the novel. I think it came out rather well, and this is probably the best rendition of the Comfort family yet. I can't tell you the pleasure it gave me writing the phrase, "Cole Comfort's farm."

The novel was optioned for the movies a number of times, and I wrote a screenplay, but it hasn't been produced yet. We've tried to do it ourselves here in Iowa, but it never quite happened. Again, easier to just rob the damn mall. A new Nolan movie deal, recently signed, may rectify that.

Mourn the Living was written around 1967 or '68, and is—in a sense—the first book in the Nolan series. (Though not the first Nolan novel to be published: that was *Bait Money* in 1973.)

Written during my undergrad years, *Mourn the Living* was set aside when an editor suggested that he would like to see either certain rewrites (with which I did not agree) or the author's next book. I followed the latter course, figuring that *Mourn* would be published later on; but the subsequent series initiated by *Bait Money* differed from this first novel—among other things, Nolan aged ten years and acquired a youthful protégé, Jon. Also, times had changed so rapidly that the novel's hippie-era time frame, so topical when I'd written it a few years before, seemed hopelessly dated.

It may sound unlikely, but I had forgotten about the book—at least in terms of it being a commercial property—until Wayne Dundee interviewed me for his fine small-press magazine *Hardboiled*. In the course of the interview, I mentioned the existence of *Mourn the Living* to Nolan fan Wayne, who expressed an interest in serializing it in *Hardboiled*.

So, twenty years after the fact, I found myself doing the necessary line-editing on the first Nolan novel. Too much time had elapsed for me to undertake any major rewriting.

While the novel was recognizably mine, I realized I was a different writer, several decades down the road; and, like any good editor, I attempted to respect the wishes and intent of the young writer who wrote it.

I hope readers will enjoy meeting the younger Nolan, sans Jon, in his first recorded adventure. As for the time period of the book being dated, I am pleased that enough years have gone by for me to present it, unashamedly, as a period piece.

My thanks to Wayne Dundee, for nudging me and giving *Mourn* an audience at last; to my late pal Ed Gorman, who brought out the first edition, in hardcover for Five Star in 1999; and to Barb, who patiently transferred the moldy, water-damaged manuscript onto computer disk for my editing.

And to Hard Case Crime, for including it in their collection of Nolan novels, and to you, for including it in yours.

MAX ALLAN COLLINS

BOOK ONE
Spree

To Bob Randisi—for wanting this book to happen.

The author wishes to thank Captain Tom Brendel, Chuck Bunn, Mike Lange and Ric Steed for research assistance; and editor Michael Seidman for a suggestion that proved crucial to this narrative. Thanks also to Ed Gorman and Barb Collins for convincing me to pay attention to Michael Seidman's suggestion.

The author also wishes to acknowledge certain nonfiction source material: *Crime as Work* (1973), by Peter Letkemann; *Crime Pays* (1975), by Thomas Plate; and *Game of Thieves* (1981), by Robert R. Rosberg.

Part One

I

Angie McFee was wary of the Comforts, certainly, but dying violently never crossed her mind. She'd dated Lyle, after all. Well, "dated" wasn't the word, really. She'd slept with him a few times. Sex with Lyle was energetic and fun, like your average aerobics workout. Unfortunately, conversation with Lyle was equally aerobic.

Before she drove out to the Comforts' on this cool October evening, she got her little silver Mazda gassed up and washed. The car wasn't quite dry, and beads of water glistened on the hood in the moonlight as she pulled off the main drag onto an asphalt road, perhaps twenty miles outside Jefferson City, Missouri. She was a petite pretty brunette of twenty-seven years, watching the moon on the hood of her car, a car the Comforts had helped buy.

It had been a shock when Lyle first suggested she meet his "pa." Christ, it had been a shock to hear anybody in this day and age refer to their father as "Pa," particularly without a trace of irony. It had similarly been a shock to see Lyle's brow furrowing in something akin to thought, that thought manifesting itself in this suggestion that she meet his "pa."

And Pa had been a shock, too. A tall, leathery farmer in coveralls and a plaid shirt with a shock (another shock!) of white hair and pale blue eyes with laugh crinkles. He had a pretty smile, Pa did, the only resemblance between him and Lyle, other than their basic lanky frame. Brown-eyed Lyle, whom she'd met in a trendy little singles bar, looked like a fashion page out of *Playboy*, he wore a creamy *Miami Vice* silk sport coat over a grayish-blue T-shirt, gray jeans, Italian shoes with no socks, a tanning spa tan, and a twenty-five-dollar haircut, when Jefferson City remained a six-dollar-haircut town. It was all so right for the fashion moment that it was a little wrong, but he had a great smile and curly brown hair and a fantastic bod and no sores on his lip. And so to bed.

Only Lyle also had a farmer drawl and a remedial reading vocabulary and a certain vacancy behind his eyes, all of which took a while to catch on to, because he was the strong silent type, the sort of brooder you assume is hiding deep thoughts behind all those pregnant pauses, when in fact those pregnant pauses prove never to give birth to anything at all, and within that pretty cranium there was, Angie had no doubt, a low and constant hum.

She had tried, on their third night together—each previous night being a month or so apart, no steady thing developing between them, just her own occasional need for some really terrific sex in the midst of her thus far fruitless search to find a better husband than the first one—to make some human connection with Lyle. She'd told him about her father's store.

"It's really pitiful," she said, smoking nervously, sitting up in bed, pillow at her back, sheet pulled up but barely covering her small, pert breasts. At least she liked to think of them as pert. "Dad had this great little place, little hole-in-the-wall, where he sold nothing but meat."

"Meat," Lyle said, nodding. Lyle didn't smoke.

"He's a terrific butcher, Dad is, but a lousy businessman. When he had that hole-in-the-wall, strictly a butcher shop, with choice cuts and all, he was doing fine. Mom was keeping the books. It was great. Then he got ambitious."

"Meat," Lyle said.

"He thought he could do better in a bigger store—you know, a small supermarket. He thought people would come in for the great meat and buy their other food as well, save a trip, even if our prices were a little more expensive than the big discount supermarkets. Going in he knew that—knew he couldn't compete with the prices that the big boys were able to give, because of, you know, volume."

"Volume?" Lyle said. He narrowed his eyes, apparently wondering what noise levels had to do with the grocery business.

"Anyway, Dad's dying with that white elephant…"

Lyle touched her arm. "I'm sorry," he said. It was clear he had taken the word "dying" literally, and that "white elephant" was some rare disease.

"No, I just mean he's losing his shirt," she said, hoping he wouldn't take that literally, too. "Our savings are gone, Mom's too sick to work, he's mortgaged up the wazoo. And there I am, with my business degree, stuck in the middle of a family business that can barely afford to pay me half of what I could get elsewhere." She sighed. "But, what the hell. You got to be loyal to your family, right?"

"Right," Lyle said, nodding again.

"So I'm keeping the books. Working in the store—sometimes behind one of the registers, which is demeaning, let me tell you. I'm glad my little boy can't see me."

"You have a boy?"

"Yeah, he lives with my ex. Steve's remarried and I'm a lousy mother. I don't think I ever want another. I mean, I love my son, but kids do get in the way."

"Kids," Lyle said, smiling, nodding.

"How old are you, Lyle?"

"Twenty-three."

"Where do you work?"

"Like you. Family business."

"Yeah, I know—you've said that a couple of times. But what do you do exactly?"

And that was when Lyle's brow had furrowed suddenly, shockingly, in apparent thought.

"You keep the books?" he said.

"Yes…"

"At a grocery store?"

"Yeah, that's right. So what?"

"You should talk to Pa."

Pa, as it turned out, was Coleman Comfort, but, as he'd said, pale blue eyes twinkling like a slightly demented Walter Brennan, "My kith and kin all call me Cole."

Cole Comfort's farm, where all of their meetings had been held over the past year and a half, was off a back gravel road, on a cinder path. The two-story farmhouse seemed ramshackle somehow, despite being freshly aluminum-sided. Maybe it was the weedily overgrown yard, in which the remnants of various vehicles rusted in the process of becoming one with the universe, or the dense looming woods behind the house, where owls' eyes and nameless critter howls seemed to invite you in but not out. Or maybe the sagging barn and decaying silo, which created suspicion as to what the house itself was like under its aluminum face-lift. Whatever the case, the Comfort place was hardly comforting and no place Angie wanted to visit.

And yet she had, once a month, for many months.

That first time, even though she had long since full well realized how thick Lyle was, the sight of the farm (and there was farmland adjacent, it just wasn't worked by the Comforts) had made her suck in a quick breath of disbelief. "There's money in it," Lyle had said, "big money." But how could there be big money here, in this Dogpatch dump? This looked like food stamp territory.

"Food stamps," Cole Comfort had said, pouring her some Old Grand-Dad, straight up, in a fast-food restaurant giveaway glass with the Road Runner on it. They sat in the living room, where reigned a giant-screen TV on which, at the moment, Billy Joel's face was the size of a card table. The pores in his nose were like poker chips.

Lyle was watching MTV. Cole, it seemed, hated MTV, so Lyle was listening through headphones. Giant images of singers silently shouting, dancers moving to invisible beats, were an oppressive flickering presence. Other images fought MTV for attention: six, count them, six black velvet paintings of John Wayne, paintings of various sizes but all in rough rustic frames with Wayne in western regalia, beat out the mere three jumpsuited Elvis Presleys, all of them riding walls paneled in a dark brown photographic wood grain. Against one wall, with snakes of cable crawling out of it toward the big-screen TV, was an open cabinet on wheels, in which stacks of stereo and video equipment perched, red lights dancing and sound meter needles wiggling. The furniture, all of it expensive, varied in style—from Early American to modern—but the chairs and several couches were consistent in one thing: they were covered with clear vinyl. The carpet was a green shag, like grass from outer space.

She drank the glass of Old Grand-Dad like it was soda pop and Cole grinned his pretty white grin and poured her some more.

"F-food stamps?" she managed to ask.

"Food stamps. You work in a grocery store. A little mom-and-pop affair, like in the good old days. None of this corporate horse-shit."

"Actually McFee's is a fairly big store," she said. "But, yes, it's not affiliated with any major chain. That's the problem. They can undersell us."

"Volume," Cole nodded. "I stopped in the place—your daddy has a right fine meat counter."

She couldn't quite tell if the phrase "right fine" was an affectation or if this guy really was the hick of all hicks. Despite the tacky decor around him, Cole Comfort did not seem stupid, or even naive. Maybe bad taste and stupidity didn't necessarily go hand in hand.

"The meat is what brings in what customers we do have," she told him. "Daddy should never have expanded."

Cole nodded, sagely this time; lines of experience pulled at the corners of his mouth. "It's the bane of American business. Expansion. Nobody's satisfied with a small success. They gotta expand till they go bust."

Bane of American business? Where was this guy coming from?

"We're in a position to help you, little lady," Cole said.

Little lady yet.

"How?"

"We deal in food stamps, my family does. Lyle and Cindy Lou and me."

She had not yet met Cindy Lou, but already an image was forming somewhere between Daisy Mae and Lolita.

"What do you mean, exactly? Your family deals in food stamps?"

"The black market, girl. Wise up. Black-market food stamps. We stay strict away from counterfeit." He waved his hands like an umpire saying, OUT! "The real thing or nothin' at all."

"Well…uh, where do you get them?"

"How we get them ain't your concern."

"I don't exactly understand what *is* my concern in all this…" Perhaps she shouldn't have gulped that Old Grand-Dad.

"You're the perfect conduit, the very conduit we been lookin' for."

Against her better judgment, she drank again from the Road Runner glass. Just a sip this time. To arm her against a man who said both "ain't" and "conduit."

"You can buy them from us at a thirty percent discount," he said. "Seventy cents on the dollar."

Now she got it. "And when I send them in…"

"The government gives you a dollar. That's thirty cents you clear, each. And you don't pay us till you get yours."

She knew that wasn't as small potatoes as it at first sounded; even with their limited business, their higher prices, McFee's had several hundred dollars a month come in, in food stamps. Other stores their size—stores with chain-style discount prices—would do a land-office business in food stamps; at least ten times what her father's store did.

Cole was patting her arm. "You could help your pa. He wouldn't even have to know. You could feather your own nest, too. The government'll never suspect a thing. We'll help you figger what you can get away with, a store your size."

"I wouldn't be your only…conduit, then?"

"No," Comfort said, his smile cracking his leathery face, "we got one or two others. But a good conduit is hard to find."

Sew that on a sampler.

"Where do you get the stamps, anyway?"

"Nobody suffers," Cole said. "They can get 'em replaced, if you're worried about poor people."

"I just want to know how it works. I know you said it wasn't my concern, but really it is. If I'm going to be involved in something... criminal...I want to know the extent of it."

Cole shrugged. Then his face darkened. "I hate that nigger shit!"

He was glaring past her. She glanced in that direction, at the big-screen TV, where Tina Turner was prancing, singing, in pantomime. Cole reached for a *TV Guide* next to him on the couch and hurled it at Lyle; the corner of it hit Lyle in the head. The son winced but did not even glance back, and certainly didn't change the channel. He was apparently used to this form of criticism on his father's part.

"Anyway," Cole said, his distaste lingering in his sour expression, "we know when the stamps go out—third of the month—and that on the fifth they're in mailboxes. Lyle and Cindy Lou just go out and about like good little mailmen, rain nor hail nor sleet, only in reverse. Taking letters out of mailboxes, not putting in."

"It's that easy?" she said. Repressing, *and that petty?*

"Yup," he said. "It ain't so small-time, either," he added, as if reading her thoughts. "There can be as much as two hundred bucks' worth in one envelope. Also, some people sell 'em to us direct. We pay a quarter on the dollar."

"People sell their own food stamps?"

"People got things they want to buy and not eat. Sure. And we got some bars that we do business with."

"Bars? You can't buy liquor and cigarettes with food stamps..."

"Of course not—not 'bove board."

"Oh," she said. It was easy enough for Angie to figure how that could work: a bartender letting a customer use a dollar food stamp for thirty cents or so worth of booze or smokes.

"It's a safe way to make a little extra bread, honey," Cole said, in his fatherly way. "You won't get caught. You almost *can't* get caught.

What are you doing, except moving some paper around? It ain't even embezzling, really."

"It is criminal," she said.

"Much in life is," Cole granted.

She said she wanted to think about it, and, after a particularly slow week in her father's store, she called Cole Comfort and said yes. She never dated Lyle again. Once a month she drove to the farmhouse and got a supply of food stamps, bringing them cash in return. The Comforts always wanted cash.

And her dad, her sweet dad, tough ex-marine that he was, was so blessedly naive. He really thought business was up.

It crushed her to have to pull the rug out.

But it was time. She'd had a call from the Department of Social Services; an investigation into food stamp abuse was underway. An appointment to "interview" her had been set up. She didn't know what this meant exactly, but she did know it was time to get out.

She'd socked a few thousand away, and bought a few toys out-right (the Mazda, for one) and got her father on his feet, even if it was only temporarily. She didn't know where she was going, but she did know she'd been in Jefferson City long enough. With her nest egg and her college degree and her looks, she could go anywhere, if she could just weather the Department of Social Services storm.

For right now, however, she was at the Comforts', for one last time.

She was greeted at the door by Cindy Lou, a cute curvy straw-berry-blond freckle-faced sixteen-year-old in a calico halter top and short jeans and bare feet with red-painted toenails. Somewhere between Daisy Mae and Lolita.

"Daddy's upstairs figuring the books," Cindy Lou said, ushering her into where John Wayne and Elvis, as always, ruled. "He'll be down in a jif."

And he was, in his usual Hee Haw apparel and his almost se-ductive smile. He said to Cindy Lou, "Take the pickup and get 'er gassed."

She clasped her hands together in front of breasts that Angie would have died for. "Can I, Daddy?"

He reached in his pocket and withdrew a twenty and, grinning shit-eatingly, said, "What's it look like?"

She snatched it out of his hands, and he patted her round little butt in a less than paternal way as she departed. Angie wondered for a moment whether Cindy Lou was old enough to have a license, before dismissing it as a foolish question.

He bade her sit on the couch again, which she did, where he poured her Old Grand-Dad and she carefully, tactfully, explained her position. Lyle was watching MTV, in headphones. Rick James was on the screen, silently screaming, but this time Cole didn't hurl a *TV Guide*. Maybe he was getting more tolerant.

Or maybe he was just preoccupied.

She withdrew from her purse an envelope of cash, which he riffled through, smiling absently; he usually gave her a thick packet of food stamps at this point. He was preoccupied tonight.

"This investigation," Cole said, tucking the money away in a deep coverall pocket, "what have you heard, exactly?"

"Nothing," she said, shrugging expansively.

"They ain't even talked to you yet."

"Just on the phone. It's only an appointment."

"Are you worried?"

"Sure I am. But I don't see how they can prove anything."

"Damn," Cole said. His smile was as rueful as it was pretty. "This has been one sweet little scam—but I'm afraid its days are numbered."

"This investigation is that serious, you think?"

"Hard to say. I can tell you this—they started registering the mail with the food stamps in it. Anything over ninety bucks gets registered. Recipient has to sign."

"So your kids can't go raiding mailboxes anymore."

"Not like they could. It's just too damn bad."

She shrugged. Smiled. "It was fun while it lasted."

"Sure was," he said, and hit her on the side of the head with the Old Grand-Dad bottle. She heard the glass break against her jaw, felt her skin tear, a flash of pain, then darkness.

She came out of it, once, for a moment, hearing: "A girl, Pa? I don't want to kill no girl. I was *with* her before."

That was when, for the first time, dying violently occurred to her.

2

In Nolan's life, right now, comfort was very important.

He'd lived hard, for fifty-some years, and it seemed to him about time to take it easy. This was the payoff, wasn't it? What he'd worked for, for so very long: the good life.

Not that he wasn't still working. He liked to work. His restaurant-cum-nightclub, Nolan's, nestled in a nicely prosperous shopping mall, was doing a tidy business and he put in, oh, probably a fifty-hour week. He did all the buying himself, and kept his own books, did all the hiring and firing as well as playing host most evenings. No, he didn't greet his patrons at the door—he had a hostess for that—but he did circulate easily around the dining room, asking people if they were enjoying their meals; and in the bar he'd move from stool to stool, table to table, chatting with the regulars.

Right now he was at home, though, in the open-beamed living room of his big ranch-style house, home on a Friday night (a rarity), a gaunt-faced, rangy man stretched out in a recliner, stroking his mustache idly, watching the reason for staying home on a Friday: a boxing match on HBO, a black guy and a Puerto Rican bashing each other's brains out on a twenty-seven-inch Japanese TV screen. Nolan's idea of world unity.

The room around him was cream-color walls and modern furnishings and soft browns. What he wore matched the room, though he hadn't intended or even noticed it: a cream-color pullover sweater and brown corduroy trousers and brown socks and no shoes, vein-roped hands folded over a slight paunch.

The paunch bothered him, but not much. He'd been a lean man so long that in his mind he still was. Eating the food at his own restaurant had done it to him, and he'd taken up golf to halfheartedly work the budding Buddha belly off. Toward that end, he rarely rode in the cart, walking, trying to make it feel like a real sport.

He was enough of a natural athlete to break one hundred the first month he played, which frustrated the rest of his regular four-some, who, like him, were in the Chamber of Commerce, with stores in or near the Brady Eighty mall. Harris owned a nearby Dunkin' Donuts outlet, a twenty-four-hour operation, and fre-quently handed Nolan a free dozen, which didn't help his weight, either. Levine owned the Toys 'R' Us franchise in Brady Eighty. DeReuss, the wealthiest and quietest, was a Dutchman who owned a jewelry store in the mall. After eighteen holes, the foursome would go to the country club bar and drink and talk sports and women. Nolan liked the three men. He felt, at long last, as if he'd joined the real world. The legit world.

He sometimes wondered, in rare reflective moments, for instance between rounds tonight, what his friend DeReuss who owned the jewelry store would say if he knew Nolan had, in his time, heisted many similar such stores, albeit never in a mall. He didn't know where his three golfing chums had got their financing, but Nolan had done it the good old-fashioned American way: he'd gone out and taken it.

For nearly twenty years, prior to this current respectability, Nolan had been a professional thief.

Jewelry stores—along with banks, armored cars and mail trucks—were his pickings, though not easy. He prided himself on the care he took; he was no cheap stick-up artist, but a pro—big jobs, one or two a year, painstakingly planned to the finest detail, smoothly carried out by players carefully cast by Nolan himself. Nobody got hurt, especially civilians; nobody went to jail, especially Nolan. He ran the show. He always had.

Well, not always. He'd started with the Family, the *Chicago* Family that is, but not in a criminal capacity. And certainly not in the heist game; in his experience, Family guys themselves rarely got into honest stealing, though they frequently bankrolled it. Unions and vice were where the Family was comfortable doing their stealing, and Nolan wanted none of either.

He hadn't meant to go to work for the Family at all; he didn't know that the Rush Street club where he was hired as a bouncer was Outfit-owned until he saw the manager paying off one of Tony Accardo's cousins.

That same manager was stupid enough to short the Family on its piece of the proverbial action, and left in a nervous hurry one night. Nolan never knew whether the little man had made it to safety or the bottom of Lake Michigan, and he didn't much care which. All he knew was it opened up a slot for him—soon he was managing the club himself, and still doing his own bouncing, making a name with the made guys, who eventually tried to get Nolan to join the Sicilian Elks himself, only he passed. They resented that, and tried to pressure Nolan into bumping off a guy he knew pretty well, and Nolan balked, and somebody else killed the guy, which somehow led to Nolan shooting (through the head) the brother of a Family underboss. Messy.

That had sent him scurrying into the underground world of armed robbery, which—with the exception of the aforementioned occasional bankrolling, a money source Nolan never sought—rarely touched Family circles. In that left-handed world he'd made his mark, and a lot of money. And, eventually, time cooled his Family problems—he had outlived the bastards, basically, and was now on more or less friendly terms with the current regime. He'd even operated a couple of clubs for them.

But he wanted to have something of his own. He didn't like having Family ties; it wasn't his idea of going straight, and straight was where he had always hoped to go, deep in the crooked years.

So here, finally, in the Quad Cities, a cluster of cities and towns on the Iowa/Illinois border, which is to say the Mississippi River, he had settled down and bought his restaurant and gone there: straight.

Funny. It all seemed so long ago—half a dozen guys standing around looking at maps and blueprints and photographs spread out on a motel-room bed or somebody's kitchen table. Cigarette and cigar smoke forming a cloud. Beer and questions and arguing and bragging. Some really great guys—like Wagner and Breen and

Planner. And once in a while a real asshole—like any one of that crazy Comfort clan. Well, Sam Comfort and his boys were all dead now, and their vendetta against him was just as dead. Nothing to worry about.

The black boxer won, and Nolan was yawning through some situation comedy, of the cable variety—stale pointless jokes and naked female breasts, not pointless—when the phone rang. He used the remote control to turn down the TV sound and walked to the kitchen where the phone was on the wall.

"Nolan," he said.

"Hi. Is the fight over, or am I interrupting?"

It was Sherry. The hostess at his restaurant. She lived with him, a beautiful twenty-two-year-old California blonde from Ohio, young enough to be his daughter. But she wasn't.

"The fight's over. You're not interrupting anything. How's business?"

"I love you, too. Business is fine. You wouldn't want to come down and work a few hours, would you?"

"Need me?"

"I always need you. But at the moment I'm thinking of the bartender."

"Crowded," he said, smiling.

"There's money in your voice," she said. "You really love the stuff, don't you?"

"What else is there?"

"Me."

"You're in the top two."

"You really know how to sweet-talk a girl. Get down here, will you? The regulars are asking for you."

"It's nice to be loved."

"So I hear," she said, hanging up, but there was no real bitterness in her voice. It was just a game they played.

She knew he loved her, or at least he assumed as much. That is, assuming he loved her. He wasn't sure. He wasn't sure what love was, exactly, except something in movies and on TV, and on his TV right now, sound down, were some girls soaping themselves in the shower, which wasn't love exactly, but was close enough.

He showered, too, alone, and shaved and splashed on Old Spice, an old habit, and put on a blue suit and a dark blue tie and a pale blue shirt, all of them quite expensive. He bought them locally, at the mall, where he got a discount; and he only wore such clothes to his restaurant, enabling him to deduct them.

Nolan loved money so much, he hated to spend it. He knew it was ridiculous—he wasn't going to live forever, and these were the years where he was supposed to be enjoying himself, and, damnit, he was. He'd bought this fucking house (he only thought of it as a "fucking house" when he remembered what it cost him) and had expensive toys, like his silver Trans Am and several Sony TVs and stereo equipment and the sunken tub with whirlpool and like that. But he knew each one of the toys had taken Sherry's nudging to get bought.

He smiled, thinking of her, slipping into a London Fog raincoat, twenty percent discount from the Big and Tall Men's shop at the mall. He'd met her at the Tropical, a club he ran for the Family a few summers back. She was a waitress and he'd fired her for spilling scalding hot coffee in a customer's lap. Then she sat on his, and they wound up spending the summer together. When she wasn't in a bikini, poolside, she was in his bed and wasn't in a bikini.

He pulled the silver sporty machine out of the garage, closing the overhead door behind him with a push of a button, wondering if some smart crook would come through the neighborhood trying various frequencies on some homemade open-sesame doohickey till he got it right and got in. More power to him, Nolan thought, and besides, my alarm will nail the bastard.

He glided down the hill—it was a cold clear November night— and turned left, toward Moline, coasting along a stretch that alternated between parks and commercial and residential, a Quad Cities pattern. He was still thinking about Sherry. Still smiling.

What had started, that one summer, as two people using each

other—a cute lazy cunt who wanted to stay on the payroll and was willing to do it by screwing the boss, lecherous dirty old man of fifty that he was—had turned into something else. Something more.

They liked each other. The sex was good, and the summer was over too soon. He had asked her to stay on, and she almost had, but her mother had a stroke and she had to go home, so they parted company, reluctantly, and he promised her she'd hear from him again. A year ago or so, when he bought Nolan's (which had been the name of the place even before he bought it, and she often accused him of buying it so he wouldn't have to spend money on a new sign), he had thought of her and invited her to work for him and, if she liked, stay with him. Despite her scalding-coffee-in-the-customer's-nuts past, he made her hostess. And she'd done very well at it. She was beautiful, of course, but she had that mid-western gift of making immediate friends out of strangers. She, more than anyone or anything else at Nolan's, was responsible for the heavy return business, the regulars who haunted the place.

He crossed the free bridge at Moline. The river was choppy tonight; the amber lights of the cities on its either shore winked on the water. Did he love her? He supposed so. He liked her, and that somehow seemed more important.

He stayed on Highway 74 and curved around onto Kimberly, a wide street whose valleys and hills were thick with commerce; he glanced at the little shopping clusters, wondering how they were doing. He knew Brady Eighty was hurting everybody else—but it might be temporary. New kid on the block always got more attention—for a while.

He turned right on Brady Street, a four-lane one-way clear to the Interstate now, and enjoyed the almost Vegas-like glow of fast-food franchises and other prospering businesses. The Quad Cities economy wasn't good—the farm implement industry, a major component of the area's economy, was withering away, and other local industries were suffering as well. But Brady Street glowed in neon health: pizza and tacos and hamburgers; used cars, stereos and videotape rental. People always have money for the important things.

Like drinking, he thought, with a wry private smile, turning toward his club. At this point on Brady, the businesses began to give each other some breathing room, and the food wasn't so fast—although Flaky Jake's, for all its yuppie pretension, was still a hamburger joint, and Chi-Chi's peddled tacos, even if they did slop guacamole and sour cream on them. This was motel country, too: Ramada, Best Western, Holiday Inn. At the left as he passed, in a valley of its own, lay the sleeping behemoth—North Park— the massive, sprawling shopping mall whose parking lot was an ocean of cement that even after closing was swimming with cars— movies and restaurants kept it so. North Park was Brady Eighty's biggest (in every sense) competitor, and conventional wisdom had said a new mall nearby couldn't hope to compete with its scores of shops, including four major department stores.

But Brady Eighty wasn't exactly a new mall. It was a refurbished one. The Brady Street Shopping Center, an open-air plaza with two rows of shops facing each other, had opened back in the early sixties, one of the first in the Cities. Over the years it had fallen on hard times, and was almost a ghost town when a Chicago-based group, led by a smart operator named Simmons, bought everybody out but a few willing-to-stay stalwarts and remodeled the place into an enclosed mall. The Brady Street location— Highway 61, just a whisper away from Interstate 80—made it the first shopping area you saw when you got off the Interstate; provided the easiest shopping-center access for half a dozen small towns outside of Davenport; and had a varied selection of shops, within a smaller, easier-to-deal-with area than North Park's miles of mall. "Brady for the '80s," the slogan went, and Nolan wondered idly what would happen to the catchphrase now that the nineties were breathing down the decade's neck.

Nolan pulled into the dimly lit, pleasantly crowded parking lot, admiring the glow of the green neon Nolan's sign on the side of the mall wall, at the right of the front entry. The words "Brady

Eighty" in silver-outlined-black art deco letters were along the long window over the bank of doors. And speaking of banks, First National's outlet was opposite Nolan's, at left, with a drive-up window. It amused Nolan to be doing business across from a bank.

He couldn't find a parking place up close, so he pulled around back. The parking lot in back wasn't full, even on a Friday, partly because people didn't seem to know it existed yet, and partly because the rear double doors were locked up after the mall closed. His was the only business open after hours, and had its own after-hours entry/exit accordingly, under that glowing green "Nolan's" neon.

As he got out of the Trans Am, the wind whipped out at him, cutting through the raincoat, whistling through the skeletal trees behind him, beyond the parking lot. He realized how, in a way, this thriving little mall was situated in a rather desolate spot. Woods and farms and highways were its neighbors; you had to drive half a mile to run into commercial and residential again. Stuck out in the boonies, they were—making a small fortune.

He used a key to get in the double doors, and his footsteps echoed pleasantly down a hallway between Petersen's, a big department store at left, and the Twin Cinemas, which hadn't opened yet. This new addition—taking over the area of a water-bed store and an antique boutique, the only businesses at Brady Eighty to fail since its opening two years ago—was the only space not up and running. No other mall in the Cities could say the same—even North Park had its share of shuttered stalls.

He walked down the deserted mall, its walkway area quite wide, having been a plaza back in the unenclosed, pre-mall "shopping center" days, and well-dressed manikins in store windows stared at him, threatening to come to life. One of them did, only it was just the security guard, Scott, a pasty-faced kid of twenty-five who carried a phallic billy club on his belt, and no gun. Nolan liked the kid well enough, but he kept telling the mall manager to put two guards on, and make one of them an older guy, a retired cop. Nolan, like any good thief, knew what the possibilities were.

Imagine, if somebody got in here one night and just started helping themselves.

He turned the corner and walked down to the Nolan's mall entrance, which also was kept locked after hours, to keep his customers from strolling the mall. He unlocked the door and went in; music assaulted him, some vaguely British-sounding youth mumbling about love against synthetic strings and hollow percussion. Fridays and Saturdays, after ten, a deejay came in and the little dance floor, over at the left, was crowded with approval. Nolan shrugged. Whatever sells.

He felt the same about the look of the place—barnwood and booths with lots of nostalgic bric-a-brac on the walls, tin advertising signs, framed forties movie posters, the occasional historic front page; and lots of plants, hanging and otherwise. Sherry had done it, the decorating. Better she do it here than at home.

He went behind the bar and asked Chet, an older man he'd hired away from a place downtown, how the evening was going. Chet said A-OK, but had to shout. Nolan occasionally worked behind the bar, but only in a crunch; if Chet needed him, he'd say so. Nolan found a stool and looked at his crowd. Weekends were singles-dominated—meat market time. Some *Big Chill*-variety married couples, but mostly singles; he had a smaller, older crowd during the week. His friends from the Chamber of Commerce and country club would come by, spend some time, some money. He liked it here during the week.

He liked it here now, too, only in a different way. He liked the way the cash register rang on weekends; it played his favorite song. So, what the hell—these marks could listen to their favorite song, too, even if it was by some adenoidal Brit twit.

Sherry came over; she was wearing a red jumpsuit with Joan Crawford shoulders and a wide patent-leather belt. The outfit was Kamali, she said; that was a brand name, apparently.

Square shoulders or not, she looked terrific. Sculpted blond hair around a heart-shaped face with big blue eyes and long, real lashes and soft, puffy lips that pouted prettily even when she smiled.

Like she was now.

"You came," she said.

"In my pants," he said. "It must've been the sight of you that did it."

She cocked her head to one side and shook it gently, smiled the same way. "No. It was the sight of all these customers."

Nolan shrugged, almost smiled.

"You love being a prosperous businessman, don't you?" she said.

"It ain't half bad," he said.

She stood very near to him, where he sat on a barstool.

"You love playing it straight, too, don't you? You get a kick out of playing at being honest."

"Aren't you supposed to be working?"

"When somebody comes in that door, I'll be there to greet them. I've come a long way from the Tropical."

"I still don't want you pouring any coffee."

She touched his knee. "Haven't you noticed? I've gotten better with my hands as I've gotten older."

"You can get a five-yard penalty for holding, you know."

She removed her hand, and her pouty smile turned wry. "That's you, all right, Nolan. The referee of my life."

"Maybe so, but I'm always interested in a forward pass. Somebody."

"Huh?"

"Just came in. Do your duty."

She went over to the door, where a handsome well-dressed brown-haired kid in his early twenties seemed glad to see her. Then he realized she was just the hostess, and when she realized he wasn't here to dine, she merely pointed him to the bar area and dance floor, where he slipped into the crowd, just another would-be John Travolta. Or whoever this year's hunk was.

Nolan said, "I think he liked you."

"Dumb as a post. You could see it in his eyes. Well, anyway, I was saying. You're an honest man, now. Why don't you make me an honest woman?"

"Are you proposing?"

"No, just kidding. On the square. You know, we've been honey-mooning since I was in puberty. You might want to consider something more serious."

She smiled a tight little, crinkle-cornered smile, that wasn't pouty at all, and left him alone at the bar to think about this. Which he never had before. Sherry was the first woman he ever lived with, for any length of time; he'd figured that in itself was a commitment, the biggest he'd ever made to a woman, anyway.

But, hell—he was a businessman, now. A straight, prosperous businessman—who happened to be living with a girl less than half his age. How did it look? The Chamber had its share of bluenoses, after all. Maybe marriage was the appropriate thing.

Nolan asked Chet for a Scotch, a single, and smiled to himself. *I am going soft,* Nolan thought. *Seriously considering marriage. Worrying about how things look, what people would say. What would Jon say?*

Across the room, at a small table, where he sat alone, feeling the glow of the eyes of appreciative single women upon him, Lyle Comfort squinted at the man at the bar and, slowly but certainly, like fire from the efforts of a stubborn Boy Scout rubbing rocks together, a thought formed.

Lyle Comfort, who just two hours ago was burying someone he'd killed in a wooded area across the river, recognized Nolan.

Quietly, he got up and left.

3

Lyle Comfort didn't like killing people. But he did what he was told. That was his best quality: he was a good boy. He did what his pa said.

Tonight he had killed his sixth person in three weeks; that was two killings a week, though it hadn't worked out that way exactly.

The first was the hardest. The girl. Angie. He'd killed her when she was still unconscious, so it wasn't cruel. He'd shot her in the heart with a revolver, the Colt Woodsman Pa gave him for his last birthday. He couldn't bear to shoot her in the head; it might mess her face up. He had buried her in the woods, a couple miles from the house, nice and deep. Hers wasn't the only body buried out there.

But she was the first girl he ever killed. First woman. It was a good thing he didn't believe in God anymore, or he'd go to hell, sure. But Pa said God was something fools believed in to keep from going crazy thinking about dying. And he also said that dying was something that caught up with everybody, so exactly when somebody died was no big thing. It wasn't like it wasn't going to happen anyway.

That made sense to Lyle, and made it easier to do the things he sometimes had to do, for Pa. The other thing Pa said that helped was: "Business is business. Money makes the world go 'round, and a man's family'll starve if he don't do what's necessary to bring in the bucks."

So Lyle, obedient son that he was, did what was necessary to help Pa bring in the bucks.

Tonight was easy, compared to Angie. He went to the back door of the bar in Rock Island and found it open; a storeroom filled with boxes and stuff also included a little office area, where a fat man in a white short-sleeved shirt and baggy brown pants sat at a desk with a bunch of money in his hands like green playing cards. The fat man was making little piles of money out of a big one. He was balding and had a couple warts on his face. He was sweating— big wet circles under his arms. It was cold outside, but warm in here, several baseboard heaters going, and besides, a big man like that just plain sweats. He made Lyle kind of sick. There were some really awful people in the world.

"Lyle," the fat man said, quietly surprised. His name was Leo. It seemed to Lyle a good name for a fat man to have. Leo, whose last name was Corliss, smiled; his smile was yellow. Leo was a jolly fat man, but it was an ugly sort of jolly that made Lyle's stomach queasy.

"Hello, Mr. Corliss." Lyle walked over to the fat man, who sat at the desk in a puddle of light from a gooseneck lamp, and shook hands with him. The fat man's palm was wet, like his underarms. Country western music from a live band was shaking the joint, out in the bar; Lyle could hear happy boozy voices cut above the racket. And to Lyle it was a racket: he didn't know how anybody could like such terrible music, although truth be told, his pa was one of them. Lyle liked the new music from England; it was smooth and had a good beat.

"What brings you here, Lyle?" the fat man said; his face was sweat-beaded, the whites of his eyes seemed yellow. Had Lyle been at all perceptive, he'd have seen the concern in the fat man's seemingly cheerful expression. But Lyle, of course, saw only the cheerfulness.

"Pa sent me," Lyle said. "We got to talk about some new arrangements with our business."

"Well, pull up a box and sit down. Glad to talk, anytime. But, uh, Lyle—ain't it a little unusual, your daddy sending you to do business?"

"Unusual?"

"You're a nice-looking boy, Lyle." The fat man touched the sleeve of Lyle's brown leather jacket; Lyle didn't like that. "But I never knew you to have a head for business."

"Pa didn't send me to do the talking. He sent me to do the fetching."

"Oh? He's with you?"

"He's at the motel."

"What motel is that, Lyle?"

"Riverview."

"Hell, that's past Andalusia. Why so far?"

"Pa takes precautions."

The fat man shifted in his chair, a big wooden captain's chair that creaked like a rusty shutter, at least when the fat man moved in it, it did.

"Your daddy's a smart man," Leo Corliss allowed. "He's as good at steering clear of the law as any man I know."

"Right. I'll drive you."

The fat man swallowed.

Then, pushing on the desk, he rose; it was kind of amazing— like a torn-down building suddenly put itself back together. "I'll just tell my bartender I'm stepping out."

"No," Lyle said. "Pa said you should just slip out back."

"Why's he so nervous?" the fat man said, licking some sweat off his upper lip.

"My pa takes precautions."

The fat man's mouth twitched; it was irritation, but Lyle didn't know that. "Yeah, sure, right. Okay. Just let me get my coat. It's cold out."

The coat, a tentlike green parka, was on a hook on the wall by some boxes of liquor. Lyle let him get it. Then they walked into the alley and Lyle opened the door of his cherry-red Camaro and the fat man squeezed inside.

"I got the seat all the way back," Lyle apologized, getting in.

"It's okay," the fat man said, uncomfortable. "Let's make this quick, okay, Lyle?"

"Okay."

Lyle pulled out from behind the alley past the fat man's dark little bar on this dark little street, then drove down Fourth Avenue and caught 92 near the toll bridge. He played a Billy Idol tape very loud. The fat man sat and sweated and looked out the window at nothing. Lyle asked him if he wanted the heat in the car lowered and he said no. They were on Highway 92, headed to Andalusia, a hamlet on the Mississippi, when Leo Corliss finally asked him to turn the music down. Lyle did.

"Could you tell me what this is about, Lyle?"

"The food stamp business."

"Well, of course it's about the food stamp business." The fat man seemed irritated; even Lyle could tell. "That's the business your daddy and me are in."

Leo Corliss' Ace Hole was one of four bars that fed food stamps to the Comforts—the only one in the Quad Cities, however. The other three bar owners were, naturally, dead now, here and there around Illinois and Missouri. They had all had policies toward food stamps similar to Leo's. The fat man accepted a dollar food stamp as twenty-five cents toward drinks and cigarettes; he then resold the stamps to the Comforts for fifty cents. Nickels and dimes, but it added up. It added up.

"Has anybody come around?" Lyle said.

"Come around. What do you mean, come around?"

"Asking questions."

"Cops, you means?"

"Or anybody like a cop."

"No. Nobody. You expecting somebody to?"

The Mississippi River was at their right; it was a windy night, rocking the car, and the river looked rough. Moonlight danced on its surface, frantically, as if to Lyle's Billy Idol tape. At their left was a wooded bluff.

"Yes," Lyle said.

"There's the motel," Leo said, as they coasted by, a little old-fashioned motor court with half a dozen rooms and a sign saying, "Water Beds—Adult Movies."

"He don't want to talk there," Lyle said.

"Well, where's he meeting us, then?"

"Up a ways."

They didn't have the road to themselves—a car would occasion-ally weave around them, on its way from one bar to another. There were a lot of bars on this road, but the stretch outside Andalusia was free of bars, past a certain point, and rather deserted at the moment. Lyle, who'd been keeping it at an easy fifty, pulled over.

"Why are you stopping?"

With his left hand Lyle reached beside the seat and under and got out the .38, his birthday Colt Woodsman (just like Pa's) with its natural-wood stock. Lyle was always a little surprised by how heavy it felt. He never quite got over how different real guns felt from his childhood toys.

"Lyle…"

Lyle transferred the gun to his right hand. "Mr. Corliss, get out slow."

Corliss did; Lyle too.

The Camaro was parked on the side of the road near the river; a little picnic area was nearby—several wooden tables. Wind whis-tled and whipped the two men. The fat man, in his impossibly large parka, a puffy pale green thing that made him look even fatter, snugged its hood over his ears, zipped the coat and stuffed his hands in its pockets.

"I don't see your daddy," the fat man said. Lyle felt the fat man hadn't yet figured out what was going on; but of course he had, miles and miles ago.

"He's waiting over there," Lyle said, and pointed to the wooded area across from them; the bluff had given way to an area that seemed almost scooped out of the ground, thick with brush and trees.

"That's a funny place to wait," the fat man said, and something in his pocket exploded.

The bullet whizzed past Lyle but didn't touch either him or his cherry-red Camaro. Lyle's reflexes were the fastest thing about him, and he fired the .38 at the fat man, hitting him in the shoul-der, on the same side as the torn smoking parka pocket. The sound of Lyle's gun was a crack in the night, which echoed briefly before the howl of the wind—and the howl of the fat man—took its place.

Leo Corliss fell to his knees; the ground didn't shake, and Lyle wondered why. The fat man's pumpkin head was lowered. His eyes were squeezed tight and he clutched his shot-up shoulder, getting blood on his hand and smearing it on the parka.

"You have a gun in your pocket," Lyle said, figuring it out.

"You are one fucking rocket scientist, aren't you? You autistic son of a bitch…"

Lyle didn't know what being artistic had to do with anything, but he walked over there and pulled the hot weapon, a little .22, a baby gun for such a fat hand, out of the shredded parka pocket, and tossed it, tossed it hard. It splashed into the river; it reminded Lyle of a bar of soap plunking in a tub of water.

"Get up, Mr. Corliss."

Lyle helped him, pulling on the side of the good shoulder.

When the fat man got on his feet, he pushed Lyle and Lyle went down on the grass, on his butt, kind of hard. The fat man was waddling in the moonlight, trying to run, heading for the Camaro. Lyle shot the gun in the air.

The fat man stopped.

Then he turned and he spread his hands, one of them bloody, from his shoulder. "Why, Lyle? Why?"

"Pa's getting out of the food stamp business."

The man's eyes were round and yellow. "So you're going to kill me?"

"When Pa gets out of something, he gets out all the way. He don't leave no trail."

"What, killing people leaves no trail? Are you crazy as well as stupid?"

"I'm not stupid, Mr. Corliss," Lyle said. Thinking, he added, "Or crazy neither."

"You don't want to kill me, do you?"

"No, sir. Not particularly."

"I have money. You saw that money, back at my bar. I can give you that. I can give you more."

"I don't think so."

"You can get out from under your daddy's thumb. A good-looking boy like you should be out in the world, making a life for himself. Not, not living at home with your old man."

"Pa's good to me."

"I'm sure he is, but you got to be your own man, Lyle. Now, put that away, and let's get in the car."

"You'd bleed on my 'polstery."

"No, no I wouldn't do a thing like that. We'll, we'll use my coat, we'll tear my shirt, we'll stop up the wound. Take me back where I can get some medical help and I'll make you a very rich kid."

"No. I do what my daddy tells me."

"This is crazy! How many people does your daddy expect you to kill?"

"You're the last. You're six."

The fat man's mouth was open; he couldn't seem to think of anything to say to that.

Finally he did: "Over fucking food stamps?"

"My pa takes precautions. Step across the road, Mr. Corliss."

The wind sounded like a sick animal, crying down a canyon.

The fat man looked determined all of a sudden. Proud, sort of.

"No. You do it right here."

Lyle walked over to him and pointed the gun at him and said, "Turn around then, Mr. Corliss."

"Fuck you."

"Turn around."

Slowly, he did. He was trembling. His jowls were like fleshy Jell-O.

Lyle pistol-whipped him and he went down with a whump. Lyle waited for a moment, listening for cars, didn't hear any, and dragged the fat man across the road, by the feet, like the carcass of some dead animal, which essentially it was. A slimy trail of blood was left behind, but Lyle figured that wouldn't last. Traffic and weather would take care of it. That was about as smart as Lyle got, incidentally.

Pulling him through the grass and into the brush and trees was harder than across the mostly smooth highway. Lyle was only sixty yards or so into the woods when he dumped the body. He was out of breath, even though he stayed in shape. Mr. Corliss was real heavy. He thought about pistol-whipping him again, but figured the fat man would stay unconscious long enough for Lyle to go back and get what he needed.

He was right. The fat man was still out when Lyle came back and put on the yellow rubber dish-washing gloves and cut Corliss' throat with the hunting knife. Lyle was proud of himself. He didn't get blood anywhere but the ground and the gloves. He'd also brought the shovel, from the Camaro's trunk, with him. It was hard digging in this cold ground, which had a lot of roots in it. And the hole had to be plenty big, for Mr. Corliss to fit in.

But the fat man did fit. Barely. Lyle kicked him, hard, really having to shove with his foot, to make him tumble into the grave. It was only four feet deep, but he just couldn't dig any deeper. He poured some quicklime over the bulging body. That would help keep animals away, Pa said. Then he filled the grave in. Patted it down. Found some leaves and things and covered it over. It looked pretty natural when he got done. Lyle smiled to himself. *Maybe I am artistic*, he thought.

Lyle washed up at the Riverview—he really was staying at that particular motel, not having the imagination to lie about it, although his pa was not along (saying so had been Pa's idea)—and changed his clothes. Just for the hell of it, he decided to drive through the Cities, before catching the Interstate. The night was young— maybe some night spot would catch his eye. Just before he reached the Interstate, one did. Nolan's.

4

The next day, Sunday, in the afternoon, in Des Moines, Iowa, Nolan's frequent accomplice Jon—who, like Nolan, had gone straight—stepped in shit.

The shit, dog shit to be exact, a pile of it on the sidewalk just outside the New Wax record shop on University Avenue near Drake University campus, was just the beginning. And Jon, who had sensed storm clouds gathering in his life for weeks now, knew the dog shit for the omen it was. He rubbed the sole of his right tennie onto the curb and went in the door next to the record shop, over which he and Toni shared an apartment.

He and Toni were friends; they slept in separate beds, in separate rooms, though on occasion they made love. Once or twice a week. They met through rock 'n' roll—playing in a band together—and had been lovers at first, settled into being friends and, now, lived together. But it wasn't love. Jon wasn't sure what it was, but it wasn't love.

Jon was returning after two less than exciting days in Cedar Rapids, where he'd been a guest at a comics convention, that is, an organized gathering of comic-book fans. As a kid, Jon had been a comic-book fan himself—Batman, Superman and Spider-Man had been his best friends in a childhood that had buffeted him from one relative to another while his "chanteuse" mother traveled, playing the Holiday/Ramada Inn circuit—and, as long as he could remember, he'd wanted to be a cartoonist when he grew up. Now he was grown up, more or less, and was the creator of an offbeat comic book, *Space Pirates*, a science-fiction spoof, not a block-buster bestseller, but a cult item that was making him a modest living. An honest living—unlike those brief, volatile days when he and Nolan had…well, that was behind him.

He was short but had a bodybuilder's build, which made sense, because he worked out three times weekly at a health spa, and had lifted weights and such since high school, where he'd been a wrestling champ. His hair was short and blond, a curly skullcap, and he had a wisp of a mustache. On this crisp winter day, he wore chinos and a long blue navy-color coat with a big collar, a military-looking coat which he had, in fact, purchased at an army–navy surplus store. Under the coat he wore a short-sleeved T-shirt, despite the time of year; on it was one of his own drawings, as the T-shirt was quite literally the first merchandising spin-off from *Space Pirates'* cultish success: Captain Bob, the klutzy hero of his book, posed with a clunky ray gun in one hand and a bosomy alien broad in the other. He wore no gloves (Jon didn't—neither did Captain Bob, for that matter).

It was only one floor up, the only apartment up there, and the door was unlocked, which made Jon grimace. His drawing board was set up in the living room, near the stereo and nineteen-inch Sony TV. It was a spacious flat, drywall walls painted a pale green and decorated with huge posters, promo stuff from the record shop where Toni worked during the week, when they weren't out on the road with a band, which they hadn't been for several months now. Gigantic Elvis Costello and Blondie and Devo and Oingo Boingo and Kate Bush faces stared from the walls. Blondie was old history, now, but Toni's vague resemblance to Debbie Harry kept the defunct group hanging on, at least on the apartment walls.

Toni had been the lead singer of a group called Dagwood, several years ago, a mock-Blondie group formed out of the remnants of Smooch, a mock-Kiss group; like the various imitation Beatles bands—a number of which were still around—such groups could turn a steady buck on the Midwest club circuit. For six months Toni had done nothing in life but imitate Debbie Harry; even now she still admired the singer, and her own style remained heavily influenced thereby.

Jon knew that Toni had the talent to go far. She had looks and brains and drive, too. She was twenty-three, a year younger than

Jon, and was in her bedroom packing her suitcase. That was the other thing she needed, to go far: a suitcase.

She was packing stage clothes—sexy lacy gypsy-looking things she ordered from Betsey Johnson's in New York City. Right now she was in jeans and a Bruce Springsteen sweatshirt, a small woman with zoftig curves and dark spiky Pat Benatar hair.

"I was going to complain about you leaving the door unlocked again," Jon said, the words sounding empty to him.

"You still think your wicked past may catch up with you some-day," she said, not looking at him.

Jon sat on the bed. "It might. I made enemies."

She looked up from her packing and gave him a condescending smile. "Don't go all macho and mysterious on me, or I may just faint. Or puke."

"What are you mad about?"

"Who said anything about being mad? Look out." She was moving past him, toward the closet, where she was getting more of her stage clothing, Cyndi Lauper-type apparel, but sexier.

"You seem to be packing."

"You are one observant little man, aren't you?"

"Any special reason?"

"I'm leaving. Going."

"Where?"

"Minneapolis."

"And do what? Go down on Prince?"

She gave him a cold look. "I got a new gig lined up."

"What about our new band?"

They'd been rehearsing for about a month with a drummer and a guitar player, both of them college kids from Drake. Toni sang, of course, Jon played keyboards, switching off between an old Vox Continental organ and a Roland synthesizer.

"The new band just isn't happening, Jon. Those kids aren't ready to do anything but play weekends. They're in fucking college, for Godsake!"

"It's sounding good."

"Jon, we're too old to be some top-forty band playing frat parties and bars. I got to get out there and make it, really *make* it, before my tits start to sag."

Jon touched her arm. "I'd be glad to lift 'em for you."

She removed his hand like a bug that had lit. "Don't start. To you this is just a hobby. To me it's a career."

Jon stood, some anger bubbling up through his hurt feelings. "Hobby! I've given this thing three years of my life, working in bands with you, driving all over the goddamn country in that lumber wagon of a van, sleeping in roach motels, fencing with moronic club owners. Jesus! What do you want from me?"

She looked at him with something approaching regret. Sighed. Said, "Sit down."

He frowned at her.

"Sit down," she said, and she sat on the edge of the bed, pushing the suitcase back out of the way.

He sat, too.

"Jon, this isn't your dream. Music. It's always been second place to you. You've got your comic book, now. That's *your* dream. You've realized it."

"Toni…" He didn't know what to say, exactly. He supposed she was right, in a way. Music wasn't the passion of his life: cartooning was. Playing in rock bands was something he'd gotten into in junior high, for the hell of it. He'd only gotten back into music a few years ago, when his efforts to make it in the comics weren't paying off.

But now he had *Space Pirates*—a monthly comic book of his own. He wrote it and drew it. Penciled, inked, lettered it. It was a small-press book, for the so-called direct-sales market—which meant his book didn't get on newsstands, rather went only to the specialty shops catering to the hard-core comic-book fans—and what it was bringing in would, at first anyway, only amount to around eighteen grand a year. Which meant he needed another source of income, and playing in a band with Toni, weekends, could provide that.

"We made a deal, you and I," Toni said. "We said we'd try to make it together. Really make it. But I don't think you're willing, anymore. I think you want to stay in one place and play weekends. You're holding me back, Jon. You aren't ready to go back on the road full-time. You *can't,* and draw your comic book."

"Damnit, I *tried,*" he said, meaning he'd tried to make it in rock with her. "What about the goddamn record?"

With their previous band, the Nodes—which had gone through several incarnations—they had put together an album of original material, thirteen songs written by Jon and/or Toni. This was about a year ago, before *Space Pirates*, before the Nodes broke up, when they were playing a circuit throughout the Midwest and South, driving a hundred thousand miles or so a year. Like a lot of bands, they had put the album out themselves, when none of the major record companies responded to their tape, and had sold the album at their various performances. Midnight Records in New York, a record store that specialized in offbeat small-label product, had even distributed it to other specialty record shops, and overseas. It had gotten some airplay, on college stations primarily, across the country.

But nothing substantial had come of it, and the frustration of that had led to the group disbanding. Toni and Jon had been putting the pieces back together, these last six months, during which time Jon had placed *Space Pirates* with a small publisher and was spending more and more time at his drawing board and less and less at his synthesizer keyboard.

"I *financed* that fucking album," Jon said, pointing to himself, as if there were some confusion as to who he was talking about.

"I know you did," she said.

The money he'd spent came from that last job with Nolan; money didn't come harder earned than that.

"You got some major exposure because of me, Toni. You got

some very nice reviews—that guy in *The Village Voice* said you were 'distinctive and powerful.'"

She smiled at that; a sad smile. "The exact words of the review," she said. "You remembered."

"Yeah. I remember what he said about my songwriting, too, but let's not get into that."

Below them the record store's stereo was booming; they were open Sundays. Springsteen.

"Springsteen," Jon said.

"Springsteen," Toni smiled.

"I hate Springsteen," Jon said.

"What?"

"I never told you before. Kept it to myself."

"You don't like the Boss?"

"Never have. New Jersey and cars and off-pitch singing. Who needs it? I know it's like hating motherhood and apple pie, but there it is."

"Goddamn," she said. "Even your musical taste is bad."

"Sorry you feel that way," he said. "You're my favorite female singer."

"Shut up, Jon," she said. Sad.

The floor beneath their feet pulsed with Springsteen.

"Tell me about the gig," he said.

She shrugged. "You weren't so far wrong. It does have to do with Prince."

"You're shitting me."

Another shrug. "It's his management company. They heard our record. They like my singing. They came looking for me, tracked me down."

"*I* didn't see any short black guys in purple capes hanging around."

"Jon, short jokes don't become you."

"Hey, Prince is all right with me. I like anybody I can look down to. So. It's the big time."

She smiled, nervously. "I don't know about that. They're putting me with a band. We'll be doing some traveling. It's kind of like playing the minors when they're grooming you for the majors. Maybe something will come of it."

He patted her knee. "I'm sure something will. Why were you mad at me, when I came in? Why didn't you tell me, instead of just starting to pack?"

"You know how I've felt about the new band…"

"Sure. I've heard the 'you're holding me back, Jon' speech a few hundred times. But I still don't understand why you were *mad* at me. I'm the one who should be pissed; I'm the one getting walked out on."

"But you're the one who caused it! Jon, you betrayed me."

"Betrayed…"

She shook her head; the spiky dark hair shimmered. "Ah, hell, that's too strong a word, but we were supposed to be in this *together*. It's your fault we got stalled in Des Moines. It's your fault a comic book seduced you away from me and music, and your fault that I have to take off without you. Shit, if I thought you wanted it, I would've fought to take you with me…"

"They didn't want me, did they?"

She swallowed. "Jon, I figured you wouldn't want to come along, anyway. You couldn't do it without giving up your comic book, and…"

"You're right. I like doing what I'm doing. Besides, I know it's you they want. Just you. And I don't blame 'em. I read the reviews of the album. As a performer/songwriter, I make a great cartoonist."

"I…I handled this all wrong."

"There's no easy way. This place won't seem the same without you."

"Jon, uh—you forget. This is my apartment."

"Yeah?"

"And I rented it from Rick, downstairs, right?" Rick was who Toni worked for in the record store, the manager, the owner of the building.

"Right."

"And you remember when you and Rick got in that argument?"

"You mean, when we got drunk that time and I told him he liked funk because of 'liberal guilt' and he belted me and I belted him back and chipped his tooth? Yeah. I remember that."

"Good. Then you'll understand when I tell you that when I told Rick I was leaving, he refused to turn the lease over to you."

"What?"

"He really hates you."

"You could've sublet to me!"

"I didn't think of that."

"Great. How long do I have to get out?"

"Monday."

"What Monday?"

She winced. "Tomorrow."

"You mean, you're *evicting* me? You're fucking *evicting* me?"

"Well...Rick is."

"Jesus! When...how..."

"Prince's people called me Friday. I talked to Rick yesterday afternoon."

He stood; started to pace, the Boss pulsing beneath his feet; he wished he were walking on Rick's face—he wished he were walking on Springsteen's face, for that matter.

"I leave for two days," he said, ranting, raving, "and come back, and my life's shot to shit!"

Toni seemed genuinely concerned, now. "Jon—you can find someplace to crash. You'll put things back together soon enough."

"Christ, I got a deadline to meet with my comic book! I just lost two days in Cedar Rapids being civil to rude little fan boys who would've much rather met the guy who draws the X-Men! I have *work* to do, and you're telling me I don't have anyplace to *sleep* tonight."

"Tonight you do. He wants you out tomorrow noon."

"Oh, wonderful. Wonderful. It's nice to have a little *leeway*."

"You'll put it back together. Jon, it's not like we...well, we're just friends. We're not lovers."

"I guess we aren't," he said. He sat down again. "But I'm awful used to you."

"Maybe that isn't such a good thing. This'll be good for you."

"What'll I do? Where will I crash? Where the hell's my short-term future, anyway? Never mind the long term."

She shrugged. "Why don't you go visit your pal Nolan. In the Quad Cities. Stay with him awhile. It might be relaxing."

It might at that, Jon thought.

"In the meantime," she said, wickedly, pulling off her Springsteen sweatshirt, exposing the full firm breasts he would soon be missing very much, "why don't you fuck me goodbye?"

"What are friends for?" Jon shrugged, pulling off his *Space Pirates* shirt, quite sure that of the ways he was getting screwed this afternoon, this would be the most pleasant.

5

Family meant everything to Coleman Comfort. Family and money. Not that you could separate the two: Cole's loyalty to his kin was measured by money, by how good a provider he could be. As a wise man once said, there was no better yardstick of love than money.

Not that he bore the burden on his shoulders alone. He had taught his sons that you had to work in order to find your way in this world. The oldest, Clarence, had gone into construction and was making a fine living for himself and his wife and four kids, till the accident with the crane. Since Clarence's death, Cole had seen to it that his daughter-in-law got a check every month, or he had till she remarried, to some jerk who owned a motel. He wasn't bitter about that or anything: he didn't expect a fine young woman like Wanda to stay single. It was just that the family responsibility had shifted to the jerk.

As for the other boys, he couldn't complain. Willis would be out of Fort Madison in about a year; the boy had been doing just fine with that chop-shop operation in Dubuque—he just had a thing or two to learn about greasing the law, is all. You can't run a business without certain expenses, and payoffs was one of them. But, hell. Those two years inside would be just the education Willis would need to get himself back on track.

Lyle, well, he was doing good, considering. Considering he'd inherited both Thedy Sue's good looks and her meager brain-power.

Thedy, bless her soul, was the prettiest thing Cole ever saw. He'd married her during the war; he was selling tires and such on the black market in Atlanta and she was a backwoods girl come to the big city. She was waitressing but Cole knew she'd fall into hooking if some knight in shining armor didn't come along, which was Cole Comfort all over. He gave her some nylons and they were married soon after.

Thedy Sue was all Georgia peaches and cream, creamy skin, breasts like peaches, a strawberry blonde with freckles and wide blue empty eyes. Thick as a plank she was, but she kept her looks over the years; never ran to fat. She learned to cook and she had a sweet disposition. What did it matter if she thought two plus two was twenty-two, and signed her name with an X? What counted was she fucked like a monkey, and only with her lawful wedded husband.

She died giving birth to Cindy Lou. Sometimes Cole blamed himself for that; maybe they should've gone to a hospital. Hell, it was a fluke, the baby coming out feet-first and all that blood and all. Who could've predicted it? Cole had never met a doctor who wasn't a crook, anyway.

And Cindy Lou, she was the spitting image of her mother. She was her beautiful mother back again, only with something of a brain. It was all he could do to keep his hands off the child. But he did. Or at least had so far. He was weighing it in his mind: who better to educate her to the ways of the world than her pa? Who better to usher her into womanhood than her loving father?

Still, some vestige of his Bible-beating upbringing, back in the Georgia sticks, clung to him. Kept him from certain "forbidden" things. He knew it was bunk; he knew there was no God. He'd looked at the world and he knew it was as pointlessly random and thoughtlessly cruel as a child setting fire to a beetle. He'd looked at the sky and seen stars but sensed nobody up there. No grand design. No meaning to this life, at all, except the meaning you make for yourself, in your life's work, in your family. Then, dying day would come, and it would all be dust. Sweet Thedy Sue, who never harmed a fly, was dust now, wasn't she? It was stupid to think of her as being in "Heaven"—she'd have left her body behind, and cooking wouldn't be called for up there, and a good nature like hers'd be a dime a dozen in celestial circles. What use could *any* God have for a dope like her?

Heaven was hogwash, but his ma's teachings sometimes came out of the recesses of his brain to haunt him. But right there with it was the memory of Pa, who put the beating into Bible-beating— literally; he used the Good Book as a weapon, slamming it against the three boys' bare bottoms, hurling it at them from across a room. His older brother Sam, younger brother Daniel, and Cole himself received his boozing pa's discipline equally: no favorites. Even now the thought of it sent a hand to Cole's forehead; the memory of the corner of that big heavy Bible cutting into his temple was still there. So was the scar.

People would come calling and remark at how dog-eared the family Bible was. You Comforts must put it to good use. And Ma would smile modestly and Pa would just sort of snort.

Cole hated the thought of his long-dead pa; he had sworn he'd raise his brood better. He had sworn he'd be a loving father, and he kept his vow. For example, he loved Lyle, and only a truly loving father could love such a dipshit.

What you could say for Lyle was this: he did as he was told. He, and Cindy Lou for that matter (but she was less reliable, by far), had pitched in on the food stamp business. Lyle even came up with an idea, a good idea, although it was an accident.

"You'll be like a postman," Cole had said, explaining how Lyle would go to mailboxes and remove food stamp envelopes.

"Will I wear a uniform like a postman?" Lyle asked, with his mother's wide empty eyes.

Cole could hardly believe his ears. "Goddamn, boy, if that ain't a hell of an idea!"

"It is?"

It was. Cole had both Lyle and Cindy Lou wear postal employee uniforms when they were out collecting mail; that way, no one would question them going up to mailboxes, moving from this mailbox to that one, in broad daylight.

Acquiring the uniforms had been easy; in two separate communities, Lyle followed first a postman, and then a female postal worker, home. He burgled both houses, taking a lot of things among which were the uniforms. Enough things were stolen to make the missing uniforms get lost in the police-report shuffle; it occurred to no one that the uniforms were the purpose of the exercise. Cole had suggested to Lyle that he rape the woman, to further confuse the issue, but Lyle didn't want to do that. You had to give the kid that much: he may have been a dim bulb, but he had standards.

And this afternoon, Sunday, Lyle had shown signs of intelligence. Initiative, even.

Cole had been sprawled out on the couch, watching a Chicago Bears football game on the big-screen television, sipping a Stroh's, when Lyle came slowly down the steps, bare feet slapping the wood. The boy was in his T-shirt and shorts. He'd just gotten up. His curly brown hair was sticking up here and there.

"Morning, Pa," Lyle said, standing at the foot of the stairs. Stretching.

"Afternoon, son. You slept in."

Lyle yawned; sighed. "Guess so. Got in kinda late."

"I heard you get in. How did it go?"

"Mr. Corliss was no trouble."

"Didn't think he'd be. Look at that nigger! Can he *hit*!"

"He was hard to drag."

"What?"

"Sorry. Didn't mean to innerupp your game."

Cole sat up; something was troubling the boy. He patted the place next to him on the couch. Turned the sound down with the remote control. "Sit down, son. I don't mean not to give credit where credit is due. I been taking you for granted."

Lyle smiled, shyly. "Aw, Pa…"

Cole slipped an arm around the boy's shoulder. "I'm proud of you. You took care of all of 'em. It wasn't no picnic, I know that. It's messy work. It's work only a real man can do. I'm right proud."

"Pa, I saw somebody."

Cole squinted. "You mean somebody saw you…?"

Lyle shook his head no, emphatically. "No, no. Nobody saw me with Mr. Corliss. That road's real deserted. It's hard dragging a fat man like that, though. The ground was cold, too. Lots of roots in the earth. Hard digging a hole."

The boy's mind did wander, even if it didn't have far to go. "Well, I'm sure you were up to the job, son. Now what do you mean, you saw somebody?"

"Do you remember a man named Nolan?"

A red-hot poker seared through Cole Comfort's brain. His hands turned into fists and through teeth clenched tighter than Kirk Douglas overacting he said, "Do I remember a man named Nolan?" He stood. He looked at his knuckle-headed son through a red haze. "He only killed your uncle. He only killed your two cousins. Are you telling me you saw *Nolan*?"

Lyle shrugged. "I think so. I only seen him that one time."

Cole and his brother Sam had been in on an armored car job with Nolan, in Ohio; this was five years ago, anyway, and Lyle hadn't been old enough to play. But they'd met once, for one of the planning sessions, in a house where the Comforts were staying, Sam and his sons Billy and Terry, and Cole and his boys and girl. So Lyle had seen Nolan. And he'd certainly heard Cole talk about him often enough.

"Was it him?"

"Pa, don't! You're hurting me!"

Cole hadn't realized he was gripping the boy's arms; but he was: his hands were squeezing the boy's biceps red, then white.

"I'm sorry," Cole said, but didn't let go and didn't lessen his grip. "Was it him?"

"He seemed older."

The stupidity of that remark brought Cole back to his senses, more or less, and he let loose of the boy and rubbed his own face with one hand, as if trying to wash away the frustration of having raised such a thick child, and said, "You saw him five or more years ago, Lyle. Of course he looked older."

"He was fatter. Just his tummy."

"Middle-aged men can get a spread, boy. You'll learn about it, should you ever reach middle age. What else?"

"He has a thing on his lip."

"A thing on his lip? What, a cold sore?"

"No, a whachamacallit. A mustache."

Cole let some air out; Thedy Sue, your son's dimmer than you. "He wasn't wearing a mustache when you saw him, five or so years ago. But he's been known to wear one."

"So you think it could've been him?"

"I think it could've been him. Where was this?"

"Davenport. Near Interstate 80. A bar. Well, it was a restaurant, too. Pretty big place. Kinda fancy. Not snooty, but nice. Good place to pick up women."

"Go on."

"I think he might be the owner or manager or something. The woman who met me at the door—uh, what would she be called?"

"The hostess."

"Yeah. Right. She was talking to him a lot. And he was talking to the bartender, back behind the bar. Customers don't do that."

That pleased Cole; that was more or less a perception, and perceptions were rare where Lyle was concerned.

"What was this place called?"

"Nolan's."

Suddenly Cole wished he were a religious man; then he'd have a Bible handy he could hurl at the boy.

"And you're wondering if this might have been Nolan?" Cole said through his teeth. "A guy managing a place called Nolan's?"

Lyle shook his head. "Pa, I been through Davenport before. That place has been called Nolan's for a long time. I don't think it was named after your Nolan."

"*Our* Nolan," Cole corrected. He put a tight hand on Lyle's shoulder. "He's *our* Nolan, son. He'll be all ours, soon."

"You better make sure it's him. I don't want to go killing people unless there's cause."

Standards. The boy had standards. There was hope for him yet.

Cole stood up; he shut off the giant-screen TV with the remote control and began to pace.

"Lyle, you must understand…this Nolan is a bad man. You know how I feel about the son of a bitch, but I never told you, exactly, what he did. Do you want to know what he did?"

"Sure, Pa."

"Several years ago him and another man…a young man, about your age…went to your uncle Samuel's farmhouse in Michigan; they went there to rip him off. Now, one rule you got to learn, son, you don't steal from other guys in the business; it just ain't done—or if you do, leave scorched earth, not survivors."

Lyle nodded at the logic of that.

"See, Nolan worked with Sam before, and me, and we never did him dirt, never pulled a cross, nothing. He had no grudge against us. A friend of his did, though, and the fucker used that as a half-ass excuse to rip Sam off. He and this kid, Jon something, tossed some smoke grenades in the house and made it look like there was a fire."

"Gee," Lyle said.

"Your uncle didn't believe in banks any more'n I do," Cole said. The Comforts had robbed a few too many financial institutions to trust in them. "Sam kept all his money at home, cash, same as us, in a strongbox. And this he grabbed, when he thought his place was on fire, and run outside, right into the waiting arms of this cocksucker Nolan. Billy, your cousin, your young cousin, got wise to the smoke screen and was about to sneak up and put a pitchfork in this little prick Jon, when Nolan shot him. Shot him! Killed him! Your cousin Billy! What kind of man is he?"

Lyle shook his head in disbelief.

"Your uncle was fighting back, fighting for his life, when this kid, this Jon, fucking shot him. So Nolan and the kid left your uncle to bleed to death, but Sam was a tough old cookie, and he fooled 'em. He lived. And when his son Terry—your cousin Terry—got out of jail on that statutory rape charge a few months later, they went looking for Nolan, and Jon. And you know what become of your uncle and cousin?"

"They were killed," Lyle said.

Cole nodded frantically, sneered. "Shotgunned and framed for a bank heist that Nolan and this kid pulled! To this day the cops think your uncle and cousin robbed that bank, when those sons of bitches not only killed your kin but walked away with the take."

"Something has to be done," Lyle said.

Cole walked over and put a hand on his son's shoulder. "You're absolutely right, boy. And we're just the ones to do it."

"Shouldn't we get the money back, too?"

"The money?" Cole said. Sitting again.

"From the bank robbery. He looks sort of rich."

"Rich? Nolan?"

"That restaurant. I think maybe he owns it."

"You may have a point." Cole wasn't used to this, Lyle thinking. "Hmmm. Tell me more about his restaurant."

"Well," Lyle said, brow furrowed, the strain of thought starting to show, "it's in a shopping place."

"Shopping place?"

"You know—a mall? Right up at the front."

"A mall," Cole said. Smiling. "A shopping mall…"

A chirpy female voice cut in: "Are we going shopping?"

It was Cindy Lou, barefoot on the stairs, in a pink baby doll, not sheer but you could see her little nipples trying to poke through; she'd slept in, too. Her strawberry blond hair, Thedy Sue's hair, was tousled sexily.

"Are we?" she repeated, leaning against the banister. "Going shopping?"

"I think maybe we are," smiled her pa.

6

Sunday night, at 11:37 (give or take a second), Nolan sat up in bed, two pillows propped behind him, the lamp next to the bed on; he was reading Las Vegas travel brochures, looking for a bargain. There were three travel agents in the Chamber of Commerce, so he'd get a discount either way. But he wanted the best package.

He hadn't been to Vegas in years, and it would be an interesting trip; he probably wouldn't recognize the Strip—he heard the casinos were side by side there, now, jammed together, no breathing room. He had mixed emotions about that—he'd always liked having some space between casinos, liked the sprawl of that, glittery sin leisurely strung out along a desert road. But he had no argument with success, or the change it brought. Progress was progress; money was money.

The best package seemed to include the Flamingo, which almost made him smile. All roads led to the Family. He'd met Bugsy Siegel once; he'd come in the Rush Street Club with Campagna. Hell of a nice guy, Siegel was; charming. Campagna, on the other hand, Little New York himself, while nice enough, seemed menacing in that quiet way that meant the worst. Nolan had known, just looking at them, that neither of these guys was anybody to cross.

He'd also been to the Flamingo in the fifties several times, '51 the first time; but that was several years after the Family cashed Bugsy's chips in. The Fabulous Flamingo, Bugsy's dream, his pink palace which gave birth to the modern Vegas Strip, was in the red, in the early days, and word was he was skimming to sink dough back in the joint, cheating his Family friends/investors, like Accardo and Ricca and, out East, Lansky. So they killed him.

It would be fun to go back to the Flamingo, with all its memories. And it seemed to be the best buy, too.

The Vegas trip was Sherry's idea; she'd never been there and it sounded exciting to her. She deserved a vacation, so he figured why not—you only live once. What she was having trouble understanding was Nolan's attitude about gambling: he didn't. Not in Vegas, not in any casino, with the exception of poker, if he was in the right mood. Any other game was out of the question. Nolan never thought about it, but his life was lived by a strict set of rules, and one of the strictest was: You never play against the house.

Nolan put the travel brochures on the nightstand and turned off the lamp; he sat in the dark, naked under the covers, hands folded on his plump belly, which looked plumper than it was, contrasted with the rest of his lean, scarred, muscular frame.

He was waiting for Sherry. This was the ritual, on the nights they made love, which was perhaps every other night, except in her period, of course.

She would say, "I'll meet you in the bedroom in five minutes." He would say fine, and would slip downstairs to shower in the can, off the guest bedroom. She would be upstairs, readying herself. Bath; diaphragm; makeup; perfume. The perfume was this hundred-and-fifty-buck-an-ounce shit from Beverly Hills, which even with his fifteen percent discount from Petersen's was a crock. His Christmas gift to her last year. It did smell good.

Within the specified five minutes, Nolan would be between the sheets; nothing but him and his Old Spice, powder and after-shave both. Another ten to fifteen minutes would pass, during which he would either read or think. He didn't mind the wait; he liked time to himself, and with all the hours he was putting in at Nolan's, ten minutes here, fifteen minutes there, meant something. He found these lulls relaxing. Calming.

Just about when he'd given up, she'd appear in the doorway, her slim, curving form a silhouette against the hall light behind her. Sometimes she'd switch on the overhead bedroom light and be naked for him. Most women are beautiful in the dark; Sherry was beautiful with the lights on. Her legs were long, sleek—not muscular, not fleshy—sleek. Supple. Her waist was impossibly narrow. Her breasts were full, nipples very pink against her creamy white flesh, translucent flesh gently marbled blue, life flowing through her. The hair between her legs was darker blond than the hair on her head, but just as well tended; she trimmed the bush, brushed it—he'd seen her do this, from time to time; this is for you, she'd say, smiling wickedly. Driving him crazy.

The only imperfection was an appendix scar, and this, too, he liked: it made her human. Her breath was very bad in the morning, like anybody else; and without her makeup she was better than plain but less than pretty. He liked that too. He liked the fantasy of his bedroom but he also liked the reality of daily life with her, a smart, funny cookie who was getting good at helping him run his business.

Tonight she didn't switch on the light, as she stood in the bedroom doorway; tonight she was in a red and black corset affair, breasts almost spilling out the top, mesh black stockings that rose to midthigh; beneath the corset, silhouetted, was her pubic fringe. The sheet between his legs rose to salute her.

She came over and flipped the covers back and, sitting on the edge of the bed, leaned over and put him in her mouth; he closed his eyes and began to believe in a life after death.

Then she climbed on top of him and rode him till they both came; it took a while, a nice while. She tumbled off to one side and Nolan reached over to the bed stand and got them both some tissues.

"I love to fuck you," she said.

"I hate it," he said.

She kissed him and snuggled close. "Sometimes I just have to do that—take charge of you."

"A girl's gotta do what a girl's gotta do."

She kissed his shoulder. "I get tired of you dominating me all the time. Sometimes I just have to strike back."

"Feel free to get back at me this way anytime."

"I wonder if it would be any less fun?"

"What?"

"Making love. After we were married." That again.

"I don't know," he said. "I've never been married."

"Me either. Have you been giving it some thought?"

He had been.

"Not really," he said.

"I think maybe we should. Get married."

"Oh?"

"For your standing in the community, if nothing else. You're a respectable businessman. Living with a young woman."

"In sin," he added.

"In sin," she smiled.

"I could adopt you."

"Incest is against the law."

"Well we can't have that, can we. Breaking the law."

"That's right—you're reformed." Sherry was well acquainted with Nolan's criminal past.

"I'm a different man, now," he said.

"Do you really think so?"

"Sure. I like crossing the street with the light. It's a whole new thing."

"You never miss it? The excitement?"

Sometimes.

"Never," he said.

"I bet you had a lot of women."

"Yes, but you were my first virgin."

"Very funny."

"When *did* you lose your virginity?"

"Junior high."

"Some young stud."

"No. One of my teachers."

"Dirty old man, then. Should've been shot."

"Not really. He seemed old, at the time, but I think he must've been about twenty-three. He was married, but unhappy. He got a divorce, later. Wonder what became of him?"

"Doesn't seem like a memory you're troubled by."

"I'm not. He was cute. He screwed me on his desk. A bunch of times."

"I don't think I want to hear this."

"Are you jealous?"

"Are you lying?"

Getting screwed on a teacher's desk sounded like a *Penthouse* magazine letter to Nolan.

"No," she said. "I've always liked boys."

"It sounds to me like you've always liked men."

"Yeah. I always went with the older guys. In junior high, it was high school guys, once I broke up with the teach. In high school, I went with college boys. And I always put out."

"Are you bragging?"

"No. I just want you to know something—you're the first man I've ever been with who's made an honest woman out of me."

"I haven't married you yet."

"I don't mean it like that. I never lasted with anybody more than a few months; then I'd get bored. It took you to settle me down, Nolan. I haven't wanted anybody but you, since the day we met."

For a second there, Nolan expected violins; but there weren't any. That was a relief.

"What are you going to tell me next?" he said. "That the time we were apart, you were faithful to me, too?"

"Of course not. But I've stayed faithful to you, since the day I moved into this house. And I'll stay faithful to you till the day you boot me out."

"That day won't come, doll."

She smiled on one side of her face; she liked being called "doll." She told him, once, she liked those old-timey sounding terms of endearment. Doll. Baby. Sweetheart. Nolan didn't know what she was talking about.

"Have you been faithful to me?" she asked.

Yes he had.

"What you don't know won't hurt you," he said, and kissed her forehead.

"You don't have to marry me," she said.

"You're not pregnant, then?" He blew air out, as if relieved.

"You're a riot, Nolan. I just mean, I'll stay here, whatever the case. Till…"

"Till I boot you out. Right. Well, we'll think about this marriage thing. There's things to consider, you know."

"Such as?"

"Our respective ages. I'm better than twice yours."

"I don't care."

"What if we had children?"

"What if we did?"

"I don't like the idea of going to my kid's graduation in a wheel-chair."

"Don't be silly."

"Not silly; realistic. In ten years you'll be in your thirties and I'll be in my sixties."

"I don't care."

"In about fifteen years, you'll come through that doorway in a Frederick's nightie and nothing will happen under these covers."

"How do you know that?"

"It'd be like raising the dead."

She slipped her hand down between his legs. "I've been known to perform miracles."

She was in the process of performing one when the doorbell rang. Her head jerked out of his lap and she said, "Damn."

"Maybe they'll go away," he said, and guided her head back down.

But the mood was broken, and the bell was ringing.

"Goddamn," she said, getting out of bed.

"I'll get it," Nolan said. "You get back in bed."

He put his brown silk dressing robe on, ten percent discount from Mosenfelder's, and walked down the hallway. He stopped halfway, and went back into the bedroom, where Sherry was standing cinching the belt on a white knee-length terry-cloth robe.

"What?" she said.

The doorbell was still ringing.

"Sunday night," he said. "It's almost twelve-thirty."

"So?"

"Who comes calling Sunday night at twelve-thirty?" He pulled open a drawer on the nightstand by the bed and got out his long-barreled .38.

"Nolan…"

"It's probably nothing," he said, and, gun in hand, walked back down the hall.

The doorbell rang again, and this time Nolan cracked the door and looked out, .38 tight in his hand, flat against the door, out of sight from whoever was standing out there.

Whoever was standing out there turned out to be a short, curly-headed mustached kid in a long navy woolen coat with a wide turned-up collar.

Jon.

Jon with a mustache, Nolan thought, stroking his; *I'll be damned.*

He was standing there with two suitcases on the cement next to him, looking very tired, very bleary-eyed, looking like a truck driver who had just pulled an all-night run and forgot his No-Doz. Even the wispy excuse for a mustache seemed droopy.

Nolan unlatched the door and swung it open.

"What the fuck," he said.

"Hello to you, too, Nolan," Jon said, smiling a little. "Is that a gun, or are you just glad to see me?"

"Just a second," he said. Nolan leaned over to the nearby door-less doorway to the kitchen and laid the .38 gently on the counter, next to a toaster.

Back in the front doorway, he said to the kid, "What are you doing here?"

"Freezing my nuts off on your front landing. Can I come in?"

"Why not."

He helped the kid with his bags.

"My drawing board and some other stuff's in the van," Jon said, as Nolan shut the door behind him. "It can wait till tomorrow."

"What is this, kid?"

"I got kicked out of my apartment. I didn't have anyplace to go. I was hoping I could chill out here for a few days."

"What does 'chill out' mean?"

Jon was all but asleep on his feet. "I want to stay here awhile, Nolan. Get my act together."

"Are you in trouble?"

"That depends on your definition. Is somebody trying to kill me? Not that I know of; the Comforts are dead, remember? And the cops never got a make on us, that I know of. I have a normal life now. The kind of life where people don't shoot at you, but your girlfriend walks out and your landlord evicts you and you don't even have a band to play in anymore and..."

Nolan guided him by the arm to a soft modular chair in the nearby, big, open living room. "You're dead, aren't you, kid?"

"More or less. It's a pretty long drive, and I had a pretty long day before I started it. Hey, uh, I tried to call; no answer. I figured you were working."

Nolan, standing near the chair the kid sat in, shrugged. "I took Sherry to a movie this afternoon," he said. "I don't put the answer machine on, on Sundays. It's my day off."

Jon yawned, grinned. "Christ, you're leading a normal life, too, aren't you? Your day off. You went to a movie. I can't picture that. What did you see?"

"Something with a woman named Street."

"Street?"

"I think that was it. She had a big nose."

"Oh, *Streep*. Was it good?"

He shrugged. "I don't know. I slept."

"Now that restores my faith in you."

"Your girlfriend walked out. Who, Toni?"

Toni and Nolan had met, briefly, a year ago or so.

"Yeah," Jon said. He explained about the big break Toni had gotten, with Prince's people.

"That shorty faggy black guy?" Nolan asked.

"That's him."

"You can sell people anything," Nolan said, struck by the wonder of it.

Jon was blinking, trying to stay awake. "You mentioned Sherry. You're still with Sherry."

"Still with Sherry."

"I never met her," Jon said.

"You have now," Sherry said; she was standing at the end of the hallway in her short terry robe.

"Pleased to meet you," Jon said, eyes momentarily a little wide. Even with her hair messed up, as it was now from their lovemaking, Sherry was a handsome woman.

Sherry walked over and offered Jon her hand; Jon stood, shook the hand, smiled at her, apologized for barging in.

"I'm beat," he said. "I just need to crash somewhere."

"There's a bedroom downstairs," she said.

"I know," Jon said. "Two of them, actually." He'd roomed there awhile, when Nolan first moved in, before Sherry was called on the scene.

"I've heard a lot about you," Sherry said, arms folded.

"I find that hard to believe," Jon said. "What did Nolan tell you about me? No. Never mind. I need a good night's sleep before I can deal with that."

"I'll get your bags," Nolan said.

"No, no," Jon said.

"I'll get your bags," he repeated; he had them in his hands, now.

"No use arguing with Nolan," Jon told Sherry.

Jon followed Nolan down the open stairs off the living room into the big open rec room, where a competition-size pool table and a wet bar dominated, and down the hall to the right, to the guest bedroom.

"I appreciate this, Nolan," Jon said, flopping on the bed. The sparsely furnished room had three light blue plaster walls and one wall that was strictly closet with wood sliding doors.

"No problem," Nolan said.

"I, uh…may need to stay a week."

"No problem."

"You really are a good friend, Nolan, underneath it all."

Nolan said nothing. Then he turned to go.

Jon said, "Thanks, Nolan. G'night."

"Night, kid."

Nolan stepped out into the hall; then he peeked his head back in and said, "Kid?"

"Yeah?"

"Lose the mustache."

7

Two weeks later, on a colder Sunday night, snow on the ground, Sherry was feeling pissed.

She had been invaded. It was as simple as that. This Jon person shows up, out of the blue, and simply moves in. Just like that. Like he fucking owned the place.

The screwy thing was, he and Nolan weren't even particularly nice to each other. They rarely spoke. They went their own way. On no occasion in the two weeks since he'd been there had Jon ever eaten a meal with them—with the exception of Thanksgiving, last week. She'd made a turkey and all the fixings, a rarity, since she seldom cooked; she and Nolan ate at restaurants, sometimes their own, on weeknights, after the dining room closed; but more often one of the many other restaurants in the Cities: Nolan's accountant had confirmed that if he ate his meals at rival restaurants, he could deduct the meals, on a basis of "checking out the competition." So when Sherry made the grand gesture of actually cooking a meal at home—particularly something as elaborate as a turkey dinner—she would like to have the sullen son of a bitch all to herself, at least.

But, nooooooo—this "kid" (as Nolan called him—though he seemed to be in his mid-twenties) had to join them. Jon was polite enough, and praised the meal, more overtly than Nolan (but that was no big deal—her man was as stingy with his praise as he was with his money) but what little table talk there was was confined to the football game the two of them had just watched, that and the football game they would watch next, into the evening! Men. It was hard enough living with one—now she was living with two!

She and Jon had barely spoken as the days turned into weeks; he seemed to be avoiding her—and when he couldn't avoid her, when he came face-to-face with her, he'd give her a twitch of a

smile and avoid her eyes, avoid looking at her, as if he couldn't
bear to, as if she were something horrible to look upon.

It was early Sunday evening, and she was driving back to the
house after a long afternoon of solitary shopping, at Brady Eighty's
chief rival, North Park. She had shopped there primarily to figura-
tively thumb her nose at Nolan. It drove him crazy when she
shopped anywhere but Brady Eighty, because of the discounts
she could get at their "home" mall. Normally, she lived and let
live where his tight streak was concerned; after all, he provided a
good home for her, and paid her a salary, a generous one, for her
hostessing at Nolan's. So she had her own money.

But she relished the pained look that would register on that
Lee Van Cleef mug of his, when he saw the sacks from North Park
stores.

"They don't have a Limited at Brady Eighty," she'd explain innocently, shrugging.

And he'd shake his head, eyes wide.

Childish of her, she supposed, as she tooled her midnight-blue
Nissan 300 ZX across the bridge at Moline; the river tonight was
smooth, shimmering with ivory, reflecting the three-quarter moon
that rode the sky like a gray-smudged broken dinner plate. The
fuel-injected toy she drove had been Nolan's gift to her last
Christmas. She felt a fool, and an ungrateful one at that, for considering him a Scrooge.

Who cared why he had affection for Jon? He clearly had it,
despite his surly treatment of the "kid." And Jon clearly looked up to
Nolan, despite his efforts to stand up to him and be equally surly.

She knew the story. She knew Jon had been the nephew of a
man named Planner, an old guy who ran an antique shop in Iowa
City, who on antique-buying jaunts would seek out, scope out and
scheme out what Nolan referred to, euphemistically, as "institu-
tional jobs." Robberies was what they were, and when Nolan had
been on the outs with those Chicago gangsters, Planner had helped
him line up "one last job," asking Nolan to take Jon along, his green,
young nephew, whose criminal experience had been limited to a

couple of gas station stickups with several wild friends. As a favor to Planner, and out of desperation, Nolan had undertaken the job—a bank robbery—with Jon and those two wild friends, one of them a young woman who worked at the bank in question. The "job" had gone well enough, but shortly thereafter, the Chicago gangsters descended on Nolan, who got shot up, bad.

Jon, however, had stuck around after the "job" and spirited the wounded Nolan away, to safety and a doctor.

Maybe it was that simple—Jon had saved Nolan's life, once; maybe that was what linked them. She knew, too, that the old antique shop guy, Planner, had later been killed by the Chicago people, and that Nolan felt responsible, and seemed to have taken the "kid" under his wing, after that. They'd pulled a couple more jobs and faded into separate, straight lives: Nolan with Nolan's, Jon with this rock 'n' roll band he traveled with.

He was also a cartoonist, Jon was, and apparently his rock 'n' roll band had split up and his creative energy was being channeled into comic books at the moment. He had set up a corner of the rec room downstairs, by the sliding glass doors facing the swimming pool (covered over with plastic now), where he could work in "natural light," he said. He had a drawing board where he worked on big sheets of heavy white paper, drawing in pencil, then going over it in ink. He was really quite good—the drawings were realistic but pleasantly goofy; it was something about outer space, sort of a skewed *Star Trek*. She had found one of the comic books lying around and she had read it and found it amusing. She would hate to admit that, but she did find it amusing.

He was no trouble. None at all. Quiet. Living his own life. He filled the little refrigerator behind the bar with little cans of orange juice, which seemed to be his only breakfast. She didn't know where he took his other meals—he was in and out, driving Nolan's Trans Am, while his own vehicle, an old light blue Ford van from his band days, was at a nearby service station for some work. What he was doing with his time away from the house, she had no idea. Mostly he spent long, long hours at the drawing board.

The problem wasn't Jon. The problem was his presence. This Las Vegas trip was coming up in two weeks. She had counted on having a month with Nolan to work on him. To put her plan in motion. To put it simply, her plan was to get Nolan to marry her—"on the spur of the moment"—in Vegas. In one of those charmingly sleazy little wedding chapels she'd read about. She would orchestrate it so it was his idea. Nolan was the kind of man who only acted on his own ideas; she knew that well—she'd been giving him ideas to have ever since she met him.

But having that extra person in the house was throwing things off kilter. Their sex life was off—she was uncomfortable having sex while somebody else roamed the house. Even though Jon stayed downstairs, she found herself trying not to make noise during lovemaking, not wanting Jon to hear. Why she cared, exactly, she didn't know; but she did. It bothered Nolan too, whether he knew it or not—their little ritual was undone: he could no longer go downstairs to shower while she luxuriously bathed and readied herself for him. They had to share the bathroom, and sharing a bathroom is a sure way to kill the mystery.

She loved this man so. He was all she had in the world; both her folks were gone, and her life without him had been a mess: a failed attempt at college; working as a waitress at a Denny's, for Christ's sake. To every other guy she'd ever known she was just a piece of ass. Nolan treated her like a person, with a certain unspoken respect. And he treated her like a piece of ass, too, when the time was right, and she liked that as well.

She wanted his name. She wanted his child. She wanted the whole traditional nine yards.

God, he was good in bed. She loved that musclely, hairy, scarred body of his. She knew the map of him like the expert traveler she was—it excited her to think that knives and bullets and years had conspired to make the slightly surreal work of art that was his body. She even liked the potbelly; it showed he was human after all.

She was well aware that Nolan was a father figure to her. She'd always liked older men; she'd always had a crush on her own father, a steelworker, a tough, grizzled, silent man who had never once told her he loved her, but she knew he did. Like she knew Nolan loved her. Even if he hadn't ever said it, goddamn him.

When her father died, six months ago, and she went home to the funeral, alone, having told Nolan not to come, she stood at the grave and said goodbye to her one father and went back to the ranch-style house in Moline to be with her other father.

Coming back from her father's funeral, she'd decided: she was going to marry Nolan. It had been a long, slow, steady campaign; only recently had she openly tipped her hand. And he had reacted well. He would come through. All he needed was the right coaxing, the right stroking, the right nudging...

And now, two weeks till Vegas, there was a monkey wrench in the works, a short, blond monkey wrench named Jon.

Yesterday she'd finally talked to Jon about it. Saturday afternoon—Nolan's didn't open till five o'clock, and they didn't go down there Saturdays till four-thirty—Nolan and his golfing buddies were upstairs watching some basketball game on the twenty-seven-inch Sony. She had slipped downstairs where Jon was hunched at his drawing board; the drapes on the wall of windows and sliding doors were drawn, letting in the light of an overcast day, the trees that surrounded their backyard, and its pool, were brown and gray and skeletal, touched with snow.

"How can you see?" she asked him.

He glanced up from his work at her, and immediately back at it; he was inking a penciled bug-eyed monster who was clutching a half-naked female space person in one clawed hand.

"Too busy to get up and turn on the light," he said, stroking his upper lip, where his mustache had been, squinting at the page as he laid graceful strokes of ink on his penciled drawings.

She turned on the Tiffany-shaded hanging lamp over the pool table.

He smiled, without looking at her, and said, "Thanks."

She went behind the bar and got herself a Coors Light from

among his orange juice cans in the little refrigerator. She was wearing Calvin Kleins, very tight, and a yellow Giorgio T-shirt, and no bra. She looked like a million dollars and goddamn well knew she did. And this little twerp paid her about as much attention as if she were Ma Kettle.

She swigged the beer, mannishly, and crossed her arms on the considerable rack of her breasts. "Am I so tough to look at?" she asked.

He winced; whether it was from confusion or the distraction of being interrupted, she couldn't tell.

He said, "You're a knockout. And you know it."

"What's that supposed to mean?"

He sighed; smiled at her politely. "You're a dish, okay? Now, I don't mean to be rude, but if I don't have this book done by Monday, I'm going to miss deadline. And since I'm paid on publication, my paycheck would in that case be a month late, and I can't afford that. Excuse me."

And he turned back to his work.

She swigged the beer again. "How long are you going to be staying?"

"What?"

"How long are you going to be staying?"

He got up from the drawing board and went to the sink behind the bar and ran the water and cleaned his brush. He said, "Do you mean, when am I going to be leaving?"

"Maybe I do."

"Soon," he said, passing by. He smiled tightly, politely, and sat at the drawing board and dipped the brush in a little black bottle of black ink. He began laying smooth strokes down, bringing the monster and the girl to life.

"You've been here two weeks," she said.

"It'll be two weeks tomorrow."

She swigged her beer. "So what's the story?"

Without looking at her, he said, "The story is I'm behind deadline. I don't have time to go out and find a place to live right now. I have checked around some, with no luck. Monday, I'll start making some serious rounds."

"You're going to live here in the Quad Cities?"

His eyes stayed on his work. "Just temporarily. I'd kind of like to move out to California, but I just can't take the time to drive out there, with no place lined up to stay. I have a monthly comic book to produce."

From behind them, a voice said, "As long as you're in the Cities, you'll stay here."

Nolan.

He was wearing a white shirt, sleeves rolled up, first two buttons open, black-tinged-white hair curling up from his chest; and gray slacks, which fit him snugly. He walked by her without a word. He had such a nice ass. He went over and looked at what Jon was drawing.

"You get paid for that?" he asked.

"Not enough," Jon said.

Nolan shrugged, then said to Jon, but looking sharply at Sherry, "Don't waste your money on some hotel room or apartment. Till you're ready to move on, you'll stay here."

"Nolan, I'm a big boy. I can take care of myself…"

"You're practically a midget. You'll stay here."

Jon was shaking his head, smiling but frustrated. "I appreciate you bailing me out like this, Nolan, but fish and company stink in two days. It's been almost two weeks, and I'm starting to reek."

"I don't want to talk about it," Nolan said, and went upstairs.

Sherry felt her eyes welling with tears, but it was anger as much as hurt. She swigged the beer; slid open one glass door and stood and looked at the brown plastic covering the pool. She was very cold but she didn't give a shit. Her nipples dotted the i's of her yellow Giorgio's T-shirt. She didn't care.

"A little cold for a dip, isn't it?" a voice behind her said.

Jon.

"Go away," she said.

"Look. I'm sorry."

"What do you have to be sorry about?"

"You have a right to be mad. I just moved in like I owned the place. You have a relationship going with Nolan. I'm messing that up. I'm sorry."

"Nobody has a relationship with that man. It's like having a relationship with a chair."

Jon touched her arm; she looked at him. He was smiling.

"He's a fucker," he said, matter-of-factly. "But he's our fucker."

That made her smile, and she allowed Jon to take her by the arm back into the rec room, where she realized, suddenly, she was shivering.

"I'll be out of here, early next week," he said. "Soon as I find a place."

"You don't have to," she said. "I'm just feeling bitchy. I get a little irritated before my period. For three weeks, before."

He grinned at that, glanced at her chest, glanced away.

Then she understood.

He sat at the drawing board and began to work. "I am moving," he said. "Soon. That's been my plan, that's been my intention. Nolan can't make me stay."

She put a hand on his arm. "You're attracted to me," she said, rather breathlessly, like she'd just figured out the meaning of life.

He glanced at her, quickly, rolling his eyes. "No kidding."

"I...I thought you hated me."

"You could make a man out of Boy George."

She pulled a barstool over and sat and smiled at him. "I get it, now. You're afraid of me."

He sighed. "I'm uncomfortable around you."

"I make you feel uneasy. And a little guilty."

"Quit it."

She was grinning. She liked this. "Because you look at me and certain thoughts go through your mind. We're about the same age, aren't we?"

"Give or take a century."

"And I'm Nolan's woman."

"That's a little arch, isn't it? Is that how you think of yourself?"

"Sure," she said. "I love the guy. And you do, too."

Jon looked at her and made a disgusted face.

"I understand why you've been avoiding me," she said. She slid off the stool, leaving the now-empty can of beer on the bar. "Out of respect."

"Respect?"

"I'm Nolan's property."

"Oh, please…"

"And the one thing in this world neither one of you would steal… is something from each other."

He looked away from the drawing board; looked at her hard, with a slow, barely-there smile.

"No wonder he likes you," Jon said. "You're smart."

"I got nice tits, too."

"Yes, and I'd thank you to quit driving me crazy with them. I got work to do."

She went over to him and held out her hand.

"Friends?" she said.

"Why not?" he said, and shook her hand.

But the handshake lingered, and they both felt the danger. And in a look they told each other that they would still keep their distance.

Now, pulling the blue 300 ZX into the drive, the smudged three-quarter moon painting the landscape ivory, Sherry was confused. Talking to Jon had done no good; she didn't dislike him, now—but she'd traded her negative feelings for feeling attracted to him. Now she had another man in the house to distract and attract her, complicating the situation even more. She had work to do; she had to concentrate. She had a man to marry. A man she was currently pissed off at, by the way. Yes, she was good and pissed at Nolan—for standing up for Jon yesterday, and quietly putting her in her place.

And despite what Jon said, she had the nagging feeling he'd be underfoot for weeks yet. When was her life going to get back to goddamn normal?

She gathered her Limited sacks and stepped out of the car and somebody grabbed her, a hand slipped over her mouth, an arm looped around her stomach, yanked her into the bushes. Something wet smeared her face and she smelled chloroform.

Somebody was dragging her, through the bushes, over the rough, viny, snowy ground, down the incline; she heard a motor running, a car.

She heard a voice, an older man's voice, very smooth, very soothing, very folksy, saying, "Nice work, son."

And a younger voice, an immature voice, said, "Thanks, Pa."

She saw the moon above, that broken-plate moon, go smudgier and gone.

8

Nolan, getting hungry, walked downstairs and found Jon at the drawing board; the drapes were drawn, but the sliding glass doors let in nothing but night.

"Did Sherry say anything to you about when she'd be getting back?"

Jon reached over and turned the sound down on his portable radio; he'd been listening to an oldies station—"Mack the Knife" continued brassily, but softly.

"She doesn't say that much to me, Nolan."

"Hmm."

"Is she late? What time is it, anyway?"

"After seven. She went shopping. Stores close at five-thirty."

"Could she have stopped for a bite to eat?"

"Maybe. We were supposed to eat together. But she is ticked at me."

Jon shrugged, said, "Sorry," and returned to his work.

Nolan was going up the steps when Jon said, "That's funny."

Nolan, one foot on the third step, other foot on the fourth step, said, "What is?"

"I was upstairs stealing a beer out of the kitchen about an hour ago. I thought sure I heard her pull in."

Nolan thought about that. Then he shrugged, too, and went upstairs.

A little after eight he looked out the front entrance, which was actually a door along the side, as the garage took up the front end of the house; he had to stick his neck out to see the driveway. Which he did, and saw her red Jap sports car.

He also saw the white shopping sacks, scattered on the driveway, like rumpled oversize snowflakes.

He turned his head back into the house and called, "Jon!"

And rushed out into the cold night.

Streetlights and moonlight conspired to make the outside of Nolan's house as bright as noon. He could see everything—except Sherry. She wasn't in the car; the rider's side was locked—the driver's side wasn't. He opened the door and reached under the dash and sprung the latch that popped the hood. He felt the engine. It wasn't warm. This car had been sitting awhile.

He heard Jon's footsteps crackling on the icy cement behind him; then Jon was next to him, coatless, hands dug in his jeans pockets, breath smoking, saying, "What is it?"

"I'm not sure."

The drive had been shoveled and salted, but a light snow had fallen that afternoon and he could make out where something—or somebody—had been dragged through the dust of snow. He quickly followed the trail to the edge of the drive, to where the bushes started.

"Fuck," he said.

Jon had been kneeling, looking at the discarded sacks, one of which contained a Ralph Lauren blouse, another a man's pale blue Van Heusen dress shirt, another a box of Maud Frizon shoes. Now he joined Nolan.

"What?"

"I think she was dragged through here." He pointed to the brush; a sort of path had been made, if you looked close: bushes were bent back, branches broken, snowy earth disturbed.

Nolan followed the path, pushing roughly, impatiently, through the foliage, twigs and branches snapping like little gunshots. Jon followed, sometimes taking a branch in the face, as it boomeranged back from Nolan's forward push.

At the bottom of the incline was the curve of the road that went up into Nolan's exclusive little housing development; of course that road went in the other direction as well, and the other direction was where Sherry had been taken.

And she *had* been taken.

"Oil," Nolan said, pointing to a black puddle glistening on the icy pavement. "A car was parked here awhile. She should have noticed it when she drove by. They were waiting for her."

"Waiting? Who? What are you *talking* about?"

Nolan bent and poked around in the snow at the edge of the curb. He found what seemed to be a frozen wad of white tissue or cloth; he picked it up, sniffed it.

"Jesus," he said.

Jon said, "Will you please quit saying 'fuck' and 'Jesus' and tell me what the hell is going on?"

He held the thing under Jon's nose. "Sniff," he ordered.

"Jesus fucking Christ," Jon said. "Chloroform."

"They snatched her," Nolan said.

"Who snatched her?"

"If I knew that," Nolan said, "I'd know who to kill."

Cars were streaming by on the nearby cross street, Thirty-fourth, a main thoroughfare. The world was going on as usual.

"Why would anybody kidnap Sherry?" Jon asked, his face contorted with confusion.

"Ransom," Nolan said. "Somebody thinks I'm rich."

"What will you do?"

"Pay them off."

"In what sense do you mean?"

"Every sense you can think of. Let's go back up to the house. It's cold out."

They didn't walk back up the wooded slope; they walked up the slickly icy street and cut to the right, up Nolan's drive.

"Are we going to call the police?" Jon said.

Nolan just looked at him.

Jon squinted at him. "Why, do you think this might be something from the past?"

"Maybe."

"What do we do now?"

"Wait. They'll call."

The phone on the kitchen wall rang at 9:37.

"Nolan," Nolan said.

"Lose something?"

The voice was male, rather soothing; an older man. With a faint, very faint southern accent. Nolan felt sick to his stomach; it was an alarm bell of sorts.

"Yes," he said.

"Do you know who you're speaking to?"

"No," he said.

A warm chuckle. "You will soon enough. Is there some...neutral place we can meet? To discuss terms?"

Nolan thought for a moment. Then he said, "Downtown Rock Island, the Terminal Tap. Next to the bus station."

"That sounds nice and public. Bring your little friend."

"My little friend."

"That curly-headed kid. He's part of the deal."

"I can't speak for him."

"You better. Twenty minutes?"

The line went dead.

Jon was sitting nearby, perched on the edge of the kitchen table. "Nolan..."

"Sherry is in very deep shit."

"What's going on?"

"That was Coleman Comfort."

Jon's brow knit a sweater and his mouth dropped to the floor but he said nothing.

"Sam Comfort's brother," Nolan explained.

"I didn't even know Sam Comfort *had* a brother!"

"Now you do. Cole makes Sam look like Sister Mary Teresa."

"Oh, Jesus..." Jon's head was lowered and he was running a hand through his hair.

"He wants you to come to the meet."

Jon looked up and his eyes were round with fear, panic. "Me?"

"You don't have to."

Jon twitched a half smile. "Sure I do." Then, trying to build Nolan's confidence back up in him, said casually, "I don't get invited to enough parties to afford turning down any invitations."

"Right."

They took Nolan's silver Trans Am and on the way he filled Jon in on Coleman Comfort.

"I did one job with him and Sam both," he said, as they rolled by a peaceful snowy park. "A long time ago. I always felt they would've crossed me if they weren't a little afraid of me."

"But you never had any real trouble with him," Jon said, meaning Cole Comfort.

"None before now. But Jon—remember: he thinks we killed his brother."

Bitterly, Jon said, "Even though we didn't."

"He also thinks we killed his two nephews, and he's a little more justified on that score."

"Shit, that's right." Jon shook his head.

Nolan knew that the kid had done his best to put this part of his life behind him, to forget about the darkness there.

"God help us," Jon said, "we *did* kill one of them."

"Not 'we,'" Nolan said. "*I* killed him."

"Same difference."

"In Cole Comfort's mind, yes."

Jon sighed. Weight of the world.

"Anyway, that's what this is about," Nolan said. "Revenge. Sherry may be dead already."

Jon looked over with some panic back in his face. "But he's set up a meet in a public place…"

"That may be to throw us off. He's crazy. He may pull a shotgun from under the table and start blasting."

"Oh, wonderful. And us unarmed."

"No," Nolan said. "There's a .38 in the glove box. Get it."

Jon opened the glove box and rustled around; under several maps and behind sunglasses and a flashlight he found a .38, a snub nose.

"Short barrel," Jon said, checking to see if it was loaded, which it was. "Not your style."

"Good enough for the car," Nolan shrugged.

"What about you?"

He took his right hand away from the wheel and patted his gray leather topcoat, where his left arm met his shoulder.

"Is it going to come down to that?" Jon asked. "Shooting it out with some crazy old fucker in a bar?"

"Maybe," Nolan said.

"And you think she may be dead already."

"Yes."

The Terminal Tap was a dump—a narrow dingy dark hole where stale, smoky air mingled with loud country western music; half of the usual neon signs and plastic beer signs were burnt out. So was most of the clientele, which seemed largely blue-collar, probably out-of-work blue-collar mostly, considering the Quad Cities economy. Comfort wasn't there yet, at least not at a booth or table or at the bar. Nolan checked both the men's and women's cans, his gun in his overcoat pocket, and a woman fluffing her bouffant glared at him in the mirror and said, "Do you mind?"

Then Nolan and Jon took a back booth. A pockmarked barmaid of thirty-seven or so in a checked blouse and too much makeup and badly permed mousy brown hair took time out from chewing her gum to take their order. Nolan said, "Anything draw," and Jon nodded the same.

"Okay," she said, but Nolan grasped her arm. He held up a ten-dollar bill for her to see.

"What's that for?" she asked. She had brown eyes. Pretty eyes under a shitload of makeup.

"This booth next to us, and this table," Nolan said. "They're empty."

"Yeah," she said, "right. So?"

"So keep it that way," he said, and pressed the bill into her hand.

"Sure," she shrugged, smiled briefly at Nolan. It wasn't busy. She'd have no trouble keeping them clear.

The beers arrived in five minutes, and in ten so did Coleman Comfort.

He was a tall, lean, white-haired man with a craggy but almost handsome face. He was wearing a western-style denim jacket with yellow pile lining and an off-white Stetson-type hat with a rattle-snake band; he stood just inside the door, pulling off heavy gloves, stamping the snow off his cowboy boots, unsnapping the denim jacket, revealing a blue plaid shirt, looking for Nolan.

Nolan leaned out of the booth and crooked a finger.

Comfort grinned like a wolf and came to them, slowly, holding his fur-lined leather gloves in one hand, slapping them into the palm of the other.

Comfort stood next to their booth and gloated. His blue eyes crinkled at the corners as he said, "Nolan. Been a long time."

The jukebox, which was in the corner just across from them, blared a Gatlin Brothers song.

"Sit down," Nolan said, and motioned for Jon to slide over and make room. That put Jon and the snub nose to Comfort's right, and Nolan and his long-barreled .38, which was in his left hand, under the table, directly across from Comfort.

"You might've ordered me a beer," Comfort said, eyes narrowed, affecting a mock sad expression, like a friend just a little disappointed in another.

"Don't fuck around," Nolan said.

The smile returned, and it was colder than outside. "I'll do what I please. It's my goddamn show."

The pockmarked barmaid came over and Comfort ordered a shot of whiskey. Old Grand-Dad, he insisted.

"Your little girl is just fine," Comfort said, slapping the gloves nervously against the cigarette-scarred, graffiti-carved wooden tabletop between them. He was still wearing the rattlesnake-banded hat. "Tucked away in a quiet spot, safe and sound. I'm not going to hurt her."

"Good. What do you want?"

He leaned back against the booth and gestured with a thick, gnarled hand. "You know, when my boy Lyle spotted you—he stopped by your fancy joint, you know, not so long ago—and told me he seen you, well, first thing I thought about was getting even."

So that was it. You couldn't live the straight life without something from the past, something bent, turning up now and then. And this time, it was a Comfort.

Nolan said, "I didn't kill your brother."

The smile faded. "Don't shit me, Nolan. You ain't in any position to shit me."

Nolan knew trying to reason with a Comfort was like lecturing a tree stump, but he tried anyway. "Your brother and his son Terry tried to hijack a job of ours; they got killed trying, but it wasn't me, and it wasn't Jon, who pulled the trigger. It was somebody else on that job, who's dead, now. So you're trying to settle a score that doesn't need settling."

"Let's suppose you're telling me the truth," Cole Comfort said, his eyes slits. "Even so, it don't justify you trying to heist Sam at his house that time; you killed Billy in the process, so don't go talking about scores that don't need settling."

Billy Comfort. The redneck pothead who'd been poised to stick a pitchfork in Jon outside Sam Comfort's rustic digs, when Nolan put two .38 slugs in him, killing him.

"Sam ripped off a partner of mine," Nolan said, knowing he was fighting a futile battle, but trying anyway. "I was getting his money back for him."

Comfort slammed a fist on the tabletop; the beers jumped, and Cole's smile, his cool attitude, fell away to show the rage beneath. "Bullshit! It was no business of yours. You don't steal from your own kind! It ain't done. You don't fuckin' do it!"

The barmaid brought Cole his whiskey. He paid her, then gulped it down like medicine.

"A lot of people who worked with your brother, over the years," Nolan said, "just flat out disappeared. The same is true of people who worked with you."

Cole shook his head, his expression now stern. "I'm a businessman, don't you forget it. I treat my business associates fair and square."

The Statler Brothers were booming out of the jukebox.

"What do you want for the girl?"

"Nothing. Nothing at all."

Astounded by all this, Jon entered the conversation: "Then why in hell did you take her?"

"Inducement," Comfort said, looking at Nolan, not Jon.

"Inducement," Nolan said.

"You see, we've had some bad blood, you and me—all three of us, matter of fact. But that's bad blood under the bridge, far as I'm concerned."

"Really."

He folded his hands. "I have a business proposition for you, Nolan."

"An offer I can't refuse."

"That's right. Not if you want to see that little piece of tail again."

"Don't even think about hurting her."

Comfort took off the Stetson-like hat and scratched his head, fingers lost in the thick pure white hair. Then he put the hat back on and said, "Oh, I don't think it's gonna have to come to that. I think you'd have wanted to go in with me on this job in any event —but, just in case, because of the bad blood, I took the girl for inducement sake."

"Get to the point."

"Like I said—revenge crossed my mind. I won't lie to you and say otherwise. But then I thought, Cole—stealing well is the best revenge. Ain't that the truth?"

"Point being?"

Cole Comfort's smile was a crease in his leathery face; his eyes twinkled, like a psycho Santa Claus. "I spent some time, recently, at that fancy mall of yours."

"It's not mine."

"Sure it is—you got your restaurant there. You know all about that place, and what you don't know, you can find out. I watched you. You got friends. You're a regular pillar of the community, ain't you, Nolan? They love you—butchers, bakers, candlestick makers. Bankers, too."

"So what?"

"I have a dream," he said, and it wasn't Martin Luther King's. "I think maybe everybody who ever was in a shopping mall has had this dream—namely, what would it be like to have the place to yourself some night? To just go shopping from store to store, taking what you want, and best of all—not paying for anything."

"That's an interesting dream. But maybe it's time you woke up, Cole."

He smiled big. "Dreams come true, sometimes. You're going to help me make mine come true. You're going to help me go shopping at Brady Eighty. We're going to loot the entire goddamn place."

Jon said, "You can't be serious."

But Nolan knew he was.

Cole Comfort, waving a hand in the air, grandiosely, said, "We're going to bring trucks in, semis, right into loading docks. We're going to steal every appliance and electronic plaything in the place. We'll hit the bank; the jewelry stores. We're going to empty everything but the pet store, and if one of us wants a god-damn dog, well, we'll take that, too."

"It can't be done," Nolan said.

"Sure it can," Cole said. He painted an air picture with a sweep of a gnarled hand. "Think of it—an all-night shopping spree—and we leave without paying the bill."

Silence; silence but for the Oak Ridge Boys, blaring.

"Let the girl go and I'm in."

"No. First we loot the mall. Then you get the girl."

Nolan looked at Jon. Jon rolled his eyes.

Nolan said, "When did you plan on taking this shopping spree?"

"Thursday night."

"What Thursday night?"

"Next Thursday night."

Jon said, "You're nuts. You're fucking nuts."

Comfort smiled at Jon, a nasty smile. "Children should be seen and not heard," he told him.

"How do you plan on going about this?"

"Oh, I got some ideas, but most of it, you're going to figure out, Nolan. You got the inside track, after all. You're going to run the show, like always."

"I'm the director," Nolan said, "and you're the producer."

Comfort grinned like a good ole boy. "That's right. Now, I've spent two weeks doing my own homework, and putting things in motion. We'll have three semis and ten men, ourselves included. Everybody'll be in town by Tuesday night. We'll have a great big get-together and you can tell us just how we can get this turkey shot."

"It's not enough time."

"It'll just have to be. Besides, sooner the job goes down, the sooner you get your piece of tail back."

"Don't call her that."

"I'll call her what I like."

"You do what you think is best, Cole."

"You're in, then?"

"I'm in."

"And the kid?"

"Ask him yourself."

Comfort looked at Jon and Jon said, "I'm in."

Comfort put both hands on the table and pushed out of the booth, smiling. He tipped his snake-banded hat to them. "Thank you, gentlemen. You'll be hearing from me."

"Cole."

"Yes?"

"If the girl is returned with so much as her hair mussed, I'll shoot you in the head."

"Will you, now?"

Nolan just looked at him.

Comfort's smile disappeared, and then so did he, out into the cold night.

Part Two

9

The mall was decorated for Christmas. At every entrance, including the one in back where Jon came in, a wreath-ringed red placard greeted customers, like a yuletide stop sign; it sat on a treelike post growing from a Styrofoam-snow base, saying, in a white Dickensian cursive, *Our Merry Best—Brady for the '80s*. Considering the lettering style, Jon thought, maybe that was the 1880s. Muzak dreamed of a White Christmas from unseen speakers above, as if God were Mantovani. Red and green banners hung from the ceiling, rows of them extending the width of the aisle, every six feet or so, swaying ever so slightly, looking more like grotesquely oversize military ribbons than anything having to do with Christmas. Or so thought Jon, anyway, who was in a very bah-humbug mood.

It was Monday afternoon, a few minutes after two. He had just come from the post office in downtown Davenport, where he express-mailed a package containing the original art for *Space Pirates*, issue #5, to his publisher in California. Normally that would have put him in a relaxed state of mind—knowing he had another issue behind him, thinking that a month sounded like plenty of time, a luxurious amount of time, to write and draw another twenty-two pages of outer-space comic-book whimsy. It wasn't, of course, but he liked to spend a day or two pretending it was, getting a leisurely start on the scripting of the next issue, picking up speed so that by week's end he'd be ready to start drawing.

This week wouldn't quite work that way.

For one thing, he was in no frame of mind to think up funny stuff—and for another, his time wouldn't be his own for a while, not till Friday, and chances were Friday wouldn't find his frame of mind any more conducive to thinking up funny stuff than it was today.

This week was spoken for; his time was taken up.

He had a mall to help heist.

This mall he was strolling through right now, Casual Corner, Radio Shack, Mrs. Field's Cookies, Kroch & Brentano's, Barb's Hallmark, weaving through the swarm of seasonal shoppers, in and out and around the mock rustic carts perched periodically in the middle of the wide mall aisle, cute carts filled with Christmas knickknacks, quilted Christmas stockings and little wooden reindeer and lots and lots of candles, seasonal shops on wheels overseen by teenage girls dressed as elves. In the central area of the mall, where the ceiling rose an extra half story to a mirrored height, tiny twinkling white Christmas tree lights, arranged in circular chandeliers, hovered like plastic ghosts; a white picket fence decorated with gay red bows surrounded Santa's cotton-covered slope, in the midst of which steps rose to the Christmas occasion. The fat man in red and white sat on a red and white throne with an eight-year-old girl in his lap; you can be arrested for that in some states, Jon thought. Teenage girl elves atop the slope were charging four bucks per Polaroid with Santa. Maybe stealing *was* in season.

Ho ho ho.

Christmas was Jon's favorite holiday, favorite time of year, for that matter; usually the commercialism didn't get him down, it was just part of the Christmas package—only this year he felt cynical and angry, because Nolan's Sherry was in the hands of that crazy murderous son of a bitch Comfort. Maybe she was dead already.

He had thought he'd left this behind him. He had thought those days, with Nolan, were over. He liked Nolan. He respected him, and supposed he felt something like affection for the guy, though you'd have to take Jon's toenails out with pliers to get him to admit it.

But those days with Nolan seemed a nightmare to him now. A vivid nightmare, easily recalled, but nothing he wanted to dream again. He had seen people die, violently; he had done violence himself. He had felt no exhilaration during the handful of heists Nolan had taken him on—only nausea and cold, clammy fear.

Already, he had the butterflies; like he always had before a performance. The trouble was, the resemblance between rock 'n' roll and heisting ended there: once on stage, music all around him, the butterflies flew; on a heist, impending violence around him, the butterflies grew.

How did he ever get mixed up with a guy like Nolan? He had his criminal uncle to thank for that; thanks, Unc. RIP. Merry Christmas.

He turned left at Santa's Kingdom and walked down a wide short corridor where, near the front entrance and separated by another *Our Merry Best* stop sign and a fenced-in patch of cotton snow with electronic big-eyed smiling-face rosy-cheeked puppets riding a sleigh, was the First National Bank branch, on the right, and at left, Nolan's. The restaurant wasn't open yet, but Nolan was waiting there for Jon. When Jon raised his fist to knock, in fact, Nolan's face appeared in the glass door and he opened it up.

Jon stepped inside, glanced around the place. This room (one of two, not counting the kitchen) seemed to be largely a bar, and there was a nice parquet dance floor, room for a band to play, if some tables were moved out. The walls were busy with nostalgic bric-a-brac and lots of yuppie-ish hanging and potted plants; it wasn't much like Jon pictured a place called Nolan's would look. Sherry's touch, he supposed.

"Nice place," Jon said.

"It's a living," Nolan said. He was wearing a pale blue dress shirt and black slacks; no tie or jacket. He pointed to a nearby table, and they sat.

"You want a beer or something?" Nolan asked.

"No."

"Did you take a look around?"

"Yes."

"What do you think?"

Jon gestured with two cupped hands, as if grabbing the balls of a giant. "I think this is nuts. Heisting a goddamn *shopping* center? It's looney! Why not Fort Knox, other than Goldfinger already tried it. And, shit, man, Comfort's crazy. As a fucking bedbug."

Nolan moved his head to one side, slightly; that was his shrug.

"You're right and you're wrong. Right about Comfort. Wrong about the mall heist."

Jon looked at Nolan carefully; the lighting was dim, and Nolan seemed even harder to see than usual. "You're kidding, right?"

"I don't kid, kid."

Jon smirked. "Really? I seem to recall a few thousand sarcastic remarks directed in my general vicinity."

"Sacking this place can be done," Nolan said. "It's nagged at me ever since I took space here, how easy it would be."

"Nolan, this place is fucking huge. And now this alternate-universe Jed Clampett wants to pull a couple of trucks up to the back door and go shopping? A couple days from now? And you think that's a good idea?"

Nolan folded his hands on the table and looked at them. "It doesn't matter what I think; it's Comfort's party. But the job is workable. It's also nothing I want any part of. It endangers the life I got going here."

Jon sat forward. "You mean, you figure an investigation after the robbery might be serious enough that somebody could uncover your checkered past?"

"Investigation is hardly the word. And neither is robbery. There are fifty shops in Brady Eighty. Two of them are jewelry stores. Plus three major department stores—Petersen's, J. C. Penney and I. Magnin. There's also a bank."

Jon shrugged. "Sure there's a bank, but there's no way to get in the vault. They're sure to have a big mother with a time lock. Right?"

"Right. But they got two night deposit safes, and an instant-cash machine. That's three safes—modest-size ones. You know what they got in 'em?"

"No idea."

"I'd say, twenty grand in the instant-cash machine. And as for the night deposits, you were out in that mall. You saw the kind of business they're doing."

"It's crowded, all right."

"It's December. The month that makes the rest of the year possible, for businesses. There could easily be fifty grand in night deposit money—not less than twenty-five."

Jon shrugged again. "So there's serious money in this. But there's also a ten-man string. Assuming Comfort won't pay the two of us, that still leaves eight, which is a lot of ways to split the take."

Nolan got up. He paced slowly beside the table. That bothered Jon; Nolan wasn't the pacing type.

"I don't want to go into it in detail right now," Nolan said, still pacing, "but I figure this for a half-mil haul, conservatively, after goods are fenced."

This time Jon didn't shrug. "So if this goes down, it's going to be major. Major media coverage; serious cop action."

"Yes. My being the inside man on the heist could well come out. So could my 'checkered past.'"

Jon was nodding. "The bank robbery will bring in the feds; state and local police will enter the other robberies; the department stores will have insurance investigators on the case…"

Nolan stopped pacing, looked around him. "I could lose everything."

"Is this place what's important to you?" Jon said, disgustedly. "What about Sherry?"

Nolan looked at the floor. "I said I could lose everything."

Jon sighed. "I'm sorry. I know she's what's important in this."

"She's more important to Comfort than she is to us."

"How so?"

"She's what's keeping him alive." Nolan checked his watch. "Come on. I'm having coffee with a guy at two-thirty. I want you to meet him."

They turned right at Santa's Kingdom toward the Walgreen's, half of which was drugstore, the other half cafe, whose outer wall was lined with booths looking out on the mall. Jon followed Nolan into the cafe, where they joined a ruddy-cheeked balding blond man of about twenty-five, who wore an expensive-looking gray suit and a red-and-green-striped tie; the gray coat was supposed to say executive, and the tie was supposed to say Christmas, or so Jon assumed. The guy wanted it both ways: authority figure and nice, regular guy.

"Nolan," he said, putting down the coffee cup he was sipping from, half rising, extending a hand to shake. "Good to see you."

"How are you, Stan? Stan, this is Jon Ross. He's an old friend of mine."

Stan half rose, grinning, extended a hand to Jon and they shook; too firm a grip, Jon thought, an overcompensating grip.

"*Old* friend?" Stan said. "He's as young as I am."

"We're none of us getting any younger, Stan," Nolan said, smiling faintly. "Jon's the nephew of a friend of mine. Late friend. Neither of us have much family, so we like to spend Christmas together."

"Right," Jon said, smiling blandly at the guy, thinking, gee, Nolan, what a crock of shit.

Nolan gestured toward Stan and said, "Stan Jenson is our new mall manager."

"Well, six months new," Stan said, embarrassed, as if Nolan had been praising him effusively, as if "mall manager" were a designation on a par with "ambassador" or "astronaut."

"He's the guy who thought up that 'Our Merry Best' slogan," Nolan said to Jon, deadpan.

"Really," Jon said.

"No big deal," Stan said, waving it off, as if Jon had said "Wow."

"Snappy," Nolan said, nodding.

"The advertising firm said they couldn't have done it better," Stan admitted, with a modest little shrug.

A waitress came and Nolan, who hadn't had lunch yet, ordered the chicken fried steak. Jon, who hadn't had lunch yet either, was still in no mood to eat; he ordered a Coke.

"Stan," Nolan said, "I appreciate you getting together with me. I missed last month's Mall Merchant Association meeting."

"I know," Stan said, smiling, "and we met at *your* restaurant!" He was grinning, as if he'd pointed out the biggest irony of them all. This guy was harmless, Jon thought, but a jerk. If a jerk can ever be harmless.

Nolan said, "What I wanted to talk to you about was mall security."

Jon squirmed in his seat.

Stan put on an exaggerated "oh no" look, shook his head. "Not that again. Are you singing the same old song, Nolan?"

"I think security here is lax, Stan."

Stan's expression turned somber. "Nolan, I appreciate your concern. And as a merchant yourself you have every right to voice your opinion. But I wish you wouldn't denigrate our fine staff."

"I'm not denigrating anybody. On the other hand, I didn't want to embarrass anybody, either. That's why I wanted to talk to you, one on one. Not at a meeting."

Stan nodded, appreciating that.

"Virtually every store out here, including the bank, is tied into the same security system," Nolan said.

"A-1 Security," Stan said, smiling tightly, nodding some more.

"They're a good outfit. But did you ever stop to think that all of our alarms are carried on one phone line? All it would take is for a thief to snip that one phone line and he could have carte blanche."

Stan smiled wide now, shaking his head, waving a hand as if to quiet a child. "That's not the way alarm systems work, Nolan—if the wires are cut, the alarms are activated—at both the A-1 office and the police department."

"It's possible to jump the alarm, Stan."

"Jump the alarm? You mean, cross the wires to bypass the alarm?"

"Yes."

"Wrong again, Nolan. This just isn't your area."

"How am I wrong?"

"Well, this is going to get a little technical. But bear with me."

"I'll do my best."

"A-1 tells me that if their alarm is jumped, the 'pulse rate' of the current flowing through it will set off the alarm."

The waitress put Nolan's chicken fried steak platter down in front of him; it included a generous portion of mashed potatoes with brown gravy, and Jon, whose Coke she also delivered, thought it was no wonder Nolan was getting a belly on him.

"Well, that's reassuring," Nolan said, cutting a bite of meat. "But I'd like to put another alarm system in, at the restaurant—not just a silent one, connected to A-1, but something nice and loud."

Stan lectured with a pointing finger, friendly but firm. "Check your lease. We don't allow any audible alarm systems."

Jon couldn't stay out any longer. He said, "Why not?"

Smiling, Stan looked at Jon patronizingly. "It's been our experience, in our other malls, that when such alarms go off during business hours, by accident, as they sometimes do, it can be very unnerving, alarming, if you will, to the shoppers." He stopped to chuckle at "alarming."

"With our location, on the edge of the city, with so little else around, who would hear such an alarm after hours, except the burglar himself, who would beat a hasty retreat? A silent alarm, on the other hand, which A-1 assures us that it can react on within minutes, will keep the burglar there and unaware."

"What's wrong," Jon asked, "with scaring him away before he has time to take anything or do much damage?"

Stan shrugged matter-of-factly. "What's wrong with capturing him? The five minutes it would take A-1 to dispatch a car, not to mention the police who may well be there just as soon, isn't that big a deal."

"Okay," Nolan said, his chicken fried steak eaten, just starting his potatoes, "you've convinced me. But one thing you will never convince me on…"

Stan laughed softly, shaking his head in friendly frustration. "You still think we should have a security man on duty twenty-four hours a day."

Nolan nodded, swallowed a bite, said, "I think you should hire four more men, and two should stay on night shift. Patrolling inside and out."

"That's simply not necessary. The corporation has malls all over the Midwest, and security measures in those malls are exactly like those here. When was the last time you heard of a robbery at a mall?"

"Hell," Nolan said, grinning, which was something Jon had rarely seen, "maybe I'm just paranoid."

"Well," Stan said, finishing his coffee, "at least you didn't suggest our security guard be armed, for pity's sake, like you did at that one merchants' meeting."

"I just suggested that for after hours," Nolan said. "And by the way, that kid you have on the job just doesn't have the experience."

"He was an M.P. in the service."

"You should hire some retired ex-cop to work with him."

"How is some paunchy old guy going to do going up against the young punks who cause problems in a modern mall?"

Nolan pushed his clean plate away from him. "If you had a young guy plus an old pro, you might come up with a winning combination."

"It would never work," Stan said. He glanced at his watch. "Got to run. Have a meeting with the marketing director at three." He got up and out of the booth, shook Nolan's hand, thanked him for his concern, shook Jon's, smiled, said it was nice meeting him, left.

"Jesus," Jon said.

"His father is vice-president in charge of personnel for the home office, by the way. Not that security would be any better around here if somebody competent were in his job."

"No armed guard at night?" Jon said, dumbfounded.

"No guard at all, after ten P.M. One maintenance man, who's a woman, who mops and does windows. Who could *Windex* a 'burglar,' if she ran into one, I guess."

"What about that 'pulse rate' business?"

"He's right, but it can be got around."

"Are you saying this is going to be easy?"

"No. There are plenty of problems. But problems can be solved. That's what our business is about."

"Are we back in that business?"

"Yeah. Just in time for Christmas, too. Come on. Let's walk."

They walked the mall, tinsel and plastic greenery all around them. Hickory Farms. Record Bar. Ann Taylor.

"Comfort called this morning," Nolan said.

"Yeah?"

"He told me some of the people he has lined up. I know two of them. Pete-man named Roger Winch, who usually works with a locksmith named Phil Dooley—Comfort didn't mention Dooley's name, though, and I didn't ask if he was a player; and an electronics guy name of Dave Fisher. Good people. That may make the difference for us."

"Well, good."

"I told Comfort that getting Sherry back wasn't enough. That I had to be in for a full share. And you, too."

"Well…uh, why did you do that?"

"I want him to think I buy into the notion that all he wants out of this is my help on the heist."

"And you don't?"

"Of course not. I'm convinced Comfort intends to keep Sherry alive only till after the job goes down. You see, I told him I wouldn't play unless I talked to Sherry on the phone right before the heist happens. That keeps her alive till Thursday, anyway."

"Damn."

"We're going to try to find her, Jon."

"I figured as much."

"Because once we've helped Comfort, he'll kill her. And me."

"Don't say it."

"And you."

"I asked you not to say it." Muzak played "Jingle Bells." Jingle all the way.

10

Andy Fieldhaus, forty-five years old, five ten, balding, slightly over-weight, wearing a leather bomber jacket under which was a pale pink shirt with a leather tie, co-owner and manager of the Haus of Leather at the Brady Eighty mall, was enjoying the happiest—and most frightening—days of an existence that (save for his glory years as a high school quarterback of some local renown) had largely been a disappointment.

What made his days happy was his girlfriend Heather.

What made them frightening was his wife Caroline.

Heather was twenty-two years old, and his assistant manager at the Haus of Leather. Heather had a lot of frosted brunette hair and large breasts and a small waist and nice hips and a good head on her shoulders, in every sense of the word: a good head con-taining an above-average brain; a good head on the front of which was a pretty face consisting of big green eyes and a small nose and a small mouth with small very white teeth that made for an enchanting, childlike smile; and, last but not least, a good head capable of giving good head. Very good head.

She had been a cheerleader in high school, and in junior col-lege too, before she had dropped out to get married to a basketball hero. She had divorced her fading-jock husband, who had turned to drinking when he got laid off at John Deere, at which time he began beating her. They'd had one child, before she dumped him, a sweet little girl named Tara, who was now two.

Andy liked the little girl. It reminded him of when his two girls were small; he liked the energy of little kids, how unquestioningly loving they could be. Heather was young enough herself to take him back, to make him feel young again. He hated being forty-five years old, but if he had to be forty-five years old, let him be forty-five years old with a shapely, sexy young girlfriend.

Caroline, who had once been a shapely brunette with large breasts herself, was simply large now. Oh, Andy knew he wasn't perfect himself—while he still possessed his square-jawed all-American good looks, he also carried the usual middle-aged spare tire, and his hair was thinning. But ever since her first pregnancy, so many years ago, Caroline had really let herself go; eating was her only hobby—eating and soap operas. Her idea of a good time was an evening in front of the TV with a box of caramel corn in her lap. He no longer loved this woman. He didn't hate her. He just didn't feel anything much toward her at all, except repulsion during sex.

He would have left her five years ago if the inheritance from her grandfather hadn't gone into the Haus of Leather. She was co-owner of the store, though she rarely set foot in the place, and a divorce settlement would be ungodly expensive. She might even end up with the store itself; or so had said the attorney friend he'd quizzed on the q.t.

Once a week, Saturday night usually, they would make love. Making love to this obese woman, who had once been so lovely (though the image of that version of her was fading in his mind), was a nauseating chore. But when she clung to him in the darkness, the voice was the voice that went with the not completely faded image of a lovely shapely twenty-year-old he'd married a lifetime ago, and he felt a pang of something—guilt, remorse, longing, something.

The joy he felt in Heather's arms, however, overwhelmed such pangs. What they did not overwhelm was his fear—the fear that Caroline would find out that the long hours he put in with the store were frequently not at the store, but at Heather's apartment, the other employees covering for him if she called; that he was invariably accompanied by his pulchritudinous assistant manager on his various buying trips and, of course, the annual leather convention in Fort Worth; that on those evenings when he was doing inventory and working on the books at the store itself, he spent most of his time in the office in the back room, with Heather, where they were frequently on his couch, which oddly enough was covered in vinyl.

Vinyl was fine with him. Leather meant nothing to him except customers. The smell of leather in the shop, overpowering as it was to the customers, was something he'd long since stopped noticing, his sense of smell dulled to it. And he'd never been into leather, sexually speaking, though he did turn a pretty penny on the side special-ordering bizarre leather goods, for some of the straightest-looking customers.

You never knew about people. Andy figured he was no different than anybody else: he had secrets; he wasn't as straight as he looked. Heather was his secret, or anyway the reason for all his secrets. She was no dummy, Heather. It had been her idea to keep the money for the sexually oriented leather goods "off the books," to deal only in cash where that stuff was concerned; and from there he began to play other tricks with the books.

Brady Eighty was a prosperous mall, and the Haus of Leather was the only store of its kind in the entire area—and its goods were top-quality and expensive, leather pants and jackets and boots for men and women both, and every accessory you could imagine. None of that western shit, either; class all the way.

The Haus of Leather was making a killing, in fact—but Andy was watering that fact down in the books. Heather helped him do it. She had accounting in junior college.

The idea was not just to salt money away. The idea was to make the business look less prosperous than it was, so that when the time came, Caroline's divorce settlement wouldn't amount to so much. And so that Andy might end up with the business, which could then openly prosper.

It wasn't stealing. You can't steal from yourself, and this was his business. What did Caroline do but sit on her fat ass, munchies in her lap, watching daytime soaps till the nighttime soaps came on?

His girls, Tabatha and Tammy, were both in college; sweet-looking girls, who had taken after their mother, but fortunately had not yet shown signs of her tendency to run to fat. Trust funds set up, from the grandfather's estate, were bankrolling the girls' schooling, so his responsibility to them, God love them, was met. He hoped they would understand when he started his new life with Heather. He supposed it was too much to ask that they ever accept Heather as their stepmother, when she was only two and three years older than they were, respectively.

He'd had an affair once before—early in the marriage; during Caroline's first pregnancy. She had found out about the girl—a little blond high school student, a senior (legal age—he was no pervert), who was a frequent customer at the gas station where he was working at the time—and Caroline had been enraged. The memory of the seven months pregnant Caroline lumbering after him around the trailer with a carving knife in hand was etched in his mind, like the place on his shoulder where she'd cut him. That's when he stopped loving her, he thought; the night she made him beg for his life. He'd sworn fidelity (and who wouldn't, facing an enraged pregnant woman with a carving knife) but it had never been the same after that. They had stopped communicating, and she started eating. Well, no—they had made something of a come-back, resulting in the second girl; the parental experience had drawn them back together. He liked little kids. He was a good dad.

He was a good businessman, too, now that the Haus of Leather had given him a chance to prove it. After high school, it had all been downhill; he'd gone to Augustana on a football scholarship—he couldn't make it at a bigger school, despite his record, because of his size—and by the second year he'd been dropped from the team and lost his scholarship and flunked out soon after. He'd worked a lot of jobs—blue-collar and white-collar both, and starting fifteen years ago had a little success in real estate till the economy went to shit and the market got glutted with houses; and then finally he got a break: Caroline's grandfather died.

Caroline was one of three grandchildren—some money was left to the two surviving children, too, but that didn't include Caroline's father, who died of the Asian flu back in the fifties; the grandchildren pooled together and sold the farmland they'd inherited; so she ended up with a chunk of money. One thing in Caroline's favor was she had never considered Andy a loser, as some people did; she believed he could make a go of it.

They had bought the Leathery, as the shop was then called, for a song—Andy had heard through his real estate buddies that there was a good chance the Brady Street Shopping Center would be bought up, by a Chicago firm, and refurbished into an enclosed mall. Andy knew they'd have to honor his lease or buy him out of it, which was his initial plan; but, doing some checking with his real estate contacts, he finally decided to stay a part of what would become Brady Eighty. Which had become the hottest mall in the Cities, overnight, and his Haus of Leather one of the most profitable shops in the mall.

Just don't tell his wife or the IRS that.

Anyway, tonight Andy was tooling his year-old dark blue Corvette (Caroline never rode in it—she couldn't; it was the station wagon for her) across the bridge at Moline, on his way to Nolan's house. There was a poker game tonight. They usually got together once a month on a Sunday night, early in the month, but for once, last minute, Nolan set it up for a Monday. Unusual, but the other guys were making it, so he better, too.

He had left the store a little after 8:00 P.M., shrugging and looking glumly frustrated as he turned the till over to Heather. No time even for a quick blowjob in back of the store. If Nolan hadn't got a bug up his butt to have their poker game tonight, he and Heather would've had at the very least a rendezvous on the couch in his office. Maybe even a run to her apartment, in Rock Island.

But he never missed poker with the guys, and he didn't want anyone—including them—to suspect his secret life, so here he was, pulling into Nolan's driveway, behind DeReuss' Lincoln Continental, that lucky Dutch bastard. Where did his money come from?

Harris' Toyota was in the drive as well, and Levine's Caddy. He wondered if the game had started without him; he wondered if Nolan had won all the money yet.

Nolan didn't always win; he just usually won. The hell of it was, he played so conservatively. Took so few risks. Played the odds, and embraced winning streaks, and backed off losing streaks. Nolan was a winner, sure, but he lacked imagination. Whereas Andy liked to win big, and he didn't mind losing big nine out of ten times to win big once. Playing it conservative was dull.

Like Nolan himself. Nice enough guy, but really dull.

He rang the bell, and Nolan answered, sleeves of his pale blue shirt rolled up. The game was already on.

"Any money left for me?" Andy asked him.

"Some," Nolan said. "Come on in."

Andy stepped inside. "Where's your lovely lady?"

"Away," Nolan said, as if that explained it.

"Well, I'll miss her charming presence. She has so much more personality than you, Nolan." But then so did a doghouse.

"Figured with her away," Nolan said, taking Andy's leather bomber jacket, hanging it in the closet, "it'd be a good time for us to get together for some cards."

"You know me," Andy said. "Always ready for a friendly game." He followed his host into the spacious living room, where a round table was set up over by the wall of picture windows looking out on the backyard and trees, a view reflections obscured; the living room walls were devoid of pictures or decoration of any kind—a room with no personality, Andy felt, like Nolan himself.

DeReuss, Levine and Harris were sitting at the table playing, Nolan having folded when he went to answer the door. They were playing dealer's choice, and the game—Levine's choice—was seven-card stud. The chips were fairly evenly distributed, except Nolan's piles were a little higher. Stakes were quarter for whites, fifty cents for reds, buck for blues.

Andy sat to the right of DeReuss and, when the hand was over, bought in.

DeReuss was a solemn man of about fifty-five with lots of lines in his face, especially around his pinched mouth, and thinning dark blond hair, combed back severely. His eyes were china blue behind designer wire-rim glasses. He kept his narrow dark tie snugged up to his collar, but his sharkskin suit coat was slung over his chair, as he studied the cards (five-card draw, his deal) like a blueprint. He looked German. Maybe that was where the money came from for his jewelry store, Andy thought; Nazi parents.

To DeReuss' left was Levine, the Toys 'R' Us guy, a small dark man with a ready smile and a good sense of humor; he wore a gray turtleneck sweater and looked a little like a turtle, in fact. Like Andy, he took risks playing, but only at first; as he started to win, or lose, Levine got almost as conservative as Nolan.

To Levine's left was Harris, the owner/manager of the Dunkin' Donuts near the mall, a heavyset guy with dark hair and a mustache and a doughy complexion; he wore a University of Iowa sweatshirt. Nice guy, but quiet. Not as quiet as Nolan, but quiet.

Andy was the most gregarious of the lot, but Levine was no wallflower, and enough beers into the evening and Harris would turn talkative, and even DeReuss would open up. Not Nolan, though. Andy never ever saw him drink enough to get really loose.

What made a guy like that tick? As Nolan dealt a hand of Black Maria—seven-card stud with high spade down splitting the pot with the poker-hand winner—Andy studied the man, wondering how anybody could be so goddamn straight. It was all business with this guy. He didn't smoke. He barely drank. The only kink at all was this dish he lived with, Sherry, who wasn't that much older than Heather, really; so the guy at least liked to get his ashes hauled. But if the subject turned to women, Nolan never had much to say; Andy kidded him now and then, called him pussy whipped and Nolan would just smile, barely, and that would be the end of it.

"So where's Sherry?" Andy said, dealing five-card draw, jacks or better to open, progressive.

"Visiting a friend." Nolan never looked at his cards till they'd all been dealt. That drove Andy a little crazy, too.

"She's a pretty lady."

"Yes she is," Nolan said.

"You going to marry her, or what?"

DeReuss glanced up from his cards, sharply; evidently he found Andy's question to Nolan rude. Tough shit.

"Maybe," Nolan said, then turned to DeReuss. "Know where I can get a diamond?"

"I think so," DeReuss said, with a faint dry smile. "Fifteen percent discount."

"When the time comes, I know where you can get your toys at a twenty percent discount," Levine grinned, adding, "I can open—bet a blue one."

An hour later, while he was shuffling the cards, Nolan said, "I talked to our mall manager today."

"That pinhead," Andy said.

"He's not so bad," Levine said.

"He's a child," said DeReuss.

"I got on him about mall security again," Nolan said. "I don't suppose I could get any of you guys to line up with me."

"You think it's that big a problem?" DeReuss asked. His accent was faint, but there.

"Yeah. Our security sucks. We should do something about it. One unarmed inexperienced kid who goes home at ten."

Harris said, "This cold weather, you're not even getting the cops patrolling much."

"How do you know?" Andy asked, somewhat irritably. This line of conversation bored him. "You're not even in the mall."

Nolan began dealing Black Maria.

Harris shrugged. "The cops always stop for coffee and doughnuts, my girls tell me. Once around midnight, and again around four. Then they make a run around the mall."

"Every night?" Nolan asked.

Harris swigged some Coors. "Not at all, since this cold weather and snow; they haven't eaten a doughnut in a month. They just don't get out that far. There's nothing else for them to patrol out so close to the Interstate, no housing developments, so few other businesses. I don't like it. I'm easy prey for stickup guys, dope addict crazies; I like having the cops drop by for doughnuts."

"Well, at the mall we're tied into A-1," Andy said, hoping to close out the subject. "They patrol."

"No," DeReuss said, shaking his head. "They did, for a time. But they wanted more money to continue it. The Mall Merchant Association voted it down."

"A mistake," Nolan said. "Ante up, gentlemen."

An hour later, Nolan brought the dull subject up again; Andy couldn't believe this guy.

"You have a lot to lose," he said to DeReuss. "All your diamonds and such."

DeReuss, who was shuffling, shrugged facially. "Our inventory is considerable, yes."

"I can imagine." He began dealing Black Maria. "How much?"

"Approaching three hundred in jewels and merchandise," he said, adding, "Thousand," to clarify three hundred what.

Jesus, Andy thought, and I thought I was in a lucrative line.

"The other jewelry store carries somewhat less," DeReuss added, faintly regal.

Nolan smirked darkly. "And you're protected, if you call it that, by an alarm on one easy-to-snip phone line."

DeReuss looked at his hole cards. He smiled on one side of his face; whether it had to do with his cards or the subject at hand, Andy couldn't tell. "I have my own security measures."

"Oh?"

"Tear gas. Anyone opens my vault, he'll cry all the way—and not to the bank."

"Good idea," Nolan said. "But I'd still appreciate your support at the next meeting."

"What," Andy said, "are you running for office?"

"I just think we need an armed guard on duty, twenty-four hours a day. Preferably two guards."

God, this guy was a stick in the mud.

"Let's play cards," Andy said. "Fuck business."

DeReuss said to Andy, "How's your assistant manager working out? What's her name?"

"Heather. Fine. I'll open for a buck."

DeReuss looked at his hole cards again, smiled privately. Did the Dutchman suspect about him and Heather? Andy hoped to hell not; he'd tried so hard to be careful. He wished he were with her. He was losing heavily tonight. Twenty bucks in the hole, only three hours into the game.

The game broke up around one-thirty. Nolan had cleaned up. On the last hand, which he dealt, a hand of Black Maria, he'd had the ace of spades in the hole and won the poker hand as well; it was a big pot, biggest of the night. He seemed embarrassed about it, as he was showing them out.

"For the big winner," DeReuss said, smiling just a little, "you seem less than overjoyed."

"That doesn't make sense," Levine said to Nolan, grinning, "'cause nobody I know loves the green stuff more than you."

"Next time I'll let you pay for your goddamn doughnuts," Harris said, good-naturedly.

"Hey, you won," Andy said, patting Nolan on the shoulder. "Loosen up. Enjoy being so goddamn lucky."

Nolan opened the door for them; he shrugged, smiled. "You're my friends," he said. "I hate taking your money." And Andy and the rest went home.

11

Roger Winch felt uneasy about working with Cole Comfort again. The only time he'd worked with the guy was one money-desperate month, ten or eleven years ago, when Comfort pulled him and his partner Phil in on some supermarket heists.

Heists, hell—burglaries was more like it: Comfort and some lowlife trucker pals of his would pull up in back and load up all the beef from the meat freezer, while Roger and Phil were up front, Phil—having picked the locks to get them inside—now playing point man, watching for cops and such, while Roger blew the safe. Which was usually a snap, because virtually every one was a J. J. Taylor where he could do a simple spindle shot—knock off the dial with one swift hard blow of the sledge, and then tip her over on her back and use an eyedropper of grease, and hell, in five minutes he was in her.

Small-time jobs, those grocery "heists," although they took thousands of bucks out of them, because Comfort knew when to time it—Thursday nights, when the stores allowed the money to pile up to cover cashing paychecks on Friday.

Still, Roger hadn't liked the Comforts—Sam and Cole—because they were small-timers and mean and smelled bad. He didn't trust them. They never cheated him. They never tried to pull a cross. But he didn't trust them, anyway.

He always had the feeling the Comforts would have just as soon killed him as look at him. But for some reason—perhaps because they thought he might be of use to them again one day—they had never pulled anything on him.

Nonetheless, he would have passed on this gig but for two reasons: Nolan's presence; and he needed the money.

Nolan made any job worth doing. Roger was about the only pete-man in the business who'd never done time, and that had a lot to do with working so often with Nolan, who beyond a doubt was the most careful and tediously precise organizer in the business. No little old lady in the entire U.S. of A. was as cautious, as conservative as Nolan.

And Roger liked that. He liked going into jobs knowing the lay of the land—the specific safe, the floor plan, the alarm system, the security guards (if any), the proximity of patrolling cops, the whole megillah. He didn't like carrying guns. He didn't like anything that smacked of armed robbery. Night work. That was Roger's style.

Roger's style was playing it safe. He was, in every sense of the term, a safe man. He lived in a safe neighborhood in a safe city and he had chosen a safe, low-key, respectable lifestyle, which included a ranch-style split-level home in West Des Moines, a homemaker wife and three well-behaved children, Vicki, twelve, Ron, eight, and Joe, four. He didn't run around on his wife—she was a little plump, but he liked her plump, and she was pretty as the day he met her, a waitress in a bar in Seattle, where he and Phil worked a job.

Even Roger's appearance was unthreatening: he was forty-six years old, five seven, 137 pounds, usually encased in pastel Banlon shirts and polyester slacks, his brown hair cut very short, his face filled with reassuring character lines, his brown eyes lidded sleepily, his nose straight and never broken, his smile gentle. He had a safe, respectable business—locksmithing—which he maintained with his longtime partner Phil Dooley, a middle-aged, rather stout confirmed bachelor who somewhat resembled a smaller, balding Walter Matthau.

Phil was an excellent locksmith, and lived as quiet and low-key a life as Roger. Phil, who lived in a tastefully art-deco-appointed sprawling apartment on the top floor of an apartment building he owned, was a homosexual, which was something they had never discussed, rarely even alluded to, in twenty-some years of business and friendship. Phil lived with no one, although he seemed to maintain relationships with various young men attending Drake

University, though such boys moved on with graduation and nothing permanent ever came of it.

Roger had grown up in Massachusetts, in the Boston area, living in a safe little neighborhood in safe little Malden—where his parents, who ran a stationery shop downtown, had raised him. He'd lost his parents long, long ago—while he was still in high school; they had been on their way for a safe, quiet weekend in the Hamptons when they were killed in a head-on collision with a semi that was passing another semi. He'd gone to live with an aunt, briefly, before going to Drake on a track scholarship.

During his freshman year, he'd met Phil, who'd invited him up to his apartment; they had met in a pizza place and found a mutual interest in what was then called "hi-fi" equipment. Phil invited him up to show him the latest in hi-fi, and to listen to Kingston Trio records—in stereo, no less. Unfortunately, Roger soon found that the hi-fi stuff was the equivalent of etchings, and he had to set Phil straight about some things.

Phil had apologized profusely, saying he'd misread Roger and was so very sorry, so very embarrassed; and they'd become friends. Roger didn't much care about Phil's sexual bent. Roger'd had his own secrets. One of which was that he'd been a shoplifter for as long as he could remember.

He had shared this secret with Phil, one evening when they were both in their cups; and Phil, who already had a hole-in-the-wall locksmithing shop, admitted he had certain criminal leanings himself. He'd done time, in fact. That was where his homosexual leaning had flowered, Roger gathered. Anyway, Phil had used his locksmithing abilities on a number of burglaries, back in St. Louis where he'd grown up; he'd been involved with a ring that broke into stores and businesses. Phil used to work with a pete-man—safecracker—named Harvey Watters; they'd lived together for a time. But Watters was "inside," as Phil put it.

Watters had taught Phil a lot about the safecracking business, but Phil didn't have the nerve for it—specifically, for making the necessary grease—that is, the nitro—and working with knockers (detonators) and explosives in general.

But Roger had no such fears—the Fourth of July was his favorite holiday—and through Phil, Watters' expertise was passed on to Roger, who in the meantime had lost his scholarship and was expelled from Drake when he was caught cheating on his chemistry finals.

And so they had begun, through Phil's St. Louis contacts and a few others right there in Des Moines, doing jobs. Three or four or five times a year. Roger was a natural pete-man and, despite the relative infrequency of their jobs, gained a real reputation in the trade. He and Phil made a lot of money. Soon they had expanded the locksmithing shop and had a healthy legit business going.

They always planned to phase out their "other" profession, but they had never quite got around to it.

Because what Roger and Phil had in common, besides hi-fi and business and crime, was a love of gambling. Gambling was the only part of Roger Winch's life, besides crime of course, that couldn't be classified as safe. He and Phil—on three or four times a year "convention" trips—went to Vegas or Tahoe or Atlantic City, and played high-roller. They tended to go their separate ways—Roger concentrating on blackjack, and Phil on roulette. Now and then one of them came home a winner. Frequently neither did.

At the moment, Roger's savings account (he couldn't speak for Phil) was flatter than a blackjack dealer's ass. It needed replenishing, to say the least; Doris—Roger's wife—was oblivious to their finances, but he had promised her that condo in Florida, and unless he came out of semi-retirement, criminally speaking, and made a score, he'd have to disappoint her, and that was one thing Roger didn't want to do.

Neither he nor Phil had done a job in a year and a half. They were getting older (Phil was sixty) and, Roger's gambling losses aside, had built comfortable lives for themselves. Their locksmithing business was tops in town, and could be sold for a nice piece of change, when they went into retirement, a few years from now, something they were already discussing.

But Phil, Roger could tell, missed the excitement of doing a job; Phil might not have had the stones to handle explosives, but he obviously loved night work: unlocking doors and going in places and taking things. And there was, Roger had to admit, a thrill to it. There were, Roger could not deny, few things sweeter than seeing the door of a safe, which you've punched or blown, swing open.

But the business had changed. There just wasn't as much work as there used to be. Oh, it wasn't technology—changes in safe design were no big deal—nitro can beat any style of vault; and being in the locksmithing business gave them access to all the inside info for the finer points.

But too many safes these days were out in full view, floodlit at night, often near windows at the front of stores, where the cops could see you working. And the credit card was putting pete-men like Roger out of business, anyway: there just weren't as many cash transactions as there used to be. Also, businesses routinely used bank night depositories, rather than stick the day's proceeds in an on-site safe. So even if you could get to the safe, there wouldn't likely be much in it.

So Roger, broke, frustrated, was pleasantly surprised to receive the phone call from Cole Comfort, of all people.

"It's a big job," he said. "We need you and your pansy pal, too."

"Don't say that," Roger said.

"Say what?"

"Don't say anything unkind about Phil. He's a real gentleman, and I expect you to treat him that way."

"Why, of course. No disrespect meant. We need his special talent—there's going to be lots of doors that need unlocking."

Hearing Comfort's soothing, southern-accented tone made Roger queasy; the man was a liar, and a small-timer to boot. Roger couldn't think of Comfort without thinking of heisting grocery stores, loading frozen meat into trucks. A nickel-and-dimer, Comfort was, and a dangerous one.

"I don't know, Cole," Roger said, wanting very much to take the job, but not feeling it prudent.

"It'll be fifty gees each, minimum," he said.

"Hmmm."

"It's an inside job. Very safe. More than that I dare not say."

"Who else is in?"

"Nolan."

That decided it.

"Count me in," Roger said.

"How about the…your pal?"

"He's in."

"You can speak for him?"

"I can speak for him."

Now it was a week later, in Davenport, Iowa, in the restaurant/nightclub called Nolan's. It was just past three o'clock in the morning. They had come in two cars; he and Phil had been picked up downtown, at the Hotel Davenport, where they shared a room (he had no qualms about sharing a room with Phil—Phil never fooled around on the job). Cole Comfort himself had been driving, a blue Ford pickup; Roger sat next to driver Cole, and Phil sat next to Roger. In the other car were the three Leech brothers (as it turned out) and Dave Fisher, the slightly nerdy electronics guy.

They sat at a big table in the dimly lit bar area of Nolan's. Nolan himself, in a pale blue shirt and dark new-looking jeans, stood off to one side, leaning against a pillar, among hanging plants, lurking in the foliage like a jungle cat. Cole Comfort sat at the head of the table, a white-haired, blue-eyed near coot in a plaid shirt and overalls. Overalls, God help us. Roger glanced at Nolan, wondering why the man would lower himself to work with Comfort. Nolan, as usual, was expressionless.

Next to Roger was Phil, looking professorly in a tweedy brown sport jacket over a sweater-vest and tie; sitting like a student next to him was Fisher, a serious, earnest man in his late thirties, wearing thick glasses with heavy black frames and a white shirt and black tie with pens and gizmos in a plastic pouch within his shirt pocket, a pocket-size notebook on the table in front of him. Across from them were the Leech brothers—Ricky, Jerry, Ferdy— three lumberjack-brawny guys in their late thirties with five-o'clock shadow and dirty sweaters and stocking caps, which they were wearing indoors, just as they were wearing the same blank-eyed expression. They were triplets. No one on earth, outside of their family, could tell them apart.

Seeing them here had not made Roger's night. They were the same truckers who'd worked with Comfort on the supermarket heists. They were not really stupid men; they showed signs of being smart. But they were brutes—crude, lewd and rude, as Phil had once put it. Roger knew Phil would be equally less than thrilled to see the owners and operators of Leech Bros. Trucking of Sedalia, Missouri.

"I don't like working with faggots," a Leech said to Comfort.

"I don't neither," another Leech said, also to Comfort.

The third Leech merely nodded.

"Shut up," Comfort said. "Phil's good at what he does. We need him."

"Thank you," Phil said. The sarcasm in his voice was faint, but there. The Leeches missed it; no one else did.

One other person was there—a young guy of about twenty-five, with short blond curly hair and a sweatshirt with some sort of space-cadet comic-book character on it. He wasn't sitting at the long table—he was at a small table for two nearby, sitting in a chair that was turned around, leaning over it, head on his crossed arms, like a kid in study hall. He did not want to be here.

"Do we all know each other?" Comfort said.

"I don't know *him*," a Leech said, pointing back to the blond kid.

Nolan said, "He's with me."

"Does he have a name?" a Leech said.

"Jon," the kid said. "I caught your names earlier. Huey, Dewey and Louie, isn't it?"

The Leeches didn't get it.

One said, "I'm Ricky."

Another said, "I'm Jerry."

Another said, "I'm Ferdy."

Nolan said, "We're supposed to be ten. I only count nine."

Comfort looked over at Nolan and said, "My boy Lyle can't be with us tonight." Then he said, "Come join us, Nolan," waving him over.

Nolan walked past Comfort to the table for two and joined the kid named Jon.

"How about some beer?" a Leech said, pointing over toward the bar.

Nolan said, "We're not socializing. We need to make this as short as possible. I don't like hanging around here."

Comfort smiled at Nolan and said, "I just thought this was as good a place as any to meet."

"It's a stupid place to meet," Nolan said.

Comfort glared at him, then the glare melted into a seemingly sincere smile. "You're mistaken, Nolan. It's a real smart place to meet. We'll meet here tomorrow night, too. It's better than meeting at one of our motel rooms where we might be seen together. This is real out of the way and private." Comfort smiled like Daddy at the men sitting at his table. "Nolan's nervous about meeting here because this very mall we're sitting in is our target."

That confused Roger, who said so: "You mean, the mall bank here's our target? I don't do banks…you can't blow a vault like that without noise to raise the dead—"

"Shush," Comfort said gently. "I mean, we're gonna take this whole dang mall. We're going shopping; a regular moonlight madness sale, only it's all on the house. Thanks to Nolan, here."

Phil was sitting forward; even the generally bored-seeming Fisher was shifting in his seat. The Leech brothers weren't impressed; they obviously were already in the know. Nolan and Jon, too.

Fisher said, "What exactly do you mean? This mall has, I would guesstimate, fifty-some stores."

Comfort turned to Nolan, who then said: "Fifty stores exactly—not counting the bank, this restaurant or the three major department stores."

A rather stunned Phil asked Comfort, "How in God's name do you heist a mall?"

Comfort said, "Nolan?"

Nolan, still seated at the nearby table, said, "Right now, as we sit here, there are no security guards on duty. Only a single janitor. The alarm system is silent—no audibles at all—on a phone line to a security company and the cops."

"Lead me to it," Fisher said, smiling smugly.

Nolan cautioned him: "I'm told the change in pulse rate, if you jump it, automatically sets off the alarm."

Fisher shrugged. "Not with one of my little black boxes wired in, sending them the right pulse rate. Go on."

Nolan did: "The security guard goes off at ten. He doesn't even come back on duty till one o'clock the next afternoon. The maintenance man opens the doors at seven A.M. Merchants start arriving around eight-thirty, and stores open at ten."

"We would have from ten till six-thirty or so," Roger said, "inside this mall, to do what we pleased."

"That's exactly right, friends and neighbors," Comfort said.

Nolan said, "I don't think we need that long. Cole, here, wants to use the Leech brothers and three semis to loot the place. I don't think that's necessary."

Comfort glared at him again. "You don't?"

"No," Nolan said. "You got two jewelry stores—each with at least a quarter million worth in their safe. The bank has three safes—Roger is right, the main vault is out—but they have an automated cash machine, which has twenty-some thousand bucks in it at any given time. And two smaller night depository safes, which at this yuletide time of year could have anywhere from ten to fifty grand each in 'em."

Phil said, "So you're saying, fuck the small shit."

"Right," Nolan said. "Even allowing for fencing the diamonds, we can clear three hundred thousand, probably more, for a few hours' work. And no heavy hauling. Roger just goes in, blows all five safes, and you don't need trucks to haul away diamonds and cash."

A Leech said, "Where does that leave us?"

"You're in," Cole said. Anger hung off his voice, as cold and brittle as icicles. "You're a fool, Nolan. We got *all night* in this place, to do as we like, take as we like, and you want to stay for a few minutes and play it safe grabbing the easy stuff."

Roger said, "Blowing five safes isn't easy, Cole."

Comfort nodded, saying, "And it takes time. During which, we're taking advantage of the situation. We're going the whole fucking route. This place is Disneyland for thieves, and we got all the free tickets we want. We're all gonna pitch in and help the Leeches, here, load their three semis, which'll be pulled up to loading docks out back, and fill 'em with refrigerators and microwave ovens and TVs and VCRs and stereo shit and computers and washing machines and furs and leather goods and cameras and designer clothes and sterling silver and china and Cuisinarts and every other goddamn thing we can lay hands on, before this place opens the next morning, at which time there'll be tumbleweed blowing through this goddamn place, it'll be so empty."

"You forgot jockey shorts," Nolan said.

"What?" Comfort said.

"You can probably get a quarter each for jockey shorts," he said. "You wouldn't want to leave any of them behind."

"You just cooperate," Comfort said, raising a lecturing finger.

That was weird, Roger thought. It was almost like Comfort had a hold over Nolan...

Fisher was taking notes; he looked up from them and said, "You have a fence lined up who can handle a load like this?"

"Burden in Omaha," Comfort said, "for everything but the stones. We got to go to Chicago for the stones."

"What's the rate?" Phil asked.

"We're getting thirty percent of wholesale on the goods; forty on the stones."

"Not bad," Phil admitted. "And this goes down how soon?"

"Thursday," Comfort said.

"This Thursday?" Roger asked.

"This Thursday," Comfort said.

"What's the rush?" Fisher asked.

"No rush," Comfort said. "I been working on this for weeks, now. We got all the inside dope we need. Christmas money is flowing, out there. We're all here. Thursday's as good a time as any."

Roger looked at Nolan. "Nolan? Opinion?"

Nolan shrugged. "Thursday's fine."

Fisher looked at Nolan sharply. "Why are you doing this?"

Nolan said, "Why else? The money."

"You have a good thing going here," Fisher said, looking around the place like a tax assessor. "Why risk it?"

Comfort said, "You can never have too much money, right, Nolan?"

"Right," Nolan said.

They talked till after four, and agreed to meet back here at two-thirty tomorrow night. In the meantime, Comfort instructed, they would all, on their own, walk around the mall tomorrow during business hours. Each, in his own way, casing the joint.

"We could have jerseys made up," Jon said, "that say 'Mall Heist' on 'em—and maybe walk arms linked. That'd be a nice touch."

Comfort smiled kindly at him and said, "Remember what I told you about children, son?"

Jon, still sitting backward in the chair, gave him a sullen look, then looked away.

Roger got up and went over to Nolan's small table and asked a few questions about the bank.

"The instant-cash machine is an NCR," Nolan said. He dug in his shirt pocket for a slip of paper and handed it to Roger. "There's the model number and a sketch. You can walk right in the bank and look at it tomorrow."

"Don't forget your jersey," Jon said.

"What's with you guys?" Roger said.

"Nothing," Nolan said. "The jewelry store safe is tear-gas rigged."

"I'll talk to Fisher," Roger said. "He'll know how to get around that."

"Fine," Nolan said, smiling tightly. "See you soon."

Roger smiled back, glanced at the slip of paper Nolan had handed him; it did indeed include the model number of the safe—but it also had a Moline address jotted down and said: "Come to my house now. Say nothing to Comfort."

Roger nodded, folded the paper and slipped it in his pocket; he collected Phil, said his goodbyes all around, and left with Comfort, who dropped them at their hotel. Saying nothing to Phil about where he was going, he took the car, found an all-night gas station that could direct him to the Moline address, and when he got there Nolan was waiting.

12

The light blue Ford van was hardly ideal for a stakeout, but it was all Jon had. Neither of Nolan's cars was usable, as Comfort had seen Sherry's red 300 zx, and had probably ID'ed Nolan's silver Trans Am by now as well, whereas Jon's van had been dropped off for a tune-up at a garage near Nolan's place the morning after Jon got there—where it had sat ever since.

And now Jon sat in it—that is, the blue Ford van (which at least no longer said "The Nodes" on the side), in the parking lot of the Holiday Inn on Brady Street, just a few blocks from Brady Eighty. He didn't have the motor running, and it was cold today—this was Wednesday afternoon, the first Wednesday of December—but he was warm in his bulky army-navy surplus store navy coat, and fur-lined gloves, and ski mask.

The ski mask was almost too warm—it was certainly too scratchy —but it was necessary. He couldn't afford to be recognized by Comfort, whose red Chevy pickup, parked just across from him, he was watching. They'd seen Comfort climb into the driver's seat of this pickup, Missouri plates, last night in front of Nolan's.

It was a little after five o'clock and getting dark already. He'd been here damn near all day—since around nine this morning. He had a Thermos of hot chocolate (he hated coffee—that was for grown-ups) and the snub-nose .38 and a science-fiction novel by Walter Tevis, *Mockingbird*, which he'd finished an hour ago. The book was good, but reading a couple paragraphs and then glancing up at Comfort's parked pickup, and then reading a couple more paragraphs, and then glancing up at Comfort's parked pickup again, was a grueling process which he repeated to the point of a stiff sore neck. He kept the van doors locked, because if Comfort spotted him, a door might be yanked open and Jon jerked out; and the Comforts, of course, were capable of anything—which was why the .38 was snugged in the side right pocket of the navy coat.

He also had a mobile cellular phone in the car, a toy Nolan usually carried in his own car (he'd gotten it at a discount from the Radio Shack at Brady Eighty). Jon checked in every hour with Nolan, who was nearby at his restaurant at the mall.

Nolan had dropped by once, around noon, stopping quickly to drop off a sack of McDonald's food, and to give him a fresh Thermos of hot chocolate.

Jon had been reading the science-fiction paperback when Nolan appeared in front of the windshield, just standing there before the van like Mad Max in the middle of a post-nuclear-holocaust road.

Jon opened the door for him, Nolan handed in the food and Thermos and said, "You shouldn't read."

"I can't take the boredom otherwise."

"Boredom is one thing. Bore of a gun barrel's another."

"Cute, Nolan. He hasn't touched his fucking pickup yet, in case you're interested."

Nolan nodded and shut the van door and was gone.

Finding out where Comfort was staying was a break, or had seemed to be at the time; now that it was dusk and Comfort had stayed inside the motel all day, it seemed less significant. Time was running out. Tomorrow was the day. Operation Mall Haul. If they didn't find Sherry tonight, they might not find her at all.

But at least they had an ally in Roger Winch.

Jon had just listened, last night, while Winch sat on the couch in the living room, Nolan standing in front of him like an attorney pleading his case.

"I'm taking a big chance, Roger. If Comfort knew I was talking to you, somebody could die."

Winch, who was a low-key guy, didn't like hearing that. He said, "I knew I shouldn't get involved with Comfort. I only came in 'cause you were part of it."

"Comfort wouldn't have asked you in," Nolan said, "if he'd known how many jobs we worked together."

And Nolan had filled Winch in about Sherry's kidnaping, explaining that his own participation in the heist was strictly coerced.

"I'm retired," Nolan said. "I want no part of this."

"It's a sweet score," Winch said, shrugging, smiling mildly. "It could go down in history."

"So did the Manson murders. Comfort is a double-crossing murdering son of a bitch who's likely to kill all of us when this is over."

Winch's expression was pained. "Maybe Phil and I should just go…"

Nolan patted the air with one hand. "No. Stay in. But I have to warn you—if I have the chance to stop this before it goes down, I will."

"This is bad. I don't like violence. You know me, Nolan—I never carried a gun in my life."

"Yeah, but your pal Phil does."

Winch shrugged again. "That's part of a point man's job. He's never killed anybody."

"It's always a possibility, Roger. Look—I'd like you to stick. Play along. If you don't, my girl's going to die."

"It sounds like she's going to die anyway."

"Not if I can find her before the heist goes down. He has to keep her alive to keep me part of this. Without me, there's no score."

Winch thought about it. Then he said, "What's in it for me? I hate to say that, but if you're going to try to stop this from going down, why should I play? Friendship doesn't quite cut it. I like you, Nolan—but I like living more, and I got to agree with you: Cole Comfort is planning to do some killing before this is over."

"I'll make this worth your while," Nolan said. "I can guarantee you a minimum of ten grand for sticking. Out of my own pocket. If we scrap the heist, consider it a kill fee."

"What if the job goes down? If Comfort's planning a double cross like you say, then—"

"Then a triple cross is called for. He thinks he's on top of every-thing—he won't expect us to be on top of him. I'd like to pull Phil in on this, and talk to Fisher, too. I've worked with him. Not as often as with you, but I've worked with him."

Winch was nodding. "I think he'd line up with you. But it's going to be tricky. And dangerous."

"Yes it is. Remember—you're not supposed to know about Sherry. As far as you and Phil know, this score is something Comfort and I put together as partners."

"Could you make it twenty grand?"

"Fifteen."

"Five up front?"

"No. Fifteen after."

Winch shrugged. "Done. What now? The thing is supposed to go down in less than forty-eight hours."

"I'm going to try to find Sherry and steal her back. I figure he's got her stashed someplace being baby-sat by his boy Lyle."

"Yeah," Winch said, "his boy's in on this—Comfort says so. But he wasn't at the meet last night."

"I only saw the kid once," Nolan said. "Years ago. He was just a teenager. I don't remember much about him."

"He was around when I worked with Comfort, five years ago," Winch said. "The boy was on the fringes of the supermarket jobs I was in on—he was in his late teens, then. He's a nice enough, nice-looking kid, but a little thick."

"Is he dangerous, do you think?"

"Nolan, he's a Comfort."

"Yeah. Stupid question. Do you know where Comfort's staying?"

"No. I got a phone number, though." Winch dug in his pocket and found a slip of paper. "Here. Copy it down."

Nolan did, and Winch went back to his hotel, and Nolan looked in the Quad Cities directory, yellow pages, hotels and motels, and compared the number to the numbers listed there.

"He's at the Holiday Inn," Nolan said. "Figures he'd stay close to Brady Eighty, close to the Interstate, his getaway route."

Jon looked at the slip of paper. "It says extension 714."

Nolan nodded. "Which is probably his room number."

"Could he have Sherry there?"

"Almost no chance. She's stashed somewhere. Lyle's looking after her. I'm sure of it."

"Could we break in Comfort's room tonight and just put a gun to his fucking head?"

"Sounds like fun," Nolan said, "but all we'd have at best is a Mexican standoff. We can always try that—grabbing Comfort himself and threatening to kill him if he doesn't call and have Sherry released."

"Wouldn't that work?"

"If Comfort wasn't crazy, maybe. Who knows what he'd say when at gunpoint he called Lyle or whoever's holding her? And he's got firepower. He's probably got the Leeches in his corner, and they're violent crazy fuckers too. He's got his son. Too many unknowns."

"I don't know. It's tempting to bust in his room in the middle of the night, and—"

Nolan was shaking his head no. "We don't know what or who is in his room. Sherry might be there, and we don't want to start a shooting war. Cole Comfort could buy it, and we'd never get Sherry back from Lyle once that happened. Too risky. She's safe for the moment."

"So what do we do?"

Stake out the Holiday Inn. Which was how Jon had spent his day today. The plan was, if Comfort went to his pickup and left, Jon would tail him, calling Nolan on the mobile phone. Nolan would then search the room at the Holiday Inn—despite the slight chance Lyle might be in there with Sherry, which was a situation he could better control than one that included Coleman Comfort.

If Nolan could get in that room, without Comfort there, something might turn up—a phone number, a room key, a matchbook, something that would lead them to where Sherry was being held.

But so far Jon had done nothing but sit on his ass in this van, reading his paperback, calling Nolan briefly every hour, drinking hot chocolate, eating McDonald's food and, every now and then, leaving the van to use the Men's off the Holiday Inn lobby. Nolan had wanted him to piss in a tin can, but you have to draw the line somewhere.

By eight o'clock his bones were starting to ache; it was colder, and now and then he would turn the motor on and get the heat going. He was starting to think Comfort wasn't going to leave his motel room until the second meet, tonight, which would once again be at 2:30 A.M. at Nolan's. He was contemplating getting out and going into the lobby for another piss, when somebody approached the parked pickup.

And got in and started it up and pulled away.

"Holy shit," Jon said to nobody in particular, and pulled out after the pickup.

"Nolan," Jon said into the phone.

Nolan's voice came on, tinny: "What?" The sounds of the restaurant/club, now open for business, were a muffled presence in the background.

"I'm tailing the pickup truck."

"Good. I'll toss the room."

"No! Nolan, it isn't Comfort driving! He isn't even in the goddamn thing."

"Who is?"

"Some girl."

"Some girl."

Jon was having trouble keeping up with the red pickup, zooming along up ahead of him on the one-way that was Harrison. "She must be about seventeen. I just got a glimpse of her, is all. Good-looking. Great ass."

"Reddish-blond hair?"

"Yeah!"

"He has a daughter. She was just a little kid when I saw her. It was years ago. She was cute."

"You think this is Comfort's daughter?"

"Probably."

"What should I do?"

"Just what you're doing: follow her. She may be headed for where they got Sherry."

"Do you think so?"

"Follow her. Call me when you got something."

"Nolan—"

"Give it your best shot, kid. I'll be waiting."

The phone clicked in Jon's ear; then he put it back in its bed on its black battery pack. He was right behind her, as they headed down the one-way of Harrison toward Davenport, the vast North Park Shopping Center whizzing by at their right (never say "whizzing" to a guy who has to pee). She was moving fast. Speeding, actually. For a moment Jon wondered if she'd made him; but he didn't think that was the case. He could see her up there, looking straight ahead, no discernible rear-view mirror glancing, no turning her head to look behind her.

He allowed a couple of cars to get between him and the pickup, but she was traveling too fast for that to work without losing her. He had to keep his speed up. Which was just swell, considering he had a .38 in his pocket. He pulled the ski mask off. Comfort's daughter—if that's who this was—didn't know him from Adam. Why risk being a guy in a ski mask with a gun in his pocket stopped by a cop for speeding.

At the foot of Harrison, she turned left onto River Drive. Soon she pulled into the riverfront parking lot near the Dock, a fancy seafood restaurant, and the Loading Ramp, a nightclub in an old remodeled warehouse adjacent to the restaurant. He cruised by her, as if looking for a parking place, just as she was getting out of the car, a strawberry blonde, hands tucked in the short pockets of the denim jacket, which was much too light for this cold, to which she seemed oblivious; she had a nice tight little ass encased in denim paint. She wore red spike heels. Yow.

Jon saw her go in the big wooden door of the Loading Ramp, and then he pulled the van into a parking place not far from her pickup, but not next to it. He called Nolan.

"I'm going in there," Jon said.

"And do what?"

"I'm not sure. Talk to her."

"Better keep your distance."

"Trust me on this, Nolan."

"Jon—"

"Sometimes I know what I'm doing."

"Take the gun."

"I was planning to. I always take a gun into heavy-metal bars."

Which is what the place was; the sounds of Mötley Crüe were blaring forth from speakers left over from when this joint was a disco, and down at the far end of the smoky barely converted warehouse, a band, five skinny males in heavy-metal war paint and sparkly skimpy clothes, was preparing to play a set. They were called Hellfyre and Jon had heard of them; second-raters all the way.

He had paid at a caged window, coming in, and had been carded, which now that he was getting into his mid-twenties actually sort of pleased him. Drinking age in Iowa was nineteen, so the possible Comfort daughter was either of age or had a fake ID.

Getting a close look at her, as she sat at the bar, a beer and a smoke before her, he figured it was a fake ID. This was a kid. She had the denim jacket off, slung over the back of her high-backed barstool, and she wore a yellow RATT T-shirt under which nice high handfuls poked, and her hair was a long and teased and heavily sprayed mane, and she was smoking a cigarette, apparently from the pack of Camels before her; but this was, nonetheless, a kid. With her cute features, big blue eyes, pug nose dusted with freckles, Kewpie-doll lips: a kid. She didn't yet have the hard look the nineteen-year-old girls in this place did. The crowd was blue-collar all the way, guys in Skoal painter caps and scuzzy work clothes (the latter signifying unemployment) and girls in tight slacks and revealing tops and lots and lots of eye makeup.

The bar was a squared-off area at the back, and beyond it were tables and dance floor and stage; at the left and back a balcony surveyed the smoke and darkness. The place was about half full. Okay Wednesday night business, bar-band veteran Jon thought; typical.

He sat next to her.

She looked at him, noncommittally, looked away, sipped her beer, smoked her cigarette.

There had been no recognition in the look at all; Jon was quite relieved.

He said: "You ever hear these guys before?"

"Hellfyre?" she said. She had the faintest southern accent. She'd be from Missouri, if she was Comfort's daughter; and sometimes you ran into a bit of a southern accent down there.

"Yeah," he said. "Have you heard 'em before?"

She was a very cute kid; she was the kind of cute kid you think you've met before, Jon thought, even though you haven't.

"Yeah, I heard 'em." It was a nice voice, sultry and childlike at once. "They play down where I come from, sometimes."

"You're not from here?"

She shook her head. "I come from Missouri."

He risked a grin. "Does that mean you're going to show me something?"

She smiled back, warming to him; she had small, childlike teeth, very white. And her pink tongue licked out as she said, "Time will tell." The slight southern lilt made the words sound great.

Fuck, could this little vision be a *Comfort*?

"I just love heavy metal," she said.

"Yeah, uh, me too."

"What's your favorite heavy-metal band?"

"Hard to choose. What's yours?"

"I like that band Spinal Tap. They had a special on HBO. But I can only find one of their records."

"Uh, that's a satire, isn't it?"

"What?"

"Nothing. Good band."

"I like all kinds of music, though. Except country and western.

My daddy listens to that all the time and I could just barf some-times."

"It's not my favorite, either. I'd like to buy you a beer, when you're through with that one."

"Why not? Say. Don't I know you?"

He slipped his hand into the deep pocket of the navy coat; the handle of the .38 felt rough and cold.

"I do know you." She was pointing her finger at him, waggling it at him, and pointing her nipples at him, too; he was pointing the .38 at her from within his coat, though she didn't know it.

"Isn't your name Jon?"

"Why don't we just leave here quietly," he said, his gun poking at the pocket; but she didn't seem to see that.

"You played with the Nodes!" Her face lit up like Christmas. She squealed like he was the Beatles. "You're the organ player!"

His gun hand went limp in his pocket; something like relief coursed through him.

She leaned over and looped her arm in his.

"Don't you remember me? I'm Cindy Lou."

"Cindy Lou…"

"Cindy Lou Comfort. But maybe you didn't catch my name. Year or so ago, in Jefferson City? It was at that place out on the highway."

Shit. It was coming back to him.

She touched her hair. "I had my hair all cut off, then. During a break, you and me sat in this little dressing room under the stage and kissed and stuff."

He'd felt her up. He'd felt up Cole Comfort's daughter. Cole Comfort's underage daughter.

"I remember you, Cindy Lou," he said, his mouth dry, his dick erect.

"Is that a pistol in your pocket," she grinned nastily, "or are you just glad to see me?"

"You'd be surprised."

"I think that was a good idea you had," she said.

Hellfyre began playing "We Ain't Gonna Take It" by Twisted Sister.

"What was that?"

"Leaving here quietly."

And they did; her arm around his waist and his around her shoulder.

13

Cindy Lou just couldn't believe her luck. Running into the keyboard player from the Nodes! She loved that band; when she heard they broke up it made her sad. They'd always played a lot of oldies and some new wave and even a little heavy metal. And they jumped around on stage, and the guys were really cute. Especially that keyboard player. He reminded her of Duane, from the seventh grade, who popped her cherry. He was a little blond hunk, too.

They stepped outside into the chilly air, walking side by side, arms around each other. You could smell the river. You could see it too, moon dancing on the little waves. Real romantic, Cindy Lou thought, surprised at herself, surprised she could get it up after last night. But she put that out of her mind.

"Where do you want to go?" Cindy Lou asked.

"Where are you staying?"

"At the Holiday Inn." She paused, then added, "With my daddy. He's here on business."

"I see."

"We better not go back there. He doesn't even know I'm out."

"Really?"

"Yeah. He's been keeping me cooped up at that motel, and finally when he wasn't looking I just took the pickup keys and went."

He led her to a sky-blue van.

"We could just climb in back of there," she said.

"We could. It's not fancy, but I got some blankets back there."

She smiled, hugged his waist. "This used to be your band's van, didn't it?"

"Yeah."

She pulled away from him, traced her finger on the side of the van. "You can almost see where your name used to be. The Nodes.

You guys were real good. What happened to that girl that sang with you?"

"Toni? We were still in a band together till recently. She's up in Minneapolis playing in one of Prince's groups."

"Really? That's cool! That Prince guy is so sexy."

He opened the rider's side of the van and she climbed in and crawled between the seats in front into the back of the van, where the cold metal floor was warmed by several quilts and blankets. Some corduroy pillows were piled up against one side. Jon got in on the driver's side, turned on the engine, started the heater going, locked the doors, and joined her.

"It's going to take a while for that heater to get going," he said, sitting on his knees, watching her as she arranged a little makeshift bed out of the quilts and blankets. At the head of the "bed" she placed two of the cord pillows and invited him to lie next to her, which, after removing his big navy coat, he did. She slipped out of her denim jacket and kicked off her heels, but otherwise left her clothes on as they got under a quilt and lay facing each other, smiling in the near dark, leaning on an elbow, some moonlight and streetlights filtering in through the back van windows.

"You don't know how glad I am to see a friendly young face," she said.

"Oh?"

"Yeah." She shrugged. "I been having some family trouble. Nothing serious."

"Oh?"

"I'm getting too old to live at home, anyway."

"How old are you?"

"Seventeen."

He smiled, a cute little smile on half his face making a dimple. "I didn't *think* you were of drinking age."

"Seventeen's old enough."

"For what?"

"Anything I want."

"What are you, a senior, Cindy Lou?"

"Naw. I stopped going to high school."

"Why?"

"Daddy didn't want me to go."

"Why?"

"Needed some help in the family business. Needs me to run the house. My mom's dead."

"I'm sorry."

"Don't be. I never knew her." She sighed. "I sorta killed her."

"You…what do you mean?"

"She died having me."

That seemed to bum Jon out; she touched his face.

"Don't be blue," she said. "You got any drugs?"

"No. Sorry."

"It's okay. That gets old after awhile, anyway. Boy, I sure do miss your band. Why'd you break up?"

"We weren't getting anywhere, I guess."

"What are you doing now? You playing with a new band?"

"I was. Mostly I'm working as an artist. Cartoonist."

"You draw cartoons?"

"Yes." He smiled; seemed a little proud of himself.

"Like on TV, you mean. G.I. Joe, He-Man, those things? They're awful violent. You think little kids should watch those things?"

"I don't work on animated cartoons, Cindy Lou. I draw a comic book."

"Oh, like Archie or Batman."

"Something like that."

"Are you good?"

"Yeah. I'll draw your picture sometime."

"In the nude?"

"If you like."

"It's getting warmer in here." She pulled off her T-shirt; it was still cold enough to make her nips stand out. She looked at his face; looked at his eyes on her boobs. She knew she didn't have the biggest boobs around, but they were real firm and had a nice shape and pretty pink nips. She liked the expression they put on his face—like he was struck dumb by her beauty. She'd seen that expression many times, and relished it.

Then she leaned back on her elbow and started making small talk again, pretending to be matter of fact about her nudity but knowing she was making him crazy. It was a sort of teasing, although she was no tease: Cindy Lou liked sex. She had put out since she was twelve. Screwing was fun, and besides, it put a guy in your back pocket, for as long as you wanted him there. And she'd had "encounters," as she liked to think of them, with a lot of guys who played in bands.

"Your band played a lot of your own songs, didn't you?"

"Yeah," he said. "About a third of what we carried was original material."

"Who wrote it?"

"Mostly Toni. I did some of it. We made a record, you know."

"No! Really? Can you get me one?"

"Sure. How long are you going to be in town?"

"Just till Friday. We're leaving real early Friday morning."

"You and your dad."

"Well, and Lyle. He's my brother."

"He's staying at the motel with you?"

"No, he's over on the Illinois side somewhere, looking after business for Daddy."

"I could drop an album off at your motel tomorrow."

"You best not stop by the room. Daddy's funny about boys. He doesn't know, uh…"

"What?"

"Nothing," she said.

Cindy Lou's daddy didn't know she put out. He thought she was pure as the driven snow; he had no idea she'd drifted, in the seventh grade. And he sure as hell didn't know she and her brother Lyle used to do it together, either. She was thirteen and he was eighteen. Not often. Just now and then, when Daddy was out of the house, till she missed her period once and got scared about having a Mongoloid. It was a false alarm, but she and Lyle got the fear of

God put into them, or as near to it as possible for two kids raised to believe in nothing.

Lyle was a great lover; he made her come like a four-alarm fire. One time they made love in a rainstorm, with the water running down the window next to them all streaky, throwing spooky shadows on their naked bodies, with thunder cracking out there. Daddy was home, that time. It made it real dangerous and real exciting. But eventually the fear was stronger than the love of danger and excitement and even of her brother Lyle's long lovely pecker, and now she and Lyle didn't even mention it. Didn't even talk about it. It was like it never happened, except for an occasional glance between them that said it did.

She never thought of it as incest, exactly, at least not till that month her period was late, and she didn't believe in sin, but she did believe, vaguely, in right and wrong. That much had crept in through her schooling. She sometimes lay awake at night thinking about the stealing her daddy and Lyle did, which she sometimes helped them with, like the food stamp deal she quit school to pitch in on. She wondered if that was any kind of way to make a living.

Her daddy had always treated her like a princess, and had never been mean, except to spank her bare butt when she was bad. Daddy defined "bad" as disobeying, and she'd learned not to do that early on. She hadn't had her bare butt spanked (by Daddy) since the seventh grade—coincidentally, it stopped about the time she started putting out.

Once, about three years ago, she had sat in Daddy's lap and, reverting to the manner of a child, which always charmed him, asked: "Is stealing wrong, Daddy?"

"You shouldn't steal from your kin, darlin'."

"People go to jail for stealing."

"People go to jail for getting caught. Everybody steals, darlin'. The government steals from the public, and the public steals from the government. What goes around comes around."

"Do you hurt people when you steal from them?"

"Your daddy has to make a living in a cruel, cold, hard world. And sometimes that takes being cruel, cold and hard."

"Does that mean you hurt people?"

"If I have to. Only if I have to. I could lie to you, darlin', but it wouldn't be right of me to. You got to be true to your family. That's all there is in this old world that can be trusted; that's all there is that's worth holding on to. Family."

"I love you, Daddy."

"I love you, darlin'," he'd said, and gave her a big old sloppy kiss.

She thought her daddy was handsome; she'd seen the pictures of him and her mom, before his hair turned white, and he and her mom—who looked a lot like Cindy Lou, so much so it was spooky —looked so happy together. Such a handsome, happy couple. Sometimes she felt guilty for coming between them. Sometimes she cried herself to sleep over it, holding her mother's picture in her hands. Usually during her period, this was.

But sometimes Daddy scared her. When he drank, he got "handsy." He would put his hands on her and want a kiss. It didn't go any further than that, but she sometimes went to bed early and slid the dresser across the door. He'd never tried to come in the room, but she'd grown afraid, lately, that he would someday. Some night.

Ever since she quit school and was around the house more, she noticed Daddy looking at her. Looking at her in that way she knew so well. She figured the only thing keeping him off of her was his foolish mistaken notion she was still a virgin. She was afraid of what he'd do if he found out she wasn't.

He had his foolish old head in the sand, Daddy did. What did he think she did, when she went out on the weekends and didn't get home till three in the morning? He bawled her out about it sometimes, and threatened (just threatened) to "whack" her if she didn't mind. She could always sweet-talk him out of his mood, though.

"Daddy," she'd say, archly, "I'm just a poor country girl all cooped up on the farm all week, doin' chores. You gotta let me raise a little hell weekends!"

He'd laugh at that, and let her get away with it. But that was because she'd never had a regular guy, that he knew of—she'd never (except once) had a guy call for her at the house, she always met him (and there was quite a succession of hims) at a movie or a dance hall or bar or maybe motel. She had followed this route because the one time she did have a guy pick her up, back when she was in the ninth grade, Daddy had given the guy such a hard time, it spoiled the whole night. And the next day her daddy had been in a foul mood and snapped her head off at every turn.

So she'd decided to keep her private life her own. And she'd continue to sit in her daddy's lap and baby-talk him when she wanted something, and that would be that.

And it was—until last night.

She was staying in this motel room with him, a nice room at a Holiday Inn, just her and Daddy, with two double beds, one for each of them. He'd had some business meeting real late, way after midnight, and didn't get back till after four in the morning. He stripped to his longjohns and climbed in bed—with her. He started cuddling up to her. She could smell liquor on him, but she didn't think he was drunk. She turned her back to him and he started bumping up against her. And he started saying things.

Things like how she was going to be a woman soon. Something about educating her to the ways of the world, about ushering her into the glory of womanhood.

And she knew what he meant: fucking.

"I gotta pee, Daddy," she'd said, and got up and scurried into the bathroom and sat on the toilet, seat down, feet up on the cold seat and hugging her legs to her, shaking like to have the palsy, staring at the locked door, afraid of her own father. Her own daddy.

She'd sat there like that a long time. He never knocked on the door or tried to open it or anything. She just knew he was in bed on the other side of that door, thinking about her, in that way. But finally she heard him snoring out there, and peeked out, and he was dead asleep, mouth open, sawing away at those logs.

She slipped into the cool sheets of the other bed and waited to see if anything was going to happen. Nothing did, except over in that other bed her father kept on snoring, and pretty soon so was she.

Today, Daddy had slept in till ten. She was awake at eight, and was all showered and made up and dressed and ready for a day of shopping when he woke. But when Daddy got up, he informed her he wanted her to stay right here, in the room and around the Holiday Inn; no shopping spree for her, this trip. She'd asked him why.

"I got to keep an eye on you," he said.

"What do you mean, Daddy?"

"There's some terrible people in this world. A lot of girls your age just disappear and never get seen again."

She could tell from the tone of his voice there'd be no arguing with him; so she'd let it pass, and joined him for a late breakfast in the coffee shop. The rest of the day Daddy and his friends the Leech brothers—creepy people—sat in the room and talked business, while she either watched TV (she had a couple soap operas and game shows she'd started following since quitting school) or walked around the motel, snooping. She spent a couple of hours in the video arcade room playing Galaga and Donkey Kong Jr. A day dull as spit.

They had supper in the motel restaurant (those yucky Leeches, too), and Daddy bought her a filet mignon, her favorite, and said, "I miss your mother, sometimes."

She hadn't said anything; just sat and cut her meat up into little pieces.

"Even after all these years. You look so much like her, darlin'."

And she knew she wasn't out of the woods yet. Tonight would be another long night. It was awful to be scared of your own father. Maybe it was time. Time to get out of the house and start her own life, like her friend Ginger who was out in L.A., now, doing great probably.

After supper, Daddy and the Leeches went to the hotel bar to do some drinking, and she felt she had to grab her chance and just get out. She'd seen in the morning paper that Hellfyre was in town playing at a riverfront club and that knowledge had been nibbling at her brain all day. So she went and got the keys to the pickup from the room, leaving Daddy a note saying she'd be back before midnight, and now here she was, in the back of a van with a cute guy from a band. She'd kind of figured it would go this way, only with that bass player from Hellfyre; but what the hell—she liked this Nodes keyboard guy even better.

"Getting warm in here," he said.

"Sure is," she said. "Take off your shirt, why don't you?"

He had a great build, a little mini Rambo. What a hunk! She eased on top of him and started kissing his smooth chest, which was as hairless as Don Johnson's. His hands were on her ass, which was still in the jeans, making circles, rubbing. She was getting hot. He kissed and fondled her breasts, and she got hotter.

She unzipped his pants, pulled them down under his pecker, which was medium size and pretty. She went down on him awhile, and he tasted salty and good, and made him moan; she liked doing that. He was all hers. Then she let him pull the tight jeans off her, then her black lacy panties, and soon he was on her and in her, filling the hollow spot.

She fucked with an animal urgency, as if trying to prove something, pumping with her hips, and he was hot, too, slamming it home. They came together, noisily, rocking the van. It wasn't just another fuck to her—it was special; it was about something more than just a quickie in the parking lot. She was proving to herself that her horny old daddy hadn't ruined sex for her.

She wondered if it had been just another fuck for Jon.

14

Nolan hadn't slept more than a couple of hours in a couple of days. He was using his drug of choice—caffeine—to keep on top of things. It was 2:25 A.M. and he was drinking his seventh cup of coffee of the night. This would be the last cup. He had to be able to let the tiredness through, once the meet was over; he had to get some sleep tonight. Everything rode on tomorrow.

Last night he'd sat up planning this elaborate fucking heist he wanted no part of. It was part of the deal; Comfort expected it of him. And in a sense he was relieved to be planning it: Comfort had the balls to sack Brady Eighty, but he certainly didn't have the brains.

Not that Cole Comfort wasn't smart. He was—or anyway, he was shrewd. But Comfort's lowlife penny-ante instincts would have defeated him, had he not pulled Nolan in for organization and strategy; he'd have been the proverbial kid in a candy store, Nolan knew—running pell-mell through the mall taking things right and left, your typical American consumer gone berserk, a manic shopper with a credit card from hell.

And if Nolan had to be in on this goddamn thing, at least let it be done right. He found himself using muscles he hadn't used in a long time; he found some part of him that liked being back in the old life. He found himself caught up in the planning, thinking it through, studying each detail, making lists and maps and charts, getting lost in the work.

It also helped him keep his nerves and emotions in check. He wasn't thinking about Sherry in any other terms than doing what was needed to get her back. He wasn't letting himself deal with what the bastards might be putting her through. He wasn't contemplating life without her. He was doing what was needed to get her the fuck back.

And that required doing two things: cooperating with Comfort, or anyway pretending to, planning his heist; and working behind Comfort's back to find where they were keeping Sherry. He might on some level be caught up in the momentum of the heist; but his goal was still to shut it down and get the girl safely back. He had Winch and Dooley on his side, on the sly; and tonight he would talk to the high-tech guy, Fisher, after the meet.

Fisher was a good man—clueing him in would be a risk, but a minimal one; Nolan knew from past experience that Fisher shared Winch's distaste for violence, and Comfort's kidnaping of Sherry to coerce Nolan's participation would not likely sit well with the slightly stuffy electronics whiz.

And some light, however faint, was showing up down at the end of the tunnel. Jon had gotten a piece of something. In more ways than one.

Jon had showed up at the restaurant just after midnight and Nolan took him into the cement-walled back room where Nolan's desk and file cabinet kept company with boxes of liquor and food. The kid seemed dazed, confused.

"What the hell happened to you?" Nolan had demanded. The kid hadn't checked in with Nolan in hours.

"I couldn't use the phone in the van," Jon explained, breathlessly, "because I had company in there, till just a few minutes ago."

And Jon had told him about Cindy Lou Comfort, who turned out, of all things, to be a groupie of sorts for bands like Jon's; she'd even gone to see Jon's band on occasion, and knew him from it.

"I was in the van with her for two hours," Jon said. "I didn't find out where Sherry is exactly, but some of what I did learn is going to be helpful."

Jon filled him in, including the news that Sherry wasn't at the nearby Holiday Inn: she was somewhere on the Illinois side, being watched by Lyle.

"You've narrowed the state down, anyway," Nolan said, darkly.

"She's kind of an innocent kid," Jon said, "for a little slut. I get the idea she's only vaguely aware of what her father does. She's also having some problems with him—she made some vague references that I think may mean he's hitting on her."

"Hitting on her?"

"Sexually," Jon said, shrugging, embarrassed.

"He's a class act, our Cole. She doesn't know who you are?"

"She knows my name is Jon and I used to play keyboards for the Nodes. That's it. She's a troubled kid—she's thinking about hopping a bus to California, to go live with some friend of hers out there."

"So is every other teenage girl in the Midwest."

"I suppose. But how many of 'em have a homelife with Cole and Lyle Comfort in it?"

"We could snatch her."

"What?"

"We could snatch her and swap her for Sherry."

"Jeez, Nolan—"

"If you're thinking that would make us no better than Comfort himself, kid, you're dead bang full of shit. On our worst day we're better than that evil worthless cocksucker, who started this, remember. He grabbed Sherry, so all bets are off!"

Jon did something unusual: he touched Nolan's arm.

"I'm with you," Jon said. "Whatever it takes."

Nolan's hands were shaking; he looked at them shaking and shook his head disgustedly. "Goddamn coffee," he said.

Now it was just after two-thirty and everybody was here, most of them sitting at that long table—including Nolan, who had taken Comfort's position at its head; Comfort sat to Nolan's left, on the corner of the table, as if almost sitting at the head reminded everybody he was really in charge—just deferring to Nolan for this one planning session. Jon again sat off to the side at a small table.

But the big change was the presence of Lyle Comfort, who sat next to his father; Lyle was a handsome, well-groomed kid in expensive clothes—he wore a rust-colored leather jacket and a shirt with a faint yellow and gray puzzle pattern, had curly brown hair and brown eyes and a tan and a blank fashion-model expression. He looked like a city kid, on first glance, but if you looked hard, Lyle was a dumb-as-a-post country kid, who learned how to dress from TV and magazines.

The Leeches were again lined up on one side of the table, but Fisher was sitting on their side, tonight, down at the far end, still with a shirt pocket full of pens and gizmos, still with a notepad in front of him—open to a page of notes he'd already taken. Neither the slight, easygoing Winch nor the dour, basset-faced Dooley, sitting next to Lyle Comfort, gave anything away; they seemed completely at ease—what they knew about Nolan's situation, they kept close to the vest. Nolan's favorite kind of people: pros.

Tonight the Leeches had taken their stocking caps off, and spoiled their uniformity: one was sandy-haired, one was brown-haired, the other was brown-haired balding. They were sitting there putting the beer away pretty good. Nolan had relented and put two pitchers of beer on the table—this meet would take a while, and a nod to sociality wouldn't hurt.

Lyle Comfort's presence here, however, was disturbing.

If Lyle was here, who was watching Sherry?

Before the meet began, Nolan cornered Cole Comfort and put a hand on his shoulder and said, "Nice to have your son with us tonight, Cole."

Comfort nodded, not knowing what Nolan was getting at.

"Who's minding the store?" Nolan asked Comfort.

Now Comfort got it. "Never you mind," he said.

Nolan whispered in Comfort's ear. "If she's dead, so are you."

Comfort pulled away, shaken, nervous. "She's fine. Don't talk about that here."

Nolan laughed harshly. "Here? Meeting here at all is moronic, meeting at the place we plan to hit in twenty-four hours. Less than twenty-four hours."

"We're here," Comfort said. "Let's have our meet."

"You know, if the cops prowl the parking lot, this will make two nights in a row that pickup of yours and that pimpmobile of the

Leeches'll be out in front of my restaurant in the wee hours."

The Leeches drove a yellow Camaro with gaudy racing stripes. Very inconspicuous—if this were Tijuana.

"You said the cops don't prowl the mall," Comfort said, irritably.

"My information is that they haven't been lately, yes. But that information was casually obtained. We didn't stake out the lot like we should have, seeing if they are prowling, and if so, what the pattern is, if any."

"Aw shut up," Comfort said. He prodded Nolan with a pointing finger. "And leave this negative horseshit behind, when you're running through your plans, front of the others."

"Don't poke me, Cole," Nolan said.

"I'll do what I fuckin' well please."

"I'm sure you will. But I'd ask you to keep in mind, I've been upholding my end of the bargain. I'm helping you heist your mall—*my* mall—and I'm giving it my best shot."

"Yeah, yeah, I know you are. I appreciate that."

"I expect Sherry back—unharmed—and my full share. Jon's, too."

"We been through all that…"

"Just so we understand each other."

Now Nolan was talking while the seated group studied photocopies of a map he'd made of the mall.

"The stores with the X's," Nolan said, looking down toward Dooley, "are the ones we'll need opened, Phil."

"No problem," the locksmith said.

Comfort said, "Were you out to Brady Eighty today, Phil?"

"Yeah. I walked the mall. They use those sliding glass doors that lock together; a few have metal cage doors. In either case, picking the locks is no big deal."

Nolan asked, "How long will it take you to open each shop?"

"Five to fifteen minutes."

A Leech said, "Fifty stores, that's a lot of time."

Nolan said, "We won't be opening fifty stores."

Comfort scowled at Nolan and slammed a fist on the table and the beer pitchers sloshed. He said, "How many times do I have to say it? We're looting the whole motherfucker! We're taking it all!"

"Cole," Nolan said, smiling tightly, "as much as you may wish to take every spool of thread and Snickers bar and Slinky, we got a finite amount of time, and finite manpower. We got to pick and choose."

Comfort thought about that, just momentarily, waved a hand at Nolan dismissively, and said, "You're right." Then he looked at his photocopy of the map. "These places you X'ed are the targets, then—"

"Twelve stores," Nolan said, "not counting the three big department stores, all of which are worth hitting."

"And not counting the bank," Winch said.

"Right," Nolan said. "Not counting the bank."

"What's this double X," Dooley asked, "near the back entry, on the east side of the building."

"That's where the maintenance and security people work out of," Nolan said. "The security guy will be off duty, and we'll drop a Mickey Finn in the janitor's coffee."

"Who will?" a Leech asked.

"I'll take care of that," Nolan said. "Now, note the three major department stores—Petersen's on the east end, Penney's in the middle, and I. Magnin at the west end. I. Magnin, of course, is the most important of these. Expensive merchandise."

Another Leech said, "And that's where the loading docks are."

"Right," Nolan said. "Behind each of the major department stores. Which is perfect for us. Easy loading access to one of the semis, no matter what store you've been 'shopping' at."

He went on to explain why he'd chosen the various stores—the leather shop, for example, carried an inventory of leather goods and furs amounting to well over a quarter mil—and indicated a priority list, which shops to hit first, and began making assignments. To best utilize manpower, the truck cabs would sit empty with the exception of the middle one, where Jon would sit, as point man.

"Why him?" Comfort said.

"Why not?" Nolan said.

"Somebody's gotta watch," a Leech said. "Let him do it. He's just a little guy."

"What about guns?" Dooley asked.

"What about them?" Nolan said.

Comfort said, "Whoever wants to carry, carry. If you need something, just ask; I got some extra pieces. I'll be packing and my boy will and the Leeches. I assume you will too, Phil."

Dooley nodded, but Winch said, "I don't have shit to do with guns."

Comfort shrugged. "Up to you."

Fisher looked up from his note-taking to say, "I have a stun gun. I don't like bullets. Very crude."

A Leech said, "Why ain't the Walgreen's got an X?"

"Why should it?" Nolan asked. "That's dime-store stuff."

Another Leech said, "They got a pharmacy."

Yet another Leech said, "Meaning drugs."

Nolan looked at Comfort, who shook his head no, violently.

"No, sir," he said. "That's one thing I won't abide. I never dirtied my hands with dope."

The Leeches looked at each other, doing comic takes, as if to say, "The guy's crazy, but what are you gonna do?" Nolan tended to share that sentiment; the notion of Cole Comfort drawing the line somewhere was pretty fucking absurd.

Fisher said, "I was in DeReuss Jewelry today. I spotted the teargas alarm. It's a wall-mount—turns on and off with a cylindrical key."

"I saw it too," Dooley said, nodding. "I could pick it, like any lock."

"I'd suggest not," Fisher said. "It could have a time sequence of some kind—turn the key right for three seconds, back three seconds, and right again, or whatever."

"It's bound to be a simple sequence," said Dooley, nodding, "but that doesn't make it easy to guess."

"I'd suggest just knocking the metal plate off," Fisher said, "and jumping the wires. Not much different from hot-wiring a car, actually."

"And that would take care of the tear gas," Nolan said.

"Should," Fisher said.

"You know, a mall's a big place," a Leech said, making as profound an observation as Nolan guessed a Leech could make.

"And we're going to be all spread out," another Leech said.

"How'll we keep in touch?" the final Leech said.

"Yes, Uncle Donald," Jon said. "How?"

Nolan almost smiled at that, but again it was lost on the Leeches. "Walkie-talkies," Nolan said. "Clip right on your belt. Radio Shack has plenty in stock; I checked."

"Did you buy them at a discount?" Jon asked wryly.

"No," Nolan said. "They're the first things we'll steal. That's called five-finger discount, where I come from."

The meeting went on one more hour and two more pitchers of beer. Nolan answered questions and they went over the details. It was a big job, but simple in many ways, particularly once it had been broken down into man-by-man tasks. The hardest thing was the loading they'd all be doing—particularly hauling the larger appliances on dollies and carts to the waiting semis. It would be a long hard night of physical labor. The hourly wage would be considerable, however.

As the party began breaking up, Nolan saw Fisher head for the john and followed him in. As they were pissing at adjoining stalls, he told Fisher he needed to talk to him privately, and Fisher agreed to drive out to Nolan's house, once well shy of Comforts and Leeches.

Before he left, Comfort patted Nolan on the shoulder and said, "You're doing fine. Keep it up, and everything's gonna work out."

"Keep up your end and it will."

Comfort only smiled his disarmingly engaging smile and left. Why did that sadistic son of a bitch have such a warm, friendly smile?

When the restaurant was empty, Nolan, who'd had none of the beer, poured some whiskey in a shot glass and asked Jon if he wanted any. Jon, who rarely drank, said, "Fuck yes."

They sat at a small table and drank the whiskey and Nolan said, "Did you notice Comfort's thick kid Lyle didn't say anything all night?"

"You're wrong, Nolan," Jon said, swirling his whiskey in his glass, staring at the dark liquid like it was a crystal ball hiding his future. "His presence spoke volumes."

"What do you mean?"

"If he's here, who was baby-sitting Sherry?"

"It occurred to me she might be dead."

"I don't think so."

"You think your new squeeze Cindy Lou was watching Sherry. Sitting in for brother Lyle."

Jon nodded and kept nodding. "Yeah. I sure do. And I don't think she's going to like it."

"You don't."

"She may be a little slut, but she didn't strike me as a bad kid. She didn't strike me as somebody who'd get much of a kick out of playing jailer, either."

"She's a Comfort."

"Yeah, but she's disenchanted with her family, with her old man. And tonight they made her an accomplice in a kidnaping. She isn't stupid. She'll figure that out."

"What are you saying?"

"Let's not snatch her. Let me try to link up with her tomorrow and, shit, try to get her on our side."

"I don't know."

"I think I can get it out of her."

"You mean you can get it in her."

"No, I mean I can get it out of her—where Sherry's being kept."

Nolan thought about it. "We could also just grab her and trade her to her father even up for Sherry."

"If that's the way you want to go, I'm in. But you were right—on our worst day we're not as bad as that evil cocksucker. And that evil cocksucker knows it."

"Meaning?"

"Meaning he knows that he's capable of killing your girl. And he also knows you're not capable of killing his daughter."

"I'm capable of cutting off her fingers one at a time and sending them to him."

"No you aren't."

Nolan drank some of the whiskey.

Then he said, "We'll try it your way. Talk to her. Fuck her again. When she's coming, ask her where Sherry is." He let some air out. Finished the whiskey. "Come on. Fisher's probably invented a black box by now to open my garage door."

And Jon went out to the van, and Nolan to his silver Trans Am. Nolan wishing he had it in him to kill Comfort's daughter, knowing he didn't.

Part Three

Jon had started the stakeout midmorning. As late as the meet last night (this morning, technically) had broken up, he didn't figure Comfort would be going anyplace at the crack of dawn. Nolan hadn't argued with Jon's logic on that point, and over a breakfast of scrambled eggs and sausage, which Nolan prepared, Jon asked Nolan what the game plan was if Sherry's whereabouts could be ascertained.

"We go in with guns and take her back," Nolan said.

That didn't seem like much of a plan to Jon, but on the other hand, until the exact circumstances of how and where she was being held were known to them, coming up with anything more elaborate was a waste of time.

Jon shrugged. "Well, how hard can it be, with only that lunkhead Lyle guarding her?"

"Hard," Nolan said. "Lyle may be a lunkhead, but he's also a Comfort. That makes him a dangerous lunkhead."

Jon was, as usual, impressed by Nolan's businesslike attitude, even in the face of something as emotionally wrenching as the kidnaping of a woman Nolan may well have loved. There had been a moment, last night, in the back room at the restaurant just before the meet, when Nolan betrayed some emotion bubbling under that stoic surface; and Jon sensed the rage behind Nolan's occasional quiet remarks about what he would do to Comfort if Sherry were harmed. But mostly Nolan seemed to be sublimating his emotions and anger into working on those two conflicting goals—planning/organizing the heist, and getting Sherry back.

Now it was Thursday afternoon, a little after two, and a light snow was dusting the Holiday Inn parking lot, powdering the immediate world, making it look better and not so real. Jon sat in the parked light blue van in his ski mask and navy coat, his Thermos of hot chocolate between his legs. No paperback today. His full attention was on Comfort's red pickup truck. The Leeches were apparently staying at the Holiday Inn, as well, as Jon had spotted their yellow, racing-striped Camaro parked alongside a room on the west side of the motel. If the Leeches and/or Comfort left in the Camaro, they would have to drive through the parking lot past where Jon sat in his van. So he had it covered.

Butterflies were aflight in his stomach, however; time was running out: the mall heist was set to go down in a matter of hours—a little over eight hours. Before that time, if things went well, he and Nolan would rescue Sherry, very possibly in a blaze of gunfire and dying Comforts. And that was if things went well. He'd been in situations where he liked the options better.

He thought about Sherry. He hadn't let himself do that, much. He liked her—he was attracted to her, no question, but it was an attraction he'd never do anything about. A stunning-looking woman, and no dummy. He'd never seen anyone handle Nolan better. She didn't exactly have him wrapped around her little finger, but close. Surprisingly close.

What sort of hell was she going through? He'd been there himself—he'd been held hostage before, and knew firsthand of the helplessness, the hopelessness, the all-pervasive fear it engendered. And her captors were Cole and Lyle Comfort—he shivered at the thought, and the cold day.

Presumably Comfort would keep her alive and well till tonight's heist, at least, to keep Nolan playing. Comfort's own reputation was so rotten it had obviously forced him to call on people who'd worked with Nolan—Fisher, Winch, Dooley—pros who would put their misgivings about working with Comfort aside when they heard Nolan was aboard. (The Leeches were another matter.) This put Nolan's importance beyond providing inside information and planning; Comfort had—no doubt reluctantly, but of necessity—made Nolan the linchpin of the heist.

Without Nolan, the mall haul simply would not go down. If Nolan failed to show, Fisher, Winch and Dooley would walk.

What Comfort didn't know, of course, was that those three already knew the real score; Fisher, like Winch and Dooley before him, had last night promised to follow Nolan's lead, even down to aborting the job (in favor of Nolan kicking in a fifteen-grand payoff —business was business).

At just after four o'clock, Jon decided to take a chance. He pulled off the ski mask and replaced it with a gray beret and wrapped the black muffler around his neck up higher, so that it covered the bottom of his face, like a stagecoach robber. He tucked a square flat brown-paper-wrapped package under his left arm, locked up the van and walked across the snowy parking lot and into the Holiday Inn. His gloveless right hand was on the snub-nose .38 in the deep pocket of his coat.

Cindy Lou had mentioned, yesterday, that her father and the Leeches had spent a good deal of time together, in the lounge, which was off the restaurant, and Jon peeked in. It was just a bar and some booths and a few small tables and a middle-aged mustached pianist playing "Just the Way You Are." A couple sat at the bar, and some businessmen sat in one of the booths. But in another of the booths the Leeches and Cole Comfort were sitting, countless bottles of beer before them. They were going over one of Nolan's photocopied maps of the mall. Right in front of God and the pianist and everybody.

Jesus Christ, Jon thought, ducking out before he was seen. Finding them confabbing there meant he'd hit pay dirt; but he couldn't get excited about it because he was too struck by the notion that he just might possibly be pulling a job with these morons in a few hours.

He walked the halls till he found 714—the numbering system seemed to apply to wings, not floors—and knocked on the door. He knocked with his left hand, brown-paper package still tucked under his arm, his right hand still clutching the revolver, which remained in his pocket but pointed toward the door, because if Lyle Comfort answered it, Jon just might have to shoot the fucker.

No answer to his knock.

He sighed. He was trembling. He simply was not cut out for this life. What was he doing, hanging around with a guy like Nolan. What the fuck was he doing with a *revolver* in his pocket.

He knocked again.

The door cracked open and Cindy Lou's faintly freckled face peered out, and broke into a lovely smile, the small, childlike teeth whiter than outside. She was lovely, but seemed a little haggard. Was it the light of day, and lack of makeup—or had she had a rough night?

In any event, she was dripping wet, except for her reddish-blond hair, which was pulled back from her face. She was wearing a white towel.

"Hi, Cindy Lou."

Her smile disappeared, and the door chain was still between them. "You shouldn't oughta come here," she said, big blue eyes going smaller as she tightened her expression.

"I brought your record."

The eyes got as large as they were blue again, and she smiled; but then the smile faded, and her eyes became merely huge. *"Daddy's* around. It's dangerous."

"I think I spotted him in the lounge. He seemed settled in."

Her brow crinkled. "How would you know which was my daddy?"

"Let me in, Cindy Lou. I got to talk to you."

Her face tightened further, in thought; under those remarkable eyes she had dark circles. Then the chain was drawn aside, and she opened the door; he stepped inside and chained the door behind him. He handed her the brown package and she opened it greedily, saying "All *right!*" as the towel dropped to the floor.

Her body, in the light of day, looked just fine. Very pale flesh, very pink, very erect nipples, peachlike breasts, her strawberry blond pubic hair trimmed into a heart shape, something he hadn't seen in the near-light of the back of the van last night. His dick said boy, howdy, and he told it, down boy.

And she just stood there, not caring a whit about her nudity, jiggling, bouncing as she grinned and looked at the cover of the Nodes album, front and back.

"I *remember* some of these songs," she said, "from hearing you play!"

"Maybe you better get dressed," he said.

She stood there with her weight on one hip, a hand on one hip, holding the album in her other hand like it was a tray and she was an amused but bored carhop at a topless drive-in.

"Or maybe not," he said, and took her in his arms and kissed her; she immediately began taking his coat off, even as she was putting her darting tongue in his mouth, and the coat dropped to the floor like the dead weight it was, the gun-in-pocket clunking. Her hands worked on his zipper and she went down on her knees in front of him.

Jon stood there, shaking his head, wondering how he lost control of the situation so fast, and he was in her mouth, but only for a second when he pulled away and said, "No."

Still on her knees she looked up at him with utter confusion. "No?" she repeated, as if she didn't understand the meaning of the word.

Certainly in this context, the word seemed out of place, but Jon forced himself back in his pants and said to her, "Get dressed. We got to talk, and I can't talk to you when you're like that."

She smirked humorlessly and got up and picked up her towel and dried herself off a little, and he watched her, every cell of his body aching with regret, as a beautiful naked teenage female, as yet a stranger to cellulite, put on panties and jeans and a loose-fitting red sweater with a scoop neck that showed just enough cleavage to make him simultaneously wish he were dead and could live forever.

She stood there, weight on one hip again, both hands on her hips this time, smirking, but good-naturedly now, challenging him to find something to talk about that was more important than her giving him the best goddamned blowjob the state of Missouri had to offer, in Iowa yet.

He put his coat back on, put his hand on the .38 grip within the pocket, and looked around the room. The signs of Cole Comfort living here were few; his clothes were apparently either in the dresser and closet or still in suitcases. There was a half-empty bottle of Old Grand-Dad on the dresser. Her clothes were also put away, and her personal items must have been in the bathroom, because there was no particular sign of Cindy Lou, either, except her denim jacket slung over a chair, and on a table a *Hit Parader* magazine with heavy-metal groups on the cover, a publication he didn't figure was on Cole Comfort's subscription list.

The side wall of the room was orange-vinyl-curtained sliding doors, leading out to the pool area. Jon reached behind there and unlocked one of the sliding doors; the swimming pool (like Nolan's) was covered with plastic and a fresh layer of white powder, shimmering in the daylight like a vast coke-covered mirror.

"Sit down," he told her, pointing to the nearest bed.

She did. He sat next to her.

"Can I trust you?" he asked.

"To do what?"

"To keep a confidence."

She shrugged. "Sure."

"It's not going to be that easy. Last night you talked a lot about you and your father not getting along. You talked around it some, but that's the general drift."

She sighed heavily; the dark circles under her eyes weren't the whole story—she seemed weary, troubled.

"It isn't that simple," she said.

"He's hitting on you, isn't he?"

She said nothing for a moment; looked at the floor. Nodded.

"Was it worse last night?"

She nodded. She shook her head. Pointed toward the bathroom. "I spent four hours locked in that goddamn toilet. He started pounding on the door. He was crying, after awhile…"

Jon couldn't quite picture Cole Comfort crying.

"Was he sorry?" Jon asked.

"He said he was. He said he had…demons. He begged me to forgive him. I forgave him—but through the door. He wanted to fuck me. I know he did."

Jon looked at her with awe. Her frankness was startling, and he wondered how, after a nightmare night hiding behind a locked bathroom door from a father who probably wanted to rape her, she could so easily go down on her knees and take a casual lover like him in her mouth.

She smiled a little, reading his mind, or anyway his eyes. She touched his leg. "I like lovin'. Daddy ain't gonna spoil that for me. It's not that I don't want to have sex again—it's just that I don't want to have it with Daddy."

"That's not a bad policy."

She looked at the orange vinyl curtains. "I'm thinking about leaving. I called my friend out in California—Ginger—she's got a job and everything. Not hustling, either. She says she can get me on at the Taco Bell, too. It's a better future than I got at home."

"I think leaving is a good idea."

"It is. I just can't take it. This…it's getting…I can't take it."

"There's more, isn't there? Than your daddy pawing after you."

She seemed to almost wince. Another sigh. Another nod.

"Your father's a thief, isn't he?"

She looked at him sharply, pulled away. "What are you?" Her voice turned as harsh as a heavy-metal guitar solo. "Are you some fuckin' narc or something?"

He laughed a little. Very little. "No. I'm not a narc or any kind of cop."

"Then…what?"

"I'm another thief. I'm in on this mall heist with your father."

She looked at him like they looked at Columbus when he said the world was round. "What? You are?"

"Yes. And if he knew I'd made contact with you, he wouldn't like it."

"Is that what you call it? Contact? I thought you fucked me. And, brother, he'd kill you, for that."

"I know he would. I know he would."

She looked at him, taking him seriously; something in his voice had brought her around.

"See, I'm not really a thief, anymore," he said. "I used to be. When I was a kid, and wild. I was in on a couple of bank robberies, a few other things. But I went straight. Started playing with the Nodes, working on my comic books—like I told you about last night. But now, after I thought that whole world was behind me, your father pulls me in on this fucking thing."

"Why? How?"

"I'm going to tell you the whole story, Cindy Lou. And believe me, I'm putting my life in your hands…"

And he told her. He pulled no punches. He even told her about his part in the deaths of certain of her "kin." Most of all he told her about Sherry. About how Sherry had been kidnaped to force Nolan and Jon to help heist the Brady Eighty mall.

She was silent throughout, listening raptly; but he couldn't read her.

Finally he said, "I think you already know about Sherry, and the trouble she's in. I think you were forced to stand guard on her last night, while your brother and father met with the rest of us, for our final planning session."

She winced again. Looked at the floor.

"I don't know what crimes in the past your father has involved you in," he said, "but this time it's kidnaping. You're an accessory. You're implicated in the mall heist, as well; you're a conspirator."

She looked at him, her big blue eyes wet.

"The girl's all right," she said. "She hasn't been hurt or anything. Lyle hasn't touched her."

Thank God.

"Good. But your father wants revenge against my friend and me. I think he plans to kill Sherry, eventually. And me. And my friend."

She thought about that. Then shook her head violently.

"No!" she said. "No, I don't think he'd go that far. Daddy's not a bad man, not really…"

"Jesus fuck! How did you spend last night again? Or was that somebody else who was hiding in the can from her rape-happy old man?"

"Jon…what are you asking…?"

"First, don't betray me. At the very least, just don't say anything to your father about us talking."

He waited for her to nod, but she just looked at him.

He swallowed and went on. "What I want most of all is for you to tell me where they're holding Sherry."

"Oh, Jon…"

"Where, and under what conditions. I need to know the layout of the place, so we can get her back without anybody getting hurt. That includes Lyle, and your father."

She was shaking her head no.

"We aren't murderers, Cindy Lou, Nolan and me. We're two guys who used to be crooks, who went straight, and something out of our past came back at us and whapped us alongside the head. This girl, Sherry, is innocent in this. She's done nothing to your father to deserve any of it. She's not, never was, a criminal. Her only crime was falling in love with the wrong guy."

"I been there," she said hollowly.

Tears were making tracks down her cheeks, though her face was oddly impassive.

"I think you should help me," Jon said. "You should tell me where Sherry is, before she gets hurt. Before she gets killed. You don't want to be an accessory to murder, do you?"

Now her Kewpie-doll lips were quivering. "Jon…please…"

"Help me. Don't say anything to your father. And catch that bus to California—today, tonight, as soon as you can break free from him."

"I don't have enough money…"

"I'll tell you what. From here I'm going down to the Greyhound station. It's in downtown Davenport. I'm going to buy you a ticket to, where?"

"L.A.," she said, snuffling.

"To L.A. I'll have them hold it for you at the ticket window, in your name. How's that?"

"I can't do it."

"Go to California?"

"Help you. He's my daddy, Jon. No matter what he's done, he's my daddy. I can't, I just can't turn against him. He's kin."

Jon reached out and held her hand. "Look. This isn't a matter of 'kin.' It's a matter of right and wrong."

Her mouth tightened. "You steal things. How can you say what's right and wrong?"

"Stealing's wrong. I don't do it anymore. At least, I don't want to do it anymore. Kidnaping is very wrong. Murder is as wrong as you can get."

"Going against your family is wrong."

"Not if they're the Mansons. Help me. And yourself. Tell me where Sherry is—and catch that bus."

"Jon…don't ask me this…we hardly know each other…"

"My life's in your hands."

The door opened.

Jon withdrew the gun, put a finger to his lips; Cindy Lou sucked in air, brought a hand up to her mouth.

The safety chain kept the door from opening more than a few inches. A voice out there—Cole Comfort's voice, sounding a little drank—said, "Let me in, darlin'! What you got this thing locked for? And turn that TV down!"

Jon mouthed, "Please," to her, and she got up and went to the door, saying, "I got to shut it to open it, Daddy," and she shut it, turning to Jon and giving him a pained expression and shaking her head no.

Quickly he ducked out the glass doors and sprinted through the snow back to his van, not looking back, gun in his hand and in his pocket. Wondering if he'd blown it.

Business was slow, at Nolan's, even for a Thursday night. It was cold, particularly for early December, and the roads were slick from the light but persistent snow. This was no blizzard, but people weren't used to the winter driving conditions yet, and a lot of them stayed home. Tonight it was mostly singles, out dancing to the monotonous beat and nasal sounds of some British synthesizer band. Nolan had turned the alleged music down lower than Sherry would have liked. Sherry thought loud music encouraged dancing, which encouraged general socializing, all of which encouraged drinking. It was his thinking that the couples lingering here, after a late dinner, sitting in the bar, might want to talk, or anyway hear themselves think. The loudness of the sound system was a bone of contention between Sherry and Nolan. He usually let her have her way—as long as the customers didn't complain, and they never seemed to. Without her here, he did it his way.

The regulars were asking for her: "Where's Sherry?" "We really *miss* her!" "You're a poor substitute for a pretty face, Nolan!" He told them, including several of his Chamber of Commerce pals, she'd gone home to visit family. Since her family was all dead, he hoped that wasn't really the case.

Being at the restaurant was worse, in a way, than being at home; her touch was here—the plants, the decor, even the way things were run, much of it had come from her, or from them both, talking things out, planning together. They had shared the restaurant more than the house. Funny, how the worst waitress in the world could turn out to have such a knowing touch where managing was concerned. Strange, how he could sleep in that bed and force her from his mind but in Nolan's, he couldn't. She was everywhere.

Except in the back room. That was where Cole Comfort waited.

○

Jennifer Wallace liked her job. She never admitted it to anybody, because she was, after all, just a glorified janitor. And not particularly glorified, either.

But she liked solitude—she'd grown up in a big family and hadn't had near as much time to herself as she would've liked, and now, only twenty-five years of age, she was working on her own big family, with three at home, ages two, four and seven, which was the life she'd sought, the life she loved, but solitude wasn't part of it.

She was a small but sturdy woman, with dark brown hair in a short tight perm, small dark eyes, rather large nose, pleasant smile; wearing a light brown shirt with the Brady Eighty logo on it, and dark brown slacks. It was almost a uniform, giving her a military look, and she liked that. It made her feel less a janitor, as the term bothered her a little, even though she liked the work just fine.

A lot of people wouldn't have. But all the mopping of floors and Windexing of storefronts (which was pretty much the sum of her duties between now and seven, when the shift changed and the doors opened) had a hypnotic effect on her. She got into it. She liked the feel of her muscles being exercised. She liked working hard but unsupervised, taking her time.

And she varied it. She could finish up the place in five hours, if she pushed it. In which case, she could sit in the maintenance shop—a big cement supply room, like a garage only without a garage door—with her feet up on the workbench, reading a book, or listening to the radio, or watching a portable TV.

Other nights she would take her time. Those were the nights when she was in a thoughtful mood, and let the motion of mopping and Windexing lull her. She could get drunk on work when she took it at that slow, steady pace. But not so drunk that she wouldn't think about her kids and her Doug.

She had a terrific husband and terrific kids. Doug was blond and chubby and cute as a bug's ear; they got married out of high school—a "have-to," but they neither one had regrets, at least not that Jennifer knew. Doug worked at Oscar Meyer, day shift, and she took the kids to day-care when she got home from work around 7:30 A.M. and then she'd sleep all day. She and Doug and the kids had all evening together; she came on at ten, so they'd get the kids in bed at eight-thirty or so, and have a roll in the hay, and she'd go off to work with a glow.

She loved her life.

Tonight, she'd come on, as usual, right at ten, nodding to Pete, whose maintenance shift was just ending, and Scott, that cute security guard, who was going off duty. As usual, Pete had a pot of coffee waiting for her. She needed her caffeine; that's one thing you needed in this job. That and a good attitude.

She sat in her swivel executive-style chair, which had been abandoned by one of the businesses out here and which Pete had salvaged and repaired, with her feet up on the workbench, trying to decide whether tonight would be a high-energy, five-hour night, followed by some relaxation (she had a historical romance paperback tucked in her purse, *Love's Savage Sword* by Linda Benjamin); or a reflective, slow-and-steady worknight, where she could get lost in the circular motion of mop and rag, and contemplate her kids and her old man. She sipped her coffee, and thought: I think tonight I'll whip through this place like a female Mr. Clean; maybe I can beat my record and come in under five hours—and finish reading my romance.

With that, she was deep asleep.

Nolan sat at his desk. White-haired, blue-eyed Coleman Comfort sat on a box of whiskey bottles nearby; he was wearing his coveralls with a plaid shirt underneath, looking folksy as a postcard from the Grand Ole Opry. He seemed to have developed a bit of a paunch; Nolan didn't seem to be the only one age had put a spare tire on. One odd note was struck: his high-topped black tennis shoes, over which cream-colored longjohns rose into the coveralls. Nolan understood the shoes, though: he'd suggested to all of them, last night, that they wear something comfortable and suited for the long night of physical labor ahead. And Cole Comfort had obviously taken Nolan's footwear advice to heart, and sole.

"I guess it's time," Cole said, smiling; he had such a nice smile.

Nolan glanced at his watch. Ten after ten. "I'd say the maintenance girl's out, by now." He had gone in just before Pete went off and chatted with the man, slipping Seconal in the pot of coffee. The last three nights Nolan had, just after ten, entered the mall the back way, walking past the maintenance shop's double doors, which were invariably ajar; each night he noticed the night girl sitting having a cup of coffee before getting to work.

Three nights in a row suggested, but did not guarantee, a pattern.

"How do we *know* she's out?" Comfort said, just a little irritably.

"We'll know for sure soon enough. Before this goes any further, you've got a phone call to make."

And Nolan pushed the phone on his desk toward Comfort. Comfort rose and went to the phone and pushed some buttons and, phone to his ear, stood and smiled at Nolan. It was a smile that seemed pleasant enough, but Nolan could see the smugness, the cruelty, that lurked behind Comfort's good-ole-boy veneer.

"Hello, son," Comfort said, his voice warm. "Time to put the girl on."

He listened for a while, and handed the receiver to Nolan.

"Nolan?"

Her voice was breathy; there was fear in it, but also relief.

"Sherry," he said.

"They're using me to make you help them, aren't they?" Her bitter tone of voice conveyed what she couldn't add: And I hate it.

"You know about the mall heist?" he asked her.

"I've picked up on it. You could lose everything."

"I'm not going to lose you."

"The life you've made…"

"No. I did the planning. It'll go down smooth. You'll be returned to me and we'll even get a piece of the action for our trouble."

Nolan didn't believe that, but he needed Comfort to believe he did, and it wouldn't hurt Sherry's state of mind to believe that, either.

"They haven't hurt me. They keep saying once you've cooperated, I'll be released."

"We'll be together in a few hours."

That Nolan believed; or at least, he believed it to be a possibility. He and Jon already had something in motion.

"I love you, Nolan."

"I love you, too."

"That's...nice to hear."

Was she crying?

He said, "I'll take you to Vegas when this is over and prove it."

He told her to hang on, and then he hung up.

Comfort, who again was perched on the liquor boxes, hands on his knees, smiled paternally. "She didn't complain about the treatment none, did she?"

"No."

"You're a lucky man. She's a nice girl. A pretty girl."

Nolan didn't like to hear Comfort talk about her, but he didn't say anything.

Comfort did: "When this is over, we'll be even, Nolan. We can put all our differences behind us."

"It'll be history," Nolan agreed.

"History," Comfort repeated, smiling, standing, clapping, once. "So! Let's go open the door and let our friends in, what do you say?"

Nolan remained seated. "Soon," he said.

Comfort's smile disappeared, and his mouth pulled itself in a tight line across his leathery face, but he just sat down. He'd put Nolan in charge; he had to live with it. For the moment.

°

Jon, wearing a *Space Pirates* sweatshirt, peeked in the maintenance room. The woman in the brown uniform was slumped in a swivel chair, feet up on a workbench; she was sawing logs. He had a large gym bag with him, from which he took a pair of handcuffs and some clothesline and a roll of wide-width adhesive tape. He left the woman in her chair, but slipped her feet from the bench onto the floor. He cuffed her hands behind the chair, and tied her feet to it, snug. He ran the adhesive over her eyes and around behind her hair, grimacing with the thought of how removal would hurt the poor woman. But it beat being dead, and Comfort might just as easily killed her, which was why Nolan kept this job for Jon and himself. Jon slapped another piece of adhesive over her mouth, which didn't quite silence the snoring; her fairly large nose could saw its share of logs on its own.

In the bottom of the bag was a long-barreled .38 and an UZI submachine gun and a box of ammo for the revolver, and half a dozen clips for the machine gun. Jon zipped the bag and stowed it in a corner of the maintenance shed, behind a big shiny golf-cart-like thing, which seemed to be a floor buffer.

The guns were against Comfort's rules. Despite what had been said at the meeting last night, Comfort had told Nolan privately that he and Jon were to go into this unarmed. Nolan hadn't protested. He and Jon would go into it unarmed, all right; they just wouldn't come out that way.

"We're probably going to have to do some shooting," Nolan said.

"Oh, Christ. Isn't there ever an end to it?"

"There is if Comfort gets his way. He plans to kill us all."

Jon swallowed thickly. "You and me and Sherry, you mean."

"Possibly some of the others as well."

"Why, for Christ's sake?"

"Not for Christ's sake. For the sake of revenge, in our case. In the others, for the sake of greed; for the sake of self-protection."

Jon pulled at his own hair till it hurt. "Goddamn, I blew it, I really fucking blew it. We should have tried what you said—we should have grabbed Cindy Lou and tried a trade."

"That's hindsight; don't torture yourself, kid. Besides, it might not have worked. We may have a better chance, tonight."

"How?"

"It all hinges on Lyle showing up. And judging from his father going to the trouble of including him in our planning session last night, I think the boy *will* show. And once he has, that means one of two things."

"Which are?"

"Sherry's already dead."

"Jesus."

"Or she's being baby-sat by your friend Cindy Lou."

Jon found a smile. "Who isn't at all dangerous—who wouldn't begin to hurt her."

"I'll take your word for that. Like I got to take your word she won't sell us out, after what you told her. There's no other Comfort or Comfort crony in the woodpile, is there?"

"No. From what Cindy Lou said, it's just the three of them— father, son, daughter."

Nolan shrugged with his eyebrows. "Then once Lyle is here, all we have to do is get him and Cole together and under gunpoint and make them take us to her."

That sounded like fun; if you liked skydiving without a parachute. "And we do that as soon as Lyle shows?"

Nolan shook his head. "Once the heist is underway, it'll be hard to stop. Even though they've lined up with us, Fisher and Winch and Dooley aren't going to relish working half a caper and then having it get shut down. They could even turn on us."

"You promised them fifteen grand…"

"They could take home a hundred grand each from this job, if it goes the way it could."

"Nolan—there's no part of you that wants to do this job, is there?" Jon hated to say it, but Nolan did seem caught up in the momentum of it; could it be, now that he'd planned it, he couldn't stand not to see it go down? To see if an entire shopping mall could be looted?

"All I want is Sherry back," Nolan said.

And Jon dismissed those other thoughts; he believed Nolan. Sherry was what this was about.

"We wait till the Leeches have their trucks loaded up and have taken off," Nolan said. "Then it's just the two Comforts against our side. We grab father and son, and they show us where they're keeping my girl. Or we kill one of them."

Where Cindy Lou was concerned, an innocent kid, Nolan didn't have it in him to kill or maim her; that Jon was certain of.

"After we kill one," Nolan said, "the other loosens up and shows us. And if he doesn't, we start cutting fingers off."

As for Nolan killing/maiming the male, anything-but-innocent Comforts...Jon's certainty ran in the other direction.

He walked down the empty mall, footsteps echoing; the lights in the stores were off. All the Christmas lights were off as well. But the mall was otherwise, albeit dimly, lit. The red and green banners hung limply now, no breeze from the coming in and out of mall shoppers to make them sway; they seemed faded and decidedly un-Christmasy in the dim light. The aisle carts of Christmas knickknacks and such had been abandoned by their teenage elves, empty of their goods, presumably stored away underneath someplace. Santa's cotton and Styrofoam kingdom was deserted, too.

It reminded Jon of a time he and some friends had sneaked into their junior high school after dark for a little good-natured vandalism; it had been strange, thrilling, frightening. The school was simply a different place at night. What during the day had been a building bustling with people and activity was at night a sprawling barren place filled with echoes and not much else.

Soon, however, this mall would come back to life—night or not.

He turned left at Santa's abdicated kingdom, skirted the red and green *Our Merry Best* sign, and used the key Nolan had given him to enter the mall entrance of Nolan's, which had been locked to customers since nine.

He entered through the closed restaurant side and found Nolan and Comfort facing each other in the back room; Nolan sitting quietly, expressionlessly at the desk, Comfort sitting on a case of whiskey, arms folded, grinning at Nolan like a skull.

"She's a sleeping beauty," Jon said, meaning the janitor.

Nolan stood. "Stay here and keep Mr. Comfort company."

And he left them together, and Jon took Nolan's place at the desk, but didn't speak to Comfort. After a while Comfort asked him if a cat caught his tongue.

"No," Jon said. "I'm just taking your advice about children."

Dave Fisher, Roger Winch, and Phil Dooley sat in a gray Buick which belonged to Fisher but was officially owned by a nonexistent person named Bernard Phillips. The Buick, which was parked in the Brady Eighty back parking lot, motor running, had Alabama license plates. Fisher had written to the Alabama Department of Motor Vehicles for the plates, fulfilling the requirement of a description of the car, vehicle identification number and registration fee. The Buick was a stolen car which Fisher, who lived in Minneapolis, had bought from a friend in St. Paul, who ran a chop shop. The Buick had a new VIN (vehicle identification number) and new tires; it did not have much of a heater, as the three men were finding out.

None of them was wearing a heavy winter coat—Fisher wore a dark blue polyester jacket, Winch, a brown corduroy sport coat over dingy work clothes, Dooley, a sand-color suede jacket. They needed jackets light enough to keep on, inside, during a long night of work, but protective enough to keep them from freezing when toiling in the chilly loading-dock areas.

"If I'd known this heater was down," Fisher said apologetically to Winch, in the rider's seat beside him, "I'd have fixed it." Dooley was in back.

"Fuckin' cold out there," Winch said, rubbing his hands together.

"At least it isn't snowing now."

Their breath was smoking, clouding up the windows.

Dooley said, "We only got a couple inches. I think it's lovely."

Fisher said, "What's taking so long? It's twenty after ten, already."

"There he is," Winch said, pointing toward Nolan, who could be seen behind the glass doors of the mail's east-end rear exit. He was crooking his finger at them, like a parent summoning his children.

Fisher admired Nolan; he'd done several jobs with him, oh, probably half a dozen years before, and he'd come to admire the man's logic and discipline. He had no such admiration for Comfort, with whom he'd worked on a Mickey Mouse house burglary about ten years ago—a rich guy in St. Louis with an elaborate alarm system, or so Comfort said; Fisher had no difficulty getting around it. The job wound up paying a couple grand. Whoop-de-do.

When he heard how Nolan had been forced out of retirement by Comfort, Fisher hadn't been surprised exactly, although kidnaping Nolan's lady seemed extreme even for Comfort. Fisher was on Nolan's side in this, although he was eager to do this job and even more eager for the money. This was a challenging score (because of the size of it—the alarm system would be nothing) and would bring in a sizable piece of change, one that should indefinitely underwrite him as he continued developing the computer software he knew would one day make him a millionaire.

They piled out of the car. Fisher opened the trunk and took out a large square suitcaselike affair. Winch took out a duffel bag which made metallic clinks and clunks as the tools within bumped against each other; not to worry: the safecracker's partner, Dooley, carried the knockers and grease, in his jacket pockets. Nothing was going to blow up tonight except some doors on safes, Fisher thought, smiling to himself—and, possibly, this job in Comfort's face, if the old fool crosses Nolan.

Nolan let them in, locked the door behind them. He said to Fisher and Dooley, the men upon whom the job depended, "The Leeches will be here with the trucks at eleven. We got enough time?"

"Sure," Fisher said, referring to the alarm system.

"Sure," Dooley said, referring to the minimum eighteen locks he'd have to pick in the next few hours.

Nolan directed Winch and Dooley down to the mall entrance to Nolan's, where Jon would be waiting to let them in—they'd be entering the restaurant side, which was closed; they would join Comfort in the back room, where all would wait till Nolan gave the go. The go was contingent upon Fisher's success in jumping the alarm system.

Toward that end, Nolan walked Fisher into the maintenance shop, just to their left through the double doors. The unconscious woman who was the night janitor was tied up in her swivel chair; she looked dead, but she was snoring, which was among the things dead people didn't do. The garagelike room was cluttered with cans of paint and canisters and bottles of cleaning solutions and such; the bag of guns was stowed in the corner, as he'd instructed Jon. Good.

Nolan walked Fisher up a half flight of stairs into another cluttered but low-ceilinged area, littered with unidentifiable junk and more cleaning supplies. On the wall at left was the board where the phone line came in; it looked cluttered, too, to Nolan, who knew little about such things—to him, it was just a couple of metal control boxes affixed to a board with dozens of little green wires shooting off here and there, making side trips into junction boxes. But Fisher seemed to know immediately what the various wires were for and where they were headed; he touched some of them, lightly, lovingly, smiling like a suitor.

Then Fisher opened what looked like a traveling salesman's sample case and started unloading it.

"You need any help?" Nolan asked.

"No. It's just a matter of clipping onto the phone line and measuring the pulse rate with this oscilloscope"—he pointed to a small battery-operated TV—"and, once I've got a wave reading, adjusting my little black box"—he nodded to a little black box with some dials and switches—"to that specific pulse rate and clipping it onto the alarm line, completing the circuit, fooling their so-called system."

"And if you fuck up?"

"The cops'll be here in five minutes," Fisher said, and took his pocket knife and started scraping the phone wire bare.

The small cabin, one room with bath, would have seemed cozy to her, normally. A fire was going in its wood-burning stove, across the room near the far wall; this was, at the moment, the only light source in the room, and the warm orange glow cast on the rustic, knotty-pine interior of the cabin was as homey as a Norman Rockwell painting. Sitting before the stove, in a textured gray narrow-lapel jacket, over a wine-colored shirt, with matching pleated pants, was the boy/man, Lyle. He was a stylish dresser, Lyle was. The problem was his I.Q. seemed about the same as his shirt size. He sat there now, roasting a marshmallow on the end of a long twig he'd found outside, sat there cross-legged like an Indian in designer clothes, like a new-wave Boy Scout.

Sherry didn't know whether to laugh or cry. She did neither: she didn't want to upset Lyle. She'd had some bad moments with him, over the past days, and had only today begun rebuilding. There were signs Lyle was warming to her again. He had, for example, offered to roast a marshmallow for her, just minutes ago. She declined, but thanked him for his thoughtfulness. That was one of the small pleasures of being held prisoner by a dimwit like Lyle: he never picked up on sarcasm. You could get away with any-thing—verbally. You just couldn't get away.

She shifted on the bed; her ass felt raw—bedsores, possibly. Today was Thursday—tonight was Thursday; it was dark out the cabin windows (when it was light, there was nothing to see but snow and trees). She was dressed just as she had been Sunday when she'd been shanghaied: bulky lavender turtleneck sweater and matching cords; her suede boots were under the bed—she wasn't sure what became of her gold jewelry. She was sitting up, pillow behind her, her left hand cuffed to one thick rung of the bed's maple headboard. The arm was sore and stiff, particularly her shoulder, which ached; her whole upper back ached, as a matter of fact. Sleeping that way, as she had for four nights now, was awful; the first night, she'd kept waking herself up, turning in her sleep only to yank her own chain—but she was used to it now. She had been here forever, after all.

The square room had two single beds, separated by a bed stand on which was a phone; and at the root of the other bed was a small rabbit-eared TV on a stand. Over at the right was the only door, and just left of the door, catercorner from where she lay, was a little off-white kitchenette area, the only part of the room that wasn't dark-yellowish-varnished knotty pine. Just opposite her was the bathroom. To her left was a window, nailed shut.

On the bed stand, near that teasing phone, was a Sony Walkman with assorted tapes: the Cars, David Bowie, Billy Idol, Tears for Fears and (perhaps most appropriately) Simple Minds. That Lyle listened to such tapes first amazed, then amused, and finally depressed her. She had tried to engage him in a conversation about Bowie, and Lyle had said, "I like *some* oldies." Further observations about the music he listened to included liking the beat and a "smooth" sound and "It has a cool video." Lyle was born to rate records on *American Bandstand*.

In fact, Lyle was "bummed out" (a leftover hippie phrase that seemed oddly anachronistic, coming from the lips of this eighties Li'l Abner) that the cabin's "tube" didn't get MTV. No cable out here in the country, no satellite dish either, apparently; just rabbit ears. Nonetheless, Lyle seemed able to settle into soap operas and game shows, during the day, and sitcoms and cop shows in the evening, his stupidly handsome face impassive as he watched the moving images on the screen, often while listening to his own alternative track on his Sony Walkman—*The Cosby Show* with Billy Idol voice-over, *Hill Street Blues* starring the Cars.

He had not been mean to her. He did not seem to have a mean bone in his body (nor a brain in his head, but at least he wasn't sadistic). Her first thought, upon waking handcuffed to a bed, with the two men standing at the foot of it staring at her, was rape.

But Lyle hadn't touched her. The other one had felt her up some, pretending to just be moving her around—nothing overt. This one was Lyle's "pa," an almost handsome, white-haired, blue-eyed apparition; he was in his sixties, this one, a frightening son of a bitch with a gentle, charming smile through which shone the intelligence—and sadism—his son lacked. She had only seen him once, that first night, but the threat of him hung over her captivity like a rustic cloud. Lyle, who spoke with his pa on the phone every few hours, was in the old man's sway, obedient as a well-trained dog and nearly as smart.

That first night had been the worst, or close to it. Her anger ran a race with her fear and came in a close second. She had all but snarled at the old man at the foot of the bed: "What the hell is this about?"

And Lyle's pa had leaned a hand over and patted her leg; she kicked at his hand, but he anticipated it and pulled it away and smiled sweetly at her. "This is about your boyfriend, honey. And you go kickin' people, and you'll wind up with your feet cuffed, too. Mind your manners, hear?"

She heard; she heard bloodcurdling insanity and rage churning under his phony milk-of-human-kindness tone. She knew immediately that Nolan was in at least as much trouble as she was.

"If your man loves you, honey," said Lyle's pa, "you'll be just fine. You're gonna have to camp out with us for a few days, is all. We'll treat you right. Just don't you make a fuss."

"Nolan will…" she started, then thought better of it.

"Kill us?" Lyle's pa smiled. "I hardly think so." He walked around the side of the bed and put a surprisingly smooth palm against her cheek, smiled at her, as demented as a TV preacher. "We got something that's precious to him. He's gonna do just like we say." Some edge came into the voice: "And so are you, honey. So are you."

"How…how long will I be here?"

"A few days, darlin'."

"A few days."

"Thursday. Make yourself to home. Don't cause trouble. Be a good girl."

The old man had soon left, and she was in the company of the good-looking boy. He had been polite.

"Pa says you can go to the bathroom," he said, "long as you don't overdo it. We got supplies here. There's a microwave." That meant frozen dinners, as it turned out; three a day (breakfast was scrambled eggs and sausage but in the little frozen-dinner format). At first she could barely look at the stuff, let alone stomach it; she soon learned to do both.

"Why are you doing this?" she asked Lyle, looking for humanity in this empty-headed hunk.

"Pa told me to."

This turned out to be a standard reply. Discussion of morality and ethics with Lyle was about as fruitful as exploring theology with a bust of Darwin (who would have appreciated Lyle, who single-handedly proved the theory of evolution).

Helplessness hit her in waves. She couldn't get through to this autistic twerp, and she felt sure that when the father showed back up, she'd be in deep, deep shit for the *opposite* reason: the father *was* smart. And crazy.

And he hated Nolan. She came to know that for a fact later on, but she sensed it from the beginning. She smelled revenge in this. This wasn't just about forcing Nolan into some heist. It was about getting back at him.

Lyle, on the second day, admitted that. She'd had to ask him again and again, and Lyle had winced at her persistence and retreated to his Walkman headphones; but later, when he was getting lunch in the kitchenette (minus the Walkman—he couldn't microwave and listen to music at the same time), she started in again and finally he said: "Your boyfriend killed my uncle and two of my cousins. He's a bad man, your boyfriend."

She was dead. That was her death sentence, and Nolan's. Unless he could *find* her, somehow—but how? She was out in the boonies somewhere—the state police and a fleet of helicopters couldn't have found her. And even if they could, Nolan wouldn't go to them. This was out of his old life: he *couldn't* go to the police. And she wasn't sure she wanted him to: these creatures would kill her, if he went to the police. Like swatting a bug.

She had cried, then; heaving sobs. She didn't care if the boy heard her—she'd cried the night before, from pain, from fear, but some light of hope and dignity had made her stifle the sounds, not wanting her snoring captor in the next bed to be wakened by her despair, not wanting to let him know, let them know, that they had beaten her down so soon, so easily.

But now that she knew human emotions barely seemed to register with Lyle, she just let go: the tears, the sobs, racked her body. It was a relief, in a way, and as the crying jag subsided she felt better, and a fire within her began fanning itself, bringing her back to life.

Then she got a break. Lyle's capacity for human emotion had, somehow, been tapped by her crying. He stood at her bedside and touched her arm, gently, and said, "Don't cry."

She nodded. Rubbed the tears and snot away from her face with her uncuffed hand.

He raised a finger. "Kleenex," he said, and went into the bathroom and got her some.

"Thank you," she said, using the tissues.

He smiled at her, a tight upturned line in his face, and sat back on his bed and reached for his Walkman 'phones.

"No, Lyle," she said, "please. I'd like to talk."

He withdrew his hand from the Walkman and looked at her, blankly, innocently.

"I like you, Lyle."

"I like you, too." But there was no humanity in it. Nice day. Looks like rain. Have a happy.

"Lyle, you're too nice a guy to do a thing like this."

"Pa told me to."

"I understand that. I understand your loyalty to your father. That's good, Lyle. That's admirable."

"Thanks."

"But sometimes, Lyle, you have to question."

"Question what?"

She shrugged, shook her head, searched for the words that could penetrate his fog. "Authority. The things older people say. Your father."

"I don't question Pa. He's family."

"Lyle, does he like David Bowie?"

"No."

"Does he like Billy Idol?"

"No. He hates him."

"Does he like any of your music?"

"No. He really hates it when I listen to funk. He says it's nigger shit."

"Is it, Lyle? Is it nigger shit?"

"No. It's music."

"It's good music, isn't it?"

He nodded. "I think so."

"So your father's wrong, isn't he?"

"About music?"

"About music."

"I guess."

"So he could be wrong about other things."

Logic Lessons with Lyle; a new PBS series.

"I guess," he said.

"Well, it's wrong to kidnap somebody. It's wrong to keep them against their will."

"I don't see what that has to do with music."

Score one for the imbecile.

"Lyle, it shows your father's fallible."

"Huh?"

"Not perfect. That he can be wrong."

"He told me to keep you here. We're not hurting you. We'll probably let you go."

Probably. Oh Jesus Christ; her life was hanging by probably.

"Lyle…" And she didn't know what to say. She was lost. She was lost if she thought she could talk her way out.

That afternoon, Monday afternoon, she had tried sex. She decided she'd fuck this moron, if she had to, to get out of here; or at least start to fuck him: she might be able to knock him out with his Walkman, if she got ahold of it and smacked him hard enough (the phone was out of her reach, no matter what she tried). Also, he carried a .38 with a wood stock, stuck down in his belt, which would neuter him if it went off, which seemed a good idea to her. He was thick enough, *maybe*, to take it out and put it on the night-stand, while they made it. If she could interest him in that.

"I'm lonely," she said.

He was just starting to watch *Gilligan's Island;* it was half past four. That was one of the shows where he listened to the original soundtrack, as opposed to substituting his own Walkman rock 'n' roll version.

"I don't understand," he said.

"I'm *lonely.*"

"I'm keeping you company."

"You're a good-looking boy, Lyle. Why don't you come sit by me."

He did.

"Wouldn't you like to kiss me, Lyle?" Gag me with a spoon.

"Sure," he said. "You're real pretty."

"Then why don't you?"

"Pa said don't fool with you."

"Do you always listen to your pa?"

"Yes," he said.

She grabbed the stock of the .38 in his belt, wedging her hand between his belly and the gun, trying to find the trigger, trying to get her finger on the trigger to shoot his fucking nuts off, and he smacked her.

He stood there; he was quavering a little. "That wasn't nice," he said.

"Fuck you," she said, face stinging.

"You can't be trusted," he said, shaking his head, turning to his bed and flopping onto it and watching *Gilligan's Island.*

She was trembling. With rage. With fear. With disgust at herself, for trying to seduce this retard; with astonishment that he had spurned her so readily. She had gotten everything she ever had with her looks, with her sexual attractiveness, and her cleverness in knowing how to use same, how to mate her intelligence with her good looks. It had landed her Nolan, and a sweet life. It had inadvertently landed her here, as well—in the clutches of a cluck against whom all her feminine wiles, her brain, her body, her manipulative powers, were useless. She was impotent.

He let her bathe, once a day. He let her wash out her clothes, her underwear, and the father had provided some Jordache jeans and a frilly blouse (was there a girl in this god-awful family?) for her to wear while her clothes dried. So at least she didn't have to feel scuzzy. At least she could be clean, relatively, at least her hair wouldn't be a greasy mess; it was a clean mess, but that was better than greasy. It helped her keep her spirits up, just enough to be thinking of ways out of this.

She went to the bathroom as often as she could get away with it. It was necessary, because she went through the countless cans of Diet Coke Lyle thoughtfully fetched for her upon command. And she was working on a project: the window.

The bathroom window, which looked out upon snowy ground and evergreens mingling with gray skeletal trees, was painted shut. She was working it loose. Paint chips fell, which she dutifully gathered and flushed down the toilet. She didn't work on it long or hard at any given time, except during her bath, while the water ran, covering the noise of her upward thrusts at the stuck window.

Wednesday morning, as her bath was drawing itself, she broke it loose. She slid it open, carefully, but the wood against wood made an awful screech.

And Lyle was right there, on the other side of the unlocked door: "Are you okay in there?"

Cold air was rushing in on her; goose pimples took control.

"I'm fine," she said, trying to keep her voice light, squeezing the words past her heart, which was in her throat, in her fucking throat.

He was saying, "What was that noise?"

"The water pipes, I guess. Cold today."

"Well. Hurry up in there."

She waited a few beats; the water was still running, so she couldn't hear whether his footsteps made their way across the room, back to the bed and TV. Maybe he was still on the other side of that door, .38 in his belt. Maybe he was watching *Jeopardy!* while Billy Idol sang. Who the fuck knew.

She put the stool down, and stood on it, and crawled over and out of the window and dropped to the snow, on her knees and hands, in the borrowed jeans and frilly blouse, and she began to run, at first toward the trees—then looking around, she saw down the slope, the top of a building; she curved and ran toward there, her feet crunching in snow-covered leaves, and it was a motel, a small one, just a handful of rooms, and down the hill, goddamn! Highway. Beyond that, the river, the Mississippi.

She knew where she was, vaguely; this was the Illinois side. Probably near Andalusia. She tumbled, ankle giving. Damn! Fuck!

She got on her feet again, quickly, front of her wet from snow. Her ankle was okay—she'd twisted it a little, it would slow her down some, but it wasn't bad, certainly nothing broken, and she heard him behind her. Christ!

She could hear his footsteps, as he strode through the snow, could hear him puffing, gulping in air, and she tried to pick up speed and then he was on her, tackling her, bringing her down. She looked up, saw the goal line, the highway, down the hill. No touchdown today.

He yanked her up, holding her by her upper arm, dragging her like a disobedient child back up the hill.

"That was bad," he said. "You shouldn'ta done that."

"Don't tell your father."

"I have to."

"Why?"

"I just have to."

He was amazing; he was goddamn fucking amazing. "Do you really think it was wrong of me to try to save myself? To try to get away?"

"You're supposed to stay with me."

They made her keep the door open when she went to the bathroom from then on. They let her keep bathing, but with the door open. Lyle had nailed the window shut. He nailed the other windows in the place shut as well, after that.

Wednesday night, late, so late it was Thursday morning, Lyle left for a meeting with his father and Nolan and some other people. By now she had caught the drift of it, hearing Lyle's half of frequent phone conversations with his "pa." Unless she was badly mistaken, they were planning to rob some of the stores at Brady Eighty. Maybe a lot of the stores. They were using Nolan's inside knowledge about the mall in particular, and his expertise at such robberies in general, to pull this heist. But the bottom line still seemed to be revenge. She could smell Nolan's death in this. And her own.

They left her with the owner of the frilly blouse and jeans, a cute, slutty teenage girl named Cindy Lou, perky boobs poking at a RATT T-shirt; sitting in a chair on the other side of the other bed and reading *Hit Parader* magazine and listening to her own tapes on her brother's Walkman. She seemed nervous and embarrassed and avoided talking to Sherry.

Sherry tried to get the girl's attention, to no avail, but finally the girl put her magazine down and took the earphones off and came and sat on the bed.

"What's this about?" she asked. It had taken her a long time, lost in her magazine and music, to allow some thoughts, some doubts, to push through. But they apparently had.

"Don't you know?" Sherry asked.

"I don't pay much attention to what Lyle and Daddy do. I figure what I don't know won't hurt me."

"Well, it can hurt *me*. They kidnaped me, your daddy and Lyle. Lyle's your brother?"

She nodded; she had big blue eyes and was faintly freckled. She looked innocent and worldly at once.

"They're getting you involved in it, kidnaping, leaving you here with me."

She swallowed, looked away. "I know," she said glumly.

"I didn't do anything to them. I live with a man they're forcing to do some things, by holding me captive. I think they're going to kill both of us, when this is over."

The girl shook her head no. "Daddy wouldn't do that. Lyle wouldn't do that."

"I think they would."

"Anybody rape you or anything?"

"No."

"Not Lyle? Not Daddy?"

"No."

She shrugged. "See," she said, offering that as proof of her family's good intentions.

"You weren't sure when you asked me, though, were you? You thought maybe I might have been raped."

She shrugged again. But said nothing.

"Help me."

"How?"

"They left you the key to these cuffs, didn't they?"

"Not rilly, no. They said if you had to pee, to tell you to hold it."

"Maybe we can find something to bust this rung, and I can slip my cuff off…"

"No. I can't help you. I'd like to, lady, but no."

"Will you take a message to someone for me?"

"No. I'm sorry. Now, I don't want to talk to you, anymore."

"Please!"

But the girl was already back in her chair, putting the head-phones on, turning up the heavy-metal music.

Thursday night, finally, Sherry got her hands on that bed stand telephone. But it was Lyle's doing: she had been cuffed to a nearer rung so that she could talk to Nolan, tell him she was alive and well.

Hearing his voice was wonderful and so very sad.

"They're using me," she said, "to make you help them, aren't they?"

"You know about the mall heist?"

That confirmed her suspicions; it was a large-scale robbery.

"I picked up on it," she admitted. She told him he could lose everything because of this, but he reassured her, said he wouldn't lose her, said he'd planned the job smoothly; but she could hear it in his voice, try as he might to hide it: they were both under a sentence of death.

Now she felt compelled to reassure him: "They haven't hurt me. They keep saying once you've cooperated, I'll be released."

He told her they'd be together in a few hours, and then he said something amazing: when she said she loved him, he said he loved her, too. He'd never said that before. It was nice to hear. Too bad this was what it took...

She wiped the tears from her face, and then he said something wonderful: "I'll take you to Vegas when this is over and prove it."

That was as close to a proposal as she was likely to get out of him. Suddenly she was smiling; suddenly she was believing she would live through this ordeal.

"Hang on, baby," Nolan said, and he hung up.

She put the receiver gently back in its cradle, and the world exploded and went black. She crumpled to the floor, not even knowing that Lyle Comfort had pistol-whipped her. She slept blissfully, ignorant that her captor of these past few days was now slinging her over his shoulder like a sack of something, carrying her into the woods, where the mess wouldn't matter.

18

The worst part, for Nolan, was having to mingle with his customers. Fisher had wired his black box in at 10:27, according to Nolan's watch, and they waited till 10:45, just to be safe, before assuming the cops and security guards wouldn't be showing up. Then the job had really got underway.

But Nolan's didn't close till two; the bartender and waitresses would be out of here by two-thirty, and then, finally, better than four hours into it, he could join up with the others out in the mall. Until then, he was a captive in his own club, striving to maintain the appearance of just another night, and building a partial alibi at least.

The very worst thing was DeReuss and his wife had eaten supper here tonight; thank God the jeweler had long since gone—having him here during the heisting of his own shop would've been a little much even for Nolan's nerves.

Before leaving, DeReuss had complimented Nolan on the Surf and Turf, and added, "I've been giving some thought to your complaints about the security out here—I'm ready to go to bat for you at the next Merchant Association meeting."

"Good," Nolan had said.

Now Nolan glanced at his watch. Eleven-twenty. It would be hours before DeReuss' jewelry store got Winch's attention; no safes would be blown till Nolan's was closed and the nitro noise would attract no attention.

Right now, Dooley would still be working on picking locks, although the Leeches and the rest would be well into looting stores, according to Nolan's priority list, loading up the dollies and furniture carts with goods from the stores Dooley had already unlocked.

The first thing he'd had Dooley do was pick the locks on the three major department stores and the garage doors at the loading docks therein, for the Leeches to pull their trucks up to.

He walked casually in back and used the Radio Shack walkie-talkie on his desk, checking in with Jon.

"Nothing so far," Jon reported. He was sitting in the cab of the semi backed up to the central loading dock, the one behind Penney's. He was keeping watch for patrolling cops and any stray Nolan's customers who might for whatever reason choose to pull around back on their way home. No civilian cars were parked in the rear lot—only the loading-dock trucks, Fisher's gray Buick, Comfort's red pickup, Jon's blue van and an old clunker belonging to the lady janitor. Nolan would move his Trans Am back here after Nolan's closed.

"How's the loading going?" Nolan asked.

"Nothing in this truck yet," Jon said. "Are you sure this is where you want me?"

"It makes you a free agent, not being part of the action inside. That could be helpful."

The walkie-talkies he and Jon were using were a forty-channel model; these he had purchased, at his usual discount. By now another eight walkie-talkies should have been lifted and distributed among the other players. After Dooley picked the department store and loading-dock locks, the Radio Shack store was next on the list. Nolan had instructed Dooley which walkie-talkies to steal, putting three-channel models in everybody else's hands, giving Nolan and Jon the opportunity to communicate without being listened in on.

"No sign of Lyle either," Jon said.

Nolan didn't know if that was good or bad.

"Okay," Nolan said, and signed off.

He went back out and mingled with the customers. It was a dirty job but somebody had to do it.

∗

Phil Dooley was averaging ten minutes a lock—the loading dock's garage doors had taken a little longer, but the stores were going quickly. It was approaching midnight now. He figured he should be done by two, easy. Then he would pitch in with the others and haul goods out and help load up the trucks. He would rather have worked with Roger, as usual—been there to give him a hand, say if he had to lay a safe on its back for a gut shot. But that just wasn't practical—every able body was needed to get all the heavy labor done.

Right now, Roger was helping the Leeches load refrigerators and TVs out of an appliance store; Fisher was, too.

That left Dooley the solitary job of going from store to store—according to Nolan's list—and opening them for business. The mall with its Christmas decorations and limited lighting was a strange place to be, even for somebody like Dooley, who was used to being in places after they were closed. Most places were completely dark, though—not half alive, like Brady Eighty. The sounds of the men working, the wheels of their carts, the whump of heavy appliances being set onto carts, occasional swearing, occasional ouches, echoed down the wide central corridor, as Dooley bent over the lock of the Haus of Leather.

The last place he'd opened for after-hours business was a luggage shop—Nolan had suggested it because some of the luggage was expensive, but also because they could use the stuff to transport some of the smaller items—everything from jewelry to expensive perfume.

Dooley liked the concentration, the close work; doing a marathon number of locks like this—nothing in his career to date compared to it—was the sort of challenge he relished. If the take tonight was what Nolan and Comfort indicated, this could even put the capper on his career—he could retire on his cut.

Not that he didn't feel bad about Nolan's situation. He truly hoped Nolan's woman would be returned unharmed—he had no one similar in his life right now, but he could empathize. He had never had a lasting relationship, though not for want of trying, and perhaps for that reason he was especially attuned to pains of the heart. What Nolan must be going through, behind that stony exterior. A shame, a rotten shame.

But the money at stake made Dooley secretly, if guiltily, glad the job hadn't been called off.

The tools Dooley was using, two of which were presently inserted in the lock where the sliding glass doors joined in front of the Haus of Leather, were picks—small thin steel objects with curlicue tips, not unlike dentist's tools, and used by Dooley with similar care and expertise. Dooley carried these in a custom soft-leather pouch, which was currently on the floor at his feet, should he need to use another of the fine tools. Delicate instruments, requiring a delicate touch, which Dooley had.

Even at his age, with his experience, Dooley practiced several days a week, at least; and, through his legitimate locksmithing business in Des Moines, he was able to keep on top of the latest trends in the industry, ordering any so-called burglarproof lock advertised in the trades, practicing on it till he could pick it in minutes. He'd encountered only a couple he couldn't master, and these he never went near.

Picking the locks at Brady Eighty was, thus far at least, about as hard as buttering a roll.

For example, the Haus of Leather was open for business right now.

Andy Fieldhaus, half asleep and completely naked on the vinyl couch in his back room, on his side next to and facing a half-asleep and completely naked young woman named Heather, who was also on her side, on that same vinyl couch (as fate would have it), thought he heard something.

He sat up, quickly, and nearly pushed Heather, who was on the outside, off onto the cold concrete floor; he caught her before she did, and even slapped a hand across her suddenly wide-open mouth, below her suddenly wide-open eyes, before she could say anything.

Into her shell-like ear he whispered: "I heard something."

Then, making exaggerated facial gyrations, he pointed toward the store out there, beyond the back room, where they had been legitimately working on the books since about nine-thirty, only around eleven having gotten extracurricular, thereafter enjoying the drowsy afterglow of a particularly fine fornication when Andy heard something.

They could see each other, but just barely; a single thick rose-scented candle in a small glass bowl glowed on the desk. Anytime they were in the back room and stopped doing the books and got down to funny business, Heather always lighted that one candle and otherwise doused the lights.

Now she was mouthing the word: "What?"

He whispered in her ear again; there was a rose scent in her hair, too, from shampoo. He said, "It could be Caroline."

Blood drained out of Heather's face; even in the candlelight you could see it. She was deathly afraid of Andy's wife. She had heard the story about the carving knife; hell, she had seen the scar on his shoulder enough times.

He got up off the couch, carefully, oh so quietly, or trying to do so anyway: the vinyl was much noisier than leather would have been. He tiptoed to his trousers, draped over his chair at his desk, and reached his hands into each of the pockets and removed the jingle-jangley stuff—coins, keys and such—and placed them as quietly as humanly possible on the desk, where the candle glowed. It would have been a romantic moment if it hadn't been scary as hell.

Caroline had a key to the place; she had the only other key. He put on his pants.

Then something very frightening happened: he heard the doors to his shop slide open out there.

Jerry Leech was ready for a break. He told his brother Ricky so. Ricky wiped some grease off his forehead with a heavily gloved hand and agreed they had hauled enough TVs and refrigerators and heavy shit for a while, and they left the Petersen's loading dock, where the truck there was already a fourth or so full, and pushed open the double doors leading out into the darkened department store and ran into their brother Ferdy, as well as Fisher and Winch, each of whom was wheeling a hand truck bearing stacked microwave ovens and VCRs, winding through ladies' lingerie.

"We're gonna get some lighter shit," Jerry told them.

Winch shrugged and rolled his heavily loaded hand truck on by.

Fisher, pausing with his load of electronics, said, "We've got another couple trips' worth of these. We better stay at it."

Ferdy looked disappointed, like he wanted to go with his brothers, but Ferdy was the baby of the brothers—youngest by about three minutes—and often caved in to the leadership of others. And this time he followed Fisher's lead.

"Wussy," Ricky said, once they were out in the mall.

"Yeah," Jerry said, though he was not sure whether Ricky was referring to their brother or to Fisher. "Nolan said the leather shop was ripe. Let's hit that."

"Why the fuck not," Ricky said.

As they passed the Walgreen's, Ricky said, "Think of them drugs in there. Fuckin' Comfort's a wussy."

"Yeah," Jerry said, although he didn't agree. He didn't know why Comfort had anything against drugs, but he did know Comfort was somebody he didn't intend to cross. That was one rough old hard-ass son of a bitch.

Jerry was also a little afraid of Nolan, truth be told. That guy had been around. He knew his stuff and had eyes that made you real uncomfortable. Jerry wasn't sure crossing Nolan, like Comfort planned, was such a good idea. He also liked some of these other guys pretty well. Even that faggot Dooley seemed like a regular guy. It didn't seem right, somehow, to kill them all.

But Comfort said Nolan couldn't be trusted, that he was a murdering cocksucker who killed old Cole's brother and nephews. And since the other guys—Fisher, Dooley, and that kid with the curly hair—had worked with Nolan before, and wouldn't go along

MAX ALLAN COLLINS

with offing him, they'd have to go, too. As Cole rightly pointed out, jobs with this many guys on it lots of times come undone because somebody talks; doing this Comfort's way meant less guys left alive to eventually talk if the cops got lucky. And besides, it meant fewer ways to split the take.

They got to the leather shop just as Dooley was opening it. He didn't look like no fucking fag. Well, he'd be in hell soon. And queers burned in hell, where Jerry come from.

Ricky pointed to some fat furry white coats and said, "Nolan said get these fox furs." He fingered a tag. "They're a grand each, Jeez-us!"

"Nolan knows his stuff," Jerry said, with an admiring shrug of his head, wheeling the first of several racks of furs out into the mall.

Cole Comfort, who wasn't doing any of the heavy loading, was wandering the mall, looking in the stores that Dooley had already opened, sizing things up. In his left hand he carried a large suitcase and he was pursuing his dream: he was shopping—filling the suitcase with small, expensive items; currently he was at the perfume counter of the I. Magnin, helping himself to Giorgio and Chanel and Calvin Klein's Obsession, among other scents. He himself didn't use toilet water.

But he had to agree with Nolan's assessment of what to take and what not to take. Like the Radio Shack, for instance. They'd opened it up to get the walkie-talkies, one of which was in Cole's right hand this very moment; but they were leaving behind all the TVs and computers and such. Because Radio Shack products would be damn near impossible to fence. Stick to brand-name stuff that *anybody* could carry, Nolan had said. Pretty smart, for a dead man.

And he was a dead man, Comfort thought. *A dead man who just ain't got around to stopping breathing yet.*

He checked his watch; ten after midnight. He wondered what was keeping Lyle. That girl would be dead and buried by now. That made him smile.

Not because he was glad to see a nice piece of tail like that turned to so much worm meat; no. But the thought of telling Nolan, before shooting him, that made Cole Comfort smile. He would use a sawed-off shotgun, which was currently in the cab of the Leech brothers' truck parked behind the I. Magnin. He'd gut-shoot him, to make it last longer. Maybe he'd wait till Nolan's guts were hanging out of him from both sides, shredded by buckshot, to tell him about the girl. No, best tell him first, in case he blacked out before Cole could give him the news.

The others—Fisher, Winch, Dooley—was just commonsense cleanup, and the Leeches would take care of most of it. With one exception.

The kid would be Lyle's. He'd instructed Lyle to shoot Jon in the belly with the .38, a couple of times. That kid was just like Nolan: he killed Comfort kin. Dying slow was their ticket to the next world, only Cole knew there wasn't one.

The Leeches, though, he would take no delight in. They had been helpful to him any number of times over the last ten years or so, but they weren't the most intelligent men under the sun, and now that this mall haul, this crowning Comfort achievement, would provide him and Lyle and Cindy Lou with enough money to flat out retire, well—the Leeches would have served their purpose. Cole didn't like leaving loose ends, or loose lips; those dumb-ass sons of bitches wouldn't sink his ship. They'd drive their trucks to Burden in Omaha straight from here, in the morning, and by nightfall they'd be back in Sedalia. Where Cole and Lyle would be waiting.

He closed the suitcase up; it was filled with perfume and other such niceties. He slipped one last bottle of Giorgio in a coverall pocket. That would be for Cindy Lou. He would have to settle things with the child tomorrow, back at home; after he got back from Sedalia. A peace offering would be needed, first. And then he could teach her about the beauty of the love act.

And tomorrow night would be as memorable as tonight.

*

Nolan was heading toward the back room again when his bar-tender, standing at the end of, and just inside, the bar, reached a hand out and stopped him.

"You okay?" Chet asked; the older man sometimes treated Nolan paternally, which irked Nolan no end.

"I'm fine."

"You been in the back more than out front."

"I got gas. You want me to fart in here?"

Chet smiled. "And drive out what few customers we got tonight? No way."

"Well," Nolan said, "I'd stay out of the back room, if I were you. Unless you light a match."

"What, and risk an explosion?"

And Chet returned to his handful of customers at the bar.

Nolan checked in with Jon.

"Anything?" he asked into the walkie-talkie.

"Nothing," Jon said. "They aren't even loading my truck yet."

"Well, it's too early for that, anyway. They started at one end and they'll get that truck loaded, and then move toward the center of the mall and start loading yours."

"When'll that be?"

"Around one, one-thirty."

Somebody started knocking on Nolan's back door.

Jon said, "What was that?"

"That's what I'd like to know," Nolan said.

He tossed the switched-off walkie-talkie on the desk and covered it with a newspaper. He got a long-barreled .38 from a desk drawer and held it in his left hand, behind him, as he cracked the door open.

Where he saw the flushed and very wide-eyed face of Andy Fieldhaus.

Nolan looked out at him and said, "Well, hello, Andy."

Puffing, his breath visible in the cold air, Andy said, "Jesus Christ, Nolan, let us in."

"Us?"

"Heather and me. Let us in!"

He closed the door for a moment, stuck the gun in his waistband, buttoned his jacket over it, let them in.

"Thank God for back doors," Andy said, breath heaving.

They were barely dressed: Andy had his brown leather bomber jacket over his bare chest and wore his pants but carried his shoes and shirt and under things and such in his hands. The buxom Heather was in a coat, clutched to her with one hand, her shoes in the other, and wadded up under one arm were the rest of her clothes. She was shivering, mostly from cold, but not entirely.

It was a bitter night to go barefoot.

Heather dropped her clothes to the floor and, her coat opening, she flashed Nolan, inadvertently; she had really big tits—also really erect nipples, from the cold, not Andy. She and Andy huddled together, hugging, shaking.

"What can I do for you?" Nolan asked. It was clear they'd gotten dressed—sort of dressed—in a hurry.

Now Andy and Heather broke apart and began, hurriedly, getting fully dressed. This Heather did without shame, and it was fun watching her.

"Are you my friend?" Andy asked Nolan, desperately, hopping on one foot, as he tugged a shoe onto the other foot.

"Sure," Nolan said.

"Good," Andy said, smiling tightly. "If my wife asks, will you say we've been here all evening?"

"Sure," Nolan said.

Andy was dressed now, and so, nearly, was Heather.

Rather frantically he went on: "She could show up any minute. Can you keep your cool and cover for us?"

"Sure."

"God bless you," Andy said, grinning.

Heather smiled at Nolan and kissed him on the cheek and said, "You're a saint."

Nolan followed them as they went out through the bar and watched silently from a window as they made their way to the parking lot, Andy getting in his Corvette, the girl in her Mustang, driving off separately.

Nolan went to the back room and returned the .38 to its drawer and sat at the desk.

"What was that about?" he said, aloud.

19

He was digging in the moonlight, sideways.

She didn't know what it meant: it was simply the image before her eyes, as they slowly opened. A man was digging, shovel crunching into cold ground, washed in ivory moonlight, and she was on her side, so it was a sideways view, and out of focus. Still groggy, she moved her head just slightly and looked up. She saw the skeletal branches of a tree—the tree she lay under—and through them she could see clouds moving quickly across a blue-gray night sky, like a scrim of smoke gliding across the stationary partial moon. It didn't seem real.

But the pain in her head did; it ran across her forehead, over her eyes, like a headband of hurt. And the still, cold night air seemed very real; she was only in her sweater and jeans and anklets—her bed was the snowy ground. And the sound of the shovel, that was real too, as it chopped at roots and cut through frozen earth. She moved her head back to where it had been and looked through slits and saw him, digging, in the moonlight.

Lyle.

Handsome Lyle, wearing a brown leather jacket and gray designer jeans, digging, basking unwittingly in shadows from the moving clouds.

He was, she knew at once, digging a grave. It was the right shape; he'd roughed it out and was now only a few inches in. But it was a grave. Her grave.

The pain and the cold were her friends. They made this surreal landscape real. They were something to hold on to, to steady her, while her thoughts raced, while she peeked through the slits of her eyelids and wondered what she could do to keep from sleeping forever in the hole Lyle was making for her.

She lay perhaps ten feet from the foot of the grave. This was not as far as she would have liked. As Lyle walked around the grave, working on this end and that, he often came very close to her. He seemed frustrated. The temperature had fallen; apparently this ground was harder than he had anticipated.

She wondered if she should just get up and bolt and run. She had no sense of where she was—other than lying on her side under a tree near a grave an imbecile was preparing for her. The ground didn't seem to slope, so they were a ways away, anyway, from the cabin and the hill at whose foot were the highway and the Mississippi. Lyle stood in a small open area, but mostly there were trees, here. Some evergreens but mostly gray, winter-dead ones; more death than life in these woods.

Was she supposed to be dead already? Did he think whatever he'd hit her with had killed her? Or had Lyle simply not got around to the deed as yet; the wood-stock revolver was still in his waistband, the metal catching moonlight and winking at her, occasionally. Perhaps she'd got through to him sufficiently these past few days to make killing her not so easy a chore for Lyle. Maybe he was putting it off.

No. That wasn't it. He was working at that grave with a mindless diligence; nothing was bothering him. He was that most frightening of men: a guileless dope who meant you no harm but would kill you without blinking. Lyle would do that because his pa had so ordered. To Sherry, in that frozen, surreal moment, Lyle embodied the banality of evil. It was the ultimate empty irony: she would be killed by someone who didn't even dislike her.

After fifteen minutes or so, Lyle got tired and sat at the edge of the grave, which was now perhaps five inches deep everywhere, more or less. He put the shovel down, so that it was between him and Sherry, whose eyes seemed to be closed. He sat on the ground, hugged his knees to him and looked up at the moon and the smoke-like scrim of clouds and didn't see it coming when Sherry smacked him in the side of the face with the shovel.

He tumbled half in the shallow grave, half out. Feet sticking out. She raised the shovel to hit him again, but he reacted quickly, for a stunned moron, pulling out that .38 and firing at her.

The bullet careened off the metal scoop of the shovel, with a whang, putting a dent in it as the sound of the gunshot cracked open the night and Sherry flung the shovel at him and ran.

She had no idea where she was headed; no sense of direction at all. She just ran where there was space, where the trees weren't too thick, her shoeless feet, covered only in the thin little socks, crunching and cracking the twigs and snow-and-leaves-layered earth.

She could not hear him behind her, but perhaps that was only because her own breath was heaving so, filling her ears with the sound of her life struggling to hold on to itself.

Maybe that fling of the shovel had caught him good; maybe he was unconscious, not following her at all.

This she thought, this she prayed, but she didn't slow down. She ran with strides as long as she could make them, cutting them only when a tree got in the way, and then she tripped over something, an extended root, and tumbled into the snow and leaves, and stopped just long enough to pick herself up and heard it: silence.

What a wonderful sound.

Maybe he wasn't following her. Maybe the shovel did get him. Or she'd lost him, maybe.

Nonetheless, she began to run again, her legs aching, her feet nicked and nudged and pierced countless times by twigs and burrs and acorns, but it felt so good for her feet to tingle and even hurt, her legs to burn and ache, it made her feel so alive; at the same time her head no longer ached and the cold air was just something crisp to run through. Her face stretched tight in a sort of smile and she felt a euphoria as she ran breakneck through the woods, keeping up with the rolling clouds that shadowed her.

But the second time she tripped, catching another root, she went down hard, and it knocked the wind out of her. And as she was getting up, she heard him.

Lumbering through the woods, not far away at all. Twigs and branches snapping, cracking, like he was using a machete to clear a path; but it was no machete—just Lyle. Diligent, guileless Lyle, looking for her to take her back to the hole he was digging for her. Like his pa said.

She tried to run and realized she'd turned her ankle; she didn't feel it going down: just now, trying to run on it, it made itself known. She could still run, but nowhere near as fast; this was a pitiful, hobbling sort of excuse for running, a shambling, mummy-like two-step, and the sound of Lyle moving through the woods toward her was growing louder.

She hid.

She crawled behind a cluster of thorny brush, which nicked and bit at her skin, reminding her she was alive, yes, but she was past enjoying that sensation and teetering instead on the edge of despair and desperation. Her feet were cold and bleeding, the thin socks torn to shreds from her marathon run. She crouched behind the thicket and tried not to breathe audibly. She stopped breathing through her mouth, pulling the air in ever so gently through her nose, sipping and savoring it like a priceless wine.

She was quaking with fear and cold as he lumbered by, gun in hand; he wasn't running, exactly—it was more like a jog. An idiot jogger wants to kill me, she thought.

Like a four-wheel-drive vehicle, he rolled past, woods be damned, the sound of his forward movement taking several minutes to die down. She waited. She had no idea what to do next.

Stay put? It was night, but she had no notion of the time—if dawn came soon, she'd be naked here. If nighttime lasted long enough, perhaps that dangerous dork would comb the entire woods and find her, finally. If she took off and started running again, he would hear her, quite probably, and, very certainly, take up pursuit again.

What would Nolan do?

Nolan would find a way to kill the bastard, but that wasn't Sherry's way. She'd given that her best shot with the shovel, and blew it. It wasn't likely nature would provide her with a killing tool better than a shovel. Someone who knew the woods would find something to use, no doubt; but Sherry had only stalked shopping malls before. She had never been camping in her life. This was a hell of an indoctrination.

She was shivering with the cold, now. Wondering where she was. Looking up through branches at the spooky sky, wondering how to read it, wishing, way back when, she'd been a Girl Scout and not a cheerleader.

Maybe if she just moved quietly through the woods—in the opposite direction from where Lyle had pushed on—she might get somewhere. Maybe even civilization. The road and the river were around here somewhere.

She moved out from behind the bushes and began making her way through the woods again. Not running. Moving quickly, yes, but not running; pausing at a tree every few yards to listen for Lyle. Hearing nothing.

Pretty soon she came upon the grave in progress again.

It froze her to the earth, like Lot's wife. She had no idea she'd gotten turned around. Here she was back at square one.

But—once past the shock of stumbling across what Lyle intended as her permanent home—was this so bad? There was the shovel again, sprawled half in, half out of the would-be grave, much as Lyle had been when she tried to bash him. It was a weapon. She picked it up.

And just in time, because Lyle stepped out into the moonlight and his handsome blank face squeezed in something like thought and he aimed the .38 at her and she swung the shovel like a bat and caught his wrist and the gun went flying.

"Don't fight me," Lyle said, reaching his hands out toward her as if she should embrace him. There was no malice in his voice at all.

"Fuck you, asshole!" She swung the shovel at him and caught him in the side and he went down, moaning. She moved toward him quickly, the hurting ankle slowing her just a bit, and raised the shovel to deliver a finishing blow, and the bastard reached out and grabbed that bad ankle and pulled her legs out from under her. She fell back, tumbling.

Tumbling into the grave.

It was shallow, but it was her grave, and it was no place she wanted to be; her mind filled with horror. The shovel was no longer in her hands. She was on her back in her own grave. A scream caught in her throat.

And Lyle was standing at her feet, in the grave, looking down at her, with his blank, banal pretty-boy face marred by one of her shovel blows. Good. She kicked a field goal with his nuts and he grabbed himself with both hands, howling, and pitched forward on her.

He wasn't unconscious, but he was in pain, enough pain that he couldn't do anything about her scrambling frantically out from under him, cursing him, hitting at him, clawing at him, and then scurrying off, back into the woods, a different direction this time.

Running again, hobbling on the ankle, but running, hearing nothing but her own panting, her stomach aching, her feet numb, her legs aching but pumping, like her heart keeping the blood going; she wasn't dead yet.

She paused against a tree, panting. Wondering how long she could keep this up; when her legs would go out on her. She couldn't hear him back there. That was something, anyway. Couldn't hear him shambling after her.

But then she did hear something else:

A honking horn.

Car horn; distant, but she had a good fix on what direction. She smiled tightly and began to run. Even the ankle stopped hurting, stopped hurting as much, anyway.

She was no fool. She knew that that car could belong to Lyle's father or somebody else involved in this foul fucking thing. She would have to be careful as she neared the highway. But once to the highway, she would know where she was. She could cling to the woods and bushes along the side of the road and follow it and if she saw a car that didn't have Lyle or his pa in it, she would go for it.

She began to smile again. She was going to make it. Nolan was a survivor and so was she.

He'd be proud of her. And they'd be together.

But the euphoria passed as reality set in: Nolan was in trouble. Her thoughts raced ahead of her churning legs. He was pulled in on some elaborate heist at the mall and Lyle's father was there, intending to kill him when it was over. That was obvious: she'd been the hostage. She'd been the leverage to make Nolan jump. But Lyle's father had given the order to Lyle to kill her.

Which meant Nolan would be the next to die; he was still under that sentence of death they'd both sensed, on the phone, in what might be the last time she heard his voice.

Tears streaked her face.

She had to reach him, somehow, before the heist was a wrap. She had to let him know she was okay. She had to get to him before Lyle's father blew him away.

More than her own life was at stake here; Nolan's was too.

She picked up speed. Somehow she picked up speed. The highway was up there. She knew it was. She'd take a chance. She'd try to flag the first car that came along. Hell, Lyle's father would be at the mall, and Lyle was lost somewhere in the forest. She could risk it. She ran.

She ran, and as she crossed what looked like so much snow and leaves and weeds, she felt something give beneath her. Then the ground under her broke open like thin ice, and she went crashing through rotted planks and plummeting down an endless drop, hitting her head on something hard along the side, halfway down, blacking out, landing hard on her back, with a whump, which she neither felt nor heard.

Sometime later, however, her eyes opened momentarily and she looked up and thirty feet above her, looking down into the abandoned, brick-lined well, was Lyle. With a face blank as the moon. Peering down to see if she was alive.

He was the last thing she saw.

20

Jon sipped hot chocolate from the Thermos cup, wondering how it had suddenly become his lot in life to sit on watch in parked vehicles. It was a little after 2:00 A.M., and a long night (long morning, actually) stretched out ahead of him; hell, they wouldn't be out of here till 6:30. Despite the work involved, he would have much rather been inside, helping load up the semis—this one in whose cab he sat was just in the process of being loaded. The Leeches and the others were piling on and stacking up washing machines and other appliances in the trailer behind him, much of the stuff still in cartons and taken from the back room of the J. C. Penney's whose adjacent loading dock the truck was backed up to.

Out in front of him was the wide, nearly empty parking lot, dusted with snow, and beyond it a line of evergreens and some gray trees and not much else. They really were alone out here, on the edge of the city, a whisper away from the Interstate—just a bunch of thieves and the vast storehouse of goods that was Brady Eighty mall.

The sounds of activity back there in the trailer behind him were strangely calming—particularly the occasional sounds of voices. Sitting here, watching for cops or anything else unexpected, was unnerving as fuck. All he had to keep him company was the walkie-talkie, which he used to check in with Nolan, and the truck's scanner, which was keeping track of the half-dozen frequencies in use by the Davenport police, as well as the county sheriff department and the Highway Patrol. From the silver and blue scanner box on the dash, the tinny, barely understandable cop chatter went back and forth about domestic disturbances and drunk and disorderly and cars that slid from icy roads into ditches, on what appeared to be (in every cop's opinion) a "real slow" night. Without the constant squawk-box noise, he'd have long since gone nuts.

At least he was warm. The semi's heater made it possible for him to sit there without his coat on, even if the interior of the truck was as dusty and scruffy as the Leech Bros. themselves. When Nolan first told him about this duty, Jon had assumed he'd be freezing his ass off till dawn in a cold truck cab. He didn't realize he could keep the diesel motor running virtually all night. The exhaust pipes on a semi weren't snaked under the truck, meaning no carbon monoxide danger for the men in the loading dock behind him.

He'd never been in a situation like this before—one that mingled boredom with anxiety. It was weird beyond words to sit and tremble with fear, fear generated by the sure anticipation of violence, while at the same time being bored to fucking tears. It was at times like these that he wished he'd never met Nolan. He wondered if Sherry might be thinking the same thing.

If she happened to still be alive.

He was trying to get his mind off that when, shortly after 2:30, a cherry-red Camaro roared into the parking lot and skidded and slid to a stop. A frantic-looking Lyle Comfort climbed out of the car. He was wearing a brown leather jacket and gray jeans and the side of his face was bruised and puffy and scraped-looking. Somebody had tried to knock some sense in the dumb a-hole; futile effort, Jon thought, then quickly wondered: was this Sherry's work?

Lyle saw Jon sitting in the truck and came quickly over, slipping on the ice a little; he knocked on the cab door, as if Jon hadn't seen him coming. Jon swung the door open and looked down at Lyle, who stood there with hands in his jacket pockets, breath smoking, eyes wild; he really had taken a nasty bash.

"How do I get in?" he asked.

He seemed upset.

"They're loading this trailer up right now," Jon said, and pointed back with a thumb. "Go to the side door—I'll raise 'em on my walkie-talkie and somebody'll let you in."

Lyle nodded and headed that way and Jon shut the door and did as he'd promised.

Then he used the walkie-talkie again—to check in with Nolan. On their private channel.

"How are you doing?" Jon said. The greeting was a sort of code, in case the other wasn't alone.

"I can talk," Nolan said; the metallic ring of the walkie-talkie only intensified the hardness of his voice. "I closed up the club a few minutes ago. I'm in the process of checking in with everybody, seeing how their individual gigs are going."

"Well, you can check in with Lyle too if you want," Jon said. "He just showed up—entering at the Penney's loading dock."

"Let's hope your girlfriend's sitting with Sherry."

"I don't know. Something's wrong."

"You want to tell me, or play twenty questions?"

Jon sighed. "Lyle's face was bunged up. Somebody smacked him with something."

"Could be her. Could be she got away." There was urgency in his voice, and something else—hope? Anyway, it was an emotion, and Jon wasn't used to hearing emotion in Nolan's voice.

"Nolan, we got to face the possibility she made a break for it and didn't make it."

"Of course." No emotion now.

"Lyle looked kind of dazed," Jon said.

"Lyle always looks dazed."

"Not really, Nolan. He usually doesn't look any way at all."

Silence for a few beats—no, not silence: Nolan was there, the walkie-talkie static said so. He just wasn't saying anything.

Then he did: "I'll spend some time around him and his father." Nolan paused. "Maybe I can read it."

And clicked off.

Nolan entered DeReuss Jewelry, which like most of the stores at Brady Eighty was trimmed festively for the season, and walked past the mostly empty display cases (their contents kept in the store's vault overnight—though some inexpensive items remained on display, like a countertop spinner with Caravelle watches) and found Dave Fisher in back, facing a side wall, prying something off it with a screwdriver, while Roger Winch, wearing old clothes and shoes that were obvious veterans of odd around-the-house painting jobs, leaned against a nearby display counter, arms folded, waiting, his duffel bag of tricks at his feet.

"How's it going?" Nolan asked.

Fisher glanced over his shoulder. "Just need to defeat this teargas gimmick before our friend here blows their safe."

Nolan turned to Winch. "What are you up against?"

Winch shrugged. "Standard J. J. Taylor. Built into the wall. Jam shot. It'll make some noise."

"Nobody here to hear it but us crooks," Nolan said. "Did you hit the luggage shop like I said?"

"Yeah," Winch said. He nodded behind the counter he leaned against. "I got a nice big Samsonite over there, which I intend to fill to hell and back with sparkly stuff."

"Do that," Nolan said.

Fisher had the metal facing plate off the wall alarm and was again scraping insulation from wire with his pocket knife.

"Nolan," Winch asked, "any word on your girl?"

Nolan shook his head no. "Your concern's appreciated, but don't mention it again. You never know when there's a Comfort in the woodpile."

"Or a Leech," Fisher said.

Winch nodded, winked, pointed a forefinger fleetingly at Nolan, in an affirmative gesture.

Nolan turned to go, then stopped and said, "Hit the bank last, remember."

"No problem," Winch said.

It was shortly after three when the explosion jolted Jon in his seat, and rattled the building and truck trailer behind him, causing him to say, "Holy shit!" For a second he didn't know what it was, then he remembered: the jewelry store safe. This would be the first but hardly the last of such shocks to his nervous system tonight (this morning), what with another jewelry store to go, and the bank's money machine and several night deposit safes.

The thought then occurred to him—for the first time—that he stood to get rich from tonight's haul. As much as he'd wanted to leave this life behind, he was caught up in a heist that should make all involved a bundle. Those that lived through it, that is. Small detail.

He poured himself some more hot chocolate—he'd brought along two Thermoses—but with a shaky hand. The explosion had rocked his nerves a little. He sipped the warm liquid. He stared out at the snowy parking lot with its handful of vehicles belonging to those at work inside.

Pretty soon he finished the cup, pondering whether he could get away with turning on the truck's radio for a while and listening to some music. But that might keep him from being able to follow the nonadventures of the Davenport cops and company on the scanner; and he had strict orders from Nolan to keep monitoring that, so to hell with it. Besides, he had to pee.

He put his coat on and climbed out of the cab and went back near the loading dock and had just unzipped his pants and exposed his member to the shriveling night cold when he realized he could hear voices, just inside.

Father and son voices.

Cole and Lyle Comfort.

They were talking as they stood in there, by the mouth of the trailer, which was still in the process of being loaded up. Though the truck was backed fairly flush up against the loading dock, the voices squeezed through.

"You *lost* it?"

"I'm sorry, Pa."

"Well, get another one from one of the Leech boys."

"I will. Pa, I looked all over for it."

"Is that why you were so late?"

"Well, she gave me a little trouble. That's how I lost it."

"But you did do your job?"

"Sure, Pa."

There was a pause; Jon stood there, dick in hand, bladder about to burst, and listened.

"You did good, son," Comfort said, the anger out of his voice.

"I hate to lose my birthday gun," Lyle said, woefully.

"It's all right, son. I'll buy you a new one. Too damn bad there ain't a gun shop in this fucker, or we'd just steal you one."

"Thanks, Pa."

"Here comes the Leeches. Better pitch in some."

Jon, feeling shell-shocked, moved away from the loading-dock area, and stood facing the back wall of the mall and when his urine hit it, steam rose.

Nolan did his share of loading, but mostly he supervised, making sure the right things were being taken.

For example, he put Dooley in charge of the collectibles shop. He knew the locksmith would have the right touch to handle the Hummels and the collector's plates and other valuable knick-knacks; those on display had to be put in their boxes—original-boxed goods were always easier to fence, and with collectibles like these that was especially true.

In the camera shop, he directed two of the Leeches, each lugging a couple of footlockers they'd found at Penney's, to take nothing under a hundred dollars, and later gave them exactly the same advice in the Singer outlet, where they loaded their hand trucks with sewing machines in cartons.

In the department stores, he had various of the players strip items off wheeled clothing racks to make room for some selective shopping, loading up on designer clothes. I. Magnin, though, had whole racks of designer duds just waiting to be wheeled out, and easily matched the Haus of Leather where furs were concerned—also, several display cases of jewelry (no vault there) were broken into and emptied into waiting luggage, some of it imported leather pieces from Magnin itself.

Nolan by no means lost himself in the work, however: he kept an eye on Comfort and Lyle, both of whom kept their distance from him. He had been thinking over what Jon had told him of the conversation between Lyle and his pa. Behind his cool supervisory demeanor, a storm brewed.

It was just after four when Nolan cornered Comfort in Magnin's, where the coveralled, white-haired bandit was walking down the aisle with a suitcase in either hand, crammed with who knew what, thimbles and Snicker bars maybe, heading through ladies' wear toward the double doors that would lead into the storeroom and the final loading dock.

Nolan smiled. "Satisfied with your shopping spree so far, Cole?"

Comfort stopped in the aisle, did not put down the bags; smiled back, rather nervously, Nolan thought. "I surely am. You and me, we've had our differences. But you come through for me on this. And I ain't gonna forget it."

"Good. That's quite a wallop your boy seems to have taken."

"He fell on the ice."

"Looks like he got hit with something."

"He fell on the ice. Excuse me, these is heavy."

"I keep my promises, Cole. Remember that."

"Yeah, yeah, yeah—look. We'll shoot the fuckin' breeze some other time. Time is money, Nolan! We're running out of time, here."

"Yes we are," Nolan said.

At 4:15, two jewelry stores under his belt, a tired but self-satisfied Roger Winch walked into the First National branch bank, duffel bag in hand; he looked like a bum, in his old clothes, but that just went with the territory: you had to be able to discard your clothes, after a job, as the telltale dust from a safe blowing clung to clothes, making prime evidence for the prosecution. Roger had never done time and had no intention, at this late date, of ever doing so.

A few lights were on, behind the row of teller cages, which were decked with holly and some twinkling Christmas lights. The big NCR safe, olive-colored, stucco-surfaced, was at his left as he entered, on a pedestal; this was to help facilitate its use as a card-activated cash machine, outside. A fully trimmed Christmas tree, under which were bogus gifts, stood next to it.

This automated teller machine—which was called Presto-Change-O, the sort of cutesy name these bank cash machines always seemed to have—was open twenty-four hours. That was one of the reasons Nolan had suggested doing the bank safes last—later at night, the less likely many (if any) customers would be hitting up Presto-Change-O for cash.

The computer within the safe would probably shut down, once Roger blew the door; but ATMs going on the blink was nothing new—though an answering service would automatically be called by Presto-Change-O in the machine's last breaths before doing its disappearing act, no one would service the thing till tomorrow. And any stray, late-night/early-morning customers encountering the uncooperative machine would dismiss it with a "goddamn."

The face of Presto-Change-O was actually the ass of the safe, extending out of the bank's brick outer wall to greet the public in such a way that even if some customer did come along at 4:15 this morning, he or she wouldn't see Roger Winch in the process of performing what was known in the trade as a jam shot.

Normally Roger would have laid out all of his tools and equipment on the top of the safe; but, due to the pedestal it was on, the NCR was too tall for that. So Roger pulled a desk around and removed items from his duffel bag, arranging his things carefully, in order, on the desktop, like a chef assembling his ingredients. These included: soap, Fels Naphtha brand, which was malleable and just the right consistency to keep the grease (nitro) from draining through; the grease, a couple of ounces in a medicine bottle, cushioned by twice as much water; a folded strip of cellophane, eight inches long, half an inch wide; a box of wooden kitchen matches, four of which he removed and set out; a knocker —a small metal cap with fulmonite of mercury in it (a lot of guys these days used electric detonators, but the art of this game,

Roger felt, was knowing how to properly use a fuse-type knocker) with five inches of fuse crimped in the knocker's open end; a razor blade; a flashlight; a crowbar; and some rubber gloves, which he now put on.

Whistling "Strangers in the Night," Roger inserted the strip of cellophane lengthwise into the space between the safe's door and door frame. Then he took the soap, which he'd already limbered up at the motel before coming, and sculpted a funnel-shaped cup around the cellophane strip. He made it fit nice and snug; mustn't allow any grease to trickle down the front of the door. Then he gently withdrew the cellophane, which left a narrow passage through the soap where the grease could flow.

He placed the knocker carefully in the cup, so as not to jar it, the fuse dangling about three and a half inches over the lip of the cup, about five seconds' worth. With the razor blade he split the end of the fuse, spreading it like a flower till its central vein of black powder showed.

He reached for the medicine bottle of grease. He began to pour it slowly into the soap cup—smiling to himself as he did; here was where Roger shined—here was what separated the pete-men from the boys: you had to have timing better than Bob Hope, to judge if the safe was drinking the grease right. And Roger had that sense of timing. The ability to make sure the knocker went off just as the last of the nitro was draining from the cup into the safe door.

Quickly, he lit three kitchen matches at once, producing a prodigious flame, which he touched to the fuse, and took cover twenty feet away, behind a desk.

He sat on the indoor–outdoor carpeting, his back to desk drawers, and covered his ears with pressed fingers; but he enjoyed the KA-WHOOM of the safe blowing.

He stood. He walked through the smoke to the safe. Its doors were swinging on its hinges. He smiled. Perfect. He wouldn't be needing the crowbar.

He glanced inside at the two bins of cash, tens and twenties, amid computer circuitry. The money could be gathered later. Right now he had two more safes to blow, the little night deposit safes which Nolan said would probably hold more money than Presto-Change-O, given the Christmas shopping season.

He put his tools back in the duffel bag and moved to the next safe and began again.

The explosion, the third of the night, was the loudest yet, and jarred Jon, who was out of hot chocolate and a little drowsy in the cab of the Leech Bros. truck. He decided there was no getting used to occasional explosions. No way not to jump in his seat.

A face appeared in the window next to him and he jumped in his seat again. It wasn't an explosion, but it sure was surprising.

It was also Cindy Lou.

Her big blue eyes were red and puffy, apparently from crying, and she seemed about to cry again. Then she disappeared, hopped back down to earth, or anyway the pavement of the mall parking lot.

Jon rolled down the window and cold rushed in as he looked out, looked down at her. "What are you doing here?"

She was in the denim jacket again, which against this cold snap was no defense, and her hands were buried in its pockets, and her teeth were chattering.

"We gotta talk," she said, looking up at him.

"Get in on the other side," he said, and rolled the window back up.

He reached over and opened the door for her and she climbed aboard.

"It's warm in here," she said.

"But it's a cold world, Cindy Lou," he said. "How did you get here?"

"Walked."

"From where? The Holiday Inn?"

She nodded curtly. Added, "It's not far."

"Why did you do that? Why are you here?"

She looked at him and her lower lip was trembling. The cold had nothing to do with it.

She said, "I'm afraid…I'm confused…I been up all night…thinking…"

He touched her nearer arm. "Cindy Lou—what is it?"

She gave him a look that was part innocence and all yearning. "Did you buy that bus ticket like you said? Or were you shinin' me on?"

"I bought the ticket. One-way to L.A."

She pouted. "I probably missed the bus. I already missed the boat."

"It's an open ticket. It's waiting at the window for you. You can take the first available bus out."

Firmly, now, she said, "I'm gonna use that ticket."

"Good for you."

She looked at her lap. "My daddy's a terrible man. It's a hard thing to know, but I know it. Part of me still loves him, and maybe that's why I'm scared to stick around with him. Maybe…maybe I'd like it, if he did it to me."

"I don't think so."

"I don't either. Ah, shit, I don't know what I think. I just know I gotta leave."

"What's going on, Cindy Lou?"

She squinched her face up. "Way after midnight, Lyle come back to the motel room. He was bleeding. He had me help him wash up some."

"He looks pretty bad, even so."

"He was all bloody on his face."

"Cindy Lou. Did he kill her?"

She paused. Then she nodded.

"Shit," Jon said. Tears came, at once; he fought them.

"I asked him what happened to the girl," she said, a whimper in her voice, "and he said she was dead. I asked him if he killed her and he tried at first to make out like it was an accident. But then he owned up to it."

"Jesus fuck."

She raised her hands—they made tiny fists and she pummeled the air. "I started to hit him and hit him and he got all confused. He didn't understand why I was so mad at him. Then he said he was afraid Daddy was going to be mad, too."

"Yeah. Lyle lost his birthday gun."

That startled her. "How did you know?"

Jon just shook his head. He wiped the wetness from his eyes.

"He said he'd tell me the truth," she said, "if I didn't tell Daddy."

"What's the truth?"

"He was supposed to kill the girl, but she ran away. She put up a struggle, and he lost his gun. But he finally caught up with her. He left her body at the bottom of a well."

"Goddamn!" Jon said, and smashed a fist heel-first into the dashboard.

"Don't be mad at me," Cindy Lou said, pitifully. "I didn't do it."

Jon swallowed; worked at controlling himself. He looked at her and she was a cute kid, a good kid, in spite of it all; he felt a sudden rush of warmth toward her and touched her face with his hand.

"You didn't have to come tell me, Cindy Lou. You didn't have to come here and tell me at all."

She shrugged, rather helplessly. "I didn't know what to do. I was afraid I waited too long. See…Lyle admitted him and Daddy were going to kill you and the other man, too. Real soon."

21

Five A.M.

It would be dawn soon.

They were gathered at the final loading dock, an open cement garagelike area within the sprawling I. Magnin warehouse, a backroom catacomb of boxed merchandise, stacked and shelved. The last dollies and hand trucks and carts bearing microwave ovens and VCRs and TVs, taken from this department store, were being wheeled toward the trailer of the third, the final, semi. Cole Comfort stood at the right of the truck, watching, relishing it; you could see in his face, in his eyes, that this night had been his life's dream come true. Lyle was at the wheel of a hand truck of unidentifiable boxes. Fisher had a cart piled with boxed Cuisinarts and other small but relatively big-ticket kitchen appliances. A pair of Leeches were within the truck, packing things tight, making as much room as possible for still more stolen stuff. Another Leech was having a smoke over at left. Winch and Dooley had one of the several suitcases of cash from the bank up on a waist-high stack of boxes, looking in at the green stuff, contemplating how much it would all add up to—checks had been left behind at the bank, just so much worthless paper on the indoor–outdoor carpeting, some of it scattered under the Christmas tree as if by a sloppy Santa. Everybody seemed sort of wasted, understandably so, but a little high, as well. Things were winding down.

Nolan assessed the scene. He stood at the outer edge of the open cement area, I. Magnin boxed merchandise stacked on rows of ceiling-high shelving behind him. One hand, his right, was behind him, too.

This, he thought, would be as good a time as any.

"Gentlemen," he said. Loudly.

They stopped in their tracks. Comfort seemed puzzled—probably he wasn't used to hearing the word "gentlemen" used in reference to him. Lyle seemed stunned, but then he'd seemed stunned all night. A Leech poked his head out of the back of the van, like a groundhog checking to see if this was his day; it wasn't. Fisher looked at Nolan, not making anything of it. But Winch and Dooley seemed to sense something.

"I've got something to say," Nolan said. "I'd advise you listen carefully."

Comfort glared at Nolan. The old man's usually disconcertingly pleasant face became a sphincter of irritation as his mouth squeezed out the words: "What the fuck's the idea? Don't interrupt the work!" Then to everybody else, including the loitering Winch, Dooley and the smoking Leech, he waved his hands like an insane traffic cop and said, "Get back to it. We gotta get out of this place."

"If it's the last thing we ever do," Jon said, stepping out from an aisle between shelves and stacked boxes, UZI in his hands.

Comfort's eyes were saucers, flying from Nolan to Jon and back again. "What the fuck is this?"

"No sudden moves," Nolan said, and showed them all the long-barreled .38 he'd had behind him.

"What the fuck is this?" a Leech within the truck said, poking his head out next to his brother's. They looked uglier than groundhogs.

With his left hand, Nolan gestured gently toward the truck.

"Put it back," he said.

The men looked at each other; confusion turned to smiles. Even Lyle smiled. Heads were shaking.

Only Comfort showed no signs of amusement.

"What is *that* supposed to mean?" he said, spitting the words.

"It means," Nolan said, "put it back."

He and Jon were spread apart enough to keep the men covered. The UZI could kill them all in a matter of seconds. Despite their smiles—their nervous smiles—these men knew that. Even Lyle.

Fisher, with a tiny one-sided smirk, said, "Surely you're not suggesting we put back…what we…*took*."

Nolan nodded.

"The merchandise?" Fisher said, eyebrows raised over dark-rimmed glasses. "The money…the diamonds…all of it?"

Nolan nodded.

"Nolan," Winch said, stepping forward, looking like a raggedy man in his dusty work clothes, "it took us all night to do this job. We don't have time to put everything back, even if we wanted to. What am I supposed to do, unblow five safes? Come on, man—the deed is done. So's the damage. Let's all let bygones be bygones and enjoy this coup we pulled."

"We have plenty of manpower," Nolan said, "and plenty of time. Merchants don't get here till eight-thirty. The maintenance guy comes on at seven, and if we aren't done by then, we can do something about him. We're going to work very hard, unloading these trucks. But the first thing I want you all to do is toss your guns on the floor. No offense, but do it. Toss 'em right over by Jon. Now."

There were grumbles, but they complied—all but Winch, who didn't carry a piece. Fisher threw on his clunkily futuristic-looking stun gun. Even the Leeches coughed up weapons, surprisingly small ones, .22 revolvers, Saturday night specials. Nolan kept a close eye on Cole Comfort, who tossed a Colt Woodsman .38 on the silvery pile.

"Nolan," Dooley said, "why are you doing this?"

"You all know why," Nolan said. "The Comforts took a hostage. The woman I live with. That's how they forced my involvement here. I work here, gentlemen. My friends own and operate the stores we've looted. I've been made to do two things I don't as a rule do: steal from my friends; and shit where I eat. Start unloading."

Fisher said, "Isn't this a little late…"

"You'll all be paid for your trouble. I'll even extend my offer to the Leech brothers…" He directed his words toward them: "I'm kicking in fifteen grand apiece for your trouble here tonight."

A Leech scowled from the back of the truck and said, "This is a million-dollar score. What the fuck kind of insult is fifteen gees?"

"You're wasting time. Start unloading."

Winch stepped forward. "Nolan, we worked a lot of jobs together. I got a lot of respect for you. But this isn't right. This isn't fair."

"They killed the girl," Nolan said. He didn't like saying it. Saying it was admitting it.

Winch shook his head, made a clicking sound of sympathy in his cheek. "That's a shame. The dirty bastards." He glanced at Comfort, who was standing near the semi, boiling, and Lyle, who was frozen at his hand truck, and shook his head again. Then he looked at Nolan and shrugged, "But really, Nolan, that's between you and Comfort, here."

Fisher stepped forward, too. "It's an awful thing. But, Nolan, frankly—it doesn't have anything to do with the rest of us. We worked our tails off, all damn night."

Dooley didn't step forward, but he gave his two cents' worth. "I agree it's a dirty rotten shame, your girl. But I also agree it's between you and the Comforts. Why don't you keep Cole and his kid, and let the rest of us go, and send the Leech boys on to Omaha where our fence is waiting. We can all retire on this one, Nolan. You, too."

The Leech who stood outside the truck spit on the pavement. "Who gives a shit *who* Comfort killed or *didn't* kill. We been workin' all fuckin' night. And this is one big fuckin' haul. Fuck it!"

"Yeah," one of his brothers said, leaning out of the back of the truck. "Fuck it! Let's go."

Comfort's rage had subsided; he was smiling—lapping up the way the crowd had turned against Nolan. His blue eyes fairly twinkled in the leathery face and he smoothed back his white hair with one hand and walked a few paces toward Nolan.

With mock diplomacy, he said, "I gotta throw in with the Leeches, on this one. You can't undo this thing, at this point. Even your friends are lining up against you. Listen to 'em, Nolan— they're telling you *fuck it.* Fuck it, Nolan. Hell, fuck *you.*"

Nolan shot him in the head.

It lifted Comfort off his feet and knocked him flat on his back, with a splintering splat; his skull was cracked open—whether from the shot he took in the forehead, or the fall to the cement, Nolan couldn't say; maybe a little of both. At any rate, the blue eyes stared up at nothing and his arms were splayed out and his legs asprawl and the top of his head began emptying, as if all the meanness was oozing out, a slimy trail of blood and brains draining toward the truck.

"Pa!" Lyle shouted. He ran to the body, slipped in his father's brains and fell; then he picked himself up and kneeled before the corpse, and stared at it openmouthed. "Pa?"

The rest of them stood there, on the pavement, inside the truck, mouths open, eyes wide, breathing in the smell of cordite.

Nolan, a question mark of smoke curling out his gun barrel, said, "Put it back. Please."

"Well, since you put it that way," Winch said, and he headed back toward the truck.

"No problem," Fisher said, and joined Winch.

Dooley said, "I can handle it," and reached for the nearest box.

But the Leech brothers had other ideas, at least the two inside the truck did, because they burst out the back of it like commando jacks-in-the-box, guns in hand; they'd had them stashed within the trailer, apparently, big blue-black .357 mags that spewed noise and flames and more, exploding at Nolan and Jon, the Leeches screaming their anger, no words, just anger, gunfire ringing in the concrete room.

Nolan yelled, "Hit the deck," in the process of doing so, and Dooley and Winch and Fisher did so too, even as they scrambled toward the sidelines, for cover, though all it was was boxes, but Jon just crouched and opened up with the UZI while Nolan, on his belly, fired the .38 and bullets zinged and danced across the filthy sweaters of the two men, who pitched forward and landed face-first, not far from Jon's feet, deader than dirt.

The third Leech had grabbed up one of the guns from the pile Nolan disarming them had made, and scrambled off into the warehouse and Nolan pursued him, telling Jon to cover Lyle, who through all this, impervious to it, remained crouched over his father's body, apparently wondering what life would be like without someone to tell him how to live his.

Nolan ran after the final Leech, who hurtled down one and then cut over to another backroom aisle, and was nearing the double doors that led out into the department store, when he wheeled to throw some gunfire Nolan's way.

It was wild gunfire, though, chewing up some shelved merchandise at left, and Nolan shot him once, in the chest, and the bullet burst bloodily through the Leech and the Leech burst bloodily through the double doors, flopping on his back in ladies' wear, dead as his brothers.

When Nolan returned, Jon was guarding Lyle, and the three men were dutifully unloading the trailer.

"Forget it," Nolan told the three. He allowed himself a sigh. "It's fucked, now. We'll leave the trucks loaded—they belong to the Leeches, anyway—and the Leeches aren't going anywhere."

Winch put down the box he was unloading. He shrugged. "Maybe if we leave everything, they'll think a fight broke out. You know, your classic falling out among thieves, and that'll be the end of it."

"Yeah," Fisher said. "Maybe they'll just write it off as a heist that went sour."

"Maybe," Nolan said, nodding.

"Imagine," Dooley said, dryly, "anybody mistaking this for a heist that went sour."

"Pa," Lyle was saying.

The three men exchanged glances, and walked over to Nolan as a group. Winch, who seemed a little pale, remained spokesman.

He said, "Why don't the three of us split, then. This is no place to be hanging around." He looked around him. The two dead Leeches. The dead Coleman Comfort. The bashed-up-looking Lyle Comfort, mourning on his knees, a smear of his father's brains on his left shoe. Blood on the floor and the smell of shit and cordite in the air. Winch shook his head again. "This is what I hate about this business."

Nolan said, "I promised you money."

Dooley, who was anxious to go, waved that off. "We trust you."

Fisher thought about that briefly, then agreed.

"I don't think you'll have to wait," Nolan said, and he went over to Comfort's body. He took Lyle by one arm and hauled him over by the far wall; told Jon to keep him covered. Jon was doing fine, Nolan thought; he'd come through this like a real pro.

Nolan bent over Comfort's body and pulled down its coveralls.

Winch said, "Jesus Christ, Nolan—what…"

One of the coverall pockets was soaked and the strong sickly sweet smell of perfume rose; a bottle the old man had boosted had broken when he fell, apparently. Nolan ripped open the plaid shirt to reveal longjohns; and, finally, a fat money belt around Comfort's waist. He unfastened the bulky belt, stood, and extended it toward the three men, like it was some plump, ungainly but rare snake he'd bagged for them.

"You guys carve this up," he said. "If there isn't at least a hundred grand here, I'll eat the fucker. Anyway, I want no part of it."

Winch took the belt, held it in both hands and looked at it incredulously and said to Nolan, "How did you know he'd have it on him?"

"I didn't," Nolan said. "But I noticed he'd put on some weight since Sunday—he must not've worn the money belt to that first meeting. Entrusted it to Lyle, in case I pulled something, I guess. Anyway—I never knew a Comfort who believed in banks."

"This one takes the cake," Winch said, shaking his head.

"It's getting light out," Dooley said, touching Winch's sleeve. "We better go."

"My sentiments exactly," Fisher said.

The men made brief goodbyes to Nolan and Jon, stepped over and around the corpses, collected their guns and left out the back door, going quickly to Fisher's Buick in the parking lot and disappearing into the sunrise, leaving behind a changed, rearranged Brady Eighty that would, in a short time, surprise those who would come in and take over for them, the day shift who normally inhabited the place, who would not be in for a normal day.

Lyle had said nothing through all this, except an occasional "Pa." He hadn't wept. He just stood near the wall, looking stunned, Jon holding the UZI on him, Lyle's wide eyes staring at his pa's corpse.

Nolan put the .38's nose against Lyle's.

"So you threw her down a well," he said.

Lyle looked past the gun at Nolan, like a wide-eyed child. Orphan child. He shook his head no.

"What, then?" Nolan demanded.

"She was running. She fell down one."

Nolan looked at Jon. Jon looked at Nolan.

"Show me where," Nolan said.

22

Feeling like he was in a dream, an unending awful dream, Jon drove Nolan's silver Trans Am, following the cherry-red Camaro down Highway 92, woods at left, the Mississippi at right.

He wondered if Cindy Lou was on her bus yet. He had given her the keys to his van, back at Brady Eighty, and told her to leave it at the bus station; he'd pick it up later. Was she sitting in the station even now, waiting for a bus to take her away to L.A., away from the father she feared, and didn't know was dead?

Jon shook his head; he'd tried to help her. Just like she tried to help him. But she had, not so indirectly, provided the circumstances for her father's murder—in which Jon was an accomplice.

He wondered about her. He wondered if she would find any kind of life in La-La Land. Waitress? Hooker? Something better, he hoped. He wondered how long it would be before she learned of her father's death, and how she'd react. How would she feel about Jon, and Nolan? Would she bite her lip and understand? Or would she be the next Comfort to come out of the past and want to kill them?

The sun, not at all high in the sky, glinted off the cold gray choppy surface of the river. Up ahead Nolan was driving. Comfort's son Lyle was in the back seat, trussed up like something out of a bondage magazine, but sitting up nonetheless, so he could see out the window and give Nolan directions. The excess clothesline, and there was quite a bundle of it, was on the floor in the Camaro's back seat. So was a flashlight.

"We're not going to leave her down there," Nolan had said, with a passion unlike him.

Left unsaid was the faint hope that she might be alive. But both knew that hope was so faint as to be transparent as the wishful thinking it was. The girl was dead. Sherry was dead. Nolan would have to face that.

Recovering a body wasn't Jon's idea of a great way to start a day; his bones ached, he was so tired, and he supposed hunger was behind the grinding pain in his stomach, but after his session with the UZI, eating was out of the question—the idea of ever eating again seemed in fact abstract.

He'd killed those men, those two Leeches. Nolan's bullets had been in there, too, but Jon had seen the UZI bullets zing across the chests, going in black, coming out red. His mouth was dry.

They were murdering lowlife sons of bitches but he had killed them. Self-defense, but he had done it. He had killed them. He could face that.

He could live with it.

What he wasn't sure about was whether he could live with murdering Lyle Comfort.

Nolan had left his unregistered long-barreled .38 back with the dead bodies (Jon's UZI too)—the revolver was, after all, the gun Comfort was killed with; Nolan had even placed it in the hand of a dead Leech. In return he'd taken the unfired Colt Woodsman that had belonged to Comfort; that was the gun Lyle would be killed with, Jon assumed. Nolan would do it. Dumping Lyle's body on a roadside in his cherry-red Camaro. He was planning to do it. With luck Jon wouldn't have to watch.

But he'd be a part of it, just the same, and he wished he'd never met Nolan, and wished this dream over, this nightmare which at the moment was a strangely lyrical one, sun-dappled Mississippi, starkly beautiful snowy woods, please God let it end.

They passed a sleazy little motel, the Riverview, with signs boasting water beds and XXX movies in rooms; so much for lyricism.

Up ahead the red Camaro's brake lights indicated a slowing down, and soon Nolan pulled off to the right, into one of many little picnic areas along the river. Jon pulled in behind him. The road seemed deserted; it was 6:37 A.M. Friday.

Jon got out, wearing his long navy coat, and gloves, but unarmed. Nolan got out of the Camaro, wearing no jacket or even sport coat, the Colt Woodsman stuck in his waistband, looking black against the light blue shirt, a shirt Nolan seemed to have been wearing constantly (the shirt Sherry bought him, Jon suddenly realized, the afternoon she was kidnaped!) and went around on the other side and opened the door and took out a knife and leaned in the back seat. *Christ!* Jon thought, but then realized Nolan was only cutting the ropes.

Jon walked over to the Camaro, wishing he were anywhere else, except perhaps that bloody loading dock which awaited some hapless I. Magnin employee.

Nolan hauled Lyle out of the back seat; the boy looked pale and confused but, oddly, not frightened. His expensive brown jacket and gray slacks looked a little the worse for wear. He wasn't bound in any way.

Nolan held him by the crook of one arm and smiled tightly. "You're sure this is the place, Lyle?"

Lyle nodded. "Not far from here."

A car went past.

Without looking at him, Nolan said to Jon, "Get the rope and the flashlight."

Jon got them out of the back.

"Let's go," Nolan said. Keeping his gun in his waistband, he guided Lyle by the arm like a child, across the highway. Jon trailed after, carrying the thick ring of clothesline in one hand, the flashlight in the other.

They walked up a snowy slope; leaves under the gentle layer of snow crackled beneath their feet. The sky was a slate blue and nearly cloudless. Wind whispered, but it was a chilly whisper, a ghostly kiss.

At the edge of the woods, Nolan said, "Do you know where she is, Lyle?"

He nodded.

"You wouldn't play games with me, would you?"

He shook his head no.

"Good," Nolan said. "Now lead the way."

He let go of Lyle's arm and withdrew the Colt from his waist-band and walked just a few steps behind Lyle, who led them into the woods; he wasn't moving quickly. He seemed defeated. Near catatonic. And, as Jon knew, and as Nolan most certainly knew, he was thick as a post. He wasn't planning anything. Or if he was, it wouldn't amount to much.

They hadn't walked far when Lyle stopped. He pointed up ahead, through the gray trees, where it seemed slightly more open.

"Over there," he said.

Nolan poked him in the back with the .38. "Show me."

Soon they could see it, where the sharp angles of broken planks jutted up like strange weeds. Nolan shifted the gun to his left hand and grabbed Lyle's arm and pulled him along and ran. Jon ran, too. He stumbled once, over a root, but didn't fall.

You couldn't tell what it was, at first. Weeds and leaves and snow still covered most of it, but in the center a jagged hole yawned, where the rotted planks had given way. Nolan put the gun in his waistband and cautiously crawled out to where she'd fallen through. He was on his side, his feet on the snowy ground, his trunk on the rotted wood.

"Can't see anything," he said, looking in. "Give me the flashlight."

Jon handed it to him. Lyle was just standing there, glum, obe-dient.

Nolan shot the light down there and said, "I think I see her."

He moved back off the planks. On his hands and knees at the place where the snowy earth met the planks, he started tearing the rotten boards away.

"Help me clear these goddamn things out," Nolan said, and Jon slipped the ring of rope around his shoulder and helped. The wood was so old, so weathered, so decaying, it almost crumbled in their hands.

"You help, too," Nolan demanded of Lyle, and Lyle did. He got on hands and knees and tore at the wood. Just one of the guys.

Then the opening of the old well was exposed. It was about four foot in diameter. It was quite deep; with the sun as low in the sky as it was, there was no hope of seeing down there without a flashlight. Nolan shined his down.

"I see her," he said, leaning in one side.

"I do too," Jon said, leaning in opposite him.

She was down there all right; on her back, her head to one side. She was in a lavender outfit. That was all they could make out.

"How the hell deep is this thing?" Jon asked.

"Probably thirty feet," Nolan said. His voice was quavering.

Jon looked at Nolan; a single tear streaked the man's left cheek. Nolan looked at Jon and wiped away the tear, leaving some dirt from a hand that had been tearing away rotten planks. It was a moment neither would ever forget. Or mention.

Now Nolan stood and looked to Lyle. Nolan started to smile; it was an awful smile. He walked over to the boy and gripped him with one hand by the expensive leather coat and said, "You killed her, you little cocksucker."

He shook his head side to side. "No, she fell."

"Running from *you*. Why don't you run from me, now?" And he got out the Colt.

"That's Pa's gun," Lyle said, stupidly, recognizing it.

"Nolan," Jon said. He was on his knees, leaning over the well, using the flashlight. "I think I saw her move."

Nolan stuck the gun back in his waistband and bent down and took the flashlight and shined it down there.

"Sherry!" he called.

His voice echoed down the well, the beam of the flashlight touching her body. Her motionless body.

"Sherry!"

Nolan's voice reverberated off the brick walls of the old well.

Nothing.

"Sherry!"

And thirty feet down, something—someone—stirred.

"Goddamn," he said, a disbeliever in the presence of a saint, "she *did* move."

He stood up. "Give me that rope."

Jon did.

Nolan looped one end of it around the nearest sturdy tree, knotted it firmly; then, he looped the other end of it around his waist.

"You're going down there?" Jon asked.

Nolan didn't bother answering.

"I don't know if you've got enough rope," Jon said.

"I always allow myself just enough rope," Nolan said. He walked to the edge of the well.

"This is a hand-dug well," he said. "They laid these bricks as they went. Look—you see? There's plenty of lip on most of those bricks, to cling to. That should allow me to pretty much climb down the side."

Jon was shaking his head doubtfully. "It's an old fucker. Some of those bricks'll give."

"That's why you're going to have to brace me."

"No problem," Jon said. He wasn't worried: he'd been into bodybuilding since he was eight years old and clipped a Charles Atlas coupon off the back cover of a Superman comic book.

Jon dug his feet in and gripped the rope with his gloved hands, as Nolan eased himself down into the well, and Jon put his back into it, pulling away as Nolan went down.

As they'd thought, a brick gave every now and then, and threw them a scare, and strained some of Jon's muscles, back muscles particularly, but about five minutes later, Nolan was down there. Kneeling beside her. Cradling her in his arms.

Jon called down: "How is she?"

Nolan shouted up: "Breathing!"

That was a start.

Then Jon could hear a voice; not Nolan's: hers.

Soft, so soft he could barely hear her, and he couldn't make it out at all. But she was saying something to Nolan.

Then he understood a word; her voice had managed to be loud enough to echo faintly up the well: "Nolan!"

And they were embracing down there.

"You want me to come back later?" Jon called down.

Nolan didn't respond.

He and Sherry were standing now. He was helping her, but she was standing, too. So nothing major was broken. Good. They both stood and embraced and then Nolan seemed to have his hands on her shoulders, looking right at her, telling her something.

"I'm coming back up!" Nolan shouted.

And Jon braced the rope, pulled as Nolan climbed the bricks. The trip up took a little longer, but there were no slips, no scares. Jon pulled him up over the edge of the well, and Nolan, a little winded, sat there and smiled.

"There's a soft bed of sand and leaves down there," he said. "She landed on her back, her weight evenly distributed. Nothing broken, looks like."

"That's great."

"That's lucky. She hit her head pretty bad, though. On the way down, probably. Concussion, I think. She's cold, but not frost-bitten, I don't think. She was better off down there than out on this snowy ground. She was away from the elements."

"What do we do now?"

Nolan frowned. "Where's Lyle?"

"Huh?"

Jon looked around. No Lyle.

"Oh. Shit. I sort of forgot about him."

Surprisingly, all Nolan did was shrug. "Well, we'll find him. He's not going anywhere. I got the keys to his Camaro."

Jon shrugged back at him. "I got your Trans Am keys. Think he's dangerous?"

"Is he going to go find a gun and come after us? No. He's nothing, without his 'pa.' He's just a bug. He'll get stepped on sooner or later."

"What about Sherry?"

Nolan untied the rope from around his waist, then tossed it gently into the well like a fisherman casting his line. "I told her to tie it around her waist," he said. "We're going to haul her out."

And they did. Sherry didn't try climbing the bricks, but she held on to the rope firmly and, with both men pulling, they had her out of the ground and back among the living in a matter of minutes.

Her face was smudged and bruised, her clothes torn and dirty, the socks on her feet shredded and caked with blood, but Jon didn't remember ever seeing a more beautiful woman.

She didn't say anything; she just hugged Nolan and wept into his chest.

Then pulled away and looked at Nolan and said weakly, but wryly, "I suppose you think I'm a sissy, crying like this."

Nolan glanced at Jon, who just shrugged.

Then Nolan, noting her lack of shoes, lifted her in his arms and carried her out of the forest, like a groom carrying his bride over the threshold.

23

Lyle pulled off the main drag onto the asphalt, and for the first time today, he smiled. He was close to home.

Then the smile went away, as he remembered there wouldn't be nobody there. Pa was dead. Cindy Lou took off someplace. And it was just him, now.

Just him.

And he couldn't stay long at home, no. He knew that murderer who killed Pa would come after him. Maybe he should go after them himself—Nolan and that curly-haired kid, he was partly responsible, too. Maybe Lyle should find a gun and go kill them both.

But he wasn't sure. There was no one to ask about it.

Lyle had made about all the decisions in one day he was capable of. He felt good about that; he felt good about how he got away from Nolan and the kid. They'd been busy trying to get that girl out of that well. It occurred to Lyle, in an insight that came as close to irony as he was capable, that his fucking up and not killing the girl had turned out to be something good—without her still being alive, those two wouldn't have got distracted, and he couldn't have made a quiet break for it.

He'd outsmarted them, and he nodded to himself, flushed with self-satisfaction, as he drove, his mouth a tight smug line as he pondered all the people in his life who'd told him he was stupid, including Pa sometimes, and how he'd pulled one over on that supposedly real smart Nolan.

Nolan didn't know Lyle had a little magnetic spare-key box tucked under the Camaro. Lyle had run across the road to the car and reached under for the key and there it was: right where Pa had had him put it—after Lyle locked his keys in the car half a dozen times or so, and Pa got tired of getting calls to come drive out in the truck to wherever and use the shim to unlock the car door.

First Lyle went to the Holiday Inn, to pick up Cindy Lou, only a note was waiting, for Pa and him. It said: "Goodbye, Daddy. Goodbye, Lyle. I have went to find a new life. Please don't come looking. I will try and call Christmas. Love and kisses, Cindy Lou Comfort." She had real good handwriting.

He lit out of there. Part of him wanted to crawl in that motel bed and sleep forever and a day; but he knew Nolan and the kid would be coming after him. He threw all his clothes and things and Pa's too in the Camaro trunk and took off.

When he went by the Brady Eighty mall, he said, "So long, Pa."

Then he caught Interstate 80 west, and kept the speed at fifty-five. He wanted to go faster, but Pa said never break little laws when you're on your way home from breaking a big one. Even though the mall haul, as Pa liked to call it, sort of was a bust, Lyle supposed that rule still applied.

He was headed for home. He knew that might be a mistake—Nolan maybe could find out where the Comforts lived—but Lyle just had to go there. All his things were there. All of his clothes, except the few he had with him; all his records and tapes. He'd gather his things and take off somewhere. Hide or something. He supposed he'd have to leave the big-screen TV behind.

A little after eight, the morning still young, he stopped at the Howard Johnson's near Iowa City and ate some breakfast, eggs and bacon and toast and juice. He was real hungry, but afterward, waiting for the girl to bring him his ticket, it hit him all of a sudden. Pa was dead. Pa wasn't never coming back. Ever.

He started to bawl, right there in the Howard Johnson's.

And then he ran to the can and puked up his whole breakfast.

Then he had to *pay* for the breakfast, talk about gyps.

He felt ashamed, as he drove away from the Hojo's. Here he'd been by himself in the car, where he could've cried and nobody seen him, and he waits till he's in a damn restaurant to break down like a baby. Pa wouldn't be pleased.

He caught 218 and headed south. He was traveling through

farmland and, even covered over by snow, the friendly terrain made him feel better because it made him think of home.

He knew he ought to feel angry about what they done to Pa, but mostly he just felt sorry they done it. What Pa said about it not mattering when somebody died, 'cause everybody died sooner or later, didn't seem to make so much sense to Lyle now. Maybe Pa meant, where other people was concerned.

He'd miss Cindy Lou, too, but at least she wasn't dead. He wished he could join her, wherever she was; it was too bad she was his sister, 'cause no girl fucked and sucked like Cindy Lou. Not that he was sorry she was his sister—with Pa gone, her (and Willis, who was in the pen) was all the family he had left. If she tried to call at Christmas, though, nobody'd be home. Lyle had to stay away from the house, after today, in case Nolan tracked him down.

Lyle thought of Willis again, when he saw a sign that said eighteen miles to Fort Madison at the junction of 218 and 2. He was tempted to stop by, but he didn't know whether it was visiting day or not.

And then about the time Lyle crossed over the Iowa/Missouri border, he remembered his Uncle Daniel. That was what he'd do! He'd stop for his things at the house and go right on down to Nashville. Uncle Daniel and the boys would take him in. And his Uncle Daniel could tell what to do about those murderers! His mouth was pinched with decision. He pounded the steering wheel with a fist. That was it. That was the answer. Uncle Daniel.

He wondered if they still had their record business; that's where all their moonshine money went, Pa said. It had something to do with people paying them to make records, which never got released or something. Pa said it was Vanity, but Lyle didn't think she recorded in Nashville. Pa also said it was a sweet scam. Anyway, Lyle'd have to learn to put up with country western, but that was all right. Small price to pay for a home.

And they had good-looking gash in Nashville; he'd been there before. A real foxy singles scene. He'd fit in just fine.

He had relaxed after that. He had, for the first time, hours into the long drive, pushed a tape into the cassette deck. He turned the music up real loud and filled his brain with Billy Idol. He was tired of thinking.

He ate lunch at a truck stop outside of Kirksville; he was on Highway 63, now. He didn't bawl and he kept the lunch down— two cheeseburgers and a load of fries and a Cherry Coke. Uncle Daniel. That was the ticket.

Now, hours later, midafternoon, sun reflecting off the snowy ground, he turned off the asphalt road onto the familiar gravel one. Almost home. He felt a bittersweet twinge. It would be great to be home, but sad to go in an empty house, nobody waiting for him.

Well, he'd just pack his stuff and go. He hoped he could get all the clothes and records and tapes and stereo stuff in the car. He shrugged. He'd just have to make do.

He pulled onto the cinder path, enjoying the crunching sound the tires made; he'd heard it so many times before. Then, like something on a Christmas card, there was the house—the aluminum siding Pa conned that guy out of was holding up real good. After some time passed, maybe Lyle could sell the place; his uncle would know. The old homestead looked real homey, snow touching the rusty vehicles on the overgrown lawn. The silo and the barn reminded Lyle that his were farmer roots; of course, Pa taught him early that farming was a fool's game.

He pulled up in front and locked up the Camaro—Pa taught him that; some people just can't be trusted—and headed up the steps onto the porch. He felt sad being here but a little happy, too, even if it turned out to be the last time.

He had a house key tucked away in his billfold, and he used that, but the door wasn't locked. That struck him as funny. He went on in, and the first thing he saw was the big-screen TV, and he sighed and shook his head about having to leave that behind. Then he saw the man, a stranger, sitting over at the left, on the couch, under a John Wayne western velvet painting, the real big one, right where Pa always sat.

The man was heavyset and wore white, like a doctor; but his

face looked funny—first off, he hadn't shaved in a long time, his cheeks were real stubbly; second off, his eyes were puffy and red. And he looked kind of familiar, even though Lyle was pretty sure he never saw him before. There were empty beer cans on the floor, a lot of them, all of them crushed by a hand that didn't give a shit about nickel deposit. Next to the stranger, on the couch, was an ashtray that was overflowing from crushed-out cigarettes and ashes. But the man wasn't smoking right now.

"Who are you?"

"Are you Lyle Comfort?"

"Yes, sir. Are you a doctor?"

"I'm a butcher."

That's when Lyle saw the knife in the man's lap. A long knife. A shiny knife.

"I don't understand," Lyle said.

The man smiled, but it wasn't at all friendly.

"My name's McFee," he said.

"Huh?" Lyle said.

The man rose; the knife was so long he held it by the handle with one hand and cradled the blade in the other.

"I'm Angie's father."

And as the blade came down, Lyle understood. He finally understood.

BOOK TWO

Mourn the Living

To the memory of Richard Yates—
who read this book and told me I was a writer

Prologue

The Nolan problem bothered Frank Rich, but there was a brighter side to the unpleasant coin: he'd been able to bring his mistress into his home for the first time.

Rich shifted nervously in bed, the sheet wet with his uneasiness, causing his brown-tressed bed partner to groan in displeasure at his restless turning, tossing.

"Am I bugging you, Nance, hon?"

She pulled the covers up and over her head and answered his question by peeping one runny-mascaraed eye above them, rolling it round as though she were a comic in blackface. Then she gave him another groan and turned over on her stomach, apparently wishing she'd never traded those second-rate clubs she used to sing in for the bed of an insomniac.

"Sorry, hon," Rich soothed, patting the blankets where they sheathed her well-formed backside.

"Get to sleep, Frankie," she growled, "okay?"

"Sure, hon, sure."

Damn her, he thought. An empty-head like her didn't understand, couldn't understand a thing like Nolan.

Nolan.

Rich shifted again, feeling weak-gutted and foolish that the mere name of a punk like Nolan could run a chill across his spine. He had just closed his eyes and blanked his mind for the nth time when a knock at the bedroom door shot him out of bed like he'd been jabbed with a needle.

He shouldn't have jumped, he knew he shouldn't have, he knew it would be Reese. Reese, the man he had stationed downstairs in the library, Reese coming up to make his hourly report.

"Yes, Reese," he said, his voice surface-cool. "How's it going?"

"Dull, Mr. Rich. No sign of nothin'." Reese was big, like a medium-sized barn, and he was much tougher than his smooth pink facial complexion and much smarter than his baby blue, lamb-dropping eyes. Rich had confidence in Reese's knowing when and when not to make use of the object which caused the slight bulge beneath the big man's left shoulder.

"That's fine, Reese, we want it dull, don't we?"

"You sure you want me to keep comin' up on the hour like this?"

"Yes, Reese, it's best you do. This way I know you're still down there, alive and well."

Reese glanced over toward the double bed where Nance was sitting up, the pinkness of her making a pleasing contrast against the sheer blue nightie. She was looking pretty and looking pretty disgusted.

Reese said, "You ah, you're sure I might not be breakin' in on somethin'…personal?"

Rich forced a smile. He liked Reese, but the man thought too much. "No chance of that. Just go on back downstairs, Reese, and keep an eye open for anything out of the ordinary."

"Yes, Mr. Rich."

Rich closed the door on Reese and went back to the bed. He stood before it momentarily, then turned away, starting toward the door.

From the bed Nancy looked up, her sleep-filled eyes prying themselves open. She said, "Where you going, sugar?"

"To the can, hon, don't worry about me, just get some sleep."

"Brother…this Nolan must be a pretty damn tough character to shake you up this way."

Rich's face reddened, his hands clenched into fists. "Why the *hell* don't you just *shut your mouth* and go to *sleep*?"

Then, explosion past, the blood ran from his face and the fists became hands again. He smiled shyly, like a kid who's just said his first bad word, and said, "I'm sorry."

Nancy said nothing.

Rich's face hung. "I'm sorry, hon, really I am. I wanted these few days here at the house to be a nice change for you from all the…well, you know, secrecy. I realize how tired you must be of sneaking around all the time. When this Nolan thing came up, I finally had a legit sounding excuse to get the wife out of town for a while. You got to admit it was a good excuse."

"Only it's not an excuse," she pouted. "First you tell your fat old hag that it's too dangerous for her to stick around, then you invite *me* over. I guess that shows how much concern you have about my welfare."

"Hon!" Rich was exasperated. "Don't get upset just because I'm acting a little jumpy! There's no chance at all of this Nolan showing up around here. He'll try for the casino, or maybe one of the offices. Not here."

"Sure. That's why you been having Reese share our evenings."

Rich started to answer her, then decided against it. He turned away and went to the door and left the room.

In the bathroom Rich stripped down and appraised himself in the full-length mirror on the back of the door.

He thought he had a damn fine build for a man past fifty: strong legs, trim waist, solid chest. There were some wrinkles, sure, and a little sag here and there, but a lot of men years younger, he felt confident, would trade him bodies gladly. Still had a touch of tan left, too, from that two-week summit conference with the Boys in Miami last summer.

Only his face didn't jibe with the rest of his youthful image, and of that he was well aware.

His face hadn't looked so bad to him three days before, when the Nolan threat had as yet to rise up. But now, now he looked at it and found things he hadn't noticed before. Like deathly pale skin, puckered with dry wrinkles, scattered with an occasional liver spot. And his hair, which only a few days before had seemed to him a distinguished premature gray, now looked a stark white, setting off the new oldness of his face.

Ridiculous!

In three days?

He wouldn't even think about it.

But Rich rubbed his hand over his chin (the stubble of his beard wasn't starting to grow in gray, now, was it?) and he knew that Nolan posed the kind of threat that could age a man, as they said, overnight.

Rich stepped into the shower stall, turned the faucet on both hot and cold, mixing the spray to an even lukewarm, and thought about the years he'd spent working his way up the ladder in the Boys' organization to get into this nice home in Cleveland, Ohio. Six and a half years he'd spent in Chicago, directly under the tight rein of the brothers Franco. Charlie and Sam Franco, along with Lou Goldstein, were the Boys, the three men who controlled the Chicago syndicate.

Rich soaped himself, adjusted the water just a bit warmer, and reflected on those six and a half years with the Boys, most of it spent working in various small casinos, and, toward the end, supervising the bookmakers. Then five more years he spent as Vito's second-in-command in Pittsburgh. Finally, for the past three years, he'd had his own set-up here in Cleveland, though still tied to the Boys. His operation wasn't a big one, but it was big enough to suit him: the apex of a career of hard, dedicated work in the none too safe business world of narcotics, gambling, prostitution, unionizing, and, well, other consumer services.

And now an obstacle: Nolan.

That damn renegade hood. Rich had hardly believed his ears when he'd heard that the Boys had set a price tag of a quarter mil on that punk's head.

Of course, Rich only knew of Nolan, had never met him. When Nolan had started working for the Boys in the Chicago operation, managing clubs for them, Rich was already with Vito in Pittsburgh. But Rich knew Nolan about as well as one man can know another second-hand.

He knew that Nolan was an ex-employee of the Boys, and had submitted his resignation in bullets, taking care of Sam Franco and two bodyguards when he did. Knew that for the past few years

Nolan had been traveling around looting and generally tearing hell out of the organization's key operations.

Rich turned off the shower, slipped into a terry cloth robe to sop up the moisture.

He couldn't, wouldn't let the Nolan thing shake him. Nolan was only one man and, by reputation at least, a man who worked alone. He would hit some of Rich's sources of revenue, maybe, but he wouldn't think to hit Rich at home. Would he?

Three days before, when the rumor had filtered through his grapevine to him that Nolan was in Cleveland, Rich had moved what capital was on hand and not in banks to his own wall-safe at home. For various reasons, reasons primarily concerned with matters of federal and state income tax, this money was not banked but kept on hand by the local operation till the Boys sent in a bagman from Chicago to pick it up once a month.

Now, forty thousand of this cash was downstairs in Rich's wall-safe, and Reese or someone like him had been serving guard duty on it ever since its arrival.

Rich got back into his pajamas. He hadn't thrown the case of nerves yet, but he felt a little better; he just didn't like thinking about what the Boys would do to him if he let Nolan lay hands on their money. He was halfway down the hall to his bedroom when he heard the noise.

It wasn't a very loud noise, just loud enough: a solid substantial *thump*.

Rich scrambled into the bedroom and got his .32 out from a dresser drawer near his pillow. He didn't bother Nancy; she was rolled over the other way, asleep.

He crept down the stairs and stood silently at the bottom for a while, facing the stately ivory-white double doors leading to the library, where waited the wall-safe and the forty thousand dollars.

"Reese?"

No answer.

"Reese?"

Rich opened the doors quickly, quietly, and entered holding the

.32 in close to him, like an extra appendage. Trembling, he darted his eyes around the room.

There was no one in the library except Reese, who was stomach-down spread-eagled in the middle of the floor, like an X marking the spot. Rich went over to him, bent down. Reese wasn't dead, but from the looks of the back of his head—freshly red and a shade caved in—he wouldn't be waking up for a while.

Rich glanced over toward the wall where the picture of his fat wife Lily hung over the wall-safe. No sign of disturbance, outwardly at least.

Shaking badly now, Rich struggled out to the hall again and opened the front door. He wondered why his watchdog, a large German Shepherd, hadn't let out the usual howl he bestowed on visitors, friendly or otherwise. Then he noticed, looking out across the forty yards of lawn between him and the gate, the outline of the dog in the moonlight. The dog was lying still, but not dead, he was breathing too hard for that. Drugged apparently, Rich decided, and at any rate, out as cold as Reese.

He made his way back into the house, into the library. He shut the double doors behind him, looked around the empty room and felt a wave of calm wash over him.

Nolan had been and gone!

Obviously!

Rich smiled and reconstructed it. Nolan had come and tried to make Reese open the safe, and Reese, of course, hadn't known the combination. Then Nolan had heard the footsteps upstairs coming down, and, knowing that someone would be on the way with a gun, Nolan had made a hasty retreat! Rich breathed easily, allowed himself a smile.

Relaxed now, Rich headed for his wife's portrait, pushed it aside and opened the safe.

All the money was there.

All forty thousand.

So, Rich thought, he'd been right: the bigtime punk named Nolan had failed.

And Rich laughed.

"Something funny?"

Rich whirled, swinging the .32-filled hand around to meet the sudden threat imposed by the strange cold voice from behind him. But a massive rock of a fist smashed into his face and Rich felt himself going down like a sack of grain, and as consciousness began to leave him, he felt his hand go fish-limp around the .32. The little revolver dropped harmlessly to the floor, and so did Rich.

The tall, mustached, large-boned intruder reached into the opened safe and in one sweeping motion emptied its contents into the open mouth of a satchel. He closed the satchel, stepped over Rich and walked out of the library.

In the hall Rich's mistress was standing at the foot of the stairs, her pretty mouth wearing a wry lemon twist for a smile.

"Well?" she asked.

He opened the satchel, counted out five crisp thousand dollar notes and handed them to her. She took them and folded them into a neat, small square.

He leaned over to her, kissed her lightly.

"Thanks, Nance."

"Any time, Nolan."

One

1

The manager of the Motor-Inn looked across his desk at Nolan and said, "I hope your stay in our city is a pleasant one, Mr. Webb."

Nolan nodded and waited for his room key.

The manager smiled, and the smile was like a twitch in the middle of his florid face. "Will you be staying in Dallas long, Mr. Webb?"

Nolan didn't like questions any better than he liked smiles that looked like twitches. He dug into his pocket and came up with a twenty, traded it for his room key and shut the manager off like a TV. Then he lifted his suitcase, hefted the two clothes-bags over his arm and walked out of the motel office.

Once outside in the dry late afternoon air, he glanced down at the number on the key: 16. Good. That would be on the far side of the building, away from the highway and damn truck noise.

In his room he hung the clothes-bags in the closet and found a rack for his suitcase. He laid open the suitcase and took out a bottle of Jim Beam, unopened, a long-barreled .38 Smith & Wesson, unloaded, and a box of shells, half-empty. He ripped the virginal white seal from the mouth of the Jim Beam and carried it by the throat into the can, leaving the .38 and box of shells on the nightstand by the bed as he went by.

He tore the white wrapper off one of the bathroom drinking glasses and poured it half-full with whiskey, then turned on the faucet and added an afterthought of water.

He walked over to the bed, sat down and emptied the glass while filling the .38 with shells. He laid the loaded revolver back on the nightstand and rubbed the heels of his palms over his eyes. He was beat, washed-out; but he didn't feel particularly on edge, which was a good sign.

Maybe he was getting used to the idea of having a quarter-million-dollar price tag on his head. Or as used to it as anybody could get. After all, it had been a matter of years now, since the Family put out that open contract on him, with its promise of a 250 G payoff to anybody who could make the hit.

A quarter of a million was some kind of record, he supposed. Valachi had only rated a 100 thou. But then all Valachi had done was talk: the Family complaint against Nolan represented a complex blend of personal rage and monetary loss. And Nolan wasn't sitting in prison, his damage done—he was at large, his head packed with inside knowledge—not to mention he was looting key operations as only an insider could loot them.

Nolan's smile was almost nonexistent as he reached for the phone on the nightstand. Before coming to Dallas for a short breather, Nolan had hit the Family's Cleveland branch for thirty-five thousand. Now he had to get the money safely banked in the Dallas account of "Earl Webb." He dialed the number of his local contact, a lawyer named M. J. Lange who for ten percent would gladly handle the cash for his client.

"Let me go back over it, Mr. Webb," Lange's voice said. "Tomorrow in the mail I'll get a key. The key will open locker 33 at the Greyhound Bus terminal, and in the locker will be a blue athletic bag. In the bag's the capital."

"That's about it," Nolan said. "Set?"

"Yes, Mr. Webb. One thing more…"

Nolan juggled the receiver on his shoulder as he lit up a cigarette. "What's that?"

"Sid Tisor's been after me to get in touch with you. He's phoned me long distance every night for a week and a half, and he sounds desperate. Wants you to call him. Says it's life or death."

"M. J., you know I don't want to screw around with anybody directly hooked to the Family."

"Well, I thought it best I pass it on to you. From what I hear, Tisor's made a clean break. Retired four or five months ago.

"Don't give me that crap. Nobody breaks clean from the Family. Sid is Charlie's damn *brother*-in-law. How do you retire from that?"

"As I said, I'm just passing it on to you. He told me he did you a favor once."

Nolan ground out the freshly lit cigarette in disgust. "Did he leave a number? Goddamn him."

The lawyer fed Nolan the number.

"Didn't he leave an area code?"

"Oh yes," Lange said, "here it is. 309."

"Okay, M. J. Take care of that little blue bag, now."

"Of course, Mr. Webb."

Nolan slammed down the receiver.

Great, he thought. 309 was an Illinois area code. Close to the heat. That was all he needed.

Nolan glanced down at the bed and considered diving in. He hadn't slept well on the trip—he could never sleep well on a bus—and he needed the rest.

Then he dialed 1, area code 309, and Tisor's number.

Soon he heard, "Hello, Sid Tisor speaking."

"Hi, Sid."

"Nolan? Is that Nolan?"

"Yeah."

"How, uh, how about a favor for an old friend?"

"Maybe."

"I hear you been chipping away at the Family."

"Any complaints?"

"None. Didn't you hear I retired? As a matter of fact, the favor I want to ask of you could net you maybe forty thousand of the Family's money."

"What the hell are you thinking, Sid? When the Family lets a man retire, they trust him to keep his nose out of their business."

"Don't worry about them. They got faith in me."

"They got faith in nothing and nobody. How do you know they don't have your phone tapped?"

"They don't…why would they?"

"Life or death. Whose, Sid, mine?"

"Nolan, I got good reason to risk this."

"You had better."

"You remember Irene?"

Nolan said he did. Irene was Sid's daughter. Sid's wife Rosie had died in childbirth with Irene, and Sid had raised the child by himself. When Nolan had last seen Irene she'd been fourteen. Since then Tisor had sent her off to college somewhere. She'd be around twenty now.

"She's dead, Nolan."

"Oh."

"I think maybe she was murdered."

"That the reason you got ahold of me?"

"That's the reason."

"Where you living now?"

"Peoria—the boonies."

"The Family ever send anybody around to check on you?"

"Not once."

"It's a big risk for me, setting foot in Illinois."

"I know it is, Nolan."

"I haven't been in Illinois since the shit hit the fan."

"I know."

Neither one of them said anything for a while. Then Tisor said, "Will you come?"

"Yeah."

Nolan slipped the phone onto the hook and said, "Goddamn you, Sid."

It might be an okay score, but Sid always tended to exaggerate, and that forty G's he had promised might turn out closer to four G's. And Illinois wasn't the safest place in the world for you when every greaseball out of Chicago knew your face and knew it was worth a quarter million.

Nolan said, "Shit," and lit up another cigarette.

He didn't really give a fuck about Sid or his dead kid, but Nolan owed Sid, from the old days.

And Nolan paid his debts.

2

It took four buses to get to Peoria.

Nolan took rear seats on each of them and always tried to avoid attracting attention, and he was successful, but only with the men: from women he drew stares like flies around something dead.

There was nothing particularly striking about his clothing, just a blue Banlon shirt and lightweight tan pants suited to the Texas weather, and a blue plaid woolen parka he was carrying to meet the already cooling Illinois climate. But when he stood, he stood six feet that seemed taller, a lean, hard man with muscular bronzed arms that a young woman who sat by him on the third bus had brushed against a few more times than the law of probability could allow. His thick desert-dry brown hair had begun to gray, and his angular, mustached face was deeply lined, making him look every one of his forty years. Behind black-framed, black-lensed sunglasses were gray eyes that kept a cold, close watch on everything.

On the final bus a lady of about sixty sat next to him and tried to small-talk him, but Nolan didn't small-talk easily. She seemed relieved when they at last reached Hannibal, which was her stop. She looked exhausted from an hour of making conversation with herself.

As she rose from her seat, she gave him the matronly smile of a professional grandmother and said, "Hannibal's a fascinating place, you know. Mark Twain was born here."

Nolan made an attempt at being pleasant, since she was getting off. "He wrote books, didn't he?"

She shook her head and waddled off the bus, boarding almost immediately a touring bus bound for Tom Sawyer Cave.

Nolan fell asleep for a while and woke up as the bus was passing a sign which should have read "Hello! Welcome to Illinois!" but somebody had removed the O in hello.

He closed his eyes and leaned back and rolled his past around in his mind for a few minutes.

Nolan had begun as a bouncer in a night club on Rush Street in Chicago. In a few years he climbed to manager. He was, of course, working for the Family; and the Family was grooming Nolan for bigger and better things.

At the head of the Family were "the Boys": Charlie Franco, Sam Franco and Lou Goldstein. Charlie and Sam were president and vice, while Lou held down the treasurer post. Their "outfit" was a multi-million dollar enterprise dealing in gambling, prostitution, unionizing and narcotics, among other consumer services, tied in with but largely independent of the New York mob families.

Nolan reached behind him and got his cigarettes out of the pocket of his parka. He lit one up and glanced out the bus window. He saw some crows picking at a scarecrow in a field and he thought of Sam Franco.

Sam Franco had been largely responsible for Nolan's promising future in the organization. Nolan hated the man on sight, which was natural since even Sam's brother Charlie referred to Sam as "the skinny little bastard" more often than not. But Sam was one of the Boys, so Nolan didn't advertise his feelings. And Sam, who tended to like young men more than young women, kept his admiration for Nolan platonic, because Nolan wasn't the type of man you made passes at, even if you were one of the Boys.

So for the next year and a half things ran smoothly. Nolan moved up in the organization, thanks to Sam, and Nolan kept on hating Sam's guts in silence, and everybody got along fine until Nolan met the girl.

The Illinois cornfields, already patched with snow, flashed in the bus window by Nolan's seat. He stared out the window and tried not to think about her. He didn't like thinking about her.

She was a nice girl, a very nice girl in spite of the fact that Nolan convinced her to spend the night with him during the first week of their acquaintance. She spent the night with him for two months.

She had reddish blond hair, the high-cheekboned beauty of a model, an excellent body and was extremely quiet. All in all, she was everything Nolan wanted in a woman.

But she was something else, too, something Nolan didn't want: she was a cop.

Sam Franco called Nolan in for a special meeting the day after it became known that the girl was jane law. Sam informed Nolan that the girl would have to be removed. Nolan informed Sam that he had already told her to pack her things. What he did not tell Sam was that he too was packing his things, and would take off with her as soon as this blew over.

Sam said, "You're going to have to ice her."

"I can't do that, Mr. Franco."

"I'll tell you what you can and can't do! Now, this is your fucking mess, clean it up!"

"No."

"Ice the bitch, Nolan. That's my final word."

But Nolan's final word had been no, and he meant no. He didn't kill the girl.

Someone else did.

Nolan found her the next day, in his apartment, floating face up in his tub. The tub was overflowing with water turned pink from blood.

She'd been beaten first, to near-death, then drowned. Little of her beauty in life had been retained in death.

The emotional outlet Nolan knew best was violence, and he spent the next twenty minutes demolishing the apartment. He reduced all the furniture to rubble and smashed his fists through its plaster-board walls. When he had calmed down enough to think, he went down to the lobby of the apartment building to use the pay phone, since he had torn his own phone from the wall.

"This is Nolan, Mr. Franco."

"Yes, Nolan." Franco's voice exuded fatherly patience.

"Mr. Franco," he said, his voice even, his hand white around the receiver, "you were right about the girl. I want to thank you for…letting me avoid the dirty work."

"That's quite all right, Nolan," said Sam. "Come on over and we'll talk business."

Nolan went to Sam's penthouse office on Lake Shore Drive where he found Sam at his desk, enjoying the view of Lake Michigan out the picture window.

"Nice view," Nolan said.

Sam turned in his swivel chair, said, "Oh hello, Nolan. Yes, it is a nice view, particularly in May, when…" Sam had begun to get up.

"Don't get up, Mr. Franco," Nolan said, and Mr. Franco sat back down, two bullets from Nolan's .38 in his chest.

The first man through the door caught a bullet in the stomach, the next one through got his in the head. The odds were good that Nolan had gotten the girl's killer because the two men he had shot were Sam's personal bodyguards and had taken care of most of Sam's unpleasant chores.

Nolan waited for everyone to die, watching the doorway to see if anyone else wanted to join the party. When no one did, Nolan turned to the wall-safe opposite Sam's desk. His mouth etched a faint line of a smile as he twisted the dial to the proper combination: a few weeks before he'd been in the office for a conference and had watched carefully as Sam opened the safe. As Nolan had been storing away the combination for possible future use, Sam had boasted its being too complicated for anyone but a Franco to master.

Nolan emptied the safe's contents into a briefcase and walked out into the outer office, where Sam's secretary was crouching in the corner, waiting for death. Hauling her up by the arm, Nolan used her as a shield to get safely out of the building and into a cab, the .38 in her back making her a willing if not eager accomplice.

The police noted that the incident marked Chicago's fourth, fifth and sixth gangland slayings of the month, and promptly added them onto the city's impressive list. The Boys kept Nolan's name out of it (the secretary Nolan had used as an escort ended up describing him as short, fat, balding and Puerto Rican) because of the pains Nolan could cause them if he ever chose to reveal his knowledge of their organization's inner workings to the authorities. The Boys' benevolence, however, ended there.

Charlie and Lou, shocked to see bloodshed come so close to their personal lives, placed the quarter million on Nolan's head before Sam's body had even cooled.

Nolan had taken his twenty-thousand dollar bankroll, compliments of Sam's wall-safe, and headed for a friend's place, where he holed up two weeks, waiting for the heat to lift off Chicago. The friend who hid him out was named Sid Tisor.

Nolan looked out the bus window and watched the sun go down. He closed his eyes and waited for Peoria.

3

Tisor was waiting for Nolan at the bus station, asleep behind the wheel of his Pontiac, a blue year-old Tempest. Nolan peeped in at him. Tisor was a small man, completely bald, with unwrinkled pink skin and a kind face. His appearance hardly suited his role of ex-gangster. Nolan opened the car door, tossed his suitcases in the back, hung up his clothes-bags and slid in next to Tisor. He placed his .38 to Tisor's temple and nudged him awake.

"Nolan...what the hell..." Though the .38 barrel was cold against Tisor's skin, he began to sweat.

"Sid, we been friends a long time. Maybe too long. I'm worth a quarter million dead and you're still on good terms with the Boys. If you're part of a set-up to get rid of me, tell me now and you got your life and no hard feelings. If I find out later you're fingering me, I think you know what you'll get."

Tisor swallowed hard. He'd never heard Nolan give a speech like that before—he'd never heard more than a clipped sentence or two from Nolan at a time. Never in the ten years he'd known the man.

Tisor said, "I'm with you, Nolan. I don't have any love for Lou or Charlie or any of the bastards."

Nolan's mouth formed a tight thin line, which was as close to smiling as he got. "Okay, Sid," he said, and put the gun away.

Tisor turned the key in the ignition—it took a couple tries as the weather had turned bitter cold a few days before—and got the Tempest moving. He wasn't mad at Nolan for the stunt with the .38; he'd almost expected it.

Nolan said, "I haven't had much sleep, Sid. Take me to a motel, nothing fancy, but I want the sheets clean."

Tisor said, "You're welcome at my place. I got two extra beds."

"No. I'll stay at a motel."

Tisor didn't argue with Nolan. He drove him to the Suncrest Motel. He let Nolan out at the office and waited for three minutes while Nolan got himself set with a room. Nolan came back with key 8, which put him in a little brown cabin close to the end. There were ten cabins, stretched out in a neat row. Nolan walked to his and waved at Tisor to follow him.

Nolan started unpacking his clothes as soon as he got inside the cabin. Tisor said, "You want me to leave now?"

"Wait a minute. We'll grab some food at the diner across the road. But no talk about your problem till I've had a night's sleep."

Tisor again didn't argue with Nolan. He was used to putting up with the ways of the man. He knew Nolan's mind was his own and it was no use trying to change him. He would just go along with him and everything would work out all right.

The diner was boxcar style, and the two men took a postage-stamp table by a window. The place was cheap but clean, which was all it took to please Nolan. Tisor ordered coffee, Nolan breakfast.

"You were smart to get scrambled eggs," Tisor said. "Breakfast's always the best thing a diner serves."

"Right."

Damn you, Nolan, Tisor thought. Why is conversation such a task for you, you goddamn hunk of stone?

"You care if I ask you what you been doing the last six years or so?"

Nolan lit a cigarette. "Go ahead."

Tisor leaned over the table and whispered. "What's this I been hearing about you robbing the Boys blind? I hear they can't wipe their ass without Nolan's stole the toilet paper."

Nolan decided he might as well tell Tisor everything, so he'd have it out of the way—Tisor would hound him till he got it all, anyway.

"It started," Nolan said, "with them chasing me. They sent guns wherever I went. Mexico, Canada, Hawaii. Didn't matter."

"You ran."

"Sure I did. At first."

"At first?"

"Running gets tiresome, Sid. The first month I ran. After that I took my time. I knew the Boys, knew how they thought. Knew their operations. So when my original bankroll of twenty G's ran out, I went back for more. Looted any of the Boys' operations that were handy."

Their food came and they shut up till the waitress laid the plates down and left.

"How do you work it?"

"Huh?" Nolan said. He was eating.

"When you loot 'em. How do you work it?"

"Quick hit, planned a day or so in advance. Just me. Once in a while outside help, on a full-scale operation. Lots of pros working freelance these days. Not even the Family controls professional thieves. Not many pros are afraid to help me, not with the money that's in it."

Tisor didn't bother Nolan any more. Now that Nolan had his food and was eating, he wouldn't like to be bothered.

Tisor sipped his coffee and thought about his cold, old friend. What balls the guy had! Nolan had some stones bucking odds like that. And the hell of it was, if he kept moving, Nolan just might be hard enough a character to beat the Boys at their own game.

When both had finished, they got up from the table, Nolan paid the check and Tisor tipped the waitress a quarter. The two men walked out into the raw night air and waited for an opening to jay-walk back across the highway to the motel.

Tisor stood with his hands in his jacket pockets, watching his breath smoke in the chill, while Nolan got his key out and opened the door to the cabin. Nolan did not invite Tisor in.

He said, "See you tomorrow, Sid."

"Okay, Nolan...Nolan?"

"Yeah?"

"You mind if I ask you something else? Just one more thing, then I won't ask you any more questions."

Nolan shrugged.

"How much you made off the Boys so far?"

Nolan grinned the flat, humorless grin. "Don't know for sure. It's spread around, in banks. Maybe half a million. Maybe a little less."

Tisor laughed. "Shee-it! How long you gonna keep this up?"

Nolan stepped inside the cabin. He said, "You said one more question, Sid, and you've had it. Goodnight." He closed the door.

Tisor turned and headed for the Tempest. He got it started on the third try and wheeled out of the parking lot.

He knew damn well how long Nolan would play his little game with Charlie Franco.

Till one of them was dead.

4

When Tisor got out of bed the next morning and went downstairs to make coffee, he found Nolan waiting for him in the living room. Nolan was sitting on the couch, dressed in a yellow short-sleeved button-down shirt and brown slacks. He was smoking a cigarette and looking at the centerfold in Sid's latest *Playboy*, a photo of a nude girl smoking a cigar.

"Hi, Nolan." Tisor tried to conceal his surprise.

Nolan said, "Good morning," and tossed Tisor's *Playboy* down on the table. "Nice tits, but what can you do with a picture?"

Tisor said, "When you're my age, looking's sometimes all there is."

Nolan grunted.

"Want some coffee?"

"I started some when I got here. Ought to be done."

"I'll get it." Tisor trudged into the kitchen, the tile floor cold to his bare feet. He never ceased to be amazed by Nolan. He wanted to ask Nolan how he got in—Tisor had the night before locked the house up tight—but he knew Nolan had no patience with curiosity.

Nolan had risen at 6:30, after eight hours of sleep, and had taken a cab to Tisor's place. He'd sat down across the street on a bus stop bench to watch, hiding behind a newspaper. He saw that no one, outside of himself, was keeping an eye on Tisor's house. And it didn't look like anybody besides Tisor was staying there, either. Sid looked clean, but over a single doubt Nolan would have frisked his own mother, had she been alive. Nolan sat staring at Sid's white two-story frame house, one of those boxes they churned out every hour on the hour in the fifties, and didn't get up from the bench till Sid's morning paper was delivered at 7:30. By 7:34 he had entered the house, through a basement window, and by 8:05 he'd searched every room, including the one Sid was sleeping in. Then, satisfied that Sid was clean, he had plopped down on the couch and started looking at the pictures in the November *Playboy*. At 8:30 Sid came down in his green terry-cloth robe, looking like a corpse that had been goosed back to life.

Tisor brought Nolan a cup of coffee, black, and set a cup for himself on the table by Nolan. "Be back in a minute," Tisor said, and Nolan was on his second cup by the time Tisor came back down the stairs, dressed in a Hawaiian-print sport-shirt and baggy gray slacks. Tisor sat down in a chair across from Nolan and sipped his cup of coffee, which was too strong for him though he tried not to let on, since Nolan had made it. Nolan nearly let a grin out: he got a kick out of Tisor, who had been the most unlikely big-time "gangster" he had ever known.

Tisor was Charlie Franco's brother-in-law—his wife's maiden name was Rose Ann Franco—and had lived off Rosie's relatives since the day they were married. He had been fairly respectable before that, a CPA keeping books for several small firms and embezzling just a trifle; but his wife had insisted he take part in her brother's "business." It was quite painless for Tisor, who had switched to bookkeeper for the Family—he was an efficient, overpaid little wheel. And it was just like the world of business, all numbers in columns, and the closest he ever got to violence was the occasional Mickey Spillane novel he read.

He liked Nolan, who in spite of an apparent coldness seemed less an animal to Tisor than the rest of the gangsters playing businessman games. And in one of his rare moments of courage, Sid had taken a big chance hiding out Nolan when Nolan killed Tisor's no-good brother-in-law, that swishy bastard Sam Franco.

Now Tisor was all alone. He'd been alone for two years now, since he'd sent his little girl Irene off to college at Chelsey University. Before Irene was born, there had been Rosie, his wife; and when he lost Rosie, there was Diane, till she found somebody younger and richer. And always Irene, a wild but sweet kid, ever devoted to her old man. Tisor shook his head and sipped at the bitter coffee. Now there was nobody. Except Tisor himself, a lonely old man too afraid to take his own life.

Nolan said, "I have the same problem."

Tisor shook himself out of reverie. "What's that?"

"The past. I think about it, too. It's no good thinking about it."

Tisor smiled. That was the most personal remark Nolan had ever made to him.

Nolan poured himself another cup of the steaming black coffee and said, "What happened to Irene?"

Tisor's head lowered. "Suicide, they say."

"They don't know."

"Not for certain. You see…she was on LSD."

"Oh."

"She was on top of a building, fell off. The cops say she took a nose dive…"

"Yeah. Since she was tripping, they figure maybe she thought she could fly."

Tisor's eyes pleaded with Nolan. "Look into it for me, Nolan. Find out did she jump, did she fall, did she get pushed. But find out."

"What about the local law?"

"Hell," Tisor said. "The Chelsey cops couldn't find their dick in the dark."

"That where she went to school? Chelsey?"

"That's right, Nolan. Chelsey University at Chelsey, Illinois."

"Damn, Sid, I didn't want to come to Illinois for even a day, but here I am. Now you want me to hop over to Chelsey and play bloodhound for you."

"Listen to me, Nolan, hear it out…."

"Chelsey's only eighty miles from Chicago, Sid."

Tisor got guts for once. "Goddamn you, Nolan! Since when are you afraid of the Boys? Do you want to pay a debt you owe, or do you want to welsh on it?"

Nolan knew what Tisor said was the truth; he wasn't afraid of the Boys—he just had better things to do than make like a gumshoe. But it was a debt he owed, and it needed paying.

He said, "Go on, Sid. Tell me about it."

5

Tisor's eyes turned hard and he leaned toward Nolan. "My Irene was a wild one, Nolan. She could've taken that LSD trip on her own. And if so, maybe she did try a Superman off that building. But there were some things going on in Chelsey that might have got her killed."

"Like what?"

"She was home one weekend this summer and told me about this operation the Boys got going in Chelsey."

"What did she know about the Boys?"

"Well, before she went to college I broke it to her about my connection with them, explained it all. She took it pretty good, but it must've been a shock since I was always such a Puritan-type father. You know, not mean to her or anything, just old-fashioned."

"Yeah. Tell me what she saw going on in Chelsey." Nolan could see it would be a struggle getting the facts from Tisor; the guy would just keep reminiscing about the dead girl if Nolan let him.

"The Boys' operation, yeah. Well, they're selling everything from booze to pills to marijuana to LSD. All aimed at the college crowd."

"Irene a customer?"

"She never said, one way or another. I really can't imagine her taking drugs, but then, I'm her father, what do I know? Anyway, she knew about the Boys' operation and their market. You see, there's this hippie colony in Chelsey she's got friends in. They number over five hundred and all live in the kind of slum section of town. It's got some publicity, maybe you read about it."

"I didn't. But Illinois seems too far east for a hippie colony."

"Why?"

Nolan lit a smoke. "Too cold. Communal living's swell, free love and all that. Till you freeze your ass off."

Tisor smiled, nodded. "You got a point. But these kids aren't what you'd call real hippies, if there is such a thing. Not California-style, anyway. They're rich kids, most of 'em, living off their parents' dough. They don't look so good in their beads and wilted flowers, and they don't smell so good, either. But they got money. Money for food, for heat…"

"For LSD," Nolan put in.

"And for LSD," Tisor agreed.

"Irene, was she one of the 'hippies'?"

"Borderline. She hung out with them, but she was putting seventy-five a month in an off-campus apartment she shared with a working girl named Vicki Trask. The Trask girl was laying out seventy-five a month, too."

"Hippies don't live in hundred-fifty buck apartments. Not 'real' ones."

"Well, Irene and her roommate weren't deep-dyed Chelsey hippies. But, like I said, even the most sincere ones are just leeches sucking money off their parents. Chelsey is a rich-kid school, you know."

"You think the Boys got a good thing going for them, then? Got any ideas what they're getting for one trip?"

An LSD trip took 100 micrograms of d-lysergic acid diethylamide tartrate and cost pennies to make. "I think they're getting around eight or ten bucks a trip," said Tisor.

Nolan scratched his as yet unshaven chin. "They're not making much off that. Granted, there isn't much money wrapped up in producing LSD. Any two-bit chemist with the materials and a vacuum pump can whip up a batch. But even a confirmed tripper only takes a trip or two a week."

"It's a big campus, Nolan. Almost ten thousand students."

"Still, you can't figure more than four hundred trips a week. That's less than four grand coming in."

"That isn't so bad, Nolan."

"Yeah, but that's their big seller, isn't it, LSD?"

"They're selling booze, too, to the frat crowd. Most any kid on campus might use pep pills now and then. Big market for pot."

"They selling any hard stuff?"

"Heroin, you mean?"

"Yeah."

"Hell, no. Nolan. The Commission of families in New York's got control over stuff like that. You know that. Anybody caught with a dope set-up is going to get their ass kicked hard unless the Commission's okayed it."

Nolan shook his head. "I don't understand this. LSD. Nickels and dimes. Why are the Boys fooling around with it?"

"Nolan, they got other things going for 'em in Chelsey! They got gambling, they got a massage parlor, a strip joint or two…"

"Don't bull me, Sid. Take the college out of Chelsey and there's only seven thousand people left. The Family doesn't mess with small-time operations unless there's a reason. I know they can't be pulling in even five thousand a week, before expenses."

"Nolan, I…"

"You're not telling the whole story, Sid."

Tisor looked at the floor. He didn't want to meet Nolan's eyes, if he could help it. "George Franco's running the Chelsey operation."

Nolan's laugh was short, harsh. No wonder the set-up was small-time! An LSD ring, what a joke. You could save all the money you'd make off a racket like that and go to Riverview Park once a year.

"Sid," Nolan said, "you and I both know what George Franco is."

George Franco was the younger brother of Charlie Franco and the late Sam Franco, and also of Tisor's late wife, Rosie. George: the obese, incompetent younger brother who couldn't cut it and got sent places where he wouldn't cause trouble. A glutton, a coward, and simple-minded to boot.

"Okay," Sid admitted, "it's no big set-up. It's a small operation that Charlie gave George to give him something to do."

Nolan got up from the couch. "Be seeing you, Sid."

"Wait, Nolan, will you wait just a minute!"

"Having George Franco on hand makes this too close to home where the Boys are concerned, and at the same time makes any possible score small potatoes. Be seeing you."

"Listen to me, will you just listen? It's better than you think. George doesn't have full charge, he's more or less a figurehead. There's a financial secretary, of sorts, who really runs the show. I don't know the guy's name, but he's no dummy."

"Where do you get your information?"

"George is my brother-in-law, remember?"

"Does he know Irene's related?"

"He might have met her when she was a kid, but he doesn't know I have...*had* a girl who went to Chelsey. At least as far as I know he doesn't. That dumb asshole doesn't know much of anything."

"I'll grant you that, Sid."

"Look, George talked to me on the phone last week, social call, you know? I pumped him a little. They're pulling in at least six grand a week."

"Sid, it's my life you're trading bubblegum cards against."

"Don't forget you owe me, Nolan, remember that! And there's going to be close to forty thousand in it for you, I swear."

"At six grand a week, how do you figure? The Boys send in a bagman every Wednesday and take the last week's earnings back to Chicago. That's s.o.p. with the Family. I know these set-ups, Sid."

"But they don't come in weekly! Chelsey is so close to Chicago they don't bother sending a man every week."

"How often do they pick it up?"

"Every six weeks. But I don't know where they keep it till then."

"How about the local bank?"

"Nope, I checked it. They must keep it on ice somewhere."

"So there ought to be around forty thousand in this for me, Sid, that right?"

"I think so, Nolan. Maybe more."

Nolan thought for a moment. Then: "What makes you think this operation in Chelsey has anything to do with your daughter's death?"

"Damn it, Nolan, I figure if they didn't do anything outside of sell that cube of LSD she's supposed to have swallowed, then they killed her, didn't they? Besides, because she was my kid she knew things about the Boys and the connection they had to Chelsey. If she let any of that slip to the wrong person, it could have got her killed. And…" Tisor's eyes were filmed over and he looked down at his hands, folded tightly in his lap.

"And what?"

"Nolan, I have to know why she died. I have to know."

"It's enough she's dead, Sid."

"No, it isn't! She was the only thing I had to show for my entire life, she was the only thing I had left to care about! I'm not like you, Nolan…I can't let go of something that important with a shrug."

There were a few moments of silence, while Tisor regained a modicum of control. Nolan sat and seemed to be studying the thin ropes of smoke coiling off his cigarette.

"If I find out Irene was murdered," Nolan said, his voice a low, soft monotone, "and I find the one who did it, what am I supposed to do?"

"That's up to you, Nolan."

"You expect me to kill somebody?"

"I know you, Nolan. I expect if anyone needs killing, you'll take care of it."

"I'm not making any promises, you understand."

"I understand, Nolan."

"All right, then. Get some paper and write down every speck of information you got on Irene and Chelsey. The college, her friends, the Boys' operation, George, everything you know about it. And put in a recent snap of Irene."

"Right." Tisor got a notebook and a pen and Nolan smoked two cigarettes while Tisor filled up three pages for him. Tisor gave Nolan the notebook, then went to a drawer to find a picture of his daughter.

"Here she is," he said, holding a smudged Polaroid shot.

"That's old, Sid—nothing newer? This is what she looked like when I knew her."

"She got prettier in the last couple years since you saw her. I had her nose fixed, did you know that?"

"No." She'd been a dark-haired girl, beautiful but for a nose that could have opened bottles, and it was nice that Sid had got it bobbed for her, but Nolan hardly saw it worth talking about when she was dead.

Tisor's eyes were cloudy. "They...they told me on the phone that...she...she fell ten stories...it was awful. They sent her body back on a train for the...funeral. I had to have them keep the casket closed...."

"Don't waste your tears on the dead, Sid," Nolan told him. "You got to mourn somebody, mourn the living—they got it tougher."

"You...you don't understand how it is..."

Hell, Nolan thought, dust doesn't give a damn. But he said, "Sure, Sid, sure."

"Let me tell you about her, Nolan..."

"I got to be going now, Sid."

"Yeah...yeah, that's right. I can't tell you how much I...I appreciate this...Nolan, thanks."

"Sure." He headed for the door. "See you around."

"Yeah...uh...so long, Nolan...you going by bus?"

Nolan looked at him and said, "You ask too many questions, Sid," and closed the door.

Tisor watched through the picture window and saw Nolan board a city bus routed for downtown Peoria.

There Nolan found a Hertz office and rented a midnight-blue Lincoln in Tisor's name. He drove it back to his motel, packed and cleaned up, then checked out.

He could make Chelsey by noon if he kicked it.

6

George Franco was a satisfied man.

He was not happy, but there was satisfaction, a certain contentment in his life.

He realized this as he lay on the soft double bed in his penthouse apartment, watching his woman get dressed. She was a leggy whore, with good firm breasts, and she was taking her time about fastening the garter snaps as she replaced her black hose. Her tousled black hair fell to her shoulders, and her once-pretty face wore a tight red line for a mouth. George liked the look of her hard, well-built body, but he didn't like her equally hard face which spoke of something other than love.

But she was his woman, hired or not, and he was lucky to have her and knew it. Especially when you were a repulsive glob of fat, as George resignedly recognized himself to be.

She was dressed now, as dressed as possible considering the black sheath hit mid-thigh. She did her imitation of a smile for him and said, "Tomorrow, same time, Georgie?"

"Yeah, Francie. Tomorrow. Sure was good today."

The whore smiled some more and said, "Yeah, sure was," because that was her job. Her fingers rippled a little wave at her employer and she left.

George sat up on the bed, poured the last shot out of the bottle of Scotch he and the woman had emptied during the day—the courthouse clock across the way was bonging four—and he drank it down. He held his liquor well, he knew he did; it was the one thing he could do well. Then he settled back with a good cigar and thought about his life.

Satisfied, content. Not happy, but you can't have everything.

After all, he had fifty-cent cigars when he wanted them, and a fifty-dollar woman when he wanted her. He lived in a five hundred buck a month secret penthouse (over a drugstore) with five rooms and two color TV's and two cans and two big double beds and three bars and lots of soft red carpet. His bars were well-stocked with all the liquor he could possibly drink; and he had all the food he could eat, as prepared by his personal chef, who came in twice a day. The chef lived down the street in an apartment shared with George's maid.

There were disadvantages, George realized that. People still didn't like him. They never had, they never would. It was a kind of reverse magnetism he possessed. His woman, for example. You can only buy a woman from the neck down, he told himself over and over again, but you can never buy the head, except for the mouth of course. And his men, the ones who were supposed to protect him, they didn't like him. And his chef didn't like him—the chef could *stand* George, and seemed to *kind of* like him, but that was only because George was a good eater and, as such, a pleasure to cook for.

Hell, he thought, not even his brothers had liked him.

Not to mention his father.

But Momma (*requiescat in pace*) had liked him.

The best move he had ever made was being born of that sweet woman. Being born of the woman had made him the son of Carlo Franco (*requiescat in pace*), a big man in Chicago "business." And the brother of Charlie Franco and Rosie Franco (*requiescat in pace*) and Sam Franco (*requiescat in pace*), who didn't like him but provided for him. Especially after Poppa died and Charlie and Sam took the reins of the "business."

Charlie and Sam looked out for their younger brother very well, in spite of their lack of brotherly love for him. Back in '58 they had put him on the board of directors of the business—made him one of "The Boys." But when George fumbled away over a half million dollars in his treasurer capacity, in a virtuoso display of incompetence, he was replaced by Lou Goldstein.

George cursed Goldstein as regularly as he ate. That goddamn Jew! What would Poppa (*requiescat in pace*) think about a Jew being one of the Family, for Christ's sake!

But even George knew that Goldstein could keep good books. And Goldstein was a veteran of the "business" with a talent for seeing to it that other people kept good books. George, on the other hand, had trouble carrying a number over to the tens column.

George rose from the bed and headed for the bar a few steps away; he needed a fresh bottle of Scotch. Another disadvantage of wealth, George decided, was it made you waddle when you walked. Especially when you tipped the scales, as George did, at an even two hundred and eighty. When he walked on the plush red carpet, he left tracks that took their time raising into place again.

As he stood at the bar pouring a shot of Scotch, he heard a knock at the door. He glanced at his watch and said, "It's open, Elliot," and downed the Scotch. Time for Elliot.

A man entered the room, a man as thin as George was heavy. He wore a powder blue suit, tailored, with a blue-striped tie. His face was bony and pockmarked, and his large black horn-rimmed glasses made his head seem small. Behind the lenses of the glasses were watery blue eyes. His teeth were very white.

"How are things going for us, Elliot?"

Elliot was George's financial secretary—the strong prime minister to George's weak queen. Elliot said, "Things are fine, Mr. Franco."

George poured another shot, said, "You want anything?"

"Ginger ale would be fine."

George poured a glass, dropped a few ice cubes into it and left it on the bar for Elliot to retrieve. He headed for the bed, where he sat among the unmade sheets, wondering why Elliot never drank hard stuff, wondering why he never smoked, or never seemed to have any interest in women. Maybe he was queer, who could tell about the guy?

Elliot went after the ginger ale, then found a chair.

George, sitting on the bed, said, "How's the college kid trade? They still buyin' what we're sellin'?"

"Business is good, Mr. Franco."

"How about the feds? You said last time there was a rumor about feds."

There had been a rumble that federal men were going to look into the Chelsey situation because of some unfavorable publicity concerning local college kids and LSD. There had been a girl who had jumped from a building while on a trip. There had been four trippers, it had been reported, who were in the hospital after having eaten magic sugar cubes and then deciding to stare at the sun. A day of sun-gazing, supposedly, resulted in all four going blind.

"It's still just a rumor about the feds," Elliot said. "Nobody paid much attention to the girl who went off the building, and the story about the sun-gazers going blind turned out to be a fake. Just one of those stories that got started."

"That's good to hear," George said. "No trouble about the girl who fell off the building?"

"No, it's blown over. Phil got the thing played down."

Phil Saunders was Elliot's cousin; he was also the police chief in Chelsey.

"What was that girl's name?"

"Tisor," Elliot said. "I think that's it. Tisor."

"Coincidence," George said, gulping his Scotch. "My sister married a guy named Tisor. Used to work under Goldstein."

"Is that so." Elliot was tapping his foot, not nervous, just anxious to bid George goodbye. At least that was the way George interpreted it.

George leaned back on the bed and waved his arms with a flourish. "You're doin' a good job, Elliot, and I'm gonna put in the word for you with my brother Charlie."

Elliot's smug smile stung George. *Skinny little shit! Smirking little bastard! I'm George Franco, and you're nobody!*

"Just keep up the good work," George continued, murdering Elliot over and over again in his mind.

"I have your allowance, Mr. Franco."

That damn condescending tone!

"Leave it on the bar, Elliot."

Elliot nodded, got up from the chair and laid down his empty glass and an envelope on the bar. The envelope contained two hundred dollars, George's allowance for the next week. There were bank accounts George could draw upon, and his expenses were taken care of by Elliot on Charlie Franco's orders; but to simplify things for George, this spending money was allotted him. Pin money.

"See you, Mr. Franco."

"Goodbye, Elliot."

Elliot left silently.

George stared at the ceiling and pounded a fist into the soft bed. Then he sighed and rolled over on his stomach.

Yes, it was a good life for him. His only real job was to keep out of Elliot's way. It was perfectly all right for him to pretend that he was Elliot's superior, Elliot went along with it pretty good, but his direct orders from brother Charlie were to stay the hell out of Elliot's operation.

Kissing ass didn't bother him *too* much. Not when it stayed relatively painless, like this.

Not when he was safe, content.

After all, wasn't he the smart one? Hadn't his brother Sam (*requiescat in pace*) got himself all shot to hell by that crazy animal named Nolan? Wasn't Charlie scared crapless all the time for fear death'll strike him down like Sam, either through this Nolan clown or some other maniac connected to the family "business"?

George chuckled. *He* was the smart Franco. He stayed away from trouble in a little town in Illinois, getting fat on fine foods, getting drunk on good booze and screwing nice-looking broads. He got nowhere near the fireworks, yet he got all the benefits.

Look at poor Sam (*requiescat in pace*). Shot down like a common criminal! And to think that psychopath Nolan was still running around loose, gunning for brother Charlie.

"No sir," George said aloud, "none of that crap for me."

"None of what crap for you, George?"

George rolled over and looked up. He hadn't seen the man enter, he hadn't heard him either. He was a tall, mustached man, his brown hair graying at the temples, dressed in a tailored tan suit and holding a .38 Smith & Wesson in his hand.

"Who…who the hell're you? You work for me? I never seen you before."

"Think. You've seen my picture."

"I…I don't know you."

The man sat on the edge of the bed, prodded George with the .38. "My name's Nolan."

Two

I

Nolan arrived in Chelsey, Illinois, a few minutes past noon. He let a Holiday Inn go by, and a Howard Johnson's, then picked a non-chain motel called the Travel Nest. It was a pleasant-looking yellow building, an L-shaped two stories; its sign promised an indoor heated pool, color television and a vacancy. Nolan pulled into the car port outside the motel office and went in.

"Yes sir?" The manager, a middle-aged man with dark, slightly thinning hair, gave Nolan a professional smile.

Nolan said he'd need a room for a week, filled out the registration, using the name Earl Webb. He listed his occupation as journalist and his hometown as Philadelphia. The manager asked if he wished to pay the $65 room rate when he checked out or...

Nolan gave the man two fifties. "Make it a nice room."

"Yes, sir!" The manager eyed the registration. "Are you a newspaperman, Mr. Webb?"

"No," Nolan said. "I'm with a new magazine out of Philadelphia. Planning a big first issue. It's going to be on the order of *Look,* except monthly."

"Really?" The manager's eyes went round with interest. Nolan smiled inwardly; he hoped everybody would bite his line as eagerly as this guy did.

"Come with me, Mr. Webb," the manager said. He turned to a younger copy of himself, most likely his son or kid brother, and snapped, "Take over, Jerome."

Jerome took over and the manager followed Nolan back outside to the Lincoln.

"We can park your car, if you like."

"I'll park it."

The manager told Nolan where the room was and turned and

walked briskly toward the far end of the yellow building. Nolan got into the Lincoln and drove it into the empty space near the door the manager was entering. He liked the looks of the motel, well kept-up, with separate balconies for each room on the upper story, private sun porches for the lower. He got out of the Lincoln, took his suitcase and clothes-bags from the trunk, then locked the car.

He met the manager at the head of the stairs and followed him to room 17. It was large, smelled fresh and was mostly a pastel green. The spread on the double bed was a darker green and the French doors leading out to the balcony were ivory-white. Nolan looked in at the bath and shower, found it clean and walked out on the balcony, which afforded him a view of the wooded area to the rear of the motel. There was a color TV. Nolan said it would do.

"If you need anything else, just call down to the office and ask for me—Mr. Barnes. Oh, and there's a steak house across the street. And the pool is just down the hall."

"If you're fishing for a tip, I already slipped you an extra thirty-five."

The little man looked hurt, but he didn't say anything; he just forced a weak smile and started to leave. Nolan immediately regretted falling out of character. He had to make himself be decent to people, even insignificant ones.

"Hey," Nolan called softly.

The manager, halfway down the hall by now, turned and said, "Yes, Mr. Webb?"

"Com'ere, Mr. Barnes."

Nolan reached into his front shirt pocket and pulled out a pack of cigarettes. He offered one to Barnes, who accepted it. He lit one himself, smiled his tight smile at Barnes in a semblance of good will.

"Mr. Barnes, the assignment I'm on for my magazine is important to me. A big opportunity. I could use your help."

Barnes grinned like a chimp. "I'll be happy to assist you, Mr. Webb."

"I wonder if maybe there's somewhere in town reporters might hang out."

"Well…several bars come to mind. There's a fairly good restaurant where the *Globe* guys go to talk. Called the Big Seven."

"Where is it?"

"It's down the hill from the football stadium, by Front Street bridge."

"Big Seven, huh?"

"Yes, it's a sports type hangout. The Chelsey U football team is in the Big Seven conference, you know."

"Anyplace else?"

"Some bars downtown. Dillon's, maybe, or Eastgate Tavern. What you going to write on, the hippies?"

"Maybe."

"Well, Hal Davis did a big write-up on the anti-draft demonstration last week. Hippies, yippies, the whole SDS crew. A bunch of 'em slaughtered a live calf on the steps of the student union, then tossed it at some Dow Chemical people who came down to C.U. to interview seniors for jobs."

"Interesting. He didn't happen to do a write-up on that girl who fell off the building a while back?"

"Don't know, Mr. Webb. There was a write-up on that, but I can't remember any details. Say, I'm saving my old *Globes* for a paper drive one of my kids is on. If you want to look at some of 'em, I could bring up a batch."

"Fine. Bring them up for the past couple months and you got another ten bucks."

Barnes smiled. "Don't bother, Mr. Webb. Glad to help, you being a real writer and all." Then he trotted off after the papers.

Good, thought Nolan. This way he wouldn't have to go down to the newspaper and ask to see back files. It wouldn't pay to show his face claiming to be a writer when he didn't have enough knowledge or a solid enough cover to fake it around pros.

He eased out of the tan suitcoat, hung it over a chair and started to unpack, leaving most of his things, including a spare .38 Colt

and several boxes of ammunition, in the suitcase. He hung his
clothes-bags in the closet and thought about taking a shower, but
then decided against it. He was too tired for that, so he flopped
down on the bed and closed his eyes. He yawned, stretched his
arms behind him, brushing against the phone book on the nightstand in back of him. He pulled the book down from the stand and
looked up the *Globe's* number.

When he got the newsroom Nolan asked to speak to Mr. Davis.
Mr. Davis was not in, was there a message? No message, he could
call Mr. Davis later.

There was a knock and it was Barnes with the papers. Nolan
thanked him and took the stack from him and laid it on the bed.

He leafed through the papers till he came to one published the
day after Irene's death. The notes Tisor had given him were fairly
complete, but any extra information might help. Besides, Tisor
hadn't even come to Chelsey to pick up the body; Irene Tisor's
body had journeyed home by train.

There were three articles on the death, one published the
evening after she died, one the next evening and one the evening
after that. The article printed the evening after her death wryly
commented that "certain factions in Chelsey have made LSD,
among other items, easily accessible to C.U. students." The byline
read Hal Davis. The other two articles, under the same byline,
played down the incident, largely ignoring the LSD and its impli-
cations and labeling the death "apparent suicide."

A whitewash job.

And Nolan could guess who was holding the brush.

The Chelsey arm of Franco-Goldstein enterprises was trying to
slip the LSD part of the story under a rock to keep federal men
out. This meant, one way or another, the Family branch in Chelsey
had gotten to Hal Davis.

Nolan lit another cigarette and remembered George Franco.

Would it be stupid to reveal himself to a Franco?

Nolan had never met George and had only seen him once, at a
cocktail party some years ago at Sam Franco's. Nolan knew George

by reputation, though, and from what he'd heard about the younger Franco, it should take only a few screws put to him to make him tell his life story. George had made a name for himself as a coward, and not a smart coward at that. Some meaningful threats might both pry information from George and keep his mouth shut about Nolan's presence in Chelsey.

Nolan tried the *Globe* again, couldn't get Davis, then got up from bed and, phone book under his arm, left the room, grabbing his tan suitcoat from the chair. He went out to the Lincoln, climbed in and roared toward Chelsey.

As he drove through the shaded residential streets, Nolan felt Chelsey was more a postcard than a city. He had heard there was a slum in Chelsey, but that he would have to see to believe.

In seven minutes he reached the downtown area. It was a typical small-town business district, built around a square, with all the businesses enclosing a quaint crumbling courthouse which stood in the center collecting dust. There were people bundled warmly against the cold Illinois wind, rushing up and down the sidewalks, visibly pained to move that quickly. Birds and bird-dung clung to the courthouse and Nolan wondered why the hell they didn't fly south or something. At first Nolan didn't see any old men in front of the courthouse, as he expected there to be, but after he parked his car and walked halfway around the square, he saw them at last. They were sitting in the shade of a large leafy tree, bench-bound, tobacco-mouthed, as motionless as the twin Civil War cannons in front of them.

He checked Dillon's Tap, found it empty except for a blowsy redhead talking to the bartender. No Davis, no other reporters to ask about Davis.

He didn't find Davis or colleagues in the Eastgate Tavern, where two on-duty policemen were drinking beer. He didn't want to talk to them.

Nolan went back to his rented Lincoln and headed toward the Chelsey University campus, which lay beyond the downtown district. The downtown continued on three streets north of the square, made up primarily of collegiate shops and bookstores; then the campus lay just after that, on a bluff overlooking the Chelsey River.

The river was little more than a wide stream, with several foot-bridges and four traffic bridges crossing it. The rest of Chelsey and the C.U. campus, football stadium included, were on the other side of the river. Nolan drove over the Front Street bridge and saw a large unlit neon saying BIG 7. He pulled into the parking lot and went in.

The place was dark and smoke hung over it like a gray cloud. Nolan couldn't tell whether or not, as the motel manager had said, it was a fairly nice restaurant, simply because he couldn't see it very well. All he could see clearly were football action shots trying in vain to break the monotony of the room's pine-paneled walls. Then he spotted two men in wrinkled suits, one blue and one gray, standing at the bar arguing over a long-dead play out of a long-dead Rose Bowl game.

"Excuse me," Nolan said.

The two guys stopped mid-play and gave Nolan twin what-the-hell-do-you-want sneers.

Nolan said, "Where can I find Hal Davis?"

The two guys looked at each other in acknowledgment of Nolan being a stranger to both of them. Then one of the guys, a chunky ex-high school tackle perhaps, said, "Maybe Hal Davis likes privacy. Maybe he don't care to be found."

"If you know where he is, I'd appreciate if you tell me."

The guy looked at Nolan, looked at Nolan's eyes.

"He's over at the corner table. Facin' the wall."

Nolan nodded.

The two men returned to the play and Nolan headed for the corner table, where a sandy-haired man of around fifty sat nursing a glass of bourbon.

"Mr. Davis?"

He glanced up. His eyes were bloodshot and heavily bagged and the hands around the glass were shaky. He wasn't drunk, but he wished he was. His lips barely moved as he said, "I don't know you, mister."

"My name's Webb. Care if I sit?"

"I don't care period."

Nolan sat. He looked at Davis, caught the man's eyes and held them. "You look like a man who got pushed and didn't like it."

Davis shook Nolan's gaze and stared into his glass of bourbon. "I said I don't know you, Webb. I think maybe I don't want to know you."

Nolan shrugged. "I'm telling people I'm a magazine writer, Mr. Davis. But that's not who I am or why I came to Chelsey."

"Why, then? You come to drop out and turn on?"

"I'm a private investigator," Nolan told him. "From Philadelphia. I been hired by a client...who'll remain nameless of course...to contact a Mr. George Franco."

Davis said, "You know something, Webb? You don't look like a private investigator to me. You look like a hood. You got something under your left armpit besides hair, your fancy suit isn't cut so well that I can't tell that. What's it you're after in Chelsey? You got a contract on Franco?"

"No. What if I did?"

"I wouldn't give a damn."

"You getting shoved around by the Boys, Mr. Davis?"

"The boys? What boys are those?"

So, Nolan thought, maybe Davis doesn't know about the Chelsey hookup with the Chicago outfit; maybe he's just a small-town newsman getting pressured by "local hoods."

Nolan said, "Let me put it this way...are George Franco and his associates telling you what to say in the *Globe*?"

"You mean what not to say, don't you? Sure, they're tellin' me, and they got some pretty goddamn persuasive ways of telling, too."

"I want Franco's address."

Davis downed the dregs of the bourbon. He smiled; one of his front teeth was chipped in half. "I'll get it capped one of these days," he said, gesturing to it with the emptied shot glass. "For a while I'm leavin' it like this, so I can look in the mirror when I get up mornings and think about what a chickenshit I am."

Nolan said, "Franco's address."

Davis shook his head. "It's not an address. It doesn't exist, not officially, anyway. It's a fancy penthouse deal, only it's above a drugstore. Berry Drug, right down on the square, across from the courthouse and cannons. There's a fire escape in back that'll lead you to a bedroom window."

"Any bars on it?"

"Nope. Just a regular glass window. They don't bother protecting fat George that much. Thinks his place is a real secret."

"Is it?"

"It was." He grinned his air-conditioned grin. "But it looks like the secret's out, doesn't it?"

Nolan dropped a twenty on the table and left.

He drove back across the bridge and parked his car several blocks away from Berry Drug. He went into a hardware store and bought a glass-cutter, then walked to the courthouse lawn. He sat on one of the benches by an old man who smelled like a urinal and watched the drugstore for about an hour. A black-haired whore in a short black shift came out, then a thin man in a powder-blue suit went in and came back out in less than ten minutes.

After a while Nolan strolled around behind the drugstore and climbed the fire escape and used the glass-cutter on the window. It was broad daylight, but the 'scape was at an angle and Nolan figured a daytime attack would be less expected.

He slipped into the plush red-carpeted flat, and crept over to the bed, where an extremely fat man in a silk dressing gown lay on his stomach, half-asleep and talking to himself.

Nolan got out his .38 and, after a brief exchange of conversation, introduced himself to George Franco. "My name's Nolan." It was 4:15 P.M.

Back in Peoria Sid Tisor was wondering if Nolan had reached Chelsey yet.

2

Nolan strolled over to the bar, laid his gun on the counter and helped himself to a shot of Jim Beam. He glanced over at George, who was sitting on the edge of the bed, his plump fists clenching the bedspread. George's forehead was beaded with sweat; his mouth hung loosely above two double chins.

Nolan asked George if he wanted a drink.

George tried to answer yes but couldn't spit it out.

Nolan, seeing an open bottle of Haig and Haig on the counter, poured a healthy glass of Scotch and dropped in an ice cube. He retrieved his .38 from the counter and took the glass of Scotch to George, who grabbed for it and began sloshing it down.

Nolan dragged a chair to the bed and sat.

"Let's talk, George."

"You must be out of your mind!"

"You're not the first to suggest that."

"What are you doing here? What do you want?"

Nolan shrugged. "I just want to 'rap.'"

"When my brother Charlie finds out about you bein' in Chelsey…"

Nolan lifted the .38 and let him look down the long barrel. "Your brother isn't going to find out, George. And neither are any of your associates."

George's eyes golf-balled. "You…you think you can threaten me? Me? I'm a Franco!"

Nolan, his mouth a grim line, said, "So was Sam."

George Franco looked into the flint gray eyes of the man who had murdered Sam Franco. He swallowed hard.

Nolan lowered the .38. "I won't hurt you unless I have to. I got a hunch this deal doesn't have a lot to do with you."

"What are you talking about?"

Nolan finished the whiskey, went back and poured another. "I'm here to look into a matter. The matter may concern the Chelsey operation you're involved in. And it may not."

George was trembling, like a huge bowl of fleshy gelatin. "What... what do you want from me?"

"Information."

"What kind?"

"Different kinds. Let's start with a name. Irene Tisor. What does that name mean to you?"

"A girl, that's all."

"What about her?"

"She fell off a building."

"Is that all you know about her?"

"She was on LSD."

"Did she fall?"

"I don't know."

"You said she fell."

"She could have."

"Was she pushed?"

"I don't know."

"What connection does your operation have with her death?"

"She got the LSD from one of our sellers, I suppose. So we put on some pressure to cover it up. We didn't want feds coming in and bothering us."

"What kind of pressure, George?"

"I don't know."

"Had you ever heard the name Irene Tisor before?"

"No...I got a brother-in-law named Tisor. You probably knew him from Chicago. Sid Tisor?"

"I heard the name before," Nolan said.

"You don't suppose Irene Tisor was a relative? His kid or something?"

"You tell me."

"Naw, I don't think so. Back in the old days, Sid was nicer to me than a lot of people; we keep in touch. Just last week we talked on the phone and he didn't say a word about any relative of his being killed in Chelsey."

Nolan grunted noncommittally. Well, looked like George didn't connect Irene to Sid. But then how much did George really know about the operation?

"What kind of money you getting for one hit of LSD?"

George said, "I don't know."

"You selling pot?"

"Sure."

"How much is a lid going for?"

"I don't know."

"You selling heroin?"

"I don't know."

"What percent of your income's from selling alcohol to underage buyers?"

"I don't know."

"How about barbiturates? Amphetamines?"

"I don't know."

Nolan rose, balled his fist and resisted the urge to splatter fat George all over the fancy apartment. He holstered the .38 and got out his cigarettes. Lighting one, he said, "You don't have a goddamn thing to do with the operation, do you, George?"

George's face flushed. "I do so! I...I..."

"You what?"

"I supervise! I do a lot of things...I..."

Nolan ignored him. "Who's the boss?" George didn't say anything. "Somebody's got to run the show. Who is it?"

George remained silent.

Nolan took out the gun again, disgustedly. "Who, George?"

George's face turned blue.

"I'm going to have to get nasty, now, George."

"It's Elliot!" he sputtered. "Elliot, Elliot."

"Elliot. He's your...secretary?" Nolan searched his mind for the expression Tisor had used in describing the position.

"Yes, my financial secretary."

"What's his full name?"

"Irwin Taylor Elliot."

"Where's he live?"

"In town, on Fairport Drive. It's a fancy residential district. High rent."

"What's his address?"

"I don't know…but it's in the phone book."

"He's got a listed number?"

"He's got a real estate agency that fronts him."

"Is there anybody else with power in town?"

"Just Elliot's cousin—the police chief."

"That's handy. What's his name?"

"Saunders. Phil Saunders."

Nolan drew on the cigarette, blew out a cloud of smoke. "If you're holding out any information, George, it's best you tell me now."

George shook his head no. "I don't know nothing else."

"You're a good boy, George." Nolan walked around the room for a few minutes, playing mental ping-pong. Then he said, "How do you get in this place…besides up the fire escape?"

"Through a door next to the can downstairs, in the drugstore."

"Fitting. Any of your men down there?"

"During store hours there's always either a clerk or an assistant pharmacist on duty downstairs to watch out for me." George's face twisted bitterly for a moment. "Sure do a hell of a job protecting me, don't they?"

"Swell," Nolan agreed. "You got a phone here?"

"Yeah."

"What's the number?"

"CH7-2037. Why?"

"Is it bugged?"

"I don't think so. Why would they bother checking up on me?"

"You got a point." Nolan repeated the number to himself silently. "You'll be hearing from me now and then, George."

George looked pleadingly at Nolan. "Look, I don't know anything.

You aren't gonna get any good out of hurting me. You…you aren't gonna…do anything to me…are you?"

Nolan hunted for an ashtray, found one, stabbed out his cigarette. "I won't touch you, George, unless you cross me. But finger me and you're dead."

"Oh, I wouldn't. …"

"I should put a bullet in your head right now, when I think of it. You're a bad risk."

"Oh, no, you can't.…"

"I can, and I have. I killed six men in the past eight years. Not to mention the ones I left wounded."

"I never did anything to you, Nolan. …"

"Don't sic anybody on me and we'll get along fine. But you tell your brother about me, or that Elliot, or anyone else, and you'll die wishing you hadn't."

"Nolan, I wouldn't.…"

"Shut up. You don't think I'm working alone, do you?"

"What?"

"I got three men watching you," Nolan lied. "They'll kill you the moment anybody puts a hand on me. So getting rid of me would only assure you of dying."

George lay back on the bed and moaned. He looked like a beached whale, only whales didn't sweat.

Nolan finished his whiskey and headed for the window.

3

The National Anthem woke Nolan and he sat up on the bed and checked his watch. Quarter after twelve. He had returned to the Travel Nest after eating at the steak house across the way and watched television until it put him to sleep. Now he felt wide awake; and his shoulders, his back, felt tense.

He got out of the now-wrinkled tan suit and put on his black swim trunks. He grabbed up a pack of cigarettes and matches, draped a towel over his shoulders and headed down the hall.

The door leading into the pool was closed but not locked. A sign hung on it reading "Life Guard on Duty 9 A.M. to 9 P.M. The management cannot be responsible for after-hour swimmers. Swim only at your own risk. T. C. Barnes, Manager."

It was a small pool, filling most of a small room. From the door to the pool was an area where people could stretch out beach towels and dump their belongings while swimming. Other than that initial area beyond the entrance, there was a scant three feet around the pool's edge bordering it. Paintings of sea horses rode the blue walls, and the air hung thick with heat and chlorine.

He dove in the deep end and swam several laps and turned over on his back for a while; then he climbed out and dove off the little diving board at the far end of the pool.

Swimming on his back again, Nolan relaxed and enjoyed the warmth of the pool, the all-encompassing feeling of the water around him. Even in a thimble like this, Nolan got a sensation of freedom when swimming. It gave him room to reach out.

Several minutes later Nolan heard the door open. Another late swimmer, a young lady perhaps? That'd be nice, Nolan thought, floating on his back. Then his fantasy was over before it began when his ears reported heavy, plodding footsteps splashing in the dampness of the room.

"Everybody out of the pool," a harsh voice grated. Nolan swam to one side, set his hands in the gutters and pushed himself out. He stood and looked at the intruders.

Two men, obviously local color. A Mutt and Jeff combination.

The short one, a pale, bloodless-looking specimen, owned the low voice. He wore a pink shirt with red pinstripes, with a thin black tie loosened around the collar, and a gold sportcoat. His brown slacks were uncuffed and ended a little high over his white socks and brown shoes.

His companion was a tall and beefy dope who wore a gray business suit a size too small. His eyes were expressionless brown marbles under a sloping forehead; his features were hard and battered, his cheeks acned. His mouth, though, was surprisingly delicate, almost feminine.

The short one said, "Mr. Webb? You are Mr. Webb, I assume?" He had dark plastered-down hair with motorcycle sideburns to contrast his chalky complexion. A hick trying to look hip.

"I'm Webb. What do you want?"

The big ox nudged his partner's shoulder and smirked. The smaller man, who seemed to think himself intelligent, smiled sneeringly at Nolan.

"Care to let me in on the joke?"

"You *are* the joke, Mr. Webb," the short one said, then he and the ox shared a round of laughter.

Nolan remained calm. This was a situation he could handle, but he was pissed with himself for allowing it to happen. Amateurs, damn it, he'd let amateurs catch up with him. And the maddening thing was he too had acted like an amateur, by coming unarmed for his impromptu late-night swim.

"Allow me to make an introduction," the sideburned spokesman said. "I'm Dinneck. And my partner here is Tulip."

"A rose by any other name," Nolan said.

"Is he making fun of me, Dinneck?"

"Tulip, keep quiet, okay?"

"Okay."

Dinneck smiled again, the smile of a guy who sells watches on a corner. He said, "Mr. Webb, we don't want any trouble from you. All we want is answers."

Nolan said, "Who sent you? George Franco?"

Dinneck nodded to Tulip, who removed his coat. Tulip's chest was massive and his short-sleeved white shirt was banded by a leather strap which supported a shoulder holster cradling a .45. Tulip folded his muscular arms like a guard protecting a Sultan's harem. There was an innocent smile planted on his bud of a mouth.

Dinneck said, "From now on, Mr. Webb, I'll ask the questions."

"Well ask, then," Nolan snapped, leaning against the wall, still a good fifteen feet away from them. Voices echoed in here. "I don't like standing here dripping wet."

"Yeah," Dinneck grinned. "You might catch your death."

Tulip said, "Might catch his death," and laughed to himself for a moment.

"Why don't you just walk over here, Mr. Webb…slowly…and stand next to Tulip and me."

Nolan shrugged and joined them, picked up his towel and began to dry off.

"Now, Mr. Webb, would you call it common for a journalist from Philadelphia to travel in the company of a thirty-eight caliber revolver?"

"You missed one, Dinneck. I carry two."

"You also carry ammunition, don't you? Does a reporter commonly hide a box of ammunition in the false bottom of his shaving kit?"

"You're a sharp kid, Dinneck. Why does a sharp kid like you dress in the dark?"

Tulip said, "I think he's a smart-ass."

Dinneck nodded. "I think you're right." Dinneck back-handed Nolan and Nolan instinctively leveled Dinneck with a right cross to the mouth.

Dinneck pushed himself up off the slippery tile floor and touched his bloodied lips. His face turned a glowing red. He motioned to Tulip, who drew the .45.

Nolan said, "That's a noisy gun, friend."

Dinneck said, "What the hell's a little noise between friends? Our car is just down the steps. We can pump a slug into you and be gone so fast your body'll still be warm by the time we're snug in bed."

Nolan's mouth formed his tight smile. "Together?"

Tulip slapped the .45 against the side of Nolan's head. Nolan moved fast enough to lessen the blow, but fell back against the wall just the same, his head spinning. He wiped blood from his ear and thought bad thoughts.

Dinneck said, "We heard you were a newspaper reporter, Mr. Webb, is that right?"

"It's a magazine, and go fuck yourself."

Tulip started back toward Nolan with the .45 in hand and Nolan sent a fist flying into Tulip's gentle mouth. Tulip yiped and clubbed Nolan with the .45 again and kicked him in the back as he went down. From the floor Nolan could see Tulip spitting out a tooth. Just then Dinneck kicked Nolan in the kidney and pain won him.

He opened his eyes a few seconds later and saw Dinneck standing above him, contemplating kicking him again. Nolan grabbed Dinneck by the right heel and heaved him, hard enough, he hoped, to land Dinneck on his tail bone, snap it and kill him. But Tulip was there to brace Dinneck's fall, and train the .45 on Nolan's head.

Nolan reached for his towel and, sitting in a puddle of pool water and his own blood, cleaned off his face while Dinneck spat questions.

"What were you nosing around the Big Seven for? What did Hal Davis tell you?"

Nolan said, "Ask Davis."

Dinneck said, "He cut out. Last he was seen was talking to you. We checked his apartment and all his things were gone. His car, too. Didn't even leave a forwarding address at the *Globe*. Why did you visit George Franco?"

"You want the truth?"

"Yeah, try the truth for a change."

"I'm doing a story on the Chelsey hippie scene. For my magazine. I heard rumors that Franco was a racket boss peddling LSD to the college crowd."

Dinneck and Tulip glanced at each other as if they almost believed Nolan's story.

Dinneck said, "I can just about buy you as a reporter, Webb… just about, but not quite. I picture you more as a man running. That's the way you travel, anyway. Or hunting, maybe. Which are you, Webb? Hunter or hunted?"

"Maybe I'm neither," Nolan said. Or maybe both.

"Two .38's. Half a dozen boxes of cartridges. Unmarked clothing, not a laundry mark or a label or anything. Rented car. No address beyond Earl Webb, Philadelphia, on the motel register. Not any one thing to identify you as a living human being."

"So what?"

"So…so I begin to think you're a dangerous man, Mr. Webb. And I don't think your presence in Chelsey benefits my employers."

Nolan said, "What do I get? Sunrise to get out of town?"

"You're a man with a sense of humor, Mr. Webb. Maybe you'll like this, just for laughs…"

Nolan rose up, his muscles tensed, his back arched like a cat's.

"Tulip, toss me the .45 and we'll give Mr. Webb here a swimming lesson."

As the ox was handing the gun to Dinneck, Nolan snapped his towel in Dinneck's face like a whip. It made a loud crack as it bit flesh. Dinneck clutched his face and screamed, "My eyes! My God, my eyes!"

The .45 skittered across the tile floor. Nolan leaped for it, grabbed it. He whirled and saw Tulip coming like a truck. He waited till the ox was a foot away, then smacked the barrel of the .45 across Tulip's left temple. Tulip cried out softly and pitched backward, stumbling into the pool; he hit the water hard but got lucky and didn't crack his head on the cement. Water geysered upon the big man's impact. He wound up in the shallow section, the top half of him hanging over the side of the pool, semi-conscious, his petal-like mouth sucking for air.

Dinneck was on the floor, screaming, fingers clawing his face.

Nolan slapped him. "Shut the fuck up, before the whole motel's in here."

Dinneck quieted, still a blind man, his eyes squeezed together and his face slick with tears.

"Who sent you, Dinneck?"

"I'll...I'll never tell you...you lousy cocksucker!"

Nolan seized Dinneck by the scruff of the neck and dragged him over to the pool. Nolan knelt him down and said, "Now I'm going to ask you some questions."

Dinneck kept swearing at Nolan and Nolan pushed Dinneck's head under water for sixty seconds. Dinneck came up gasping for air.

"Who sent you, Dinneck? George?"

"You son-of-a-bitch, Webb, goddamn you..."

Nolan put him back under for another minute. When he brought Dinneck back up he had quit talking, but his breath was heavy and his unconsciousness only a ruse.

"Did George Franco send you?"

Dinneck kept his eyes closed, tried to act unconscious.

"The next time I put you under," Nolan said, "you won't be coming back up."

No response.

Nolan shrugged and pushed Dinneck toward the water. Dinneck screamed, "No!" and Nolan hesitated before dunking him again, holding him an inch above the water.

"Who, Dinneck?"

"Not George, he doesn't know anything about this...George claims he never saw you!"

"You still haven't said who, Dinneck."

"Elliot, his name is Elliot! He's the one in charge…George doesn't have any power."

Nolan released Dinneck and the man fell in a heap at the pool's edge.

Nolan grabbed up his towel, slung it around his shoulders and headed for the door. His cigarettes were in a small puddle in the corner so he let them lay.

"You…you gonna leave us? Just like that?"

Nolan turned toward the voice. Tulip, coming out of his stupor, was standing in the pool, looking puzzled and wet.

"I'm not going to kiss you good night."

Tulip, dripping wet, looking ridiculous, pouted.

"And get out of those clothes, Tulip. You'll catch your death."

Tulip crawled out of the pool. He was hefting his friend Dinneck over his shoulder as Nolan left.

Back in the room, door locked, Nolan laid a loaded .38 on the nightstand by his bed, then washed up and treated his head wounds. Next time he wanted to relax, he thought bitterly, he'd take a hot shower. Hell with swimming.

He was asleep when his head hit the pillow.

4

She wore a black beret, had dark blonde hair and was smoking a cigar. She was looking into the sun, squinting, so it was hard to tell if her features were hard or soft. Her body was bony, though she had breasts, and she was leaning against a '30's vintage Ford, holding a revolver on her hip. The woman was staring at Nolan from a grainy, black-and-white poster that was a yard high and two feet wide.

The poster was tacked onto a crumbling plaster wall in a room in what had once been a fraternity house. No one Nolan spoke with in the house seemed to know what fraternity it had been—just that about four years before the frat had been thrown off campus for holding one wild party too many—and since had been claimed by assorted Chelsey U males on the hippie kick. The fraternity symbols over the door were Greek to Nolan.

The room in which Nolan stood staring back at the stern female face was inhabited by a Jesus Christ in sunglasses and blue jeans. Underneath a beard that looked like a Fuller Brush gotten out of hand, the thin young man sported love beads and no shirt. Outside of the beard and shoulder-length locks his body was hairless as a grape.

"Doesn't she just blow your mind?"

Nolan said, "Not really."

"Bonnie Parker," the young man said with awe. He wiped his nose with his forearm. "Now there was a real before-her-time freak."

"Freak?"

"Right, man. Before her time. She and that Clyde really blew out their minds, didn't they?"

"They blew minds out, all right."

"Don't believe what the press says about them, man! They were alienated from the Establishment, persecuted by society, victims of police brutality."

"Oh." Nolan glanced at the poster next to Bonnie Parker's which was a psychedelic rendering in blue and green; as nearly as he could make out, it said, "Love and Peace Are All."

"Some of the other freaks got pictures of the movie Bonnie up on the walls. Not me. I insist on the genuine article."

"Swell," Nolan said. He lit a cigarette and said, "Got a name?"

"Me?"

"You."

Jesus thought for a moment, scratched his beard. "I'm called Zig-Zag."

"Good," Nolan said. "You're the one I was looking for."

Nolan strolled around the room, glanced at other posters hanging on the deteriorating green plaster walls. Dr. Timothy Leary. Fu Manchu For Mayor. The Mothers of Invention. Kill a Commie For Christ.

There were some paperback books in one corner, several ashtrays scattered around, a few blankets by the window. Alongside one wall a radiator spat underneath Dr. Leary's picture. The air was singed with incense.

"Irene Tisor," Nolan said. He looked out the window and watched the Chelsey River reflect the sun.

"What?"

"Irene Tisor. Did you know her?"

The mass of hair nodded yes.

"What happened to her?"

"Bad trip."

"Bad trip?"

"A down trip, straight down."

"Fell?"

"I wasn't there, man. Nobody was there but her…and she must've not been all there herself."

"What's the word?"

"Huh?"

"What do people say about it?"

"Nothin'…just that Irene thought she could fly. Guess she couldn't. Bummer."

"Was she a friend of yours?"

"So-so."

"How'd you know her?"

"She hung around the Third Eye. We talked."

The Third Eye was a nightclub frequented by Chelsey's would-be hippie element. The local underground newspaper was also called the *Third Eye* and the club was its editorial headquarters. Zig-Zag was the sixth person Nolan had spoken to that morning, and all had mentioned Irene as a regular at the Third Eye.

"What'd she like to talk about?"

"Life."

"Life."

"That's right, man. Philosophy one-oh-one."

"What'd she think of it?"

"Of what?"

"Life. What'd she think of it?"

Zig-Zag flashed a yellow grin. "Groovy."

Right.

"Was Irene Tisor one of you?"

Zig-Zag flashed the grin again. "I give, man. What am I?"

"Whatever the hell you call it. Hippie."

"I'm not a hippie, that's a label hung on my generation by a biased press!"

"Flower child, love generation, freak, whatever. Was she one of you?"

"Well, in spirit, man…but in spirit only. There's a lot of us, we live kind of foot to mouth, know what I mean? We don't want for much, but hell, we don't want much."

"Irene lived pretty good?"

"Better than that. She had an apartment, I hear, with that straight Trask chick."

"But she was thick with your crowd?"

"She sympathized. She heard the music, all right, she just couldn't take her clothes off and dance."

"She heard enough to dance off a building." Nolan walked over to Dr. Leary's picture. Down the hall somebody was playing a Joan Baez record, and though Nolan didn't recognize the voice and was no judge of music, he knew what he didn't like. Nolan ground out his cigarette in Leary's bleary left eye.

"Hey, man, what the fuck you doin', there!" Zig-Zag got up and started toward Nolan, flexing what muscle there was on his skeletal frame.

Nolan's mouth became a humorless line. "You're the love generation, remember?"

Zig-Zag brushed the ashes off Leary's face and said, "What is it buggin' you, man? You come in here all straight and polite, then you get nasty. What's *buggin'* you?"

"Irene Tisor is dead. I want to know why."

Zig-Zag shrugged. "Anybody can pull a bad trip, man."

"Wasn't she a 'straight,' like me?"

"She wasn't all *that* straight, man. But I admit I never heard of her taking a trip before this. She got a little high once in a while, blew some pot, all right, but that's all I ever saw her take on, besides a guy or two."

"Did she take you on, Zig-Zag?"

"Naw, we just shot the shit. But there's a guy in the band at the Third Eye she saw pretty regular."

"What's his name?"

"Broome. Talks with an English accent, but it's phony."

"Broome. Thanks."

Nolan turned to leave, then stopped and said, "Pot cost much around here? LSD and the rest, it sock you much?"

"Cost of living's high, man. Somebody's making the bread in this town."

"How about you, Zig-Zag? Your old man, what kind of business is he in?"

"My old man? He's a banker."

"I see. Where?"

"Little town north of Chicago."

"You get this month's check okay?"

"Huh? Oh. All right, so he sends me a little bread to help out. Big deal."

Nolan nodded to Bonnie Parker's picture. "You're lucky Bonnie and Clyde were before their time, Zig-Zag."

"Huh?"

"They were in the banking business, too." Nolan turned and left the room, went down the stairs and out the ex-frat.

It was almost noon now and Nolan, sitting behind the wheel of the Lincoln, looked back on a morning of interviews in Chelsey's quote hippie colony unquote. It had gotten him nothing more than a few scraps of information and a bad taste in his mouth.

He glanced over Sid Tisor's notebook of information on daughter Irene. He had gone through the six male names in the notes—Zig-Zag and five others like him, and now all that remained were the two female names, Lyn Parks and Vicki Trask. There were probably dozens of Irene's friends her father hadn't known about—all Tisor had was a handful of names culled from Irene's occasional letters.

Lyn Parks lived at the Chelsey Arms Hotel. Nolan parked a block away and walked toward it, passing several clusters of long-haired men and women wearing the latest thing in wilted flowers, plastic love beads and Goodwill Store fashions. The block was run-down but distinctly not tenement—secondhand stores, burger joints, head shops—though in Chelsey, Nolan had a hunch this would be as close to a slum as he would get.

The Chelsey Arms Hotel had seen a better day. Its theater-style marquee bore faded red lettering that didn't spell anything, and there was a worn carpet leading to double doors which said CAH proudly but faintly. Once in the lobby Nolan saw that the Arms was somewhat ramshackle but hardly in danger of being condemned; he'd stayed in worse. A desk clerk, in a rumpled gray suit, seemed to be trying to decide whether Nolan was a cop, or a salesman looking for female companionship.

There were Chelsey-style flower children all over the lobby, and Nolan sat in a chair across from two of them who were curled as one on a couch. Then he noticed the man standing by the cigar counter, pretending to look over the paperback rack.

Tulip.

Nolan got up and strolled to one of the pay phones to make his first contact with Vicki Trask. He would have to lose Tulip before he met with the girl, Irene's roommate, the most important name on Tisor's list. Nolan didn't imagine it would make too great a first impression to have Tulip barge in and turn his visit into a brawl.

He looked her number up in the book, dropped a dime in the slot and dialed.

A soft but somehow icy voice answered. "This is Vicki."

"Miss Trask, my name is Earl Webb. I'm a friend of Sid Tisor, Irene's father."

"Yes, of course. How is Mr. Tisor?"

"He's upset about his daughter."

"Well, I can understand…please send him my deepest sympathy."

"I'm afraid I'm asking for more than sympathy, Miss Trask."

"Oh?"

"I'm an investigator and I'm looking into Irene's death. As a favor to Sid."

"I see…that's generous of you, mister, uh…what was it?"

"Webb."

"Well, Mr. Webb, are you trying to say you'd like to see me and talk about Irene?"

"Yes."

"Right now I'm on my lunch break and I'll be going back to work in a few minutes, so…"

"Where do you work?"

"I'm a clerk at the bank."

"Would dinner be possible?"

"Mr. Webb, I don't even know you…"

"I'm ugly as sin. How about dinner?"

The voice till now cold turned warm in a gentle rush of laughter. "I must admit your voice is very intriguing…"

"What do you say?"

"…all right."

"Good."

"Might I suggest the Third Eye? The food isn't bad, the drinks are suitably damp. And you could do a little investigating on the side. That's where Irene spent much of her spare time, you know."

"That'd be fine. Stop by at seven?"

"Okay. See you at seven. Dress casual."

She hung up.

Nolan nearly smiled. A touch of promise in that voice? He glanced over at Tulip, who stood at the cigar stand engrossed in *Modern Man.*

Nolan stepped in an elevator, said, "Fourth floor," to the elderly attendant. He wondered what Lyn Parks would look like. He wasn't worried about Tulip. If Tulip cared to join him, that would be Tulip's problem.

He knocked on door 419 and immediately heard movement inside. A voice cried out, "Come on in, it's open." A feminine voice.

Nolan opened the door.

The walls, pink crumbling plaster, were covered with posters and flower power graffiti. Doc Leary put in another appearance, Bonnie and Clyde Barrow (Warren Beatty/Faye Dunaway version this time) again rode the plaster. Also W. C. Fields, Mae West, a Fillmore Ballroom poster in purple announcing Moby Grape and the Grateful Dead, and several homemade efforts, including "Legalize Pot" and "If It Feels Good, Do It." There were two bubbling "lava" lamps—one red, one blue.

Nolan sat on the bed, a bare mattress with a single crumpled blanket on it. He smoked a cigarette. The girl was in the john, making john noises. He sat and smoked and waited for her. For two minutes he stared at a chest of drawers that had been stripped of varnish and assaulted with red, green and blue spray paint.

The girl came in and was naked.

She held two small jars of body makeup in one hand, one yellow, one green, and was dabbing a tiny paint brush in the jar of yellow. There was a towel over her shoulder and her body dripped beads of water.

She said, "Oh, hi."

Nolan said, "Hello."

She appeared to be painting a yellow daisy around her navel. When he noticed this Nolan also noticed a few other things about her. Her stomach was attractively plump and her legs were long and well-fleshed. Her breasts were firm and large, with copper-colored nipples. Her face was scrubbed and pretty, surrounded by white-blonde hair cut in lengths and hanging down to partially conceal her full breasts. Her pubic triangle was dark brown.

"Have we met?" she asked, frowning in thought but not displeasure.

"No."

"Did you lock the door?"

"No."

"Lock it."

"I'm here to talk, Miss Parks."

"We'll see. Lock the door."

Nolan got up and night-latched the door. He returned to the bed and sat back down. The girl sat beside him and crossed her legs and worked on the daisy that was now halfway encircling her navel. He offered her a cigarette and she bounced up after an ash-tray and came back and accepted it. He watched her alternately puff on the cigarette and stroke her stomach with the tiny brush. Her skin was pearled with moisture from the shower, her flesh looked soft, pink…

"I don't pay," Nolan said.

"I don't charge."

Nolan drew on the cigarette and collected his thoughts. Lyn Parks stunned him a bit. He'd never met a girl who paraded around naked painting flowers on her stomach. He glanced at her again and saw the sun spilling in the window on her white-blonde hair. She smiled like a madonna.

"Lyn…okay I call you Lyn?"

"Call me anything you like."

But shy.

"Lyn, did you know Irene Tisor?"

"Yes. You have nice gray eyes, do you know that?"

"Were you a friend of hers?"

"I knew her, that's all. Your shoulders sure are broad."

"Did you hear anything strange about her death?"

"She took a bad trip. Have you ever been eaten alive?" She licked a pink tongue over her lips.

"Ever see her at the Third Eye?"

"All the time. Do you believe in free love?"

"Who's Broome?"

"Lead singer with the Gurus."

"The Gurus?"

"The band at the Eye. Don't you like girls, mister?"

"Did Broome and Irene Tisor see a lot of each other?"

"Broome sees a lot of a lot of girls. You seeing enough?"

"Enough. Was Irene a regular tripper? What'd she take, LSD or STP or speed, or what?"

"I don't know, none of it regular, I guess. Aren't you interested in me at all?"

"I'm busy right now. Irene Tisor is dead and I want the details."

She stroked the back of Nolan's neck. "Why?"

"I'm writing a story on her."

"Why not write a story on me?"

"We'll see."

"How do you like my daisy?" She had completed the flower and had added a green stem extending from her navel to the edge of the thatch of triangular brown.

Nolan got up, dropped his cigarette to the floor and ground it out with his toe. "Thanks for your trouble."

"No trouble. You're not going, are you?" She followed him to the door.

"That's right."

"So you're a writer, huh?"

"Yes."

"What's your name?"

"Webb."

"I guess you must not find me attractive, Mr. Webb."

"You're attractive."

"Well then, Mr. Webb, come on, what's to be afraid. It's free."

Nolan undid the night latch. "What if I were a killer?"

She stayed surface-cool but her eyes reflected a touch of fear. But just a touch. "What if you were?"

He couldn't figure her. Well, if she didn't scare easy, maybe she could be offended. "Ever hear the term clap? And I don't mean applause."

But that didn't faze her, either. She just stretched her arms above her head and gave him another look at her lush breasts. She said, "It's your loss."

Nolan said, "Maybe."

"You'll be back."

He said, "Maybe" again and went out.

He stood staring at the closed door. Was she for real? Did she really have the guts to let a stranger in her room and stroll around naked for him, offering him a piece of tail like it was a piece of candy?

Nolan shook his head. She couldn't be on the level, she couldn't have that kind of nerve.

But he'd remember her room number. She was right that, one way or another, he probably would be back.

6

Dinneck, who was in the john hiding in the shower, heard the door close behind the man he knew as Webb. Lyn Parks, still naked, came in and said, "Okay, lover boy, you can come out now."

Dinneck stepped out of the stall, pleased to be freed from the damp, claustrophobic cell. He shook some of the moisture from his wrinkled, uncomfortable gold sportcoat and leaned his pork-pie hat back and scratched his head. As he slipped his .45 back into its shoulder holster, he glanced at Lyn Parks as she stooped nakedly to pick up her underwear. "That's a sweet ass you got there, honey."

She sneered at Dinneck as she wiggled into her panties. "It's sweet all right, but you'll never taste it."

Dinneck laughed harshly and spat in the can. "So…your love child trip ends when that creep Webb cuts out."

"Don't try to talk like a hippie, Dinneck," she said, pulling on ski pants that left her bare to the waist. "The only thing remotely hippie about you is your fat ass."

A low blow, but just the same Dinneck flashed her what he considered to be his most charming smile. "Look, honey, you just made an easy fifty bucks, didn't you? I mean, you didn't even have to come across for Webb, just flirted a little and painted your cute tummy a flower. Now, wouldn't you like to make an extra twenty-five for something really worth your while?"

She snapped her bra across Dinneck's face and one of the metal snaps bit his cheek. "You were sent here to protect me, you little bastard, not to make passes. Now get the fuck out of here."

"What's eating you!"

"Not you, dork." She whirled out of the john, hastily fastening the hooks on the bra.

Conceited little bitch, Dinneck thought, rubbing his cheek. He followed her out into the shabby mass of posters and pop art that was her apartment. He strolled over to the window and saw Webb leaving the Arms and heading down the street toward the dark blue Lincoln. In ten seconds he saw Tulip pick up Webb's tail.

Dinneck looked back at Lyn Parks who was lying on the bed in ski pants and bra, sticking her shapely ass out at him in defiance, or so it seemed to Dinneck. She was staring at the door in a wistful sort of way, apparently wishing the man called Webb—whom she'd been paid to seduce and pump for information when he came calling on her—had taken her up on her offer.

Bitch, Dinneck thought. What the hell was it to her? She could obviously use the extra twenty-five he'd offered her. What was the difference if she gave Dinneck a quick roll in the hay?

"I suppose," Dinneck said bitterly, gnawing on a toothpick, "it's something else again when Broome tells you to diddle than when you diddle on your own."

"Oh," she said, not bothering to look back at him, "are you still here?"

Dinneck wanted her and he wanted her bad and he wanted her bad right now. "All right, baby, fifty bucks, that's tops, fifty bucks!"

"Take your fifty bucks and stick it."

"You bitch, you little bitch, if Broome okays Webb, why the hell not me?"

"What gives you the idea Broome okayed it?"

"You're Broome's woman, aren't you?"

"Part-time. I'm my own woman full-time."

"Well, if Broome didn't ask you to give Webb the treatment, who the hell *did*?"

"The same guy that sent you, dummy."

"You mean Elliot?"

"That's right. God, you're brilliant."

Elliot had sent Dinneck to the girl that morning, to watch over her in case Webb got rough when he came calling. Late the night before, after washing their wounds from the pool battle with Webb, Dinneck and Tulip had reported their findings from the ransacking of Webb's motel room to Elliot. In a notebook in Webb's suitcase had been a list of names, one of which had been Lyn Parks. Since Lyn Parks supposedly belonged to Broome, one of Elliot's hippie-town peddlers, Dinneck had assumed Elliot had gotten Broome's permission before unleashing the Parks girl on Webb. Of course, Broome was a pretty weird character and probably wouldn't give a damn who did what to his woman.

Dinneck chewed on his toothpick, thought for a while longer, then said, "How do you happen to do direct business with Mr. Elliot?"

"We're acquainted."

"You sell your goodies to him, too, do you?"

"I don't *sell* myself, scumbag. I might rent out now and then, but as far as you're concerned there's no vacancy."

"Your business connection with Elliot wouldn't have anything to do with a certain 'One-Thumb' Gordon, now, would it?"

"How did you know that, you little bastard?" The girl was surprised to hear the name, as she should be, because it was the name of her father, who was an associate of the Boys. It was a well-kept secret that she was the uncontrollable offspring of Victor "One-Thumb" Gordon. She had threatened to expose her daddy's Family ties unless he left her alone but well provided for.

"How the hell did you know about that?" she asked again.

Dinneck said, "Shut up, shut your damn mouth," and wiped his sweaty forehead.

What a goddamn fool mistake *that* was, he told himself, letting information slip like that! He had gotten mad at the bitch and let his temper flare up and expose a piece of his cover. He had to remember to play smalltimer, and he hadn't had any trouble in playing it till now. But if any of them—especially Elliot or anyone close to Elliot—saw through him, then he was washed up. If Elliot didn't get him, Dinneck had no doubt his other employers would.

And that Webb, that son of a bitch, had he seen through the hick routine? He remembered the swimming pool and how Webb had held him under water till his lungs had nearly burst. Where had he seen that face before? As soon as he took care of his job in Chelsey, Dinneck promised himself he would take care of that bastard Webb. Whoever he really was.

Dinneck walked over to the bed and looked at the girl and thought to himself that if it wasn't for the lousy clothes and the stooge role he'd had to assume, he might have gotten into that sweet bitch. As it was, the beautiful piece was sitting on the bed wishing she had made it with Webb.

"When you turned me down, sugar," Dinneck said easily, "you missed something real fine."

She kept her eyes fixed on the door. "I heard about you, needle dick. Remember a certain blonde waitress at the Eye? She says you don't fuck for shit, and I believe her."

Dinneck snarled and swung at her. She ducked and shot a small, sharp fist into his adam's apple. While he stood choking with his hands wrapped around his throat, he saw her go to the dresser, pull open a drawer and withdraw a mostly empty vodka bottle. She broke it over the edge of the dresser and turned it into a formidable weapon. She held it up in a very unladylike manner, the slivers of glass catching bits of light and reflecting it around the room.

She said, "You're going to leave now, and you're going to leave lucky that I don't call Elliot and tell him about the crap you've been giving me. The next time you come inside kicking range of me, you'll leave wearing your balls for earrings."

Dinneck choked some more and shuffled out.

She was a bitch, all right, he thought, but she was a tough bitch.

Dinneck, in the lobby, tossed away the toothpick and fought the sour taste in his mouth with a cigarette. He rubbed his throat gently, thought about how much fun he would have within the next day or two, when he'd be free to hit Webb and leave Miss Parks begging for more. But first he had to take care of the job he'd been hired to do in Chelsey.

He stepped up to the phone, dropped in a dime and dialed Elliot's number.

Elliot was in his den reading *Fortune* when the phone rang.

It was Dinneck.

"Mr. Elliot, Webb wouldn't go for Broome's woman."

Elliot said, "He wouldn't dip into the delectable Miss Parks? Strange…did he give any reason for his celibacy?"

"Just smartass shit—'ever hear the word clap and I don't mean applause.' And so on."

"A man of genuine wit, apparently. Did she get any information?"

"No, Mr. Elliot. He still says he's a writer, with a magazine. His cover is consistent, anyway. And he keeps asking questions about that Tisor twat that did that two-and-a-half gainer off the Twill building a few weeks back. The Parks girl dodged his questions and tried to get friendly, but no go. She started in pumping for a little information, then out the door he went."

"Is Tulip still following him?"

"Yes, sir."

"Fine, Dinneck. Call back in three hours for further instructions."

Elliot hung up and rose from the desk. He stared blankly at one of the mahogany-paneled walls for a moment, then went to the doorway and called for his servant Edward, a black gentleman of around fifty.

"Yes, Mr. Elliot?"

"Ginger ale, please, Edward. With ice."

He went back to the desk and waited for the ginger ale. He drummed his fingers and glanced continually over his fireplace where, instead of a landscape, his license for real-estate brokerage hung. Behind the oversized framed document was a wall-safe, where rested all the cash benefits netted by Elliot in the course of the Chelsey operation. Included was the last six weeks' haul, as yet uncollected by the Boys' periodic visitor.

Edward came in with the ginger ale; Elliot thanked him and spent a quarter hour sipping it. Then he rose, stripped off his herringbone suit and his pale blue shirt and his blue striped tie, and began to exercise. He exercised for twenty minutes, push-ups, sit-ups, leg lifts, jumping jacks, touching toes, knee bends, a few isometrics.

Then, exhausted, his bony frame slick with perspiration, he lay down on the black leather couch and tried to nap. And couldn't. His heart was beating quickly from the exercise and he took deep breaths to slow it but his nerves kept it going fast and hard.

He walked to his desk, opened the drawer and removed a glossy photo.

Elliot looked at the photo, at the hard, lined face and the cold eyes and the emotionless mouth.

The man in the photo was named Nolan.

And Elliot, in a cold, shaky sweat, darted his eyes from the wall-safe to the phone, wondering if he dare call Charlie Franco and tell him about the man who called himself Webb.

Three

At two till seven Nolan reached the address of Vicki Trask's apartment and found himself facing a door sandwiched between the chrome-trimmed showroom windows of Chelsey Ford Sales. Just down the street was Berry Drug, the upper story of which was occupied by George Franco. As Nolan glanced in one of the windows at a red Mustang he caught the reflection of a dark green Impala creeping along the street behind him, a familiar Neanderthal figure at its wheel. Nolan lifted his hand easily toward the .38 tucked beneath the left armpit of his sportscoat and looked in the reflecting glass to see what Tulip was going to do.

Tulip drove on.

Nolan straightened the collar of his pale yellow shirt, wondered absently if he should have worn a tie. He pressed the bell and placed his hand over the knob, waiting for the lock to let go. A buzz signaled its release and he pushed the door open.

She stood a full steep flight of stairs above him, displaying long, sleek legs below a blue miniskirt and she called out, "Come on up, Mr. Webb, come on up."

Nolan nodded and climbed the stairs. At the top he took the hand she held out to him and stepped into the loft apartment.

"Hello, Mr. Webb," she said warmly, "come in, please."

Her face was lovely, framed by long to-the-shoulder brown hair. She smiled invitingly and motioned him to a seat.

"Thanks," he said, refusing her gesture to take his sportscoat; she wouldn't be prepared to meet his .38.

"Drink?" she asked.

"Thanks no."

"Abstainer?"

"Just early."

"How about a beer?"

He nodded and she swept toward the bar, which was part of the kitchenette at the rear of the room. Nolan was sitting in an uncomfortable-looking comfortable modular chair; he glanced around the apartment. It was a single room, very spacious, the walls sporting impressionistic paintings, possibly originals. Overlooking the large room was a balcony divided in half between bedroom and artist's studio.

"How do you like it?"

"It's fine. You paint?"

"How'd you ever guess?" she laughed. "Yes, that's my work defiling the walls."

"Looks okay to me."

She came back with two chilled cans of malt liquor and stood in front of him, openly watching him. He took advantage of her sizing him up and did the same to her. She was a beautiful girl, the shoulder-length brown hair complemented by large, child-like brown eyes. Her body, well displayed in the blue mini and a short-sleeved clinging white knit sweater, was lean but shapely, with high, ample breasts that didn't quite go with her otherwise Twiggy-slender body. Her features were of an artistic, sensitive cast with a delicate, finely shaped nose and a soft-red blossom of a mouth.

Suddenly Nolan realized she was waiting for him to say something and the moment became slightly awkward.

He cleared his throat. "This really is a nice apartment."

"Thank you," she said, seating herself. "It's rather large for one person, and kind of spooky now that Irene is gone."

"I wonder if we could talk about Irene, if it doesn't bother you."

"No, that's all right…directly to business, I see, Mr. Webb?" She laughed gently. "Not much for small talk, are you?"

"No. Call me Earl, will you?"

"Of course, Earl." She looked at her hands, thinking to herself for a moment, then said, "I don't suppose small talk would fit your personality, would it? I mean, since I already feel as though I know you."

"How's that?"

"Irene spoke of you often."

Nolan's hand tightened around the glass. How could Irene Tisor have known the non-existent Earl Webb? "I never met Irene."

"Of course you have." She laughed again. "I'm afraid I'm teasing, aren't I?"

"I'm not much on humor, either."

"I don't know about that…Mr. Nolan."

Nolan didn't answer.

He reached over and gripped her hand and looked into her eyes and locked them with his. Fear took her face.

"I…I suppose…suppose you want me to explain."

"Yes."

She tried to smile, stay friendly, but his hard icy grip and the gray stone of his eyes froze her.

Her voice timid, forced, she said, "Irene and I, you see, were… extremely close…like sisters…"

She stopped to see if that explained anything, but all she got from Nolan was, "So?"

"Well, Mr. Nolan, she…she carried your picture in her billfold, all the time."

Nolan hadn't seen Irene Tisor for years, had hardly known her even then. There was no reason for her to carry him around with her. "Keep going, Vicki."

"She idolized you, Mr. Nolan."

"It's Webb and why should she idolize me?"

"She said she knew you when she was growing up. That you were a…gangster…but that you had gotten out. By defying your bosses."

"Suppose that's true. Suppose I did know her when she was a kid. Who was Irene Tisor that a 'gangster' would know her?"

"Her father…her father was one himself."

Nolan released her hand. "Okay, Vicki. Let's suppose some more. Let's suppose I did know Irene Tisor when she was growing up and her father was what you say he was. But let's also suppose I hadn't seen her for years and this part about me quitting the outfit didn't happen till eight months ago."

"She knew about it because her father helped you. Her father wasn't a very brave man, she told me, but he *had* helped you. She remembered it. It made an impression."

"How did she know?"

"Her father told her."

That was like Sid. Nolan nodded and said, "All right."

"All right what?"

"All right I believe you."

There was another awkward moment, then she managed, "Well?"

"Well what?"

"What are you going to do?"

He picked up the can of malt liquor and finished it. "Decide whether or not to kill you."

She sat back and let the air out of her as if someone had struck her in the stomach. She said, "Oh," and shut up and sat, worry crawling over her face.

"Don't sweat it," Nolan said, with a faint trace of a smile. "I'm deciding against it."

She sighed. Then, reprieve in hand, she attacked. "That's very big of you, you bastard!"

Nolan grinned at her flatly. "See? I do have a sense of humor."

She shook her head, not understanding him at all. Her eyes followed him as he rose and went to the door, opening it. She got up and joined him. She looked up at him with luminous brown eyes.

"Just my natural curiosity," she said, tilting her head, "but why?"

"Why what?"

"Why in hell did you decide thumbs up for this skinny broad? I thought hard guys like you always threw the likes of me to the lions."

Nolan hung onto the flat grin and shrugged. "I need you, for one thing."

"How about another?"

"Well, you're not the 'type' of person who ought to end up a casualty in the kind of war games I play. Anyway, I hate like hell to kill women."

"That's pretty goddamn chivalrous of you." She smiled, a mild in-shock smile. "Does that mean you plan to keep me out of your life?"

"Hardly. Later on I'm going to ask you if I can move in with you for a day to two."

That stopped her for a moment, then she got out a small, "Why?"

"I need a new place. There are some people who want to kill me and the motel I'm staying at now is getting to be a local landmark."

She touched his shoulder. "You're welcome to share this mausoleum with me for a while, Mr. Nolan."

"Webb, remember?"

"All right. Earl? Earl it is. Is that all you want? A place to stay, I mean?"

"There's more. I need information on Irene, of course."

"Of course. Is that all?"

"We'll see," he said. "You need a coat?"

"Yes, just a second." She came back with a bright pink trenchcoat and he helped her into it. She plopped a Bonnie Parker beret on her head and said, "You know the way to the Third Eye?"

He gave her half a grin. "You eat a mushroom or something, don't you?"

"Maybe I should lead the way," she said.

She led.

2

The Third Eye was a red two-story brick building along the Chelsey River, surrounded by a cement parking lot and assorted packs of young people, early teens to mid-twenties, milling about in cigarette-smoke clouds.

Nolan drove around front, in search of a parking place. He took a look at the brick building and said to Vicki Trask, who sat close by, "That looks about as psychedelic as an American Legion Hall."

She nodded and said, "Or a little red schoolhouse."

At a remote corner of the parking lot, Nolan eased the Lincoln into a place it shouldn't have fit and said, "What the hell's the occasion?"

"You mean the crowd?"

"Yeah. It always like this?" He turned off the ignition, leaned back and fired a cigarette. As an afterthought he offered one to Vicki and she took it, speaking as she lit it from the match Nolan extended to her.

"It's always crowded on nights when they have dances. The Eye runs four a week, and this is the biggest night of the four."

"Why?"

"Tonight's the night they let in the teeny-boppers. You'll see as many high-school age here as you will college, and one out of four of the hard-looking little broads you spot will be junior high."

"Why're the young ones restricted to one dance a week?"

"Because they run a bar—Beer Garden, they call it—on the other three nights. Serve beer and mixed drinks. And they serve anybody with enough money to buy."

"Drinking age in Illinois is twenty-one."

"Sure, but nobody cares. However, they don't serve booze on the night they open the dance to high-school and junior-high age. Chelsey's city fathers, pitiful guardians of virtue though they may be, even they would bitch about the Eye serving booze to that crowd."

Nolan nodded and drew on the cigarette. He looked out the car window and stared blankly at the river. He watched the water reflect the streetlights that ringed the entire area. The suggestion of a smile traced his lips.

"What are you thinking, Earl?"

"Nothing."

"Come on...don't tell me you couldn't use a friend. You're not that different from everybody else. Spill some emotion."

Nolan shifted his eyes from the river to the glowing tip of his cigarette. "Emotion is usually a messy thing to spill."

She edged closer, putting a warm hand against his cheek. "I'm lonely, too, Nolan."

His jaw tightened. "It's Webb."

She shook her head, turned away. "Okay, okay. Be an asshole."

He opened the car door and she slid out his side. He paused for a moment and looked out at the river again. It had reminded him of a private place of his, a cabin he maintained along a lake in Wisconsin, near a resort town. It was one of several places he kept up under the Earl Webb name, for the times between, the times of retreat from the game he played with the Boys. Even Nolan had need for moments of solitude, peace. He hadn't meant to hurt Vicki Trask, but he didn't know her well enough yet to share any secrets.

They walked along the riverfront, casually making their way toward the building a block away. They walked where the river water brushed up easily against the cement, lapping whitely at their feet. In spite of himself, Nolan found his hand squeezing hers and he smiled; she was lighting up warmly in response when Tulip stepped out from between two parked cars.

A scream caught in Vicki's throat as she watched the apeish figure rise up and raise his arm to strike Nolan with the butt of a revolver.

Nolan dropped to the cement, the gun butt swishing by, cutting the air, and shot a foot into Tulip's stomach. Tulip bounced backward and smashed against a red Chrysler, then slid to the pavement and lay still. Nolan picked the gun from Tulip's fingers and hefted it—a .38 Smith & Wesson. Tulip made a move to get up and Nolan kicked him in the head. Tulip leaned back against the Chrysler and closed his eyes.

Nolan shook his head, said, "When they're that stupid, they just don't learn," and tossed the gun out into the river.

They walked on toward the Eye, Nolan behaving as if nothing had happened. When they were half a block away from the entrance, she managed to breathlessly say, "Did...did you kill him?"

"Tulip?"

"Is that his name? Tulip?"

"Yes, that's his name, and no, I didn't kill him. I don't think."

She looked at him in fear and confusion and perhaps admiration and followed him toward the Eye.

There was a medium-sized neon sign over the door. It bore no lettering, just an abstract neon face with an extra eye in the center of its forehead. From the look of the brick, Nolan judged the building wasn't over a year old. The kids milling about the entrance were ill-kempt, long-haired and smoked with an enthusiasm that would have curdled the blood of the American Cancer Society. Nolan saw no open use of marijuana, but he couldn't rule it out—most all the kids were acting somewhat out of touch with reality.

Inside the door they pushed through a narrow hallway that was crowded with young girls, most of them thirteen-year-olds with thirty-year-old faces. One, who could have been twelve, extended her non-existent breasts to Nolan in offering, giving him a smirky pouty come-on look. Nolan gave her a gentle nudge and moved past with Vicki through the corridor.

At the end of the hall they came to a card table where a guy sat taking money. He looked like an ex-pug, was around thirty-five and had needed a shave two days before. Nolan looked at him carefully and paid the two-fifty per couple admission. Nolan smiled at the ex-pug, a phony smile Vicki hadn't seen him use before, and moved on. Nolan followed Vicki as she went by a set of closed, windowless double doors, then trailed her down a flight of steps.

"Where the doors lead?"

"To the dance floor and Beer Garden."

"Oh."

She led him through two swinging doors into a shoddy room, cluttered with a dozen wooden tables.

"This it?" Nolan asked.

"Don't let it fool you," she told him, leading him to a small table by the wall, "the food's not bad at all."

Nolan looked around. The room was poorly lit and the walls concrete, painted black. The naked black concrete was partially dressed by pop-art paintings, Warhol and Lichtenstein prints and a few framed glossies, autographed, of big-time rock groups like the Jefferson Airplane and Vanilla Fudge. The tables were plain wood, black-painted and without cloths, and each was lit with a thick white candle stuck down into a central hole. The far end of the room, the bar, was better lighted, and the doors into the kitchen on either side of it let out some light once in a while. Other than that the room was a black sea of glowing red cigarette tips.

Nolan lit a fresh cigarette for both of them and they joined the sea of floating red spots.

"You notice the guy taking money as we came in upstairs?"

She nodded. "The one who looked like a prizefighter?"

"That's the one."

"What about him?"

"I used to know him."

"What? When did you know him?"

"A few years back. In Chicago." He looked at her meaningfully.

"You mean you knew him when you worked for…ah…"

"Yeah."

"Did he recognize you?"

"Hell no," Nolan said. "He doesn't recognize himself in a mirror. Punchy. Surprises the hell out of me he makes change."

"What's he doing here?"

Nolan stared out into the darkness and said, "You tell me."

"How?"

"Start with the man who runs this place."

"The manager, you mean?"

"Not the manager. The owner."

"As a matter of fact…I *have* heard the owner's name. I've heard Broome mention it. It's Francis, or something like that."

"Franco?"

"Yes, I think that's it."

Nolan withheld a smile. "Fat George."

"I believe his first name is George, at that."

A waitress came to the table, put down paper placemats and gave them water and silverware. She handed them menus and rolled back the paper on her order blank.

Vicki asked for a steak sandwich, dinner salad and coffee, and Nolan followed suit. They ordered drinks for their wait, Vicki a Tom Collins, Nolan bourbon and water.

Nolan sat, deep in thought, not noticing the silence maintained between them until the drinks arrived five minutes later.

Vicki cupped her drink, looking down into it, and said, "Do you want me to talk about Irene now?"

"That'd be fine."

"Well…she was wild, Earl, not real bad or anything, but a little wild…I guess you could blame that on her father."

"He isn't what I'd call wild."

"But…isn't he…a gangster?"

"The deadliest weapon Sid Tisor ever held was a pencil."

"Oh. Well, anyway, Irene and I used to be quite close. You have to be, to live together, share an apartment and all. Both of us were artistic, using that same balcony studio in the apartment. Some of those paintings on the apartment walls are hers. Once in a while she wouldn't show up at night, she'd sleep over with some guy or other—no special one, there were several—but that was no big deal, I'm no virgin either. It was just this year that it started getting

kind of bad. Not with guys or anything. It was when she started
getting in tight with some of these would-be hippies. I went along
with a lot of it, because some of these people are witty and pretty
articulate. Fun to be with. For example, they meet upstairs here
during the day, and put articles and cartoons and stuff together
and put out a weekly underground-style newspaper, called the
Third Eye."

"What you're trying to say is they're not idiots."

"Right. I'm friendly with some of them. If you leaf through
some back copies of the *Eye* you'll see some of my artwork. But
not all of these Chelsey hippies are well, benign. Some of them are
hangers-on, bums, drop-outs, acid-heads. Like this Broome creep
who runs the band here. Irene fell in with characters like Broome
this last month or so, and I saw less and less of her…she was exper-
imenting that final week or so, with pills mostly. And she kept
saying, threatening kind of, that she was going to try an LSD trip."

"And?"

"She did, I guess."

"You think it was suicide?"

"Her death? I think it was an accident."

"Oh."

"You sound almost disappointed, Earl."

"To tell you the truth, Vicki, I don't give a damn one way or
another. I'm just doing Sid Tisor a favor."

She looked at him, shocked for a moment. "But you knew her,
didn't you? Don't you care what happened to her?"

He shrugged. "She's dead. It begins and ends there. Nothing
brings her back, it's all a waste of time."

She squinted at him, obviously straining to figure him out. "You
came to this stinking little town to risk your life when you think it's
a waste of time?"

Nolan drew on the cigarette. "You don't understand. It's a debt
I'm paying. Also, there's a chance for me to make some money off
the local hoods. But I'm not doing this for me, I'm doing it for Sid
Tisor. He cares, and that's what counts."

"Because you owe him."

"Because I owe him."

Their meals were brought to them and they ate casually, speaking very little. She watched him, beginning to understand him better.

He paid the check and they went upstairs.

3

The large gymnasium-sized room was filled with cigarette smoke, unpleasant odors and grubbily dressed kids. Nolan stood with Vicki at the entrance and looked around, over the bobbing heads.

The black concrete walls were covered with psychedelic designs, varicolored, abstract, formless but somehow sensual, done in fluorescent paints. The lighting consisted of rows of tubular blacklight hanging from the ceiling; a strobe the size of a garbage can lid was suspended from the ceiling's center, but it was turned off at the moment. At one end of the room, to the left of the double doors, was a shabby-looking bar with an overhead sign that read "Beer Garden." It was open for business but serving soft drinks only. The other end of the room was engulfed by a huge, high-ceilinged stage piled with rock group equipment.

"Let's take a look," Nolan said.

Vicki nodded agreement and pushed through the crowd with Nolan till they reached the foot of the stage.

On stage were three massive amplifiers that looked to Nolan like black refrigerators. A double set of drums was perched on a tall platform, and various guitars were lying about as if discarded. An organ, red and black with chrome legs, faced out to the audience showing its reverse color black and white keyboard. Boom stands extended microphones over the organ and drums, and upright stands held three other mikes for the guitarists and lead singer. The voice amplification was evidently hooked up to two large horns the size of those found in football stadiums.

Vicki said, "You look at that stuff as though you know something about it."

"I do," Nolan told her. "Been everything from bouncer to manager in all kinds of clubs. You get to know musicians and their equipment."

"What does that equipment tell you?"

"They have money," he said, "and they're going to be too god-damn loud."

She laughed and a voice from behind them said, "That, my friend, is a matter of opinion."

They turned and faced a six-foot figure resembling a coat-rack hung with garish clothes. The coat-rack spoke again, in a thick, unconvincing British accent. "Aren't you going to introduce me to the gent, Miss Trask?"

She began to answer, but Nolan shushed her. "I can guess," he said, looking the coat-rack up and down.

The boy was emaciated, the sunken-cheeked Rolling Stone type that shouted drug use. His hair was kinky-curly and ratted, making him look like a freaked-out Little Orphan Annie. His face was a collection of acne past and present, and the sunkenness of his cheeks was accented by a pointed nose and deep-socketed eyes that were a glazed sky-blue. He wore a grimy scarlet turtleneck with an orange fluorescent vest and a tarnished gold peace sign hung around his neck on a sweat-stained leather thong. His pants were black-and-white checked and hung loose, bell-bottomed, coming in skin-tight at the crotch.

"You're Broome."

A yellow smile flashed amiably. "Right you are, man."

"Who picks out your threads," Nolan asked, gesturing at Broome's outfit, "Stevie Wonder?"

Broome's laugh was as phony as his English accent. "You can't bum me out, dad. I groove out at everything, everybody, every-where. Bum *me* out? No way—I'm too happy, man."

Nolan looked into Broome's filmy, dilated eyes and silently agreed. "When you play your next set?"

Broome pulled a sleeve back, searched his wrist frantically for his watch, which turned out to be vintage Mickey Mouse on a loose strap. "In five, man, in five."

Vicki pointed Nolan to the stage where the rest of Broome's band was onstage already, four boys just as freakishly attired as

Broome but apparently less wigged-out—they were tuning up, generally preparing to begin their next set. Teeny-boppers crowded in around the stage, shoving to get as close to the band as possible, and consequently pushing Nolan, Vicki and Broome into a corner to the left of the stage.

Broome was small-talking with Vicki and getting a cold-shoulder in return, Nolan having turned his back on both of them to watch the band set up. From the corner of his eye Nolan saw Broome light up a joint.

Nolan said, "That one of the things that makes you so happy?"

Broome lifted his shoulders and set them back down. "It helps a little, dad, you know?"

"I know."

Broome spoke to Vicki. "I didn't catch your friend's name, love. What is it?"

"His name is Webb," she told him. "Earl Webb."

Broome looked at Nolan and something flickered behind the gone eyes. After a moment's hesitation, he said, "I hear you get around, Mr. Webb, is that right? Do you get around?"

"I get around. How about you, Broome? Ever hear of Irene Tisor?"

Broome's face tightened like a fist. "Maybe I have, Mr. Webb, maybe I have. So what?"

"What do you know about her?"

"She's dead, haven't you heard?"

"I heard." Nolan smiled, the phony smile this time. "You just smoke that stuff, or do you sell it, too?"

"Hey, dad, I'm a musician."

"Yeah, right. Who sold Irene Tisor that hit of acid? Whose music was she dancing to when she did her swan dive into the concrete?"

Broome dropped his joint to the floor and stomped it out, his face a scowl and in one motion thrust his middle finger in Nolan's face defiantly.

"Make love not war," Nolan reminded him.

Broome farted with his mouth and hopped up onto the stage, joining his band, keeping an aloof air when speaking to the other members, and mumbled "One, two, test" into his mike. He gave the band four beats with his booted heel and they roared into a long, loud freaky version of a rhythm and blues number called "In the Midnight Hour." The amps screamed as if in pain, emitting feedback and distortion, while Broome tried to sound black, crouching over the microphone, as if making a kind of obscene love to it. The Gurus, his four man back-up band, seemed vaguely embarrassed by him, with the exception of the bass player, a blond youngster who wore a pageboy.

Toward the middle of the first number, somebody turned on the ceiling strobe, which flickered, flashed, making everything look like an acid-head's version of a silent movie.

Nolan said, close to her ear, "I've had enough. I won't get anything out of Broome. Not in public."

Vicki followed Nolan as he burrowed through the crowd toward the doors. Above the deafening music she shouted, "Didn't you get anything out of this evening?"

Nolan waited till they were in the hallway with the double-doors closed behind them before he answered. "I got a few things out of it. Saw some pot being smoked, and not just Broome. Did you smell it? Bittersweet, kind of. And I'd put a thousand bucks down that Broome is an addict."

"An addict? Can you get addicted to LSD?"

"LSD, my ass. He's riding the big horse. Heroin."

"Heroin? Are you kidding?"

"I don't kid much, Vicki. He may have Mickey Mouse on his wrist, but he's got needle tracks on his arm."

They moved back through the hallway, past the ex-pug who still didn't recognize Nolan, and out into the open air. Just as they started to walk away from the Eye, Nolan spotted a familiar face— Lyn Parks, whom he'd last seen in her apartment, as she sat naked, painting a flower 'round her navel. As she went through the door

she caught Nolan's eye; she said nothing but her smile said everything.

Touch of jealousy in her voice, Vicki said, "They all give you the
eye don't they, teeny-boppers on up?"

"Sure," Nolan said. "Even Broome."

They walked back to the Lincoln and drove to Nolan's motel.

4

Nolan pulled the Lincoln up to the Travel Nest's office, where through the glass he could see Barnes, the manager, at the desk inside.

"I'm going to pick up some of my things," he told Vicki, "and see to it the manager keeps my room vacant and my name on the register for the next few days."

"But you'll really be staying with me?" she asked.

"Right."

She leaned forward and caught his arm as he began to get out of the car. He glanced back and she moved forward and they kissed. A brief kiss, with a touch of warmth, of promise. He squeezed her thigh and climbed out of the Lincoln.

He had barely gone through the door and into the motel office when an ashen-faced Barnes started babbling.

"I'm sorry, Mr. Webb, they made me let them in, believe me, I couldn't help it...."

Nolan grabbed him by the lapel. "What the hell are you talking about?"

"Those policemen...they made me let them in...."

"What policemen?"

"The officers who searched your room last night!"

Nolan said, "Plainclothes? One tall and fat, the other short and dressed for shit?"

"That's right, that's them."

Tulip and Dinneck. That was how they had gotten into his room last night, before the pool skirmish. He hadn't bothered to check with Barnes; he'd assumed Dinneck and Tulip had gotten in on their own.

"Why the hell did you let 'em in?"

"They had a search warrant...I...I couldn't refuse them."

Nolan let him go. Of course. Of course they'd have a warrant. That financial secretary of George's, that Elliot, had a cousin for a police chief. A guy named Saunders. No trouble getting Dinneck and Tulip a police cover and a search warrant.

"Okay," Nolan said. "It wasn't your fault. But you should've told me about it later."

Barnes was dripping sweat; his bald blushing head looked like a shiny, water-pearled apple. "I was afraid, Mr. Webb, I'll…I'll tell you the truth. They told me you were a killer, a dangerous psychopath."

Knowing that Barnes was high-strung, scared easily and would bite almost any line fed him, Nolan leaned over the desk and looked the manager in the eye.

"What I'm about to tell you is confidential, Mr. Barnes," he said. "I need your sacred oath that you won't repeat the following to anyone."

Barnes was confused, but he nodded.

Nolan continued. "I'm an FBI special agent, investigating the illegal sale of hallucinatory drugs here in Chelsey."

Nolan could see in Barnes' face that he bought it. It rang true to Barnes; there was a lot of funny business about drugs in Chelsey. He believed Nolan.

Just as Nolan was ready to hand more FBI bullshit to him, Barnes' eyes lit up like flares and he began to shake.

"What's wrong?"

"Have…have you been up to your room yet? You have, haven't you, Mr. Webb?" Barnes shook like a bridegroom at a shotgun wedding.

"No, I haven't. What the hell's wrong with you?"

"Then you better get up there quick! I told you they made me do it!"

"What are you talking about?"

"They came in again tonight, didn't you know? I thought that was why you barged in here!"

He grabbed Barnes by the lapel again. "When?"

"Ten minutes before you came in, Mr. Webb...I thought you knew...."

"Damn!"

Nolan turned and ran to the door, spoke over his shoulder to Barnes. "Keep everybody away from that room as long as you can. No cops—they're crooked!"

"Should I call your superiors..."

"Don't phone anybody, don't do anything. Just keep your mouth shut."

Nolan flew out of the office, sprinted to the Lincoln and pulled open the door. "I got visitors in my room, Vicki. Sit tight till I get back. Be alert and make a fast exit if things start looking grim."

He left her with her mouth open, left before she could stop him to ask questions. He ran lightly across the motel lot and stood in an empty parking space beneath the balcony of his room. He looked up. The lights were on inside, shadows moved behind the curtained windows of the French doors leading from balcony to room. Nolan put his hands in the iron grating and his grip crumbled the crisp brown remains of the vined flowers that had climbed the trellis before the air had chilled. He tested the grating and it felt firm. He inched up slowly, the metal X's cutting into his hands; only the very ends of his shoe toes would fit into the X's, and they provided unsure footing. He edged his way up the iron trellis and in a minute and a half that seemed much longer, he found himself parallel to the balcony.

Clamping one hand tightly in one of the grating openings, Nolan withdrew his .38 from the underarm holster and slipped one leg up and over the side of the balcony. He fought for balance, shifted his weight and landed on the balcony cat-silent.

Nolan faced the four-windowed French doors and watched the shifting shadows on the curtains. He peered through the crack between the doors and saw Dinneck sitting in a chair with his back to Nolan, tossing things from a suitcase over his shoulders, angry because he wasn't finding anything. Tulip had stripped the bed and was in the process of gutting the mattress with a stiletto.

Dumb bastards, Nolan thought. The room hadn't told them anything the night before and tonight wouldn't be any different. Well, a little different maybe.

Nolan slammed his shoulder into the French doors and they snapped open. He kicked Dinneck's chair in the seat, turning it over on him. Nolan leapt on the chair, heard bones and wood crack simultaneously, and sat on it, pinning Dinneck beneath. He leveled the .38 at Tulip, who stopped frozen, knife over mattress, with the bug-eyed expression of a punk caught stealing hubcaps.

"Raise them, Tulip," Nolan ordered. "Slow and easy and no games with the knife."

If Nolan hadn't mentioned the stiletto, Tulip probably wouldn't have remembered it, but Nolan had and Tulip did. Like a reflex Tulip whipped the knife behind his ear and let it fly. Nolan ducked, losing control of the overturned chair, and hit the floor. Behind him the stiletto quivered in the wood paneling. Nolan fired the .38 at a fleeing Tulip, caught him in the arm with the shot, which spun him around and sat him down.

That put Dinneck out of Nolan's mind just long enough for the man to crawl out from under the smashed chair and step up behind Nolan.

And when Nolan remembered Dinneck, it was too late to matter. He turned and saw the toe coming at his face and when he tried to turn away it caught him in the temple and things went black.

He woke thirty-some seconds later and stared into the barrel of his .38, which was now in Dinneck's hand. Tulip was sitting a few feet away on the partially gutted bed, whimpering, mumbling. "Need it, Dinneck, I tell ya I need it bad…let's just finish him and get out, huh? What d'ya say?"

Nolan looked past the gun barrel and into Dinneck's cold, uncompromising eyes.

Nolan said, "What's Tulip need, Dinneck?"

"Shut up."

Tulip was rubbing his mutilated arm. The bullet had caught him in the lower shoulder and he was stroking below the wound.

The blood from his shoulder was all over his hands and partially on his tear-streaked face, where he'd tried to wipe the moisture from his eyes. He was moaning, "I need some, gotta shoot up, need it bad, real bad...."

"He need a fix, Dinneck?" Nolan asked.

"Shut your goddamn mouth, Webb."

"Little shot of heroin?"

"I said shut up, you son of a bitch!"

"Where's Tulip getting his heroin, Dinneck? Is it..."

Dinneck interrupted Nolan by slamming the barrel of the .38 into Nolan's temple again, then smashing him across the mouth with it.

Nolan's body went limp, but he wasn't out. His mouth, his lips felt like a bloody wad of pulp, but he wasn't out. His temple ached, his head pounded, but he sat back and waited to make his move. He sat back and waited and watched Dinneck's eyes.

Tulip seemed excited, the pain momentarily forgotten. "Let *me* shoot 'im, Dinneck—let ol' Tulip put him to sleep forever—"

Dinneck smiled and shook his head. "Sorry, pal. I got a special grudge against Mr. Webb here."

Tulip stood up, clutching his bloodied arm. "*You* got a grudge! Last night that bastard set me on my ass every time I turned around, he knocked out one of my teeth, and a coupla hours ago he kicked me in the fuckin' head! Now he half shoots off my fuckin' arm and *you* gotta grudge."

"Sit down," Dinneck said, "and shut up."

Tulip sat, frowning, caressing the wounded arm again, and Dinneck consoled him with, "Take it easy, man, I'll see you get your shot, don't worry, stay cool. Let me handle it."

Nolan had been looking past Dinneck's tacky clothes and into the authority of his face, the competence of his actions, the hardness of eyes that spoke professionalism. Nolan told himself he'd misjudged Dinneck, whose dress and even manner to a degree had been calculated to elicit such misjudgment. Beyond that, Nolan saw a coldness in Dinneck, and a need to inflict pain.

"I read you wrong, Dinneck," Nolan said.

Intrigued by the comment in spite of himself, Dinneck said, "What?" Then remembering his previous commands to Nolan he said, "Just keep your mouth shut while I figure what to do with you."

"Who are you, Dinneck?" Nolan asked.

"I told you to shut your mouth."

"Tulip, how long's Dinneck been working with you? He been in town very long? How long's he been with Elliot and Franco?"

"You're only making it tougher on yourself, Webb," Dinneck told him evenly.

Tulip's face showed the strain of thought, then he said, "He's only been with us about two, maybe three months. He's somebody the Boys sent in from upstate somewhere."

Nolan looked at Dinneck again. "Who are you?"

"Just keep trying my patience, Webb, keep going at it...."

"You some kind of Family inside man, checking up? Just who the hell are..."

Dinneck's face exploded into a red mask, veins standing out on his forehead like a relief map. He raised the gun up over Nolan's head and brought it down fast.

But not fast enough. Nolan sent a splintering left that caught Dinneck below the left eye and followed with a full right swing into his throat. Dinneck rolled on his back, wrapping his hands around his throat, and he tried to scream in pain but that only made it worse. Nolan tromped down on Dinneck's wrist and the man released his grip on Nolan's .38—he'd forgotten it anyway.

Nolan stood over the sprawling figure, leveling the retrieved .38 at Tulip, who had sat back down on the bed.

"You didn't have to hit him in the throat, did you?" Tulip's voice was like a child's; he wasn't holding onto his arm anymore and the blood on it was beginning to turn a dry brown. "You didn't have to hit his throat. It still hurts him from this morning when some broad hit him there. What a hell of a place to hit him. You sure are a mean son of a bitch, Webb." Tulip shook his head.

"You and Dinneck came to the wrong man for sympathy," Nolan told him. "He should've got his tonsils out some other day."

"What are you gonna do now?"

Nolan didn't answer Tulip. He lifted a barely conscious Dinneck by the collar and dragged him to the can, keeping one eye (and the .38) on Tulip all the while. Nolan dumped Dinneck in the tub, turned on the shower full blast, on cold, and pulled the shower curtain down over his head.

"You sure are a mean s.o.b.," Tulip repeated.

"It'll relax him," Nolan said.

Nolan left Dinneck in the tub, shower curtains around him and shower going on full, ice-cold. Dinneck was a mass of whining, hysterical pain, fighting the shower curtain and the cold with what was left of his will. Nolan shut the bathroom door.

"I bet you could use a shot, couldn't you, Tulip?"

"Mean s.o.b., sure are a mean s.o.b...."

"How long you been riding that horse, Tulip?"

"...mean s.o.b., you sure a..."

Nolan gave up on getting any information out of Tulip; at the moment the big man was practically catatonic and talking to him was a waste of time. Besides, pretty soon Barnes would get worried enough to call the cops, despite Nolan's advice to the contrary, what with the gunshot and all the violent noises that had been coming from the room. He wondered if Vicki had taken off. She should have.

He collected his things, picked his suitcase up off the floor and hastily re-packed it, got his clothes-bags too. He rubbed his temple; his head was still pounding like hell, but his balance was okay. A few aspirin would help the head as long as there wasn't a concussion. His mouth was bleeding and hurt like a bastard, but he ran a hand over it and didn't think he would need stitches.

Out in the hall, he could hear a muffled Tulip in there saying "Mean s.o.b." over and over. Nolan lugged his suitcase and clothes-bags thinking he could have been a lot meaner than he'd been. He wouldn't have lost much sleep over killing that pair.

The Lincoln was indeed waiting and he walked easily over to it. Vicki was at the wheel, the engine running. He got in the rider's side, tossed his things in back.

When she saw him her eyes rolled wide and she gasped. "What happened! Your face, your mouth…"

"Hard day at the office," he said. "Beat it the hell out of here."

Sometimes, when insomnia hit him and he spent half the night fighting for sleep, Phil Saunders almost wished his wife were alive.

This was a night like that. He'd gone to bed at twelve, as soon as the late-night talk show had signed off. Now it was two-thirty and he was still awake.

Yes, too bad, in a way, his wife wasn't alive any more.

At least if she were there she could have bitched him to sleep.

Now there was no one. No one to talk to, have sex with, live with. A little old-fashioned nagging never killed anybody. At least you weren't alone.

Not that it was bad, living alone here. He had a nice apartment, six rooms, luxury plus. And very nicely furnished, too, in a conservative sort of way. But then, Phil was a conservative sort of person, outwardly upright, honest. But on the inside? Life had grown a sour taste lately.

A year and a half ago life had been sweet. A year and a half ago when he had been Police Commissioner of Havens, New Jersey, a legit aboveboard job he'd worked his ass off over the years to get. A year and a half ago his wife had been a drying-up prune he put up with out of habit and for appearance sake. A year and a half ago his affair with Suzie Van Plett, that succulent soft little seventeen-year-old, had been in full bloom.

Too bad his wife had walked in on him and Suzie that time. There's nothing like the sight of a naked seventeen-year-old blonde sitting on the lap of a naked forty-nine-year-old balding police commissioner to give a really first-rate instantaneous and fatal heart attack to a fully-clothed fifty-two-year-old gray-haired police commissioner's wife. Then the reporters, the disgrace, the friends deserting him, the question of statutory rape in the air and finally the humiliating midnight escape.

His name had been different then, but it died with his wife and his reputation in Havens. He turned to his cousin, a longtime con artist going by the name Irwin Elliot. Elliot had a sweet set-up going in Chelsey, Illinois, through the Chicago crime syndicate. Cousin Elliot was good at documents and he forged the defrocked Havens police commissioner a good set of references, pulled the proper strings, opened and closed the right mouths, and the newly named Phil Saunders sprang to life, full-grown at birth. He filled the puppet role of Chelsey Police Chief and watched his cousin Elliot control the town as the brains behind another puppet, that fat fool George Franco, who was a brother of some Chicago mob guy.

It was a rich life, and an easy one.

But there were no succulent seventeen-year-olds in his Chelsey life, nor would there be, on Cousin Elliot's orders.

Just a conservatively furnished six-room apartment that even his dead wife could have brightened with her presence. At least if his wife were around there would be someone not to listen to, not to talk with.

The door buzzer sounded, startling Saunders. Then, knowing who it would be, he went to the door and opened it.

He smiled and said, "Hi, buddy," and then he noticed the .38 in his visitor's hand.

The gun went to his temple, the visitor fired and Saunders joined his wife.

Lyn Parks had been with Broome long enough. He was a lousy bed partner, he smelled bad and his manners were nonexistent.

They were in the backstage dressing room at the Third Eye, and it was three o'clock in the morning. Broome had been trying desperately to get her to come across since after the band's last set and his failure was getting him angry, despite the fact that he'd shot up with horse a few minutes before and should have been feeling quite good by now.

"Get your goddamn hands off me!" She shook her head in disgust with him, with herself. "You're really a sickening bastard, Broome, and it's pretty damn revolting to me to think I ever let you touch me."

"Come on, babe, you ain't no cherry...." He groped for her and she was sick of it. After seeing him shoot up with H—he'd never had the poor taste before to shoot up right in front of her—she was almost physically ill with the thought of her few months of close association with the man. She was ready to move on—life with Broome and these sick creeps was worse than life with her father, "One Thumb" Gordon, a gangster who pretended respectability. She hated phonies, like her father, and she hated Broome as well, for his brand of phoniness.

"You aren't anything but a pusher, Broome," she told him bitterly. "Flower power? Some of the kids in this town are on the level with their peace and love, but you...you're a bum, a peddler, a cheap gangster worse than my father ever was."

"Your father? Who's your father?" Broome wasn't having much luck with trying to speak, everything was coming out slurred.

It was disgusting to Lyn, this rolling around with a doped-up lowlife on a threadbare sofa in a backstage people closet with dirty wooden floors and graffitied walls. Broome was no threat, he was already on the verge of incoherence, sliding into dreaminess. She started for the door.

Then heard the footsteps.

Somebody banged on the door.

Fear caught her by the throat and she instinctively ducked in the bathroom, where Broome had so often shot up, his works still on the sink.

She heard Broome mumble something out there, maybe a greeting. A few more words.

Then a gunshot.

Kneeling tremblingly, she peered through the keyhole and saw a person she recognized pocket a revolver and turn and go. She waited three long minutes before opening the closet wide enough to see Broome, lying on his back like a broken doll, his freaky blond

Orphan Annie curls splattered with blood and brains, skull split by a bullet.

She puked in the sink.

She wiped the tears from her eyes, found control of her retching stomach, wondered what to do...

Webb.

That was it, she had to find Webb.

He could do something about this.

At least he could take her away from it....

She ran.

George Franco was pissed, in several senses of the word.

He sat by the window and stared down the block at the extended sign of Chelsey Ford Sales, the building he'd seen Nolan enter several times during the day—the last time around midnight with a pretty girl, a girl George thought he recognized.

It was too late to be drinking, but George was. He sat in his red and white striped nightshirt like a colorful human beach ball and nursed a bottle of Haig and Haig.

That fucker Nolan. Who did he think he was, pushing George around? And why hadn't Nolan called? One whole day gone since he and Nolan had made their pact, with Nolan saying he'd check in every now and then. Well, why the hell didn't he?

George had decided he wanted a favor from Nolan—in return for keeping quiet about the thief's presence in Chelsey. It was only fair...and it would be a favor that Nolan would get something out of in return....

George swigged the Scotch, looking out at the blank street, the naked benches by the courthouse cannons. He didn't see anybody watching him; Nolan said he had three men taking turns watching George, only now George wasn't so sure. The tower clock read three-fifteen, but George wasn't tired. He was all worked up. And he was thirsty.

It had come to him tonight, how he could use Nolan to better his position. To make his brother Charlie reconsider his opinion of

George; to have some responsibility again. To get rid of that smug bastard Elliot and have the last laugh....

If he could only remember that girl's name! That girl who'd been with Nolan, it was *her* apartment they'd gone into!

He'd met her once in the drugstore below. She was a friendly little thing, she said she'd seen him and she guessed they were neighbors and how was he? But that was a long time ago, a year or so, and he couldn't remember....

Vicki something.

More Scotch. It would help him remember, more Scotch...

Trask.

Vicki Trask.

He waddled to the phone book, a pregnant hippo in a night-shirt, and thumbed through the pages.

Sure it was late, and Nolan would be pissed, but that was just too bad. He couldn't push a Franco! Why, George could have his brother and an army down from Chicago in a few hours, with just a snap of his fingers! He could erase Nolan, have him wiped out like a chalk drawing on a blackboard! It was that easy.

He dialed. Nolan would talk to him, he knew he would.

It rang a long while and a female voice answered. He asked to speak to Mr. Webb and she said just a minute.

He waited for Nolan to come to the phone. The female voice had been pleasant. Like his whore's, Francie, only more sincere. He'd been mean to Francie today, edgy over the thing with Nolan, and she'd walked out mad. He'd called her twice and asked her to come back and let him try and make it up to her. She'd hung up both times, but he still hoped she'd show. Maybe he could patch things up with dollars and Scotch.

Then Nolan was on the phone.

"Yes, I know it's late, Mr. Nolan...sorry, Mr. *Webb*...but I have to talk with you...I can help you take Elliot down...."

There was a soft rap at the door.

George said, "Just a second, Nolan, I mean *Webb*...the door, I think my girlfriend might be back, jus' a second."

George stumbled to the door, thinking to himself about how fine it would be to see his Francie at the moment, have a nice drink with her.

He opened the door and an orange-red blossom exploded in somebody's hand and burst George's head and he went down, a sinking barge.

Four

Nolan reached out in the darkness and stroked the sleeping girl's breast. She stirred in her sleep, a smile playing on her lips. He ran his hand under the sheet and over her smooth body, over her thighs to the flat stomach, across the soft rises of breast, nipples now relaxed, the tightness of passion a memory.

Vicki Trask's eyes opened slowly; then blinking, yawning, she said, "Are you still awake? It must be after two in the morning—"

Nolan flipped back the sheet. He took a gentle bite out of her stomach, nuzzling her. His lower lip cradled the dip of her navel, his upper lip tickled by the tiny hairs on her flesh.

"Salty," he said.

"Hmm?"

"You taste salty."

"I ought to," she replied. "You worked me hard enough."

"It's good for you." He moved up to her breasts and nibbled. The tips, remembering, grew taut again.

"Ouch! Take it easy!" Then she laughed and looped her arm around his neck.

He looked into her little-girl face and said, "You were good, Vicki."

The faint light from a street lamp poured through a circular window into the balcony and gave her skin a glow, an almost mystical look, like a textured photograph. She sat up in bed and propped her knees up and rested her chin on them, locking her hands around her legs. She stared at him, her smile slight.

"You were wonderful," she told him. "I…I never felt so much a woman before." She leaned over and brushed her lips across his cheek.

"You're a woman all right," he said. Not entirely true, but she had been a lot less girl than Nolan had expected.

Boredom from the so far sleepless night mixed with the infrequency of sexual activity in his life of late tempted Nolan to go another round with the girl. She'd admitted she wasn't a virgin, but she'd been close to one, and he didn't want to press her unduly.

But then her lips were on his chest and her fingers had found their way to his back, where they were digging in. She looked at him, resting her head against his chest, her expression one of sweet shame, asking him if…? He reached his arms around her and covered her mouth with his.

Twenty minutes later Nolan was sitting in the dark smoking, his back against the headboard, his mind adrift. His left arm was around her shoulder, his hand cupping a breast. The other arm rested on the nightstand by the bed, where he'd laid his unholstered .38. Vicki had floated into sleep a few minutes before, but he remained awake beside her, thinking and smoking, smoking and thinking…

Around three A.M. Vicki awoke suddenly and found Nolan still sitting back against the headboard with the fourth, maybe fifth cigarette tight in his lips. His gray eyes were open, two dead coals in the darkness.

"What's the matter? What is it? Why are you still up?"

He didn't look at her. "Have to be leaving soon."

"Is it getting to be dangerous for you to stay around Chelsey, or what?"

"No, that's not it…it's always like that for me. It's just that I got a feeling there's nothing here that needs to be found out about Irene Tisor."

Her hands played with the blanket. "When do you have to leave?"

"Soon, I said." He had to figure a way to hit the Chelsey operation first—he had to get his hands on this Elliot guy and make his hit for the cash on hand and the hell with Chelsey and Sid Tisor's dead kid.

"Will I see you again? After you leave Chelsey?"

"Sure."

"You're not telling the truth."

There was no answer to that.

She buried her head in his chest and he felt her tears on his flesh.

He smoothed her hair. It was soft and fragrant. "Don't pretend to yourself that you want me to stay."

"What do you mean?"

"I mean I'm one or two nights in your life and that's all I am. Accept me that way."

She studied him, her eyes moist. "You know something, Nolan? No, don't object to me calling you Nolan, you're not Earl Webb you're Nolan and in my bed I'll call you Nolan if I damn well please. I have you pretty well figured out. You walk around like a mobile brick wall. So cold, the ice forms on your shoulders. And you know what you are under all that ice, Nolan?"

"You tell me."

"You're all the emotions you despise to show. You're like that gun over there. You're a hunk of metal until you get in a demanding situation, then you explode. I've been with you only a few hours, but I've seen you kick a man in the head and later come out of your motel room looking like you just wrestled a grizzly and won. And I've shared my bed with you, and you were tender enough, I guess, but that damn gun of yours remained on the nightstand beside you all the while. Anybody as violent as you, and as passionate, is a fire-bomb of emotion. Now...what do you think about that?"

He was silent for a moment. Then said, "I think you talk too much."

She laughed her warm laugh and nodded that she guessed he was right and leaned her head against his shoulder.

"You going to stay in Chelsey, Vicki?"

"I don't know," she said. "I have...have a problem or two that may keep me here."

"It's your business," Nolan shrugged.

She smiled. "I guess you think I was out of line a minute ago with my dimestore psychology. Now here I am keeping secrets from you. But…everybody needs a few secrets."

"Sure."

The phone rang.

"Who the hell would call you at this hour?"

"Nobody."

"You better get it."

"Are you here, Nolan?"

"Earl Webb is."

"Okay…"

"Careful," he told her. "Too goddamn late for a phone call. It's going to mean something, whatever it is."

"Even a wrong number?" She laughed.

"Answer it before they give up."

She climbed out of bed and threw a filmy negligee over her creamy-white skin. She flew down the spiral staircase that connected the balcony to the living room and grabbed up the phone, which was on the bar in the kitchenette. Upstairs, Nolan leaned back and took a cigarette from the half-empty pack and popped it into his mouth.

From below, her voice came, "It's for you, Earl."

He got out of bed, slipped into his pants and shoes and went down the spiral staircase, taking his .38 with him.

"This is Webb."

"This is George, George Franco…"

"What do you want, George? A little late for you to be up, isn't it?"

"Yes, I know it's late, Mr. Nolan…"

"Webb."

"Sorry, Mr. *Webb*…but I have to talk to you!"

"About what?"

"I can help you take Elliot down."

There was a hesitation at Franco's end.

"What's wrong, George?"

"Just a second, Nolan, I mean *Webb,* the door, I think my girl-friend might be back. Jus' a second."

There was silence and Nolan looked at Vicki and said, "Think he's been into the cooking sherry again."

She smiled in confusion and Nolan half-grinned and the receiver coughed the sound of a gunshot.

Nolan dropped the receiver as if it were molten and ran out the door and down the steps to street level. He wasn't wearing a jacket —just a T-shirt—and the cold air hit him like a pail of water.

From the doorway above Vicki called down, "Nolan...what are you doing...?"

"Wait here," he said. "Somebody just got shot. Stay put, don't let anybody in but me."

"But..."

"Shut the door and wait, Vicki," he told her, wheeling around to face the deserted courthouse square, marked only by a few scattered parked cars whose owners lived in apartments over stores. Down the street a light was on in George's penthouse above the Berry Drug.

Nolan ran to the corner, turned and slowed into the alley. He kept the .38 in front of him and made sure the alley was empty. Then he jumped up and pulled down the fire escape and climbed to where he had used his glass cutter to get in the day before. He elbowed the cardboard patch and it gave way easily. He slipped in his hand, unlocked the window and crawled into the apartment.

There was no one inside except George, and he was over by the door, dead, his head cracked like a bloody egg.

The killer had used a .45, Nolan thought, or possibly a .38 at close range. Plugged George right square in the forehead with it. Effective. Not particularly original, but effective.

The killer hadn't bothered to hang up the phone, which was making the loud noises the Bell people use to persuade you to hang the damn thing up. Nolan slipped it onto the hook and heard sounds coming from the drugstore below.

He climbed back out the window and down the 'scape and dropped silently to the ground. Cautiously he made his way around to the front of the store, wondering if the killer had made his way out yet.

Then Nolan heard tires squealing away from a curb down the street from behind him.

In the alley he found a back door, still open, where the killer had hot-footed it from the drugstore to a car parked along the side street. Nolan could see it in the distance, blocks down. It was a dark blue Cadillac having no trouble at all disappearing.

He stood there for a while thinking, cold as hell and just as he was wishing he'd brought his cigarettes along, a blue-and-white squad car sidled up next to him. "Chelsey Police" was written on the door in small print, as if they were ashamed of it.

A man in a nicely pressed light brown business suit stepped out of the squad car, flanked by two uniformed officers. The plain-clothes cop had a tanned, weathered face, a shrewd, tough cop's face, and that was one of the worst kinds. The cop being a plain-clothes meant he was probably one of the smartest, most experienced officers of the Chelsey force. Which didn't necessarily mean much. Nolan figured being a top cop on Chelsey's force was an honor akin to being the harem's head eunuch.

The cop motioned the uniformed pair up the 'scape and into George's apartment, everyone obviously knowing just what to expect. A few minutes after they went in, one of them, a scrubbed-faced type, looked down at the cop who was standing below with Nolan and said, "Yup."

The cop smiled. "What's that you got in your hand?"

"It's a gun."

"You got that filed with the city?"

"I got," Nolan said, stuffing the .38 in his waistband, "a closed mouth till I see a lawyer."

"I'd tell you to keep your shirt on, pal, if you were wearing one." The cop's tough face broke into a wide grin. "I sure hope you haven't fired that thing lately."

Nolan didn't say anything. Why didn't the cop take the gun from him?

The cop kicked at the loose gravel in the alley, like a kid kicking pebbles into a stream. "You might be interested to know that within the past hour, hour and a half or so, the fair city of Chelsey has been seriously blemished. Blemished by three, count them, three... murders. Murders committed, strangely enough, with a .38."

"Who's dead?"

"So you decided to open your mouth? I don't see any lawyers around."

"Who?"

"You're a regular owl, aren't you? Okay mister, I'll tell you. The Police Chief, one Philip Saunders, found dead on the floor of his apartment, a bullet in the head. An alleged musician at the Third Eye, one Broome, no other name known, found dead on the floor of his dressing room, a bullet in the head. And I assume we have a similar problem with George Franco, up there. You might say fat George has a weight problem—a dead weight problem."

"You might say that," Nolan said, "if you were a fucking comedian."

"You're getting nasty, mister, you aren't in any position to get...."

"I got an alibi."

"Swell," he said.

"An on-the-level alibi. She's got a name and everything."

The cop's mouth twisted. "You really do have an alibi, don't you?"

"That's right."

He scratched his head, shrugged. "Well, then...you're free to go. Nice talking to you...mister, uh, Nolan, isn't it?"

Nolan froze.

"It's Webb," he said. "Name's Earl Webb. From Philadelphia."

"Tell me all about it."

"You going to charge me with something?"

The cop scratched his head again. He did that a lot. "I would, but I can't make up my mind between breaking-and-entering, carrying a handgun without a permit, and, well, murder. You got a three-sided coin on you?"

"Take me in or don't take me in."

"What if I said I got a deal to make with you, mister...ah... Webb. And that if you keep your side of the bargain, I'll let you walk. Without so much as a citation for loitering. Interested?"

"Maybe."

"You got somewhere private we could go?"

"Maybe."

The cop was through talking. Now he was waiting.

"Okay," Nolan said. "Let's go."

2

The cop's name was Mitchell. Nolan introduced him to the now fully awake, fully clothed Vicki Trask, who looked much fresher than four o'clock in the morning. She was wearing a blue and red candy-striped top and a white miniskirt.

"I'm sorry to barge in on you so late, Miss Trask." Mitchell tried to look embarrassed and was fairly successful.

"That's all right, Mr. Mitchell. Would you two like anything to drink?"

"Something soft would be fine," Mitchell told her, "if it wouldn't be any trouble."

"Cokes, Vicki," Nolan said.

The girl walked to the bar and iced two glasses. Mitchell and Nolan sat, the cop wondering with his eyes if they should begin speaking and Nolan shaking his head no. When Vicki brought them the Cokes, Nolan told her quietly to wait for him in the bedroom and she followed his command, scaling the spiral staircase wordlessly and disappearing into the balcony above.

Mitchell said, "I'll put it to you straight, Nolan. You are wanted for questioning in half a dozen states...Illinois one of them. Matter of fact, it's kind of a coincidence, because just this afternoon I was glancing at a bulletin on you..."

"Can it."

"What did you say?"

"I said can it. I'm not wanted for a goddamn thing."

The cop bristled. "Who the hell do you think you..."

"Okay, Mitchell. You want to haul me in?"

"I..."

"You don't have a thing on me."

"I have half a dozen circulars..."

"Bullshit."

"Now wait just a damn…"

"Bullshit! How'd you know who I was?"

Mitchell swallowed thickly. "Anonymous tip late this afternoon. We were told you were in town. Of course we recognized the name…."

"Oh? What's my real name?"

"Your real name?"

"My real name. You don't know it. How about military service? Got anything on my distinguished service medal?"

"Of course I know about your medal, what do you take me for?"

"I take you for a piss-poor bluffer," Nolan said. "When I was in the service, I got a little mad and beat the hell out of a military cop. Got a bad conduct discharge. That was under my real name, which nobody I can think of knows outside of me. And even I forget it sometimes."

"You're a real smart fella, Nolan."

"You aren't. What do you want?"

Mitchell's jaw was tight, his teeth clenched. "I could run your ass out of this town so quick, your head'd spin…."

"Then do it."

"What?"

"Do it. Run my ass out. Make my head spin. Put any more pressure on and I'll leave on my own." Nolan leaned forward and gave the cop a flat grin. "But I don't think you want me to leave."

Mitchell's face split into a wide smile and he helped himself to one of Nolan's cigarettes in the pack lying on the table. "Okay, Nolan. I guess I'm too used to dealing with punk kids who scare easy. You see through me like a window. You're right. I don't want you to leave."

"What do you want from me, Mitchell?"

"Your help, in a way. Look, I got no bulletins on you, but I sure as hell know about you. A lot of cops across the country've heard the scuttlebutt about you and your one-man vendetta against the Chicago outfit."

"It's no vendetta."

"I heard..."

"You heard wrong. I steal from them. That's it. I get a kick out of upsetting their applecarts. For money. And I'm staying alive when they send people to kill me."

"You admit you've killed?"

"I'm not going to lie to you. There's no court stenographer sitting here. I've killed in self-defense and skipped hanging around for an inquest, sure. I stick in one place that long I get dead quick."

"You don't look like the type who's afraid of much of anything."

"Only idiots fear nothing. If I can fight something, then no sweat. But you can't hold ground and fight a bomb in your room. Stay in one spot long enough and they find a way to get you."

Mitchell leaned back and smoked slowly and thought.

Nolan reached for a cigarette and said, "Make your pitch, Mitchell. Let's have it."

Mitchell smiled. "You know how long I've lived in Chelsey, Nolan?"

"No, and do you think I give a damn?"

"I was born here. It was a nice little place for a long time, friendly, homey, very Midwest, you know? Called it the intellectual corner of Illinois, too, because of the university...."

"Get to the point," Nolan said. "If there is one."

"All right." Mitchell's face hardened; it was deeply lined, more deeply lined than that of the average man of thirty-five or so years. "I could make things rough for you, Nolan, if I wanted to. I could hold you long enough to find out who you are, especially since you kindly informed me of your trouble during your stay in the army. The army keeps records. Fingerprints and such. A bad conduct discharge shouldn't be hard to trace."

"If I was telling the truth," Nolan shrugged.

"I don't know what you're after, Nolan, but I know enough about you to have a general idea. You came to Chelsey to hit the Family's local set-up, right?"

Nolan just looked at him.

"Now, off the record, as they say…what I want is the man in charge. Give him to me. Then maybe I can start cleaning this town up a little bit."

"And you'll give me a free ride home, I suppose?"

"As long as I get the goods on the head man, you'll be free to go. With anything you might relieve him of in the way of cash."

Nolan said, "You don't have any idea who your 'head man' is?"

"I've been trying to find that out for over a year, since I first started to realize just what kind of corruption was going on here. You don't mean you already know who he is?"

"Found out the day I got here."

"How?"

"Never mind that. You said your police chief, Saunders, was killed tonight?"

"One of three dead…so far."

"Well, Saunders wasn't in charge, but he was in up to his ass."

"I knew it!" Mitchell slammed fist into palm. "That son-of-a-bitch has been crippling the force since the day he took office."

"What about the next man killed?"

"Broome? We think he was involved in some kind of narcotics ring. There was heroin in his blood stream at time of death, and we found a hypo in the room and some H. Couple hits worth."

"Broome was a junkie and a pusher and a creep. But my money says he's outside help linking Chelsey to a drug supplier."

"Broome?"

"That's right. The Boys in Chicago, the mob in New York, they wouldn't send a punk like Broome in, because he was a user. But maybe he used to work for the Chicago or New York mob before he got hooked, and still had connections to a supplier."

Mitchell was confused. "This is beginning to go over my head."

Nolan didn't like explaining things, but to handle Mitchell properly, the cop had to be told what was going on. Narcotics, Nolan told Mitchell, were hard to organize; by nature they were a sprawling thing, a pusher here, a pusher there, nothing that could be controlled easily. For years the Commission hadn't bothered even trying to control it. But the last seven, eight years, Nolan explained, had changed things: the eastern families had put on a big push to organize narcotics once and for all, and with large success.

"But it's tough to hold rein on narcotics traffic," Nolan said. "The difference is that now, if you're a non-Commission sanctioned narcotics dealer and they find you out, you get leaned on."

"Leaned on hard?"

Nolan's look was that of a father dealing with a backward child. "The Commission of Families doesn't know how to lean soft."

"So this Commission has to authorize narcotics trafficking, or it's no go. And the Chelsey operation is an extension of the Chicago Outfit, which is a Commission member. Are you suggesting the Commission doesn't know about the narcotics trade in Chelsey?"

Nolan nodded. "And the Chicago Boys don't know it, either."

"Now I am lost."

"That's because you don't understand what the Chelsey operation was for. George Franco, brother of one of the Boys or not, was a big nothing. The Chelsey set-up was supposed to be a minor deal, just to give worthless George something to do, make him look good, save a little face for the Francos. But this operation is obviously making money. A lot of it. Money the Commission in New York doesn't know about. Money the Boys in Chicago don't know about. And when they find out, both the Boys and the Commission are going to be pissed. But good."

"Who's behind it? Who's getting the money?"

"Not George Franco, that's for sure."

"Then who?"

"Who brought your late police chief to town?"

Mitchell thought for a moment. "That real estate big shot. Supposed to be Saunders' cousin or something. Elliot."

Nolan nodded. "Him."

"You can't mean it," Mitchell said. "Elliot's as legit as can be...."

"No. He's the one. Elliot. He's your boy."

Mitchell rose. "I'll be damned if I don't believe you." His face twisted with a big grin. He shrugged and said, "Well, Nolan, since you told me all this, I guess there isn't much left for you to do. I'll go out and arrest Elliot...."

"Go out to Elliot's place without hard proof, Mitchell, and you're fucked. Wait around while you collect evidence, and you won't see Elliot again. Except maybe in a travelogue of Brazil."

"I can't let you go out and..."

"You were willing to five minutes ago. How about those murders tonight? Elliot pulled 'em, you know. Any idea what those murders were for?"

Mitchell shook his head.

Nolan grinned, his first full-out grin for a long time. "He was house-cleaning," he said. "Taking care of anyone who could spill anything that could lead Boys, Commission, cops or feds to him. And five will get you five hundred he'll be out of the country by tomorrow morning."

Nolan got up and called for Vicki. He asked her to get the rest of his clothes and she did. He sat on the sofa and checked his .38, which he stuffed into the shoulder holster under his arm. Then he slipped into the blue plaid parka and walked to the door. Mitchell stood there and didn't say a word.

"Do I have to tie you up, Mitchell?"

"No."

"Stay away from Elliot tonight."

"You going to take him?"

"Yes."

"Alive?"

"I don't know."

"I'm going with you."

"Forget it."

Mitchell fought himself, finally accepted it, saying, "If it has to be that way, all right. I guess I suggested it myself, didn't I?"

"That's right. Stay here and watch Miss Trask. She's been seen with me and could be in danger. If I need you, I'll call."

Mitchell nodded reluctant agreement and Nolan said goodbye

to Vicki and went out the apartment, down the steps and to street level. He walked to the Lincoln and got in.

He heard the heavy breathing in the back seat instantly and his hand was over the butt of his .38 when he heard a voice say, "Take me with you, Webb! Let's get the hell out of this hick town."

3

"What the hell do you want?"

Lyn Parks crawled up off the floor in back and sat on the seat. She leaned forward, shook her head of blond hair and stroked Nolan's temple. She said, "I think you know what I want, Mr. Webb, but I don't want it in Chelsey."

Nolan said, "Get in front," his jaw firm.

She crawled over the seat and sat beside him. She was wearing a man's white shirt and tight tan jeans. She wore no shoes and her blond hair was tousled. Coppery nipples were visible beneath the white shirt and Nolan had an urge to take her up on it, to drive straight out of town with her and forget the whole goddamn fucking thing. But it passed.

He said, "Why do you want out of Chelsey?"

Her eyes were wild saucers. "Elliot!" she scream-whispered. "I'm scared of that bastard!"

"Why?"

"I...I saw him shoot Broome tonight."

"And he let you go?"

"He didn't see me. I was in the john, hiding."

"What were you doing with Broome? How do you know Elliot?"

Her eyes lowered. "This morning...this morning I didn't level with you. This morning...I guess that's yesterday by now, isn't it?"

"Skip it. Tell me where you fit into this."

"Well, when you came up to my apartment asking questions about Irene Tisor, I knew you'd be coming. Or might come, at least. Elliot paid me fifty bucks to find out who you were, what you wanted. See I used to be Broome's girl, in a way. And Elliot was Broome's boss. Elliot, the son-of-a-bitch, he even had me over to his place a few times, but he never even touched me. Is he a faggot or something?"

"I don't know. Get back to it."

"Okay. Anyway, Elliot thought you might be around because this guy named Dinneck, know him?"

"We met."

"Well, this Dinneck found my name in a notebook in your motel room or something. And he told Elliot about it and so Elliot told me to find out who you were when you came around...."

"All right," Nolan said, making the proper connections.

She swallowed. "I shouldn't tell you this, but...but Dinneck was in the can, listening, all that time you were in my apartment at the Arms."

Nolan smiled flatly. "You didn't by any chance hit him in the throat after I left?"

"Why, yes...yes I did. Hit him right smack in the adam's apple. The bastard made a pass at me. Why?"

"Never mind," Nolan said, turning the key in the ignition. "I got to find Elliot's house. I know it's on Fairport Drive. You want to tell me where it is exactly, or do I go looking?"

"You won't find it looking."

"Tell me where it is, then."

"You gonna take me along?"

"Why should I?"

"Because you might need some friendly companionship when this is all over."

"Maybe I got that already."

"Not this friendly, you don't. Besides, I know where Elliot lives."

"All right," Nolan said, "we'll see. Now let's find Elliot's house before he finds us."

"Fairport Drive's in the ritzy section across the river. By Chelsey Park."

Nolan nodded and she directed him there, over the bridge and into the upper-class residential district ringing the park.

"That one," she told him, pointing out an imitation Southern Plantation, pillars and all. The whole *Gone With the Wind* route.

Nolan drove past it, parking half a block away.

"Which bedroom is Elliot's?"

"Second story, farthest window to the left."

"He got a den, anything like that?"

"Right under the bedroom on the first floor."

"Good girl." He patted her thigh and lifted her chin until her eyes were level with his. "Sit here and keep your mouth shut. Take this, it's cold." He gave her his parka. "I'm going to leave the car here. If things look bad, call Vicki Trask's apartment and ask for Mitchell."

"Mitchell? Hey, are you a cop?"

"Hell no."

"I didn't think you were. I had an idea you were a gangster or something. Like my daddy."

"Your daddy?"

"Yeah, didn't I mention that? My daddy's name is Gordon, Mr. Webb. One-Thumb Gordon, as his business associates would call him."

"Christ." That was all he needed. Gordon was Charlie's left hand, missing thumb or not.

"Something wrong?"

"You and your father close?"

"Oh, yeah," she said, "just like this." She crossed her first and middle finger. "This is me," first finger, "and this is him," middle finger. She laughed. "Daddy's a bastard, too, just like Elliot."

Nolan patted her thigh again. "We're going to get along fine, Lyn."

She smiled and bobbed her head. Her eyes went wide as he withdrew the .38 from under his arm. "Ditch the car here if you have to go for help," he said. "I saw a phone booth on the other side of the park."

She nodded again and he left her there.

He walked along the sidewalk at a normal rate, passing two other homes, a red brick two-story and a gray stucco, before he reached the would-be Tara, which sat way back in a huge lawn, back at least fifty yards from the street and bordered on both sides by eight-foot hedges. Elliot's place was isolated, a virtual island. The Navy Band could play in the living room and the neighbors wouldn't hear a thing.

Nolan crept along the edge of the high shrubbery. He reached the house and eased along the white walls, looking into each darkened window and finding no signs of life in the house. Past two pillars, past the porch, past two more pillars and on to another row of blackened windows. Finally, when he reached the last window he found that it had been covered with black drapes so that the room would appear dark from the street.

Elliot's den.

The grass rustled behind him; Nolan whirled and swung his .38 like a battle-axe and clipped the guy on the side of the head. He went down like wet cement. He was dressed in a chauffeur's cap and get-up but he looked like a gone-to-seed hood, which upon closer examination was what he proved to be. A major league gunman Nolan had known long ago in Chicago, a gun grown soft and sent out to the minors. Nolan found a house key in the jacket of the chauffeur's uniform.

He walked to the big brass-knockered door, slipped the key in the lock and turned it. He pushed gently and the door yawned open.

He was in a vestibule, a fancy one, for though it was dark, when he leaned against the wall he felt the rich texture of brocade wallpaper. Ahead a few steps he could see light pouring out from under a door. Silently Nolan went to it and ran a hand over the surface. Plywood with a nice veneer, but plywood. Something a man could put his foot through.

He slammed his heel into it and it sprang open like a berserk jack-in-the-box and Nolan dove in, clutching the .38. Immediately he saw a black leather chair and went for cover. But there was no gunfire to greet him, or even an exclamation of surprise.

When Nolan looked out from behind the chair he saw a thin, very pale man in horn-rimmed glasses. The man was standing over a suitcase on a table by the wall, transferring stacks of money from a safe into the suitcase. There was a .38 Smith & Wesson, a twin to Nolan's, on the floor next to the man. The man eyed the gun, his trembling hand extended in mid-air wondering whether or not to try for it.

"No," said Nolan. "Don't even think about it."

The man heaved a defiant sigh and straightened out his blue double-breasted sportscoat from under which peeked an apple-red turtleneck, brushed off his lighter blue slacks. He appeared to be a usually cool-headed type who'd recently lost his cool head. And he was trying to get it back, without much luck.

"Elliot," Nolan said.

"Mr. Webb," he replied. The voice was nervous, even cracking into higher pitch once, but it was the voice of a man determined to regain his dignity.

"I'm not much for talking," Nolan said. "Suppose you just keep packing that suitcase with your money and then hand it over to me."

"And after that you'll kill me?"

Nolan shrugged.

"You don't have a chance, Webb. *Webb!* That's a laugh. You're Nolan, I know you're Nolan, you think the Boys haven't circulated your picture?"

"Pack the fucking suitcase and maybe later we'll have time for an autograph."

Elliot managed a smile, a smile that seemed surprisingly confident. The pieces of his composure were gradually falling back into place. "Your chances of survival, Mr. Nolan, are somewhat limited. You see, it dawned on me this afternoon just who you really were. I wasn't positive, of course, not having seen you, but I didn't want to take any chances. I called Charlie Franco personally. At this very moment—"

Nolan's harsh laugh cut him off like an unpaid light bill. "Who did you call after Charlie? J. Edgar Hoover?"

Elliot's face twitched.

"I got you figured down the line, Elliot. The double-cross you been working on the Boys is going to put you on their shit list, too—right next to me."

"I don't have any idea what you're talking about."

"Okay, Elliot, cut the talk. Back to the money." Nolan gestured with the .38.

Elliot returned to the safe and kept on piling stack after stack of bills into the suitcase. Nolan lit a smoke and sat in the black leather chair.

A few minutes had passed when Elliot looked up from his money-stacking and said, "Want to tell me how you got it figured?"

Nolan lifted his shoulders. "The way I see it, you took on this piddling operation for the Boys because at the time you had nothing better to do. If you were already working for the Boys, you might not've had a choice. The job was meant to make George Franco look and feel like a part of the organization. To help save face for the Franco name. And as time went on, you got bored with it, figured a way to make some easy money and retire to a life of luxury."

Nolan leaned forward in the chair, casually keeping the .38 leveled at Elliot. "The Chelsey operation was pulling in pretty good money, for what it was. Money made mostly off college kid plea-sures, booze and pep pills and some LSD for the supposed hippies. Bagmen from Chicago came in every six weeks and picked up the profits. Around thirty G, I suppose, for each six week period."

"More like twenty G," Elliot corrected.

"Okay." Nolan's information on that point had come from the initial talk with Sid Tisor, so it figured the take was only twenty G per six weeks. That damn Sid always did exaggerate.

"The thing is," Nolan continued, "you had a prime connection. A musical junkie named Broome who could get the stuff for you. So you decided to break in an extra source of personal revenue—hard narcotics—without telling the Boys about it."

Elliot had the suitcase full now and he closed the lid. "All right,

Nolan. I've been directing a little traffic in drugs. You blame me? I was getting table scraps off this set-up. They paid my bills, sure set me up good with this house and everything. But my cut of the 'piddling' action was puny."

"No wonder you got greedy. You make good money from the Chelsey narcotics trade?"

"What do you think? I've been supplying dealers from cities in three states. There's enough profit to go around, Nolan. You could have a nice cut, too."

Nolan nodded. "One hundred percent is a nice cut."

"Don't be a glutton about it. This isn't the Boys' money, it's mine! Your grievance is with the Boys, not with Irwin Elliot! I'm like you, Nolan, out to take the Boys for a ride."

Nolan shook his head no. "Forget it. You're part of the Boys. Maybe you're worse."

"We could be partners…"

"Hey, I put nothing past you, not after you wasted your three partners tonight."

"No. Dinneck and Tulip did that—"

"Dinneck and Tulip got banged up earlier tonight. They didn't kill Saunders, Broome and George. You did. Three murders in one night, a gentleman like you. And just to clean house. What's the world coming to?"

Elliot's laugh was almost a cackle. "You're amusing, Nolan, you really are. Yes, I murdered those morons tonight. When the Boys find out three of their Chelsey men were murdered with a .38 and that Nolan was in town, they'll blame you, not Irwin Elliot. And when they find out I've vacated the premises, they'll assume I was just frightened of what you'd do to me. By the time they figure out what was really going on in Chelsey, I'll be in South America."

"I don't think so," Nolan said. "Hand me the suitcase. And no fun and games."

Elliot scowled, tossed the suitcase at Nolan's feet.

"How much is there, Elliot?"

"Near a quarter million dollars."

"Not bad. How long you been planning this?"

"Long enough. I knew all along I'd have to get out sooner or later, because once the Commission got wind of narcotics action they hadn't sanctioned, I'd be a marked man. I wanted to wait near the end of a six week period so I'd have the Boys' twenty thousand take, too. And it took me a while to liquidate my stocks and bonds...I don't keep this much in cash on hand all the time, you know."

"You're not stupid, Elliot," Nolan said, "just not smart. You got the Boys who'll be after you. New York'll want your hide. And the feds will want a piece, too. You're going to be a popular boy. I'm considering not killing you. It might be fun to tie you up and leave you here and let everybody fight over you."

A voice from behind them boomed, "Drop the gun, Webb, will ya drop it now?"

Nolan turned and saw a very battered Tulip standing in the doorway of the den, holding a .45 with an incredibly steady hand.

"*Now,* Webb."

Nolan let the gun plop to the soft carpet.

"All right, you fucker...I got a score to settle with you."

Tulip's six foot frame lumbered over to him, the arm Nolan had wounded earlier hanging limp as a dead tree limb, brown with dried blood. Nolan couldn't tell if Tulip had ever gotten that shot of H he'd needed so badly hours before; all Nolan knew was that Tulip seemed in full control as he raised his good arm and aimed the .45 at Nolan's head.

There was a blur of movement in the doorway and a familiar voice cried, "Tulip! Stop, Tulip, it's me!"

Tulip smiled, turned away from Nolan and faced the door.

The slug caught Tulip in the stomach, hard, and Tulip lay down like a hibernating bear. He looked up at the smoking nine-millimeter in the hand of Dinneck and said, "What the hell did you do that for?" Then Tulip closed his eyes and stopped breathing.

"Thanks," Nolan said.

"Saving your life wasn't the point," Dinneck said. "But Tulip was

Elliot's man, and I needed him out of the way." This he said even as he stepped over the big dead man.

"Allow me to introduce myself, gents. My name is Dinneck, but you also have the right, I think, to know who I represent."

Dinneck sat down on a black leather couch and let the nine-millimeter take turns staring at Nolan and Elliot.

"I'm a native New Yorker," he said, and coughed, his throat raspy. "My employers heard some rumors about dope traffic in this part of the country. Around Chelsey to be exact."

Dinneck rose, stepping over the corpse of his ex-partner. "I work for the Commission."

4

"Won't you sit down, Mr. Webb?" Dinneck asked, his hoarse voice dripping sarcasm. "I have some business to take care of with Mr. Elliot here, before you and I settle our personal differences."

Nolan said, "Your ball game," and sat back down in the black leather chair. The gun Elliot had dropped at Nolan's command a few minutes before lay unseen behind the closed suitcase of money. Elliot seemed to have forgotten it, and Dinneck didn't know about it. Nolan would make his move for the .38, but not yet. Dinneck was in the mood to talk, so Nolan would listen and watch while he waited for the right moment to move.

Dinneck stroked his throat, which was visibly bruised from both Lyn Parks' assault and Nolan's blows of earlier that evening. He looked weak, he looked pale—almost as pale as Elliot.

"Mr. Elliot," Dinneck was saying, "I was assigned to you by my employers to work undercover until I had enough on you to be convinced positively of your guilt. Which I am. I placed a long-distance call this afternoon to a gentleman in New York who gave me instructions as to what to do about you. You see, my employers don't take it kindly when somebody opens up a business without a franchise."

"You never saw a thing," Elliot snapped. "You weren't involved with the narcotics operation at all. None of the men the Boys sent me were."

"That's right. You used me for strong-arm work. Beat people up, pressure them. Like I did with that reporter, Davis, who skipped town. Watched over people, like Mr. Franco...the late Mr. Franco, now, I hear. And Broome and Saunders, too. My, my, but you were a busy little fella tonight. Yes, I ran your errands, and you were careful to keep me away from your narcotics set-up. Instinct maybe." Dinneck coughed, caressing his throat; talking was obviously painful to him, but he couldn't resist. He coughed again and glanced pointedly at Nolan, who sat motionless, silent, like an obedient schoolboy. Then he returned his gaze to Elliot.

"You got to remember Chelsey's a small town, Mr. Elliot," Dinneck said. "Junkies and pushers aren't hard to pick out in a town this size. And the college punks have big mouths, like to brag about getting their kicks. Your bosom pal Broome was a pusher and a junkie both, he could've worn a sign it was so obvious. And my own late partner, here, was paying half his salary back to put in his arm."

Sweat was streaming down Elliot's face; his confident tones turned back into the high-pitched squeaking he'd used when Nolan first came into the den. "There's a quarter million in that suitcase, Dinneck! Take it and let me go. I'll never say a word."

Dinneck smiled. "You don't cross the Commission and live, Elliot. If I did that, even if I killed you and kept the money, my life'd be as worthless as…as yours."

Elliot was shaking his head no as Dinneck brought up the nine-millimeter; then Elliot remembered something. "Nolan," he said, "you don't know he's Nolan!"

Dinneck hesitated. He lowered the nine-millimeter, puzzled. "Nolan? What the hell are you talking about? What is he talking about, Webb?"

"Search me," Nolan said.

"He isn't Webb, he's Nolan," Elliot spewed. "There's a quarter million on his head."

"We got quarter millions up the ass tonight," Nolan said.

Dinneck coughed, covering his mouth with his hand. "Shut up, Webb…" He coughed, coughed again. "Okay, Elliot, okay. This guy here, this Webb, he's Nolan? The guy that resigned the outfit by shooting one of the Francos?"

Elliot nodded and didn't stop nodding. "That's him, he's the one, a quarter million dollars."

Dinneck gave them both a broad, toothy smile. "That's nice to know, children—that's real comforting to know."

"Look, I told you and I didn't have to," Elliot said, his eyes filled with desperation. "Give me a break. Don't kill me, don't shoot me."

"I'm not going to shoot you, friend," Dinneck told him. "Not with a gun anyway." He motioned Elliot up against the wall.

Nolan leaned back in the chair. He had a good idea of what would be coming next; he'd heard rumors of this practice among mob enforcers when he'd been working for the Boys. He eyed the .38 and knew it wasn't time to move. Not yet.

Dinneck reached into his pocket and withdrew a brown carrying case about the size of a small picture frame. He snapped it open and the light of the room caught the reflection from the tip of the hypodermic needle within the case and tossed it around.

"You a user, Elliot? You take the stuff yourself, or do you just sell it?"

"I'm no user, you know that. And I don't smoke or drink or womanize, either."

"Well good for you. You're just all virtue and no vice, aren't you?"

Nolan said, "Get it over with."

Dinneck said, "Don't be so anxious, dead man. Your turn'll come soon enough." He walked over to Elliot, shoved him hard against the wall, then held the hypo up and said, "You ever hear of a mainliner?"

Elliot didn't answer.

"Of course you have. You're in the business, aren't you? A mainliner is a shot of H, right in the old bloodstream. Into a nice fat juicy vein. My employers are of the opinion that a person dealing in drugs ought to get first hand view of what he's selling. Now that's only good business, isn't it?"

Elliot plastered himself against the wall. "You...you're going to give me an overdose! You're going to kill me with that thing!"

Dinneck nodded. "And the cops will find a poor slob who just misjudged and popped too big a cap for his own good."

Elliot began to scream and Dinneck slammed his fist into the man's temple. Elliot slid to the floor and lay there, a puddle of flesh.

Dinneck took a rubber strap from one of his coat pockets, kneeled over, bared Elliot's right arm and tied the strap around it. The hypo was already loaded and it was no trouble for Dinneck to jam the needle into a throbbing, bulging vein and press his thumb down on the plunger.

Nolan leaned over, ready to go for the .38 that waited for him on the floor a few feet away. Dinneck caught the motion from the corner of his eye and sank his heel into Nolan's hand just before it had reached the gun. Then he kicked the .38 across the room, at the same time backhanding Nolan, who flopped back in the chair and waited for a second chance that would probably never come.

Elliot was semi-conscious, crying softly and spasmodically. Dinneck kicked Elliot's head once and put him out.

"He won't be waking up," Nolan said.

Dinneck tossed the hypo to the soft carpet. "Not in this world."

"How much did you have in the hypo?"

"Enough. Enough horse to kill a horse. Hah, horse, hell, a herd." Dinneck laughed some more, but the laughter turned into a racking cough.

Nolan thought, keep coughing, pal, come on, got to make another try for you.

"My eastern employers didn't pay me to kill you, Nolan, but somehow I don't think they'll mind. You're a thorn in the Boys' side, and the Boys are part of the Commission, after all." Dinneck slipped his free hand into his coat pocket and popped a toothpick into the corner of his mouth. "Besides, I can use the money. Quarter million's gonna go a long way. It'll hurt, you know, handing in Elliot's suitcase of bills."

"I didn't figure you killed for free."

Dinneck hefted the .38. "You got a point. I'm strictly a contract man, and all my contract work's done for the Commission. A loyal soldier. But in your case, I'd make an exception, even if there wasn't a quarter million on your head."

"You talk too much, Dinneck," Nolan said, "for a man with a sore throat."

Dinneck grinned. "Two-hundred fifty G's is gonna soothe that fine."

The nine-millimeter came up and faced Nolan, and Nolan knew his move had to be fast and good and now....

The shot came from the doorway, a thunderclap that couldn't happen, slamming into the wall between them.

Mitchell stood in the doorway, a Police Special smoking in his fist. "Hold it right there!"

But Dinneck didn't do anything of the kind.

He whirled and dropped to one knee, bringing up the .38 to try to blast Mitchell out of the door. Nolan heaved the suitcase of money at Dinneck's hand, knocked the automatic flying, and the mouth of the suitcase jumped open and vomited bills. Nolan sliced through the drifting green bills and drew his foot back to kick in Dinneck's head. Dinneck, scrambling after the nine-millimeter, saw Nolan's foot coming and grabbed it and spun Nolan around and threw him over on his back. Mitchell was still in the door, forced to hold fire because of all the movement.

Nolan landed hard, on his own .38, where it had been kicked away by Dinneck minutes earlier. Nolan rolled over, scooped it up and looked up into Dinneck's face and Dinneck's gun.

Nolan squeezed off a single shot, then rolled away, ready to squeeze off another. But it wasn't necessary.

The slug had caught Dinneck in the throat, and the small blue hole that marked its entry appeared just under the man's adam's apple. The nine-millimeter tumbled from his hand, and Dinneck did a half-turn and crashed to the floor. He used his last few seconds foolishly; he tried to speak, dredging up nothing except blood, and he tried to grasp the gun, coming up with a wad of money that wouldn't be buying him anything. His mouth went slack, the toothpick fell away from his lips, and he didn't have time to close his eyes before he died.

Nolan looked at Mitchell, standing there in the doorway with the Police Special in his hand; cordite-smell was in the air.

Nolan said, "Talk about cavalry," but Mitchell didn't react. Nolan shrugged and started picking up the scattered cash that lay over, under and around the lifeless bodies.

It took ten minutes to repack the suitcase.

5

Mitchell had come alone. At Vicki Trask's he'd gotten a call from Lyn Parks saying she'd seen several of Elliot's men go into the house, and Nolan would probably need help.

Now Nolan and Mitchell stood in the hall outside the den where the remains of Elliot, Tulip and Dinneck were inside waiting for Chelsey's harried medical examiner. The chauffeur Nolan had clubbed over the head less than an hour before sat handcuffed and dazed in the den with the dead men. Since Mitchell was the only cop who'd reached the scene so far, Nolan was anxious to be on his way.

"I'm keeping the suitcase of money," Nolan said flatly.

Mitchell didn't say anything. He looked beat. He'd been up most of the night and in eleven years of police work had never run across an evening that remotely compared to this one. He was shaking his head and gazing in at the three bodies in the den.

Nolan watched the cop, who seemed practically in shock. Nolan said, "Mitchell, we made a deal. I want your word you'll keep me out of this. Just cover up the incident as best you can."

Mitchell nodded, his eyes a pair of burnt-out holes. "Okay," he conceded. "But you got to get out as soon as possible. I don't want anybody finding out I opened the door for this massacre."

"I'll need an hour," Nolan said.

Mitchell said, "Okay, okay," not giving a damn, and stood looking into the den.

Neither man said a word as Nolan left, suitcase in hand.

When he reached the car he was met by a bubbling Lyn Parks. He let her talk, reaching an arm in the open window and grabbing the keys from the ignition. He ignored her eager interrogation and opened the trunk and stowed away the suitcase of bills, where it lay innocently with the rest of his luggage, just another piece of baggage. He got back in the car, started it and headed for Vicki Trask's apartment, paying no attention to his talkative passenger.

He pulled up in front of the apartment and got out of the Lincoln. Looking in at Lyn Parks he said, "We'll have plenty of time for talk later. You got a car?"

"Yeah, but…"

"What is it?"

"An ancient Plymouth, why?"

"Walking distance?"

"Yeah, as a matter of fact it's in a parking lot over by the Arms. Couple, maybe three blocks."

"Ever been to Wisconsin?"

"No, but…"

He tossed a ten dollar bill in her lap. "If you want to go to Wisconsin with me, go get your car and fill it with gas. Drive it back here and wait for me. If you don't want to go with me, don't be here when I get back."

Nolan left her before she could say anything else and opened the door in the middle of Chelsey Ford Sales. He went up the flight of stairs that led to Vicki's apartment and knocked once. She came to the door, smiling in relief at the sight of him and throwing her arms around him.

He broke her warm clasp and led her to the couch. He told her to sit and she did.

Nolan went back and closed the door. He looked at her. She seemed tired but was still very nice to look at. He remembered how she'd been in bed.

"Like I said before, I got nothing personal in this," Nolan said. "We slept together once and I like you, but it ends there."

There was horror in her face. "What are you talking about, Earl?"

"Go ahead and call me Nolan. I haven't figured out yet what I'll be calling you."

"You'll keep calling me Vicki, of course! What are you talking about, what's wrong?"

Nolan stood over her and looked down. "I owed Sid Tisor a debt. So to pay it back to him I came to Chelsey to look into his daughter's death. If it was murder, he would as soon I kill the murderer. If suicide, or an accident, I was supposed to confirm it with him and let it go at that."

"Why are you going over all this past history?"

"Be quiet." Nolan lit a cigarette, the last of the pack. He crumpled it and tossed it on the table and went on. "My first thought was to look into Chelsey's branch of the Outfit. As it turned out, the Boys didn't have anything to do with Irene Tisor. Other than indirectly, selling the initial cube of LSD she took that night."

"Isn't that where you were? Having it out with the criminals and all? Isn't your debt paid?"

"I had it out with the 'criminals,' all right. Three more died, died before I could ask them what they knew about Irene Tisor. But I didn't have to ask, because they didn't know anything. No, Vicki, the debt isn't paid."

"What are you talking about? Why are you telling me all this, Nolan—I really want to know!"

"Maybe you should be doing the telling," he said. "Maybe you'll tell me what's going on here."

"Nothing's going on here!"

Nolan said, "You could start by telling me how the real Vicki Trask died, Irene."

She looked up, slowly, and saw in his face, in the ice-gray of his eyes, that he knew the truth, at least partially. Her mouth jerked spasmodically and she brought up her hands, cupping them over her face to catch the tears.

Nolan spoke softly. "It took a long time to recognize you, Irene."

She glared at him wildly, her eyes red, her face streaked with tears. "How…how did you know?"

"It was hard," he told her. "Your hair is different now. And you had your nose fixed. Your father told me about that, I should have remembered. And when I saw you last you were a child. Not a woman."

"When...when did you know?"

"Tonight in bed I figured it. But I must've suspected all along. You couldn't resist calling me Nolan, could you? You had to play a game with me."

"It wasn't really a game," she said, beginning to regain control. "I did idolize you, Nolan, as a child and a teenager and even now. But since I was playing Vicki Trask, I couldn't recognize you first-hand."

"Why, Irene? Why did you play Vicki Trask? Why does everyone who knows you in Chelsey know you as Vicki Trask? Why did every-one in Chelsey think the real Vicki Trask was Irene Tisor? And why is the false-Irene/real-Vicki dead?"

The tears began again, and Nolan waited for them to stop. Then he said, "Tell it, Irene."

She nodded, swallowing the hard lump in her throat and rub-bing her red eyes with balled fists.

She said, "Before I left home for college, my father had one of his infrequent heart-to-heart talks with me. He told me...told me that before he'd retired, he'd been involved with organized crime. Our whole family was, on my mother's side. That he had been involved for more than twenty years."

She stopped and Nolan said, "So?"

"I was...was ashamed. Oh, I know, I should have guessed what kind of business he was in. If from nothing else, from the kind of people who showed up now and then at the house. People like you, Nolan. But...but he was such a mild man, a gentle person...it really threw me to find out he'd been a...a criminal. I'd always thought of him as so upright...it suddenly disgusted, revolted me...with him, myself, my whole life!"

She hesitated again, but Nolan prodded her and she resumed.

"I wanted to be respectable. It made me feel...feel dirty, some-how. A dirt I *had* to wash off. He was my parent, my only parent, since my mother died when I was born. And now, I...I just wanted to start over. So I decided to go to Chelsey and on the bus I struck up an acquaintance with a girl, a girl who was headed for Chelsey herself. Vicki Trask."

"Go on."

"Vicki looked something like me, and we had similar interests. She wanted to go to college and study art, but her parents were both dead and left her without a penny. And her grades weren't strong enough to get her a scholarship. I...I didn't care about college anymore...I just wanted an anonymous life, away from my father. But I still wanted my father's monthly allowance—I felt he owed me that much. It was Vicki who got the idea...the idea to switch names and everything. She could go to college, and I could keep getting checks from daddy to underwrite my college-girl existence. It sounded like it might work, and if it didn't, the worst that could happen was she could be kicked out of a school and I could be fired from a job. Well, it did work. We made a pact. We set it up together, got this apartment and all and traded identities. It took some doing, but we managed to shuffle some papers around and fix some documents and...and just swap places."

Nolan stabbed out the cigarette. "Why didn't you just get married if you wanted to change your goddamn name?"

"It...it was a *mental* thing with me...and I wasn't ready for a man in my life. Nolan, you were the first man I'd been with since I came to Chelsey."

Nolan shook his head, said, "Okay. Go ahead and tell the rest."

"Well, everything worked out pretty well. It wasn't hard for me to get a job in a small town like this without anybody checking the references too close. Though I was kind of scared, since it was a bank I'd applied to, and I figured they might be careful about who they hired. But they didn't spot anything false in my references and I've been working there ever since."

Nolan said, "Yeah, I can believe it." He knew a lot of banks picked girls on a basis of looks and personality; he just hoped they were more cautious in the banks his money was stored in. He said, "Keep talking."

MAX ALLAN COLLINS

She stared at the floor, avoiding Nolan's eyes. "And…and my father…I loved him so much, once…respected him…but the love was transformed into hate, when I found out what he really was."

"Cover some new ground," he told her, seeing the first light of the sun coming in through the loft windows above them.

"What…what's left to tell?"

"Quit stalling. How did your roommate die?"

She tried to speak but her throat caught. The tears began again, in a violent rush. Nolan grabbed her by the shoulders, shook her. "How? How did it happen? Did you kill her?"

She bit the ends of her fingers. "I…I don't know…I don't suppose I'll ever know."

Nolan released her. "Calm down and tell me about it."

She leaned forward. "Remember what I told you about Irene Tisor? The false one, I mean, before you knew? How she was getting wild the last few months? That was true, even though I was talking about the other Irene. She started to abuse our agreement, feeling a strange sort of freedom, I guess, from living under another person's name. I began to feel…to feel I had to end the farce… take the name back and forget my pride and leave Chelsey, go somewhere, anywhere else! Anywhere but Chelsey! As long as these pseudo-hippie friends of Irene's weren't around." She laughed. "I get confused, even now. Who's Vicki? Who's Irene? Which am I?"

"What happened?"

"She wanted to try LSD. Grass wasn't enough for her, yet she was afraid of anything stronger. Except LSD. She read a lot of books, magazine articles on it…some of her weird friends were urging her to give it a try. When she finally got the nerve, she got this little sugar cube, from that Broome character, she said. It was wrapped in cellophane, like a piece of candy. She brought it to the apartment and told me about how she was going to try it and said she needed my help. Either I gave her a hand with it, or she'd call my father on the phone and expose me. What she needed was a guide, a person to be with her when she was on the stuff who would make sure nothing...nothing bad happened...while she was on the trip, you know? I said I'd do it."

Nolan sat down next to her, steadied her with a hand on her shoulder.

Her voice trembled; it was soft, distant, as she recalled an evening she'd tried to forget.

"We started out in the apartment," she said. "She ran around the room looking at things, feeling, eating, tasting, touching. She was an animal, writhing on the floor, a serpent, utterly stripped of any inhibitions she'd ever felt. She told me it was wonderful, she could feel and taste and hear and see all at once, never as before. She...she seemed almost insane, and it got worse...worse as she went along. Then she sat in a chair...that chair, the chair right across from us now...and had a conversation with someone only she could see. Claimed it...it was her soul. Then she sprang out of the chair and ran down the steps. I followed her...I didn't try to stop her, there was no reasoning with her...it was late and no one was around to bother us."

She hesitated, buried her eyes in her hands and said, "She came to...to that building. Twill Building. She pulled down a fire escape and she climbed it...climbed up, up to the top...and I followed her. She said...said she wanted to taste the stars, feel the sky. She got on the rooftop and...and she ran...ran around like a crazy woman...and chattered about God, how she was meeting God...and I snapped. I couldn't stand it anymore. I grabbed her, tried to shake her, shake her out of it...but no use. No use. She was strong...she fought me...we scuffled around...tumbled...rolled...and suddenly the edge of the building was there and we kept struggling and...and she just...she just went over. She went over, that's all."

There was silence in the room for a moment, then she said, "I got away without a single person seeing me. I came back here and went to bed, but I didn't sleep. The next day, Irene Tisor was dead. When I saw the word would get back to my father that his daughter was dead...I let it ride. I let it ride."

Nolan stood up. "I see."

She reached out for him, her eyes dry but still bloodshot. "I don't think I...I pushed her, Nolan, but...I don't know."

"Sure."

"What...what will you tell my father?"

He shrugged. "The truth, maybe. Or perhaps that his daughter is dead and to forget it. I don't know yet."

"Do you think I...I killed her? On purpose, I mean?"

"I don't know," Nolan said. "Maybe I don't even give a damn. But any way you spell it, I can't scrape up much pity for you."

"Nolan..."

"You condemned your father for being a criminal, then turned around and made a lie of your own life. You slept with me, a thief, a killer ten times over. And maybe you even killed somebody yourself."

The tears were back again. Funny how Nolan had told Sid Tisor when the thing began that it was the living to feel sorry for, and not the dead. Sid had mourned the living all along.

"Your father worked for the Outfit, all right," he said. "But he was a pencil jockey, a book man. Maybe just being a part of the Outfit makes you a criminal, but Sid sure didn't share any love for his bosses. Helping me like he did proves that."

She kept crying but Nolan didn't pay any attention.

"You took the good life on a platter from him," Nolan said, "kept it, and threw him away."

"What can I do, Nolan?"

"That's your problem."

"But Nolan..."

"My debt's paid. Kiss Chelsey goodbye for me."

"Don't leave! Tell me what to do! What should I do, Nolan, tell me!"

"You should probably go to hell," he said. "But you want my advice so bad, I'll give it. Become Irene Tisor again. Drop the Vicki Trask tag and start over. But quietly, or they'll trace you back to the death of your roommate."

"But they'll find out, won't they?"

"I don't think so. The death of Irene Tisor is a closed case. It's marked probable suicide in a file. But stick around Chelsey and your chances aren't so good. The easy days in this town are over what with the Boys not having an operation here anymore and the on-the-take police chief dead."

"How? How can I do it?"

Nolan reached in his pocket and dangled the keys of the Lincoln in front of her. "These keys fit the car I been driving around Chelsey. It's rented in your father's name. The car, with the keys in it, will be waiting at the bottom of the steps for you. When you're ready, drive it back to Peoria."

Her eyes were red, wet circles. "What do you mean?"

"I mean go back to your father. Go back where they know you and you can explain your 'death' by saying it was a mix-up and they'll believe you. Your father's a lonely old guy. Just be careful you don't give him a heart attack when you show up. He'll be so happy to find you alive he won't give a damn about what an ungrateful little bitch you've been."

"Go back to him?"

"If he'll have you."

"But…"

Nolan turned and walked to the door. "Give Sid my regards. And tell him we're even."

She swallowed and said, "Maybe I'll…I'll do that."

He opened the door. "So long, Vicki…or Irene." His lips formed the humorless line she'd come to know as his smile. "Maybe I'll stop by Peoria in a year or so," he said. "And see who you are."

He closed the door and left her.

6

It was a red Plymouth that was dirty as hell and hadn't been new for twelve years. Lyn Parks was sitting behind the wheel, her long blonde hair hanging down over the shoulders of Nolan's parka, which she still wore. The Plymouth's engine was running, the muffler sounding as if it had seconds to live.

"Well?" she called, as Nolan came from the doorway of the apartment.

"Well?" he returned, heading for the Lincoln. He opened up the trunk of the big car, got out his clothes-bags, luggage and the money-stuffed suitcase. He slammed the lid back down, tossed the keys in the open window of the Lincoln and joined Lyn Parks in the dirty red Plymouth, piling the back seat with his baggage.

"You need all that crap?" she asked.

He patted the suitcase of cash fondly. "This one's all I really need."

"What am I supposed to do?"

"Drive."

"Where?"

"Think you can find Milwaukee?"

"Eventually," she shrugged.

"I got a stop to make." Nolan's Milwaukee contact, a broker named Richmond, would see that the quarter million was properly banked/invested.

"You're the boss," she said. "I just hope this crate'll make it as far as Wisconsin."

"I'll buy you a new one on the way."

She grinned. "Sounds good." She started the car, her blonde hair bouncing, and four minutes later Chelsey was a memory.

Nolan leaned back, his hand on Lyn Parks' thigh. There would be no sweat from the Boys for a while; they'd be busy trying to figure out what had been going on in Chelsey. And that was good, he hadn't relaxed for months. He squeezed Lyn's thigh, leaned his head back and shut his eyes. Wisconsin would be cold this time of year. It would be nice to have a bed warmer.